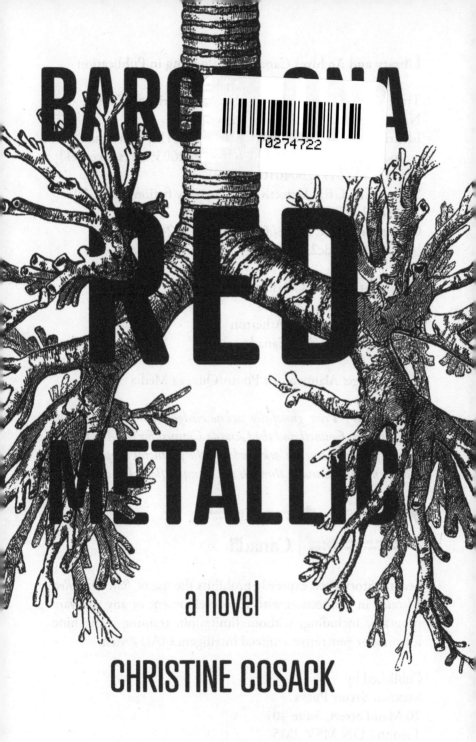

BARCELONA RED METALLIC

a novel

CHRISTINE COSACK

Second Story Press

Library and Archives Canada Cataloguing in Publication

Title: Barcelona red metallic : a novel / Christine Cosack.
Names: Cosack, Christine, author.
Identifiers: Canadiana (print) 2024038301X | Canadiana (ebook) 20240383028 | ISBN 9781772603910 (softcover) | ISBN 9781772604016 (EPUB)
Subjects: LCGFT: Detective and mystery fiction. | LCGFT: Novels.
Classification: LCC PS8605.O83 B37 2024 | DDC C813/.6—dc23

Cover image: Alamy Stock Photo/Quagga Media

Second Story Press gratefully acknowledges the support of the Ontario Arts Council and the Canada Council for the Arts for our publishing program. We acknowledge the financial support of the Government of Canada through the Canada Book Fund.

Published by
SECOND STORY PRESS
20 Maud Street, Suite 401
Toronto, ON M5V 2M5
www.secondstorypress.ca

To Bobbie Blue

PROLOGUE

1975

"Sixty-five roses." The pediatrician they had traveled to for so many hours regards Jo and Paul with solemn eyes.

"Excuse me," Jo says in a voice that does not sound like her own. "Did you say Ollie has sixty-five roses?"

The nice-enough doctor smiles curtly and shakes his silver-templed head. "Cystic fibrosis," he enunciates elaborately. And then launches into a medical jargon–filled explanation of what that means while Jo's brain is still busy supplying images of pink-hued, velvety rose petals. The next thing she hears is a number.

"Twenty-six-point-five," he pronounces, "is the maximum life expectancy for children with this genetic disease at this time."

The words seem to float down on her from a great height and settle around her shoulders, heart, and soul like judgment and sentence alike.

Twenty-six-point-five.

Twenty-six and a half.

Twenty-five plus one and a half.

How many months is that even?

She feels herself wilt under the weight of the diagnosis, sees the imaginary rose bush droop, the leaves and petals drift to the ground, and the branches become brittle. Anguish engulfs her, making her feel small and unsteady. Grief so heavy it hurts to breathe. Then, she clings to one word. Genetic. *Did we give this to him?* She learns that they had. That there is a chance other children she and Paul might have could get this, too.

Twenty-six and a half.

Sixty-five roses.

CHAPTER ONE

THE ACCIDENT

Lena puts her thumb against the lever of the bicycle bell and presses repeatedly. The melodious tinkle fills the morning stillness and follows her down the slight incline and into the sweeping, soft curve of the road. Lena likes the *tink-tink-tink* well enough but wouldn't mind a bell that makes a mighty sound, like the urgent wail of a fire truck or the long *waaaaaah* of the lighthouse foghorn through soupy sea air. The bell is silver and round, and Elsa, her favorite Disney character, winks and smiles from its surface. Oh, how Lena loves her bicycle; the jewelry pink of it, the glittery blush of silver streamers that whoosh and dance when she gets enough speed going.

The bike had been sitting in the middle of the living room the morning of her fourth birthday, and Daddy had piled all the chairs on top of the table so that she had space to practice. Before Kikki and Bruno and Angie had come over and they had all gone to the water park, Lena had already learned how to ride in a straight line, how to turn left, then right, and how not to scratch the paint on the wall in the skinny corridor by the laundry room. That first night, the bicycle slept in her room with her. But now it has moved into the garage, where Mommy and Daddy's bikes are and the car and all their helmets hang on hooks on the wall. Lena's is purple, with yellow dots that Mommy calls flecks, 'cause Mommy was born in another country and knows lots of different words.

At first, Lena was only allowed to ride in the garage and the driveway, and then Daddy took the training wheels off and said that she had great balance and was a natural. Now, when Daddy walks beside her, she rides the sidewalks around the block, and yesterday, she rode all the way to the playground. Kikki and her played on the slides and when she was tired, Daddy pushed her on the bicycle all the way home. When they got to the driveway, Daddy's phone rang.

He answered it quickly and walked behind the house, and so Lena parked her bicycle in front of the garage and went inside. She is allowed one hour of TV every day and yesterday was *Dora the Explorer*. Then there had been dinner and baby Benny was fussy, and after, Daddy read her the book about the grumpy pigeon. At night, she dreamed that a giant crow drove the school bus, which scared her a little and woke her up. She did bathroom things, then let James out, their golden retriever. He wandered around in the backyard, then squeezed through a gap in the hedge and disappeared. Lena ran through the house and opened the front door and sure enough, there was James, tail wagging and proud that she had fallen for his game. Lena didn't scold him because her eyes fell on her bicycle. It was still standing in front of the garage door. Daddy must have forgotten to put it inside; geez Daddy, someone could have *stole* it.

Here is her bike, all shiny and pink, and no one around to hold her back or make her ride on the sidewalk or call out to go slower. Lena closes the door behind James, hurries over to her bicycle, walks it away from the garage, and then gets on. A glance toward the still-sleeping house, and she is off.

At first, she stays on the sidewalk and rides around the block, Daddy's words in her ear cautioning her. But then the breeze blows through her hair and his voice recedes as she rolls off into the street by Mister Walter's house and circles the block again. It's way better to be on the road—she doesn't have to contend with all the dips of people's driveways. Lena circles her block twice on the wide street, carefully loops around parked cars, listening to the whoosh of the streamers. Then she turns off toward the playground—she knows the way well but has only ridden it on the sidewalk. Maybe that's why she had not realized how steep the road really is. She has trouble making her legs move fast enough to keep up with the spinning pedals. The cool morning air blows past her, and the little plastic rings on the spokes of the back wheel clatter a satisfying staccato. Lena is thrilled and keeps her eyes on the red slide just coming into view at the park. She'll slide a couple of turns, maybe even give the swing a go, then ride home, carefully and on the sidewalk, just in case Daddy is waiting in the driveway for her.

What an adventure she is having!

Lena has not learned about stop signs yet and rolls through the intersection without looking sideways. If she had turned her head, she would have had just enough time to see the gleaming red hood bearing down on her. As it is, her last view of this world is Elsa's smiling, winking face.

If Lena had lived, she would have seen the red car stop, the driver's door open, and a person step out. And Lena, reared like most kids by parents with Instagram and Facebook accounts, would have reflexively conjured a toothy smile for the camera. If she had lived.

He gets back into the car and places the camera carefully on the passenger seat before levering the gear stick into "D" and rolling slowly through the intersection. He is exhilarated beyond anything he has ever experienced. All his senses seem to be on high alert: he feels the cool polymer of the steering wheel beneath his hands, and its embedded ridges and curves that cup each individual finger. His heart beats hard and fast, his blood pulses in his fingers and face. His lips are buzzing. His ears hum. He notices the airflow along his calves and shins, feels the down across his chest and along his neck move. The hair in his armpits and groin are cooly wet. His eyes make out a million details all at once: the varying shades of gray and shadow that emerge with the sunrise, the claw-like tree branches jutting across the boulevard, the minuscule, star-shaped fissure in the center of the windshield where a tiny bit of gravel must have hit. He sees, again, the little figure on the bicycle, appearing miraculously right in front of him, like an answer to a fierce prayer. He had felt such a rush of pleasure at the sight of her that, even if he had *wanted* to, he could never have lifted his foot off the gas pedal and slammed on the brake in time. All he could do was watch—himself, the car, and the kid colliding in one fluid motion. There hadn't even been a jolt or much of a sound, although he thought he had heard a silvery tinkle float on the air. The car seemed to have only brushed her, hardly a bump. And he half expected, as he walked around the fender, to see the kid sitting on the curb, maybe studying a broken-out milk tooth in the gutter. But she had lain there with open, unseeing eyes, and he asks himself now, as he slowly drives the familiar streets, if it wasn't a damn shame that the kid couldn't have stayed alive long enough to *see* him. The way he has seen her. Her round face and pudgy little cheeks, the smattering of dark specks in her light eyes, the braided pink friendship bracelet circling her wrist. She was flawless and she was his.

CHAPTER TWO

A TERRIBLE DISCOVERY

Just after six, Pahal Singh slides quietly out of bed. She tiptoes out of the bedroom, past the kids' room, stops herself from peeking in lest the little one is awake and demands her attention. Aarush is a quiet, introspective soul; she might be lying still in her crib, gazing contentedly at the black and white mobile suspended above her, thinking baby thoughts. There must be a lot going on in babies' brains assimilating the giant world around them. Best to give them space and peaceful quiet to take it all in. It's really too bad we can't remember anything of this miraculous time, our own getting-to-know-the-world years. How wondrous it must have been. Pahal slips into the bathroom where her freshly laundered running gear is folded neatly onto the small bench and dresses hurriedly. *Thank you, Mām Gyanpreet*, she thinks while she brushes her teeth and sends thoughts of gratitude and love toward the old woman who sleeps in the downstairs suite. Sachdeep's widowed mother had arrived from India weeks before the first baby, Karnam, had been born and had folded herself into their household with absolute grace. She is such a kind, warm, loving woman who dotes on her grandchildren with kisses and freshly cooked laddoos, and she performs a thousand household chores every day to free up Pahal and Sachdeep's schedules. *Amazing woman*, she thinks as she slips on her runners by the back door. *How did I get so lucky with my mother-in-law, who is kinder and funnier than my own, truth be told?*

Pahal locks the door to their two-story, gabled house that differs from its neighbor only by color—blue—and placement of entry door and bay window. Sachdeep had painted the garage door a bright, sunshine yellow, and none of their visitors ever get lost in the large, multitiered subdivision. She takes a few deep breaths in and out, glances at her watch, six-fifteen, and sets off in a dash up the road. She'll run hard to the top of the hill, an arduous mile and a half along the serpentine road, and then canter on the way down. Some days, she runs the loop three times. *But today is probably not one of those*, she thinks and then spots a pink, dented kid's bicycle lying up against the curb with the back wheel spinning. She hears the *clack-clack-clack* of the plastic spoke beads as they slide lazily up and down the aluminum rods before she sees the little girl in rainbow pajamas lying motionless a couple of yards away. Pahal stops abruptly and stares, her mouth suddenly like sandpaper. Her breath sticks in her throat, nausea rising behind it. The child is dead, clearly, but Pahal forces her legs to move, stiffly, and squats next to the still form. To lay her fingers against the jugular vein that does not pulse even faintly beneath the cool, soft layer of pale skin. She looks around; who else is here? Someone needs to do something. But there is nobody, something she usually relishes during her early morning jogs. Holy Guru Nanak, why did she not bring her phone? Doesn't Sachdeep regularly plead with her to take a charged phone on her runs, and a can of bear spray, too? He is right, of course he is right, she would never again laugh at his worried, "You just never know what might happen, Pahal, my love."

Pahal runs to the nearest house, bangs on the front door, and presses the ringer. For a moment, she stares unseeing at the white door, playing a reel in her mind of a large car and a tiny pink bicycle, of a very small, red-curled head without a helmet knocking against an unyielding bumper or a headlight, of the bicycle flying one way and the little body another. Where is the car? The driver? How can it be that a human being drives away after such a thing? Pahal knocks louder, faster, and keeps ringing the buzzer. Finally, a disgruntled old man opens the door. She knows that the child cannot be alive, cannot be resuscitated, but everything in her screams urgency. After her frantic explanation, the homeowner dials 9-1-1. She can hear him shouting the address repeatedly and something about a terrible accident. Pahal hurries back to where the girl lies and sees that the wheel of the bicycle has stopped turning. She doesn't know if she is allowed to touch the child; she has watched so many television shows where high-ranking officials seem very serious about crime scene contamination. *But this is just a little girl who died all alone*, she thinks, and she squats on her heels, taking the child's hand in her own, and strokes the blood-spattered cheek with the fingers of her other hand.

"I hope your short life was a happy one, little flower," she murmurs, "and that your spirit will become one with the part of the world you loved most."

Pahal remains there, still and staring, her heart heavy, until a wailing ambulance and the police cars arrive, and other neighbors up and down the street appear on their front lawns and driveways. Two RCMP cars park in the intersection to block it from traffic, and a kind young man in a uniform takes Pahal's elbow and escorts her to the sidewalk. She tells him what she had seen while Sachdeep, who comes running from their home, his worried expression easing only a little when he sees her talking to a policeman, waits a few steps away, his eyes never leaving her face. When the short interview is over, and Pahal has spelled her name and given her contact information to the RCMP officer, she hurries into her husband's arms and buries her face in his thick bathrobe.

They walk home together, ignoring the questioning looks from their neighbors. Then they close the door behind them, draw the curtains, and light as many candles as they can find.

CHAPTER THREE

A GOOD MORNING

A sleepy mist hangs in the plum and apple trees, the grass is dewy-moist, and the bees scoot hurriedly in and out of their hives to lay in as much honey before winter as they can. Jo stands in the back-porch door and surveys her large garden with pioneer pride. She and Paul can buy all the groceries they'll ever need with their pension checks, but the abundance of food she's able to grow herself placates a deep, insistent yearning. This past summer, she harvested berries, tomatoes, peas, carrots, beans, onions, and garlic, and all manner of greens and herbs; now it's time to bring in the autumn fruits, squashes, and spuds. Another six weeks and her entire two acres will be tucked in for the winter; the beds covered in inches of straw, the fruit tree branches pruned back to protect against the weight of snow; the laying hens will travel to the humane butcher—now *there* is a contradiction—then return plucked and freezer-ready; the honey from the two hives will pour golden into ready jars and be replaced with buckets of simple sugar solution that will sustain the hibernating bee colonies safely through the long winter months. Jo loves how the ebb and flow of the seasons ordain her daily tasks and finds deep, soul-sustaining satisfaction in bending to the rules of nature. After a lifetime of fighting what had seemed inevitable, this yielding way-of-being seems like a nourishing balm.

She sighs contentedly and closes the door, her empty coffee cup in hand. Paul's porridge pot sits ready on the stove, oats and water measured into small bowls next to it, and the coffee machine is ready to percolate. Jo always has a cup or two of instant first; she developed a taste for it during interminable nights and mornings in all those hospitals. Packets of chewing gum, dextrose tablets, a mug, and a small jar of Nescafé had been staples in her purse back then, and although everything had changed completely, the pure contentment of a cup of black instant endures.

When Paul comes down to cook his oatmeal, Jo turns the radio down. It's barely six-thirty, but over more than forty years of marriage, their breakfast time only really varied when Oliver was in the hospital. When they had been newlyweds in Port Alberni, Paul's shift at the mill had started at six in the morning. Jo got up with him at five to boil an egg, make toast and coffee, and after he left their forest-enclosed small cabin, she had crawled, sighing, back into bed. Then Paul got different—not better—jobs with the mill, and they could sleep in a while, enjoy the luxury of late breakfast together. And six-thirty is the way it had remained through all of it. Through the many moves, jobs, stages of their lives. Now, both of them retired with not much pressing except keeping their house and garden, they still have early breakfast every morning, read the news, touch each other's hand every now and again, glance out the window, and comment on the weather and the daily chores. Today, the peaceful silence is interrupted by the urgent wail of sirens, and they glance at each other with worry.

"That sounds as though it's near the new subdivision," Jo says. "There've been a few early morning ambulances since they built that. I wonder if a lot of in-laws and grandparents have moved in with the young families, folks we don't see out on the streets much."

When Jo had been a 9-1-1 dispatcher, early morning calls had come in just about every day.

"Can't breathe," old, scratchy voices had whispered, followed by a short, whistling in-breath and an even shorter, barky exhale. Or, much scarier, silence. Jo would send the advanced life support team immediately and then stay on the phone. Usually, it turned out to be someone with some type of chronic cardiac condition or simply a slowly breaking-down old body who woke up to go pee and found that they couldn't catch a breath. The paramedics would use oxygen and inhaler steroids and most often, that would be enough, and the ambulance would leave half an hour later, quietly. This morning, Jo and Paul do not hear the siren again and assume whatever medical emergency had spurred the 9-1-1 call had been resolved. They cannot know that the ambulance had never been required in the first place, that a hearse instead will take the small, broken girl to a makeshift mortuary behind the clinic on Second Street, or that, at the moment Paul gets up from the table, two uniformed police officers knock on the door of 51 Crescent View, where a tired-looking man in blue pajamas opens the door, and a golden retriever wags his tail in friendly greeting.

"Grandma, can I have waffles today, please?" Nico comes into the kitchen not long after eight, just as the radio news ends. Jo had listened to the familiar voice describe the American president's latest foolishness but did not really pay attention. Instead, she thought about dinner and whether a few ripe plums would suit a thick, chunky tomato sauce. Jo loves food and usually begins to think about fixing the next meal before she has finished eating the current one. Maybe the landscape of her body would not have morphed from curvy plains to expansive swells and gorges over the decades if food had only been an aside for her, but Jo, comfortable in her size sixteen wardrobe, doesn't spend too much time considering that particular issue. Life is too precious and food too delicious not to be enjoyed, it's as simple as that. So, she makes waffles for Nico and then a couple for herself to use the batter up, and they sit together and pour maple syrup over their buttered delicacies.

"Did you sleep well?" she asks, and Nico nods.

"Slept like a log, Grandma, like I always do out here. I wish Mom and Dad would move from the city," he grumbles.

Jo smiles at her grandson and pats his hand. "Your parents both have so much going on right now with their work. Do you feel they aren't paying enough attention to you?"

"They never do," Nico says dismissively. "I just like it better here, with you and Grumps. I wish they'd let me live with you."

She laughs, remembering the many times Nico had loudly protested having to spend part of his vacation with his grandparents. He doesn't really want to live with them. He usually complains to everyone who cares to listen about his tedious boredom as soon as he sets foot in Oyster Hill. But teenagers have short memories, and his parents truly are very busy at the moment. Oliver is embroiled in setting up his business, and Gina is campaigning for the federal by-election coming up in late November. The polls favor her; she's immensely popular with young voters, and her clearly defined strategies for education, taxation, and infrastructure projects hold sway over the older demographic. Gina is a master orator, a no-nonsense policy analyst, and a marine biologist; there isn't much she can't speak to on a dime. *Poor Nico*, Jo thinks, and arranges her face into a more sympathetic expression, *he has probably never experienced the thrill of winning an argument with his mother.*

She folds her arms across her chest, and in an unconscious gesture already familiar in its furtiveness, slides her forefinger over the small lump in her left breast. Steals across the hardness of it, then circles it several times. It's been more than a week since she first encountered it, this small lump. It's been just long enough now that she has begun to form a relationship with it. With the word *cancer*, with the bigger, heavier *breast cancer*, with the lump itself. It's pea-sized, hard, and sort-of anchored. Of course, she has googled, but not much, already assured in this new awareness. Breast cancer. She doesn't see the point in researching more until she has a better sense of what to think about that. For now, she feels it with her fingertips every chance she gets. To become familiar.

Nico rewards the inhaled waffle pile with an unexpected hug before leaving the kitchen to find his bicycle, or his computer console, or perhaps the fishing rod. Jo doesn't ask him. She's determined to let the boy run loose and not engage in the imperative, controlling oversight she'd had to wield over Oliver. Over her Ollie-Golly, Goofy-Doofy, her sweet little dumpling baby boy, who had turned from being the light of her life to the weighty burden of her very existence the moment she and Paul had received the diagnosis of their son's illness.

Sixty-five roses.

Twenty-six and a half.

They'd had to move to the city where the specialists and the pediatric hospital ward were. They also quickly learned that they inhabited a different country now from those around them, where they had their own customs, rules, rituals, and vocabulary. People could visit them there, but they could never truly know what it was to live within its borders.

During a blissful four- or five-year period of relative health and easy maintenance, she and Paul did try for another child, one that could be checked for the flawed gene while still being more of a blob than a baby. Jo miscarried days before the test and bore the guilt of relief in the same hefty bag with all the other unresolved, shameful thoughts and deeds of her life. Later, she sometimes thanked the universe that she and Paul had been spared that decision. That they didn't have to become border guards to their small country of three.

CHAPTER FOUR

THE CALLOUT

Luci Miller's breakfast on the already-sunny balcony of her seventh-story one-bedroom in Vancouver's trendy West End consists of a still-warm, flaky croissant and a piping hot espresso in an authentic, white porcelain cup, replete with a sugar cube. *This really is the life*, she thinks, remembering her year in Naples; the long nights at the beach, the large, rectangular trampolines built right into the sand, the black Vespa that could manage a respectable eighty, and her Matteo. Her first real boyfriend who had been as besotted with her as she had been in love with him, and whose memory, forever after, suffused that time in Europe with a sultry, romantic nostalgia. Matteo had called her *dolce Lucia* but somehow nudged those syllables to sound like *delicious*, and she had fallen for him hook, line, and sinker.

Still smiling, Luci heads for the kitchen and extracts a second espresso from the De'Longhi. In the more than ten years since Matteo, men have come and gone, but her sense of flirtation and adventure has remained. A new beau is waiting in the wings—Grant—and he called late last night to ask her out to a waterfront restaurant today after work. Of course, she'll go; she'd go almost anywhere with this funny and kind geologist who holds a helicopter license and works in the far reaches of the Yukon.

They'd met at a curated Northern Nature photography show at the BC Museum of Anthropology only a month ago, where they both had photographs on display. Hers were of an approaching avalanche and Grant's had been of a curvy, luminous section of the Kaskawulsh Glacier under the spectral of northern lights, taken from the lofty heights of his helicopter seat. They spent the evening talking about the Yukon, one of three territories in Canada's arctic reaches. They both spent time there: Grant as a surveyor for the territorial government, where he still works, and so he only comes to Vancouver sporadically, and Luci as a fledgling RCMP recruit in Dawson City. She had toiled in grunt police work for just a few years. It hadn't been to her liking. Fresh out of college, the force had stationed her in small, northern detachments in Manitoba, Alberta, and the Yukon and had moved her around at will. Keeping the peace was not on; her work had consisted mainly of dragging drunk construction and pipeline workers off to jail, heaps of drug and sexual assault investigations, tons of traffic patrol, and many, many horrific accident scenes. Which she got to clean up, body parts and all, and then she had to bring the messages of devastation to shocked families.

She'd needed a way out of her life as a Mountie-fledgling, and so she'd transferred to the RCMP's Collision Analysis and Reconstruction Service (CARS) section, where her well-practiced skills of observation and attention to detail were in demand and appreciated. Here, coworkers don't transfer out every five minutes: the four teams of the section are cohesive, stable units of dedicated, well-trained officers who average five years in this particular deployment. Luci has been here two years now, has advanced to corporal rank, and thinks of herself as an investigator.

Her phone rings. It's her boss' number, and Luci feels a pang of regret even before she downs the last sip of her espresso, touches the green button that accepts the call, and allows Sergeant Timothy Rudinsky's booming voice to fill her ears.

"Got a callout, Luce, gotta go to Oyster Hill, up on the Sunshine Coast. Fatal hit-and-run, a dead kid. There's a reasonable detachment on the ground, someone with a bit of traffic and homicide experience, so we'll drive instead of fly. Two cars, from the office, leaving ASAP."

CHAPTER FIVE

THE TRIPTYCH

Lobaria pulmonaria, common names: tree lungwort or lung lichen. With her graphite pencil, Jo carefully outlines the spherical ridges, and then painstakingly adds the fine layer of hair on the leaf's lower surfaces. With a slightly softer tip, she adds the cephalodia between the ribs of the thallus. She has done drawings at far more minuscule scales before, but her eyes now strain peering through high-objective microscope lenses, and so she limits herself to structures that can be seen with the naked eye. She has drawn and painted the lung lichen so many times she could add the microscopic details from memory, and she still dreams about phycobiont layers of green-blue algae and mycelium from time to time.

Back when Oliver had been diagnosed, she'd begun to study in the evenings instead of karaoke-ing and dancing John Travolta in their living room until she collapsed, roaring with laughter, on Paul's lap. She had become a learner, had moved from being the understudy of nurses and doctors to a scholar in mere months, traveled to the many Cystic Fibrosis Foundation meets and conferences, was the first on her block to buy an IBM computer and quickly excelled at it. She studied anatomy and pathophysiology, followed drug trials in the States and, along the way, learned about lung lichen, which grows so plentiful in the rainy regions of British Columbia's coastal forests. She met Eloise Charleson, a Hesquiaht medicine woman, who pounded the green lobes into a paste for Jo to add to Ollie's calorie-rich cream shakes and to smear on his chest when his breathing labored. Eloise's son, Gerald, told her of the UBC professor who contracted coastal hikers to catalog lichens, and a path to a livable life opened.

Ollie needed regular, vigorous exercise to prevent his lungs from becoming sticky, and so Jo took him hiking. They clambered through forests and gorges and challenging coastal trails, sang loudly to warn off bears, feasted on backpacks full of sandwiches and chocolates, swam in lakes, rivers, and the ocean, and learned how to build functional ladders from fallen branches so Ollie could climb up to dizzying heights and photograph the loftier specimens.

The university's eminent lichenologist paid them well for their detailed, descriptive sheets and photography, and Jo supplemented this steady income with dispatch work through the winter months, when Paul took their son to hockey practice. One of her colleagues in the 9-1-1 call center ran a small art gallery, and her eyes became large and intense when Jo showed her some of the drawings.

"Wow, Jo, you're an artist. These are fantastic! If you can afford to have them properly mounted and framed, I can sell these. They're amazing!"

Jo could not afford expensive vellum or custom framing, but the spontaneous recognition by someone who wasn't a biologist spurred her to buy a drafting table and a decent set of watercolor paints and, over time, her skill as a botanical illustrator grew into artistry. It didn't hurt that lichen cataloging became a serviceable tool to recognize subtle climate changes, and her customer base grew from one—namely UBC's Dr.

Goward—to many, including noted environmentalists and conservationists, as well as their affluent admirers. These days, Josephine Nelson's delicate art adorns countless private and corporate walls, and galleries all over Canada scramble to host a showing. Even David Suzuki had sent her an admiring note after receiving a moonglow lichen print as a gift.

This Lobaria pulmonaria drawing she's doing now will be part one of a triptych, a three-paneled piece, commissioned by Dr. Len Robichaud, the pulmonologist who'd kept Ollie alive until his capitulating lungs could be swapped for a fresh pair nineteen years ago.

Nineteen years ago.

When Ollie-Golly was twenty-five.

Twenty-six-point-five, the most torturous number, had been outlived because Jo and Paul and Ollie had worked so damn hard, and because medicine and science had come a long way, and because Dr. Robichaud was a gem who had never once given up, had never once been unkind, had always been available and ready to help. You could call him at two in the morning, at home, and say your son's sputum was too thick and the wrong color and that you were on your way in, and then he was there, solid, twenty minutes later at the emergency department with a smile on his face. *Ollie*, he'd say, *come on in, buddy, we'll get you sorted.*

The second triptych piece will be a watercolor of the same lichen in shimmering hues of emerald, olive, mint, and jade—the petals and lobes flowing into each other, allowing for light to diffuse the entire gracious structure. The third painting is already finished: a set of lungs molded from a sea of flowers. *Sixty-five roses*. Petals burst from every edge of the twin ovals in soft pinks, deep whites, even heather blues. Some of the flowers have not blossomed yet and are imbued with the promise of life just waiting inside the tiny buds.

Jo smiles as she expertly applies a minuscule layer of shading to the protruding propagules of the foliose lichen. The triptych will be a celebration of light and air, of structure, shape, and harmony, and will direct the viewer's sense from wonder at the infinitesimal to the promise of renewal. Just right, then, for the waiting room of a doctor who changes lives.

CHRISTINE COSACK

CHAPTER SIX

THE VILLAGE

The news of Lena Newman's death spreads through the small town and many people light a candle in their window, in case the little girl's soul, already swept up into the heavens, might need to return to this hamlet for one last errand.

Oyster Hill counts some three thousand inhabitants in the village and surrounding hills and secluded bays. Tourists swell these numbers in the summer, but in late August, most everyone has returned to their home cities. Main Street features the usual assortment of grocery and variety shops, small cafés and bistros, a post office, city hall, and a pharmacy; on First Street, the hotel, bar, ice cream parlor, RCMP detachment, library, and elementary school line both sides of the block; and Second Street is home to the fire department, the clinic, which is staffed by a half-time doctor and two nurses, a fabric store, and a good number of two-story, gabled wooden houses typical of those the settlers had built for themselves at the turn of the century.

The town is built high into the hillside; despite its namesake, mollusks never featured much once the settlers arrived, ravenous eyes feasting on millions of ramrod-straight spruce, pine, fir, and hemlocks. A hundred years later, after the last of the old growth had been logged and before the newly planted monoculture trees could be harvested, the town's population had dwindled, just like in many other resource towns throughout the province.

After all the local mills had shut down, Oyster Hill was about to become a ghost town. But then Wi-Fi came along and a desperate mayor allowed a telecommunication company to build an enormous cell tower on a craggy hill behind the village. From the mid-nineties on, a steady stream of well-to-do, professional newcomers had moved to Oyster Hill, had built modern houses, and encouraged the growth of modern conveniences, such as a small recreation facility with a pool. Now, a veterinarian clinic, artist's studio, and a sushi bar have opened in the town's first mall, and there are rumors that a hardware store will move into the anchor space. The little town that could, some say, while others caution that too much development too fast will bring big-city problems to their village.

The dozen RCMP officers stationed here mostly patrol the highway traffic, locate lost tourists, smooth domestics, and hang out near the hotel bar after midnight to grab the town drunk before he can get behind the wheel of his Ram. They've not seen big-city crime and generally seem jovial and relaxed. Unless, of course, they are called to the nearby First Nations reserve, where they feel unsure and outnumbered, and subsequently behave like the louts and bullies they're portrayed to be on city news.

Not here, though, not this morning in this intersection. Three constables cannot contain their sorrow and tears keep spilling from their eyes. The sergeant, called out on his day off, arrives with grim determination, but he, too, succumbs to the overwhelming sadness of the broken child lying near her gleaming pink bicycle. He can see the small scratch marks where nuts had held the training wheels in place.

"Witnesses?" he barks at no one in particular, and Constable Miriam Humphreys answers that, as far as they'd been able to ascertain so far, nobody had seen or heard anything at all. She also tells her boss about the young woman who had come upon the scene and who'd held the child's hand for a few minutes.

"Well, that shouldn't have ruined anything, and the parents will be glad to know that someone was with their girl," Sergeant Stephan Gill murmurs. "Do we have a name yet?"

He learns that the neighbors know the little girl and her parents well; the Newmans were among the first wave to move into the recently finished subdivision. They're friendly and outgoing and Lorna, the mother, had participated in neighborhood activities right up until her due date in early spring. All summer, Lorna and her daughter Lena had walked the stroller through the streets, had proudly introduced little Benjamin to all the neighbors, and Lena, red-haired and mischievous, had shifted the baby's toque to expose a gleaming bald head. Soon after, she'd paraded her new bicycle for all to admire, and the residents witnessed the father jog alongside every time the child had been on it. Everyone asks the same question: would the police go to the parents' house with the news?

The officers assure them that they would and no one volunteers to accompany them. Sergeant Gill looks at his three officers and settles on Miriam Humphreys and Julian Calnan.

"You two, why don't you go to the house," he says quietly. "Bromsky and I will photograph the scene, and Mom and Dad can come down here and see her before we move her. That might be best. I doubt you could keep them in the house, anyway."

He and Peter Bromsky take dozens of pictures from every conceivable angle, and they hear the anticipated screams of anguish a few moments before both parents run into the middle of the accident scene. Constable Bromsky positions himself so that they will not knock into the bicycle, and Stephan stands over the only piece of real evidence he has found, if the little shard of red metal is related to this event. He's careful not to call it an accident in his mind, or a hit-and-run. He wants his impressions to flow unfiltered. He had put out the call to the Vancouver-based traffic team while he was still pulling on his socks in his bedroom and Sybil had just gone into the kitchen to make coffee for his thermos.

"I don't know much," he'd told the dispatcher. "But we have a dead child of about five years, and a driver who likely never even stopped. It's a small town and there are CCTV cameras at several points up and down the highway. If they left a calling card of any type at the scene, we should be able to identify the car and driver."

This little red fragment might be the calling card he'd been hoping for, and the analyst will confirm or deny it. Until then, all he and his team can do is tabulate the information and bear witness to the unspeakable grief permeating the intersection.

When the Vancouver traffic analysis team arrives, they park their cars just outside the yellow tape encircling the intersection. After handing over the accident scene to his forensic colleague, Peter Bromsky heads home, knowing he won't be able to sleep after this night shift. Miriam Humphreys and Julian Calnan drive to the office for a debrief; Miriam will spend the morning "manning" the desk and chasing paperwork, and Julian will set up radar-equipped traffic surveillance just south of town where he'll be less charitable with speedsters than usual. Only Stephan Gill remains on the scene with the CARS team, and he crouches over the little yellow plastic pyramid stenciled in black marker on all sides with the number fifteen.

"This is the larger of the two fragments we found," he says to Luci Miller, the corporal in charge of photography, and then gestures to a series of markers a few meters away. "The other one, only about half the size, is over there, number twenty-two. They both look to be the same red, but it's hard to say."

"You did a good job keeping this so contained considering you allowed the parents in," Luci murmurs while adjusting the dials and focus length on her Canon. She snaps a series of close-ups of the metal fragment lying on the pavement.

Sergeant Gill squats down next to her, scratches his neck, looks directly at Luci, and waits until their eyes meet.

"My father died in a traffic accident when I was twelve and they wouldn't let us kids see him because of his wounds. I lived immersed in a make-believe world full of space avengers and kryptonite, and so I ended up not believing that he had really died. Made up all sorts of stories in my head about what had become of him. Almost twenty years later, when my eldest was born, the grief hit me. It hit me so hard and unexpectedly that I sank into a deep depression and sort of missed my son's entire first year. Not to mention endangered my marriage and my wife's health." He speaks quietly and intently, his eyes never leaving Luci's.

"I know from my own experience how important it is for people to see their loved one in death, touch them, say good-bye, let them go. There is far more evidence of this being good practice than there are cases when a fiber transfer at the scene hampered or derailed an investigation."

"Human needs versus artificial boundaries," Luci nods. "You're preaching to the converted, Sergeant. I'm with you. And I am glad that you took all those pics before the parents… uhm…stepped in."

The parents had been manic, of course. The dad ended up holding Lena in his arms and refused to put her back on the ground. Instead, Stephan had asked the ambulance guys to prepare a stretcher for the little girl and eventually, Dad had been persuaded to tuck his child into the waiting pink flannel sheets. Lena's mom suddenly screamed that she had left the baby home alone, with the door open, and turned to run back when Julian assured her that Constable Humphreys and a neighbor were there, standing guard over little Benjamin, and that they would radio in if she was needed. Lorna turned back toward her husband and wrapped her arms around him. They stood next to the stretcher for ages, murmuring and crying, sometimes reaching out a tentative hand and stroking Lena's waxen cheek.

The hearse had come at eight twenty-five. After hushed conversations with Sergeant Gill, the paramedics, and then Mom and Dad, the attendant had scooped Lena up, flannels and all, and carried her quietly and reverently to the back of the vehicle while her parents looked on, anchored to the curb by shock and disbelief, their hands entwined so tight that Stephan could see the white knuckles.

How in all the world could he have prevented them from being at their child's side in this most crucial moment? He blinks and a tear rolls down his cheek, mirrored by the ones in Luci's eyes.

CHAPTER SEVEN

DRIVING LESSONS

The photograph he takes later that morning is sensational. The bottom third of the image is awash in the charcoal and anthracite shades of wet asphalt, the kid's pink bike is totally centered, its colors jumping out, some glitter on the streamers reflects a lucky speck of sunlight into a bright sparkle, and the top third shows the heavy, leaden sky. Two black police SUVs are silhouetted against the clouds and, more distant, sways a bit of yellow marker tape.

He takes care not to be conspicuous. There are plenty of rubberneckers about: neighbors, joggers, kids on bicycles, old folks walking their dogs, the local bit-paper journo, and their coming and going serves to shield him from being noticed. Not that he needs to linger; he just came by for a quick pass. Could not have done otherwise. This is his scene. His doing. *His.* He had only pulled out his phone because everyone else was doing it, too. Then saw how the shot would line up. Magnificent.

Jo puts her customary late lunch–early dinner on the table. Spaghetti squash with tomato sauce deepened with a handful of ripe plums, sausages, and kale pesto on the side. Pecan cookies for dessert with a side of ice cream.

"Gran, that was so good. I'm stuffed." Nico sighs contentedly and gets up from the table, puts his plate and cutlery next to the sink, and looks at the dishes like they're foreign objects. "Do you, uh, want me to do some cleaning up?"

"Why don't we go for another driving lesson?" Paul folds his napkin and sips from his water glass. "I meet the guys for a game of snooker at the pub at eight, so I have plenty of time now. Gimme five minutes for the bathroom and shoes and we can head out. Okay?"

Jo looks at the heap of dishes cluttered about the sink and sighs. Of course.

Common sense prevails. Nico is only here for another couple of days and he'll get his learner's permit soon. There is so much mayhem on the streets: just look at today's tragedy right here in Oyster Hill. Better to get in front of it.

"Driving is all about patience," Paul says for the hundredth time, and Jo suppresses a smile when she remembers him mooning over a newspaper article that described a group of octogenarians who traveled to Germany to drive rented sports cars around the Nürburgring. And so, she washes the dishes and cleans the kitchen, then prepares overnight oats with the last of the blackberries for her and Nico's breakfast. When she sits back at the kitchen table with a steaming cup of chamomile tea and the library's latest copy of *Canadian Art Magazine* in front of her, she sighs again, deeply, with contentment. She loves having Nico around. Their life is quiet here in Oyster Hill, full of her art and Paul's genial engagement with the community, but she misses the freshness and intensity of living with a young person. At fifteen, Nico is a mixed bag of emotions, intelligence, and a know-it-all attitude, but he's polite and respectful, too. And he is healthy. Totally, one hundred percent healthy. She had seen to that. When Oliver had begun to marvel at the possibility of fatherhood, Jo had taken to books and research again, had read long into the nights about genetic embryonic testing and had traveled to Seattle, again, to consult Dr. Méng-Yào Zhang, the foremost IVF specialist on the west coast. And when Ollie and Gina had become not only wistful but passionate about having children, Jo had born the prohibitive cost of ensuring, as best as science could, that her grandson would emerge from a seed that had been tested for all manner of genetic disease and did not contain any. Handsome, talented, intelligent, gregarious, funny, healthy Nico. Whose university education would not cost as much as his inception. Whose equally healthy sibling egg was implanted in 2018 but was lost to miscarriage when Gina tragically fell down the stairs at her home. Just as Ollie's brother or sister didn't survive. Survival is not to be taken for granted.

Jo has reached the bottom of her second cup of tea when she hears "the boys" tramp up the back stairs and open the mudroom door. Paul seems to be telling a tall tale involving racoons and coyotes, and both are mimicking angry critter noises and laughing boisterously. Jo is ready to join in the fun and looks at them expectantly when they come into the kitchen.

"It's gotten late, I almost asked Nico to drop me off at the pub and come home on his own," Paul says and grins when he sees Jo's face cloud in alarm. "Don't worry, love, I may think daft thoughts, but I wouldn't do it." He leans forward and kisses her on the cheek. "But I'm not sticking around. Have a title to defend." And with that he is off, throwing a "so long" over his shoulder as he traipses out the same way he had just come in. Buddies, beer, and billiards are awaiting. Jo smiles.

"Gran," Nico says from inside the fridge, because, of course, he is hungry again, it's been more than an hour since his last meal. "I managed to scrape your car a bit on the front. I'm sorry. But Grumps says that it's no big deal and you wouldn't mind, anyway." He looks at her, eyes round and questioning, a chunk of Emmentaler and a bottle of ginger beer in his hands, closing the fridge door with his butt.

"If your grandfather feels that way about dings in cars, maybe you could do your driving lessons in his from now on," Jo answers sourly.

"Yeah, I said that, too." Nico grins. "I want to learn how to drive standard, anyway." He puts the cheese and soda on the table, then gets some bread and butter, a plate and knife, then a glass before pulling out a chair and sitting opposite her. "He thinks it's his fault, anyway, and so he couldn't be mad at me."

"What happened?"

"We were at the mall parking lot, and I practiced parallel parking." Nico busies himself and speaks to the tabletop. Of course, he'd be embarrassed. Maybe that's why Paul had said the thing about letting Nico drive home by himself. To bolster his confidence after a mishap.

"I did pretty good with the shoulder checking and all, got pretty close to the curb, too," Nico continues. "But then Grumps wanted me to use only the side mirrors and because I didn't really get where I was supposed to gauge, he stepped out and stood on the sidewalk." Nico laughs, then bites into a thick slice of bread with an almost equally generous slab of cheese atop. "It was funny, you should've seen him. Whirling his arms and shouting to turn fifteen degrees this way and that." He chews for a moment, then swallows, reaching for his glass. "I was doing pretty good, back and forth, and then he waved me forward, but there was a low planter that I didn't know about and he didn't see, so...."

Jo watches Oliver's son talk and eat, drink, and laugh, and a wide band of joy encircles her heart. This boy in her life! Driving lessons with his Grumps, farm work over at the Weatherall's, learning how to can preserves here in this kitchen. This healthy, mostly carefree teen who has all the gifts to squeeze happiness out of the mundane. A frequent notion arises: is this what Ollie would have been like at fifteen if he had been healthy?

CHAPTER EIGHT

THE TEAM

The Vancouver traffic team meets at a diner on the highway, just south of town. Burgers and iceberg lettuce salads arrive in little red plastic baskets, alongside thick milkshakes in metal tumblers with wide straws.

"Gill was right when he called it in," Sergeant Rudd says. "We've got enough metal scrapings and color fragments to identify the car, and this town is small enough. Shouldn't be too hard to find."

"Maybe the driver will come forward on their own," Constable Ki-woo Park adds while she scoops up the last of the ketchup with a couple of fries. "There are no brake marks, the kid more than likely blew through the stop sign, so the driver may not have been at fault. By now, or perhaps tomorrow, they'll realize that and maybe turn themselves in."

"Yes, but don't forget about the community wrath of a small town," Constable Danielle Holtman cuts in. "I mean, can you imagine? They will always be the person who ran over the little Newman girl. There'll be little love and support for them here, whether they come forward or we identify and charge them with a hit-and-run offence. They'll have to move, no matter what happens."

"And in the meantime, they'll have to live with themselves. Maybe we can stoke the purgatory fires over the next couple of days and flush them out," Rudd mouths around his straw. "Let's split up into two teams. I'll head back to the city with the samples and start begging the lab to move them along. Even so, we won't have anything concrete for at least a couple weeks."

"I'd like to stay for the interviews and rumor mill," Luci says, with a fleeting thought of Grant and their date, "and maybe Jagwir or Danielle—one of you, too? If Rudd goes back, Ki-woo will want to go with him, right?"

"You bet, I would! I have a ton of work left on the Tesla file, and you need me at the desk, anyway, for all your pesky little questions." Ki-woo's germ and insect phobia is well-known (and ridiculed) by the entire traffic department, and any one of her colleagues who has traveled with her has a tale about the lengthy cleaning procedure Ki-woo subjects the entire room and ensuite to, ending with slipping her own, sanitized covers over mattress, blanket, and pillow.

"I'd like to stay, too," Danielle and Jagwir Malik, also a constable, say simultaneously, and so that's how they settle it.

Rudd puts two motel rooms on the department's credit card for three nights, then he and Ki-woo leave with Lena's bicycle and the rest of the material that needs to be analyzed in the forensics lab in Vancouver. Luci holds back the largest colored metal shard they found in the intersection and then she, Danielle, and Jagwir drive to the detachment in Oyster Hill where Sergeant Gill and Constable Humphreys are waiting. They gather in the little conference room that doubles as a kitchen.

"So, are you able to confirm that it was an accident?" Stephan Gill asks as soon as they're all seated.

"It certainly looks that way," Luci answers. "But I wouldn't put that in writing yet. Maybe after I've spoken to some of the neighbors and get a sense of traffic flow at that intersection, usual speeds, any gossip about known DUIers on their street.... I mean, known to them, not you," she hastily adds when she sees the scorn on his face. "Sometimes neighbors have a good sense about somebody but would never dare to go to the police about it. But when a child is dead, well, that might loosen a few tongues."

"You're right, of course," Sergeant Gill agrees and smiles, perhaps wanting to smooth over the awkward moment. Luci imagines that having a woman, both a younger and lower-ranked officer, imply that he doesn't know the people who make a habit of driving under the influence in his community has irked his pride, but he recovers.

"I interviewed the parents," he adds. "They think they must have forgotten to lock the bicycle into the garage last night and that Lena must have seen it sitting there when she let the dog out. It's not her normal routine to get up before Mom and Dad, but it happens occasionally. With the new baby, they're exhausted and so much gets done by rote."

Luci thinks he might be the only one at the table who actually is a parent, who remembers the abiding fog of fatigue during a baby's first year.

"How about the bicycle?" the sergeant asks into the solemn silence. "Were you able to spot anything on it?"

"No lacquer or metal transfer visible to the naked eye," Jagwir answers, "but I scanned it with the digital LUPE and found quite a few marks. Without proper instrumentation, I can't say what they're from, but I am sure they were no older than twenty-four hours, max. A couple of marks on the left side of the frame may be the point of impact but, again, those are tiny scratches and dents."

"The car didn't go very fast at the time of impact," Luci adds, "either they had slowed down for the sake of the intersection or they're habitual crawlers."

Miriam Humphreys looks up, startled, from the file notes she was studying. "Would you say it might be possible that the driver hadn't noticed the accident? Like, someone vision- and hearing-impaired, shrunk a couple of inches in the last few years so that they can barely look over the steering wheel. Maybe they never saw the kid and didn't notice that they'd wiped her out?"

"That's actually pretty common," Luci says, "and when we do our house-to-house tomorrow, those are the kind of people we'll pay attention to, for sure."

"And, I guess, the time is of significance, too," Danielle looks at the two local officers. "What goes on here around six? Where would our driver be headed? When we had dinner, I noticed that the diner doesn't even open until seven. What is here in town that's open at six in the morning?"

It turns out that a small convenience store on Main Street opens at six, as does the attached laundromat. As they sit and talk, the local members think of more and more people they know to be early risers. The librarian, who always goes home as soon as she closes in the afternoon because she has to cook dinner for her very elderly parents. She likes to come in early to clean up the previous day's pulled-out and wrongly stacked books. The factotum at the Anglican Church opens the door with a foot-long iron key around the same time. Shopkeepers, short-order cooks and waitresses, and "Of course, we have a few commuters who live here, too," Stephan Gill exclaims. "I can think of at least four off the top of my head. These folks head out real early, sometimes before five."

They sit around the table for hours making lists of people to interview, see if they have security cameras facing outward, and then split up the lengthy roster between the three CARS officers. "I know that you'd like to take on some of these yourself," Luci says to Sergeant Gill, who nods but remains silent. "I know I would if I lived here and knew all these folks. But I prefer to do the initial interviews just with my team, and then bring you guys in for follow-ups, if that's okay. If we think people are withholding or lying, or if you can point out discrepancies when we go over the transcripts tomorrow evening or the following morning with you—well, then a second questioning, maybe here at the detachment, would roll some stuff over. I have done it like that a few times and it works pretty well."

Although the furrowed midline on his forehead and his narrowed eyes say differently, Sergeant Gill nods. Luci wonders if he remembers being a young officer himself, with enough skill and experience to know what he was doing, but not high enough in rank to call the shots. She moves her hand to her temple in a subtle salute. "Thank you, sir."

CHAPTER NINE

INSOMNIA

Jo can't sleep. She has never met Mike and Lorna Newman, or their little girl Lena, but images of grief-wrecked parents fill her mind, and she tosses for hours before finally giving up all together. She gets up and takes her clothes to the bathroom. She needn't really be so considerate; Paul takes a sleeping pill every night and the only thing that can rouse him is his bladder. Jo envies his ability to sleep well but is loath to reach for pharmaceuticals herself. Instead, she drinks a pot of chamomile in the evenings. But today's events have upset her on too many levels for this mild panacea to work.

After she gets dressed, she stops in the kitchen to boil water for her instant and then installs herself in her studio behind the drafting table. The white walls of the large, airy room are covered in lichen drawings and paintings, some framed behind nonreflective glass, some tacked to wooden mounting rails. There are no depictions of sunsets here, nor whales, beach rock, ocean waves, or cloud formations. Wherever the eye travels, there are lichens and their components, fungi and algae. About a third of the drawings are in charcoal and graphite, delineating the characteristic thallus and foliose structures in great detail, the others are watercolors, rendered in infinite shades of green, gray, blue, brown, and orange. There are tendrils and tubules, clusters and pebbles, lobes, flanges, cups, and buttons. Here is a sea foam and shamrock–colored *Xanthoparmelia plittii*, whose maroon discs are clustered in the center with the lobes undulating outwards like glaciers extending into rocky landscapes. There a *Vestergrenopsis isidiata*, olive and hazel, with narrow, longitudinally grooved lobes that forever remind her of hippie-era macramé works. The water creature–like *Toninia sedifolia*, also known as earth wrinkles, whose body heaps into folded and puckered irregular convex warts and squamules, not unlike a cauliflower, in icy blues and light grays. But most of the wall space is given to lichen's predominant color: green, from light mint, pistachio, and spring shades to deeper juniper and forest hues. Green is the color of calm, and over forty years, Jo has perfected the art of imbuing it with light. Her customers praise her artistry, but Jo suspects they fall prey—as she does—to feelings of peace and hope invoked by a pea-green, slender strand of fragile, symbiotic life dotted with specks of dappled sunlight. She has heard about the Japanese custom of *shinrin-yoku*, a meditative approach to being in nature, and believes her paintings nourish a similar yearning.

Jo breathes deeply, pushes air into her lower belly, and counts to six before releasing it slowly. After a few of these, a slight, pleasant dizziness smooths her ragged thoughts. How many parents of dead kids has she known? Is it possible that one can lose count of such tragedies? Little Stacey from Surrey was Oliver's first friend with cystic fibrosis. They met in BC Children's Hospital and hit it off, as only nine-year-olds can. The staff tried to keep them apart, as CF kids are at risk from one another, given that they all colonize different lung bacteria and may cross-contaminate when in close contact. But these two had found ways around the restrictions and mandates, and their parents, Jo and Paul, Barbara and Ralph, hadn't really known enough, hadn't been scared enough, to force separation. They thought it was cute, important even, that their kids had found one another, had found a friend who could truly understand what they were going through. So, they advocated hard and found some money for a large Plexiglas partition and eventually, Stacey and Oliver could watch TV in the same room, provided they kept six feet apart, and they could have their lengthy chest physio sessions together, on either side of the Plexi room divider. At the end of Oliver's month-long stay, everyone had become very close, and adult hugs and phone numbers were exchanged while the kids loudly proclaimed to be besties forever and to call each other every day until college, at least. When Stacey died two weeks before her tenth birthday, Jo, Paul, and Oliver walked behind her small coffin hand in hand with her parents. After that, there had been Lenny, then Peter, Maude, Zach, and Poppy. Oliver had barely known these kids in person but there were good, old-fashioned pen pal–ships, hours-long phone conversations, and later, emails and video calls. Jo and Paul had known the parents well, had met moms and dads at conferences, hospital cafeterias, volunteer and fundraising events, became friends with all of them, and went to every funeral with sympathy and shared grief, but also in penance for their son's continued hold on life.

Twelve, Jo decides. She has been to twelve funerals where she beheld parents' grief, their devastation, where she'd searched for guidance, knowing she would walk in their shoes soon enough. Twelve times unbearable sorrow had seeped into every crevice in her, her heart folding in on itself like matter into a dark hole, her skin made tight and clammy around her neck, her carefully rehearsed words of condolence dried into a croak.

Little Lena's funeral would be large; a child taken by accident in a small community would bring out the entire village. Jo would know the parents instantly: their eyes would scream their torture, never mind the dark rings underneath or the pallid skin and hair. They would walk hesitantly, as though unsure how and in which direction to set their feet. They would look around, searching for their child in the crowd, only to be reminded over and over again that she was not there. Their shoulders and spine would sink under the weight of earth's gravity, their hands would not find a place to be restful, their suppressed screams would pulse in their veins.

Jo squints and feels the moisture of tears on her cheeks. *Release, connect, restore*, she tells herself; a mantra she had come to rely on decades ago. Breathe out your sorrow, anger, fear, or bitterness, connect with what brings you joy, and find your equilibrium. That's how you get through the toughest parts. And so, she breathes and allows her tears to flow, hooks her eyes firmly on green and light and green and green and green—and tries to imagine a little girl in pajamas gazing in wonderment at heaven's lustrous gate.

CHAPTER TEN

THE SEARCH BEGINS

Luci, Danielle, and Jagwir drive from the motel to a little bistro in town for breakfast, then walk over to the detachment to borrow a couple of cars. Their interviews will take them all over, and Oyster Hill, although technically a small town, spreads along a rugged coastline and mountainous terrain; some addresses are a twenty-mile drive apart from each other. Luci elects to go door to door in the neighborhood where the accident occurred, omitting the bereaved parents. Sergeant Gill said he'd check on them and let them know that the team, and he made a motion with his hand to indicate Luci and himself, would update the parents as soon as they had any information. This is fine with her; most RCMP members who have been stationed in a community for some time develop a certain sense of protectionism. A notion she certainly doesn't share but understands.

It had happened to her, too. As a new recruit, she'd been plunked into a small town two thousand miles away from where she'd grown up in Brandon, Manitoba. Was left to her own devices to get to know the people she had been told to serve and protect. So, she ingratiated herself, attempted to forge relationships with no shared history, no slowly developed trust and appreciation. Whenever a friendly hand was extended, she busted her ass to protect fragile bands of community immersion. When she had been invited to her neighbor's kid's birthday party, she had overlooked all manner of barely concealed drug use and even a couple of guys who really shouldn't have gotten behind the wheels of their pickup trucks. What was she to do? Screw up her very first foray into the populace with a heavy police hand? Then, a year down the road, she felt an almost proprietary sense of duty and protection toward her people, especially the ones who had welcomed her in with warmth. Had lost all objectivity in the process and understood that being the nice cop in town undid her as an investigator.

She interviews residents of about twenty homes in a wide circle around the intersection where Lena Newman had definitely been hit by a car, as opposed to some other act of violence made to look like an accident. After their meeting at the detachment last evening, Luci had gone to the mortuary to photograph and document the child's injuries. There'd been an immense hematoma that spread from the girl's left knee all the way to her shoulder. This was where the fender of a car had made contact, no doubt about it, and Lena's small, soft-boned body had actually protected the chassis from any obvious damage. No wonder they had only found a couple of tiny, fragmented paint chips on the ground, and the few dents and scratches on the bicycle had largely come from its impact with the concrete curb. There is a menagerie of stuffies now at that curb, with balloons, flowers, and cards. The community rallying their heartfelt support behind the grieving family.

This is a neighborhood of young families, and many people are not home when she knocks on their doors; she marks these addresses in her notebook to return to in the evening. Even though she already begins to get a sense of the normal traffic pattern in these streets—mainly, that there is hardly ever any through traffic from the highway that runs through town, that few tourists ever find their way here, that most folks barely turn their heads when they cross the streets on foot. Most of the cars parked in driveways this morning have child or booster seats in the back, or one of those cartoon stickers that depicts two adult- and several kid-sized stick figures on the rear window. She walks to the opposite side of the crossing and envisions a red car driving along the through street at perhaps fifteen miles an hour, the driver a short person, both hands on the wheel at the ten and two position, eyes barely above the dashboard. Given the size of the bruise, the car's fender must be massive, so the car is likely a van, SUV, or pickup truck. If a short person sits in the driver's seat of an elevated cab, their view of the area immediately in front of the vehicle would be obstructed by the dashboard and the engine hood.

"So, you could be old or young, male or female, but you're not very tall. Once I'll get the paint code of the fragments we collected, I'll know what kind of car you drive and then it won't take long. Even if you didn't notice when you hit the girl, you must have heard about it by now. You probably went out and had a look at your fender. I can't be sure about that, but if you did, you probably thought that there isn't much to see. If you're devious and a prick, you smear a bit of dirt into the scratches and think that'll be good enough. But you're wrong. It's not good enough. We will find the car and you with it," Luci murmurs, gazing at the impromptu memorial. She does this with all her cases, often right in the middle of a tumultuous scene, with firefighters, paramedics, cops, undertakers, and tow truck drivers swarming about. It serves as her mantra, prayer, and pep talk. A reminder of why she's here, in the epicenter of someone's greatest catastrophe, searching the grotesque scenery for details and clues.

She leaves the neighborhood and drives to a gas station with a repair shop on the outskirts of town. She buys a granola bar and a soda, and shows the bag with the red metal shard to the two mechanics.

"Have you seen this color before?" she asks them. "It's pretty deeply red, isn't it?"

"European cars often have brighter reds than North American or Asian manufacturers," says the younger mechanic after he studies the paint chip. "This looks like something Audi, BMW, or Opel could make, even Volkswagen. What do you think, Earl?"

The older man pulls a handkerchief from his seat pocket and cleans his glasses before examining the bit of colored metal.

"I dunno, could be Toyota. Metallic Spain or something like that," he ventures.

"You mean Barcelona Red Metallic," Luci says, her heart rate speeding up. "I've heard about that one before. It's proprietary Toyota, isn't it?"

"Well, all the car makers patent their paints, but yes, Barcelona Red is Toyota's. Been around more than ten years."

"Do you know where the nearest Toyota dealership is?" Luci asks, and Earl tells her that there are two about an hour's drive south. Of course, she could phone, but Luci believes in eye contact, and she also knows that the sight of a police uniform motivates some people to slip into their most helpful selves. So, she calls Danielle and Jagwir who are interviewing in the outskirts, then, on route in the Subaru using her Bluetooth set, checks in with Rudd.

His news is dismal. Apparently, the RCMP forensic lab is being moved into a new facility in Surrey and, in preparation, the Heather Street location has just begun to send all their cases to Edmonton and Ottawa. This will mean unprecedented delays, and they could count themselves lucky if they get anything concrete by the time their case makes it to court, but they will certainly not be able to use any potential lab results during their investigation.

"Old school," Rudd shouts gleefully, "plodding and nogging will get us there."

"Well, you can help, Rudd. Can you make me a list of Toyota vans, SUVs, and trucks that are factory-produced in Barcelona Red Metallic paint?"

"Sure, no problem. You should get it later today."

Luci makes her own list with the help of the staff at the Toyota dealership in Gibsons, an improbable place for a car franchise.

"You only think you're in the middle of nowhere," the salesman laughs when she voices this. "There are some twenty thousand people living in these parts, double that if you include Squamish."

Must be the trees, she thinks on her way back to Oyster Hill, *that are hiding the hordes.*

CHAPTER ELEVEN

TEAMWORK

When the three CARS officers meet at the diner again that evening, they are tired but confident in their efforts to whittle down the list of potential suspects. Last night, before turning in, Jagwir had spoken to the bartender at the hotel who gave him a few names of people he suspects of habitually driving after leaving his establishment.

"I always ask if I can call a cab for them, but what else can I do? They look me straight in the eye and lie—say they'll walk, and that the wife will pick them up along the way."

Today, Jagwir had dropped by the residences of these folks—and in one case, a workplace—asking about their activities yesterday and taking photographs of their vehicles. Of the six names on the bartender's roll call, he confidently eliminated five as potential suspects, and he'll revisit the last person on the list after dinner. Gordon Machensky lives alone in a small, dilapidated house in the easternmost part of town and drives an older, bright red Toyota Camry according to the neighbors.

"I'd be more comfortable if one of you could come along," he allows. "It's pitch-dark out there, not a streetlight for miles, and the guy has at least one angry dog in his house. The place is just run-down enough to give me the creeps."

"I'll protect you Jags—you know I'm a dog whisperer," Danielle laughs and sips from her large mug of hot chocolate. "But I may have to fortify myself with a piece of apple pie, first. I get an outsized sweet tooth when I'm in the country, especially in the fall."

Jagwir guffaws, his many laugh lines forming a deep, starburst pattern. "That's what you said in Golden, in July. Only, after you ate two pounds of ice cream, you said it was the summer sun that brought your appetite for sugar on."

They banter, recalling some of their best and worst diner experiences. They spend so much time in small towns, eating all their meals at Tim Hortons and sketchy hotel taverns—Luci thinks it's a miracle they don't break out in pimples, develop diabetes, or grow sideways. But all three of them glow in undeniably good health with youthful, muscular bodies, clear skin and, most importantly, fast minds. Danielle is the youngest member of the team at twenty-seven; she is short and fast, with a red Afro, freckles, and large, impossibly white, evenly spaced teeth. She probably could have made a living being a model for Johnson & Johnson but had followed in her father's career footsteps. She'd been the Regina RCMP detachment's press liaison and spokesperson, owing to her natural composure and thousand-watt smile—but a sexist, misogynistic sergeant with roaming hands and a sick sense for pornographic humor had put an end to her deployment there. She fled west and met Rudd at an internal job fair in Vancouver, took the CARS course at his suggestion, and has never looked back. She is smart as a whip, intuitive, and an extremely competent interviewer. Jagwir is thirty-one and carries almost two hundred pounds on his six-foot frame, all of it shoulder and thigh muscles from a lifelong immersion in competitive swimming. He has short-cropped hair and wears the trendiest glasses money can buy, currently sporting a rectangular frame in a light wood that seems otherwise destined to become Swedish furniture. He is a whiz in brake pattern analysis and has an uncanny ability to find loose items that have been projected from vehicles on impact. Cellphones, open beer cans or vodka bottles, bongs, one time even a small dog, injured but alive, almost thirty yards from the truck bed he had not been secured in. The vet bill had been in the thousands, but the owner had paid every penny of it, grateful and chastised, and he still sends Jagwir Christmas cards to the office.

"Was there anything particular about Machensky's place that was odd?" Luci asks him when the food talk ebbs. "Anything other than the dog, I mean?"

Jagwir nods slowly, a contemplative look sliding over his features. "Joe Illingworth, the bartender, described Machensky as volatile and short-tempered. A chronic alcoholic with bad manners. Lives alone on the edge of a salt marsh, comes to the pub at least four nights a week and drinks a few shots and a couple of Millers. Keeps to himself but will hustle tourists for the occasional pool game. He always has money—the barkeep doesn't know where Machensky works, and neither do his immediate neighbors. I say immediate, but the houses on that road are several hundred meters apart, with dense vegetation in between." Jagwir lifts the lid of his teapot, looks inside, and then signals the waitress for more hot water. Because he had charmed her earlier with his winning smile and polite manner, she brings the steaming kettle over right away, and Jagwir thanks her.

"He lives in a small house," he continues, "bungalow type, wood shingles, unkempt although the roof is newish. Blinds are drawn in all windows. Blackberry brambles and salal everywhere, but no signs of gardening or cultivated anything. There's a large metal Quonset in the back, mid-grade in terms of age and general countenance, and the driveway is free of debris and vegetation. It appears as though he uses it quite a bit. Anyway, I didn't go nearer, of course, just had a good look from the road. Overall, the place looks like you think it should after learning about Machensky's boozing habit, but this huge, steel barn is a bit incongruous in that setting. Certainly a good place to hide a red car."

"You think if there are two of us, we might talk him into allowing us access to the Quonset?" Danielle asks, brown eyes sparkling.

"Well, yes, that…and also, the place is just so dark. It was already dusk when I was there earlier and there are no street-lights, no light from the neighbors', the guy doesn't even have a porch light. I checked. So, I'll have to carry a flashlight to knock on his door…puts me at a disadvantage, physically, and him on the defensive, from the get-go."

Luci, who outranks her teammates by one stripe, grins broadly. "We'll check the bar after we're finished here. If Machensky isn't there, we'll all go out to his place. We'll tell ghoulish ghost stories on the drive over there. Reenact *The Blair Witch Project*."

Danielle continues the debrief while savoring a giant piece of apple pie. She had interviewed about a dozen of the early risers and commuters and has pages and pages of notes about what they had seen or not seen during the morning hours. Nothing stands out. Then Luci relates that first Earl from the gas station, and then every single staff member at the dealership, had thought that her paint chip could very well be Toyota's Barcelona Red Metallic, a super popular color. The car lot did not, however, have color sensor soft-ware that could confirm this, but Rudd had learned that a franchise in Kerrisdale did, and he would take one of the fragments there tomorrow.

"So, if it's so popular, there'll be a lot of them here in town and it'll take longer to check them all, right?" Jagwir asks.

"I think we can limit ourselves to only vans and trucks in the first round," Luci says. "Here, look at the picture of the he-matoma on Lena, there is no way that was caused by a sedan."

They look at the large photographs on her laptop surreptitiously, mindful to shield the images from customers and staff in the restaurant.

"Well," Danielle says frowning, "if you picture her on her bicycle, in a seated position, with her left foot on the pedal at the apex, I think even a midsized sedan or compact could cover that area if the angle is just so."

They all stare at the photograph, trying to visualize the moment of impact.

"You're absolutely right," Luci says with a sigh. "I had not considered her body position that way. So, we'll have to look at all Barcelona Red Toyotas in town, and Rudd just sent a text saying that they used the paint mainly on Corollas, RAV4s, Prii, and Camrys but that all their models are available in any color a buyer wants to pay for. And then there is the aftermarket, of course. Rudd found out that Barcelona Red Metallic is really popular and stocked in just about every body shop."

CHAPTER TWELVE

THE DOG

The massive dog is not accustomed to visitors, clearly. He throws his one hundred and thirty pounds against the front door, snarling and howling to meet the intruders head-on. Jagwir, Luci, and Danielle stare at the buckling door, the car's headlights projecting their oversized shadows on the weather-stripped shingles of the dilapidated house. Basic police training had taught them to move apart, for one to meld into the surrounding darkness, but the beast's fury activates primal nerves, and they cluster close. Luci instinctively reaches out a hand toward Danielle, then rests it on the butt of her holstered service pistol instead.

"Oh my," Jagwir croaks, "this is worse than I'd feared." He resolutely steps forward and onto the small porch when Danielle calls to him.

"Jags, there's a light on at the Quonset. Maybe Machensky is in there."

He turns around with relief, then imagines eighty- or one-hundred-year-old metal hinges busting under the dog's onslaught and hastily turns again, navigating the ten steps to his colleagues backwards.

"Dogs are smart, as a general rule," Luci says with more confidence than she feels. "He makes as much noise as possible to scare us off, just protecting his turf."

"Right. Do you think there might be an open back door he can run through to catch up with us on our way to the barn?"

"No way, Jags," Danielle answers in a whisper. "It's barely above freezing, nobody in their right mind would leave a door open for the dog in this weather."

"Right mind, my ass. Does this place look as though someone who is in their right mind lives here?"

"It's just run-down. Nothing here to say the man is crazy. Lazy, maybe." Danielle is still whispering.

Luci steps back. "Come on, you guys. As long as the dog is making all this noise, we can head around back. Let's hope he keeps it up for a while."

They turn off the car's headlights and Jagwir uses his tactical flashlight to illuminate the way back to the road, then into the wide driveway that leads to the Quonset hut. The dog's frenzied barking continues but recedes into the background and becomes less threatening as the officers slowly advance the hundred yards or so to the large metal prefab. A weak light bulb in a steel mesh casing illuminates the top half of the entrance door and not much else. Jagwir turns the flashlight off, and they stand quietly in almost total darkness. The dog's barking abruptly stops. While each of them worries about what that might mean, soft sounds emanate from inside the building. Scraping and a dull thumping and an underlying humming buzz, reminiscent of a strong mosquito light. Something resonant and tonal in the background. After searching his colleague's shadowed faces for consent, Jagwir knocks three short raps on the metal door with his flashlight.

"Mr. Machensky, are you there?" he calls out. "It's the police. May we ask you some questions, please?" he adds a few seconds later, loud enough to cut through the ambient din.

"Who's there?" The voice is gruff, hoarse, and all three of them clearly hear the resentment it contains.

"It's the police, Mr. Machensky. We need to ask you about a traffic accident that happened yesterday."

"Accident? Where?"

"In town, in the Eagles Nest subdivision."

"I don't go there."

"Could you open the door, please, Mr. Machensky? If my report states that I didn't actually see you during the interview, my boss will knock on your door first thing in the morning."

"Your boss is more than a hundred miles away and gets to sleep in," Luci intones quietly, and they almost burst out laughing. The tension of their first few minutes on the dark, unkempt property, eases into annoyance. Why won't the guy open the door?

"I'm in the middle of something. You'll have to wait." The words are muffled, as though the speaker is turning away from the door.

"How long will you be?"

The man inside doesn't answer. Jagwir turns the flashlight back on and slowly arcs it around. A large, rutted dirt yard opens wide, as though trucks or tractors routinely pull in and turn around here. The metal track of the massive sliding doors is clean and shines oily in the strong beam.

"This all looks well used. Heavy traffic in and out. What the hell does this guy do here?"

"Dope." Danielle already sounds convinced. "This place is a grow-op. Large, industrial grow-op. Maybe mushrooms, 'cause there's no smell. Or else he filters the air. That's why he always has money and nobody knows what he does."

Jagwir groans quietly. "Hence the dog. Cheap alarm system. And if he is a grower on this scale, he's probably armed."

"We'll spread out," Luci states. "Jagwir, you stay here with the flashlight on, Danielle and I will step back thirty feet in either direction."

Both women back away and disappear from sight. Jagwir searches the Quonset's exterior for any signage, cameras, or cues as to what goes on inside. He comes up empty. The metal walls are exceedingly plain and give nothing away. He knocks the rugged steel end of his flashlight against the door again, much harder this time.

"Mr. Machensky," he begins in a shout when the portal suddenly flies open and hits his outstretched hand, causing the flashlight to fall on the ground in a wide arc. Improbably, it snuffs out. Jagwir has to take two rapid steps back so that the door doesn't hit him in the chest. The building's interior, a bright, cavernous space that seems crowded with workstations and shelves, is visible only for the briefest of moments before a large man in overalls steps over the threshold and closes the door firmly behind him.

Gordon Machensky, if that's who the quarrelsome-appearing man is, stands in the weak glow of the overhead light with his legs wide apart, arms hanging loosely by his sides, and a glowering expression on his shaded face. He is tall, at least six four, with wide shoulders, a barrel chest, and long, thick arms that end in wide, shovel-like hands.

"You said 'we,' so why are you standing here alone? Is your colleague sniffing about my property?" His voice is deep, sonorous, melodious even, but contains nothing but scorn and suspicion. "I don't want anyone rifling through my place so call them back!"

"It's a tactical decision to stand apart when under threat," Luci says evenly as she steps closer but remains in the shadows. "Good evening, Mr. Machensky, I am Corporal Luci Miller with the Collision Analysis Team and this is Constable Malik. We couldn't connect with you earlier, we apologize for the late hour."

"Threat? What threat?" the man mutters angrily and then barks at Jagwir, "So, what do you want from me?"

"There was a fatal hit-and-run on O'Reilley Crescent yesterday morning, around six," Jagwir says, "involving a red car and a bicycle. We're asking everyone in town with a red Toyota to account for their whereabouts for that hour and also to allow us to check their car."

"My car is not here, and I was in bed, sleeping. Now get out of here."

"Mr. Machensky, please, just a few questions."

"No, dammit!" The man's hands ball into fists but he remains standing still. "I am pretty sure I don't have to talk to you at all, but I did and told you I was sleeping. There, that's it, civic duty done. Now fuck off!"

"It's your right to tell us to leave your property," Luci steps forward into the outer fringe of light. "But if you are not cooperating with our investigation at this basic level, we have the right to ask a judge for a warrant that compels you to answer our questions and also for a search warrant for your entire property."

"Where is your car, Mr. Machensky?" Jagwir asks quietly.

"Get off my land before I let the dog out," the man says through clenched teeth, and Luci makes the fallback signal above her head so both Jagwir and Danielle can see it.

"If you sic your dog on us, we'll shoot it and charge you with assault," she states loudly and clearly. "You'll go to jail, Mister."

Jagwir takes a couple of steps back and puts both arms out wide in a placating gesture. "How about we come back tomorrow, during daytime hours? Will you be home tomorrow morning?"

"None of your fucking business where I'll be in the morning." The man turns and lays his large, lumpish hand on the door handle. Before Luci or Jagwir can utter another word, he opens the door, slides through, and closes it hard behind him. A second later, the wilted light bulb above extinguishes and Jagwir finds himself standing in utter darkness. The building's soundscape of hums, scrapes, and buzzes resumes. He notices a slight vibration in the air around him and relaxes only when

Luci turns her flashlight on. Danielle joins them seconds later, handing him his own light that had fallen to the ground.

"That went well," she sighs with an exaggerated breath. "Now what?"

"We'll head out," Luci answers. "There is nothing to be gained from an antagonized asshole, and if he claims that he just let his dog out to pee, there'll be plenty of prosecutors who won't sign off on an assault charge."

"If Danielle is right and this is a grow-op, he might even have a remote-controlled dog flap or something like that," Jagwir adds and groans when his mind supplies an image of a stealthily approaching attack dog with elongated, super-sharp canines. "Let's go."

They retrace their steps along the well-used driveway, and Luci runs the beam of her flashlight through the ditch for some clue for what kind of freight goes in and out of this place regularly. But there is only long grass, bulrushes, salal, and impenetrably woven vines of blackberries.

CHAPTER THIRTEEN

FRIENDSHIP AND TRAVEL

It's Jo's second sleepless night. *I shouldn't have had that nap in the afternoon*, she thinks gloomily. In the faint night-light's glow, she can make out Paul's indistinct shape under the feather duvet. He had fallen asleep pretty much as soon as his head hit the pillow, having spent the whole afternoon helping a hobby-farmer neighbor with the potato harvest. The Weatheralls treat their harvest help to elaborate, communal dinners, and Paul and Nico hadn't come home until almost ten, sore-muscled, happy, and full of good food.

"I love living here," Paul had murmured contentedly, folding her into his arms and drawing her whole body close against his when they'd crawled into bed together. "We moved seven times in thirty years, but this is the first place where I feel we have truly come home." He'd kissed her on her eyes and cheek before finding her lips in the darkness. His hands began to roam her naked body, following the curves of her hips and buttocks, eventually coming to rest on her thigh. "Je ne regrette rien," he whispered softly, then his breath had regulated into soft snores and his hand on her leg had become heavy.

Jo rolled onto her cozy side, tucked deep into the blanket and thought about that. Seven times in thirty years. From Port Alberni to Victoria, to Vancouver, Langley, Abbotsford, back to Vancouver, then White Rock, and finally, to Oyster Hill. But she and Oliver had moved more than seven times. While Paul was bound to jobs that weren't exactly on a career path per se but still benefited from permanence and regular attendance, Jo's ever-increasing skill as a lichen illustrator proved worthwhile almost everywhere. That was fortuitous. Cystic fibrosis was being researched all over Europe and North America at a dizzying pace; millions upon millions of dollars were gathered through a wide network of foundations that funded innovative thinkers in medical centers and pharmaceutical companies. One such innovator was Dr. Ilse Ramsey, a pediatrician who had finished her residency at Boston Children's Hospital the year Oliver had been diagnosed and who had since moved to Seattle's Children's Hospital. Jo and Ilse had met, by chance, at a hotel bar in Cincinnati during a CF conference. Over Amaretto Sours, they found their birthdays were identical but separated by eight years. Neither had siblings and their spouses' names started with a *P*. Both were fiercely drawn to cystic fibrosis research. Ilse had studied under Harry Shwachman and had been deeply and indelibly inspired by the humanity of the man who'd pioneered global understanding of the disease and who had developed a diagnosis and treatment program that dramatically extended the lives of CF children. Both Ilse and Jo were tall, broad-shouldered, no-nonsense women who could and would move heaven and earth in the pursuit of their erstwhile goals. They were *Yes, we can!* women who eschewed makeup and perfume but enjoyed fashion and adornments, the occasional drink, meandering conversations, politics, and music, with blues and ballads taking top billing. They soon began to refer to the other as sister-friend and, when the conference ended, promised to stay in touch. And they did.

1984

Nine years after a nice-enough doctor had pronounced that sixty-five roses would kill Ollie before his twenty-sixth birthday, Ilse calls at eight in the evening.

"You have to come to Seattle," she urges without much preamble. "Walters and Vichinsky are doing a drug trial for nebulized antibiotics that target *Pseudomonas aeruginosa* and they need human subjects of all ages. This is good, Jo, really good. Something is coming of this, I know it."

Parents all over the continent clamber to get their kids enrolled in drug trials because effective treatments don't exist and no one has the luxury of time. True, kids aren't dying as babies anymore, but they still die in childhood, as teenagers, as high schoolers. Very few CF kids live to attend postsecondary graduation. Drug trials hold the only whiff of hope there is. "Yes, absolutely!" Jo replies before she has even considered the implications of moving to Seattle from their home in Victoria.

The two cities are only a border-security checkpoint and a two-hour ferry ride apart, but Paul's weekend visits are few because he has to pull every extra shift with the parks department he can get. Living in the States is expensive. Jo rents a furnished one-bedroom near Seattle Children's and hires a freshman to tutor Oliver, who is miserable and misses his friends.

"This hospital stinks," he says, "literally, Mom. It smells sick."

"Of course it does," she says. "It's a hospital."

They find Magnuson Park. It's close enough to walk to, and swimming in salt water has been Ollie's panacea forever. It's part of his exercise regime at home, now it becomes his ultimate focus. The water is punchy but he swims every day, in all kinds of weather. He swims in the dark. He swims when the waves are white-peaked, when they leap onto the shore, each wave like a hand reaching out and grabbing the shoulder of the one in front of it. He swims in early morning fog when the water's surface is still, glass-like, and there is nothing but an almost imperceptible tidal roll. His body glides through the water like a blade through silk. Jo is here, too, but her cold-water tolerance is waning. Sometimes, after just a few minutes, her core warmth slips away as if someone had opened the window to let the winter air in. She gets back to shore, rubs herself dry with a hard towel, dresses in layers. Then sits on a log and watches her boy be a seal. Sometimes, there are real seals about, curious, and their rounded, sleek heads pop up next to him, accompany him across the bay then head off into the tangle of algae and sea grass where the fish are.

One of the hospital's physiotherapists, Glen, is an avid hiker and takes them on many trips to Mount Rainier Park. In volcanic soil, Jo and Ollie find lichen they have never seen and take hundreds of photographs, then some of themselves as they clamber on nearby glaciers.

Participating in a drug trial is ridiculously hard. And boring. Before they can even get started, Ollie's baseline has to be assessed by the team. There are rounds of blood tests, spirometry, X-rays, a bronchoscopy, a pulmonary function test, an ECG, a treadmill test. Then they have to show up at the hospital three times a day for the nebulizer treatment; after two weeks of that, the team gives them two days' worth of inhalers to take away, and they celebrate being "off-leash" with an overnight camping trip to the Cascades. Luck would have it that Ilse is off on those same days, so they bring her along. The two women sit by the fire, roast marshmallows, drink tea spiced with dark rum, and talk into the morning hours while Ollie practices rappeling from trees in total darkness.

They don't know if Oliver is receiving the new inhaler medication or a placebo. Any change in his breathing is noted, measured, and fawned over by the medical team, but Jo and Ollie can't tell if an improvement in symptoms is caused by rigorous swimming or perhaps longer-than-usual chest physio sessions. Longer, because they don't have to hurry everything in order to get to school on time. As weeks lean into months, their away-from-home life begins to feel stale, and their motivation to keep up with their intense exercise, swimming, and hiking schedule wanes together with their can-do attitude. Ollie has a flare-up and needs to be hospitalized for two weeks to receive intravenous antibiotics; he's pale, sore, bored, and irritable when Jo brings him back to the rental.

"I'm tired, Mom. Can we go home?"

"Soon, baby. Dr. Vichinsky said to hang in for one more month, then it's done."

After Ollie falls asleep, Jo calls Paul. The next Friday, Paul arrives for a surprise visit, bringing Lou and Danny along, Ollie's best friends. They spend the weekend watching movies and eating pizza, going to the beach, and roaming Seattle's Pike Place Market. When Jo looks at her son questioningly Sunday afternoon, he shrugs. "It's okay, Mom, I can manage another month."

There had been two more drug trials. One in Montreal, in 1990, that lasted almost a year, another earlier one, when Ollie had been thirteen, in Miami of all places, over eight months. Both times, it was too expensive for Paul to come out and visit, but Lou's parents dug deep and sent him, his sister Stephanie, and Danny out for half their summer break to join her and Ollie in Florida. Ollie was ecstatic. The Miami beaches were amazing—all sand and sun, all the time. The kids were in the water day and night and Ollie acquired a layers-deep, bronze tan. Jo couldn't take her eyes off him and, for the first and only time, used her illustrative skills to capture her son's likeness. The picture now hangs in the stairway, exactly where her gaze slides over it every time she turns on the landing. Sun-drenched water with a playful, knee-high rolling surf. A hint only of skyward buildings, bars, cars, tourists. The pride of place to the bronzed, glowing boy, who is just about to throw himself into the water. There is purpose in his stride, vibrancy in every muscle, ease and strength in his movement. You can look at this picture from any angle you like but you will never see stillness. The water rolls and tugs, the sun arcs, the light suffuses, and the boy leaps. Here are his shoulder blades rising to lift his arms above his head, here the shaggy, wet hair that sparks with droplets. One leg high, foot extended toward the hidden sandy landing, the other limb airborne as well, leaving a momentary imprint of toes before frothing water devours it. Ollie had always been a good-natured kid who sought joy above all else, but thousands of sickbed and hospital hours had made him bookish and cerebral, moody and withdrawn at times. In the picture on the landing, there is only bliss.

Jo looks at it in the darkness as she finds her way between bedroom and kitchen. She had lain next to Paul for the past hour, remembering the many times she and Ollie had moved around the continent without their husband and father and how, surprisingly, these separations had fused them as a family. Their aching need for the other had enlarged their hearts and fortified the emotions within. When they were apart, they really, really missed each other. Their phone bills were astronomical, and Jo sent a thousand postcards. They had whispered phone sex under the covers, and Oliver and Paul would call one another twenty times during one hockey game, in jubilation or to tear a strip off a numbskull move.

Paul contacted strangers in hospitals and apartment buildings and finagled they drop off a bottle of wine or a bunch of flowers. She'd call him then and cry with missing but also with love and happiness at his thoughtfulness.

In spite of everything, we survived, she thinks as she watches the kettle boil. *Ollie is still Ollie, and we are still a family. How lucky we are.*

CHAPTER FOURTEEN

A LONG LIST

They'd all slept like logs and when they meet up in the diner just after eight, only Danielle, who had been out at six-thirty for a run and then spent half an hour showering and twisting her Afro into a bun, appears awake and alert. Jagwir's lids droop heavily, and Luci eyes the oily sheen on her coffee with distaste.

"Machensky has a juvie record, sealed, and then a few run-ins into his early thirties...nothing in the last twenty years, not even a parking ticket. Model citizen. No social media accounts, no registered weapons on file. He is the registered owner of four vehicles, three of them currently insured: a '99 red Camry, a 2015 Ford F-150 with an elongated flatbed, and a 2012 Harley-Davidson Roadster. Not one accident report on file." Danielle looks at her colleagues and rolls her eyes. "Come on, guys, wake up! I'd like a drumroll, please."

"For what?" Jagwir spits the words but manages to add an eye-smile that takes the sting out. Classic Jags. "You're telling us we are at mile zero and this is our third day here. What's there to celebrate?"

Danielle beams. "I have been texting Rudd since six. There are thirty-eight red Toyotas registered in Oyster Hill. Machensky's is one of them. Rudd talked to a judge, and she said...." Danielle nudges Jagwir across the table, "this is where your drumroll comes in," and waits until he taps his two pointer fingers rhythmically on the table. "She said that we can have a warrant to inspect and photograph, but not seize, any BRM Toyota in town where the owner won't allow access."

"Bravo, that is good morning news, indeed," Luci grins and Jagwir whistles, then high-fives Danielle.

"Alright," he laughs, "well done, Miss Marple Mophead! Now we're getting somewhere!"

Rudd's list arrives complete with owners' names and addresses; Luci and Danielle split it evenly. It'll take them all of today to visit each residence, inspect the vehicles, measure and photograph any front-end scratches they find, and take tiny lacquer samples. Keep up with their notes. In court, the only maxim that counts is: where are the notes? If you don't write it down, it didn't happen. Simple as that.

Jagwir will drive by the detachment on First Street and arrange with Sergeant Gill for two locals to accompany him to Machensky's house.

Just as they are leaving the restaurant, the chime for a video call from the Vancouver office alerts, so they quickly crowd into the Subaru and open the laptop. Ki-woo grins widely at them from the screen.

"Good morning, bedbug smorgasbord. How is the local mountain air?"

"We're at sea level, Ki-woo, just like you."

"But so far north, and there are big mountains right behind you. I saw them myself." Ki-woo laughs and points to her sparkling eyes. "Twenty-twenty, dear ones. My optometrist-uncle still copies my vitamin list for all his patients." She giggles then looks down and appears to be typing.

"I am sending you a list of red Toyotas that showed on the four highway cams north and south of Oyster Hill between five-thirty and eight on August 28, the day of the accident. I cross-referenced insurance records and the list Rudd sent and grouped the cars into local and away. Where you see check marks, the car has no record of any accidents. Exclamation marks for drivers with more than one recorded accident, double exclamation marks if they had been at fault. A star for DUIs, double stars for suspended licenses."

The screen splits and a columned list appears, in color. Jagwir sighs deeply when he sees *page one of four* appear in the bottom corner.

"Seriously, Ki-woo? Four pages?"

"Mmh, yes, and you could be grateful that I spent an hour manually cross-checking the early license plate numbers against their insurance data when it was still too dark to differentiate colors."

Luci turns the tiny Bluetooth console printer on, and the first page begins to emit.

"This is great, thanks, Ki-woo. Looks like there is quite an uptick in traffic from just after six for about an hour."

"Yes, very noticeable, especially when you look at the cam video at high speed. A definite cluster, all those commuters heading south."

They print out two copies of Ki-woo's list and Luci and Danielle mark the commuters on their sheets with an asterisk; places they would have to visit in the late afternoon and evening, perhaps even tomorrow, when those who work in the city would begin their weekend with a comfortable lie-in. That still leaves more than ten addresses each for this morning.

"Jags, maybe Machensky is a pussy cat by daylight, and you can help us out after lunch?"

Jagwir smirks. "It's more likely I'll call a code FUCK! Am not really looking forward to this, but who knows, maybe it'll close the case." He gets out of the car, waves, then heads for the borrowed marked cruiser parked in front of his motel room.

CHAPTER FIFTEEN

LUCI MEETS JO

"Hello, is anyone home?" Luci calls out after knocking twice.

"I'm in the back!" a woman shouts. Luci follows the sound around the side of the house.

A woman with long gray hair is hanging up laundry on an old-fashioned spider when Luci comes through the garden gate. She turns around when she hears the gate swing open with a faint look of anxiety at seeing Luci.

"Hi, I'm Corporal Miller, but please call me Luci. I am here about the accident over on O'Reilley Crescent the day before yesterday. You heard about that?"

"We all have," the woman replies, the hint of fear in her eyes shifting to sadness. "I'm Josephine Nelson, but please call me Jo. You're not from our detachment, are you?"

"No, I'm not," Luci responds for the fifth time today, "I'm on loan. RCMP units are a bit like your local library where you can get just about everything through the intra-library loan program. Just put in for Jamie Oliver's latest and voila!"

"So, you cook and fight crime? And you're not a cranky old man in an ill-fitting suit. Bravo!"

"I detect a reference to Hercule Poirot? Or Nero Wolfe, perhaps?" Luci smiles.

"Don't forget the 'Gourmet Detective.' Those were fun, too." Jo slings the last couple of towels over the line and faces Luci with her hands clasped together. "Okay, take me then. I'm guilty of everything. Take me to a nice city jail where they'll give me three squares, I get to meet lots of interesting women, and have a wretched affair with a handsome guard. Or guardette. I'm not picky."

"You have watched too much *Orange Is the New Black*," Luci laughs, "real prison is boring, trust me, I have that on good authority."

They look at each other, grinning widely. Luci is aware that this gray-haired, straight-backed old woman with bright eyes and laugh lines all over her face reminds her of her favorite aunt, Michelle. The animation in the woman's eyes wanes when Luci says that she's here because Jo's RAV4 is of the same color as the vehicle that hit the little girl.

"Barcelona Red Metallic," Jo says with a wry smile, "the name appealed to me as much as the car. Well, and the color actually. When I drive around, I imagine that I'm a *capote de brega*, which is what the Spanish call the cape the matador swings about to ire the bull. Not that I like bullfighting," she adds quickly, "I'm more about the irritating part."

Luci laughs. "You are a card," she says, "I've got an aunt in St. John's, Newfoundland, who'd have your number."

"That girl's parents have been on my mind all day and night," Jo says, sorrow clouding her features. "I can imagine what they're going through, and my heart aches for them."

"You can? Imagine their grief, I mean?"

"Yes, sadly. Our son was born with cystic fibrosis, and we lived for more than twenty years anticipating his death. And of course, all the people we befriended over those years were parents of CF children, and we walked behind a lot of coffins. Parental suffering after a child's death is its own circle of hell. I have always believed that."

Luci looks into the older woman's wide, expressive eyes and strikes Josephine Nelson from the list of people who might smear a bit of mud across scratches on the front of their cars. If this woman had smacked into Lena, whether with acute awareness of the incident or a growing suspicion afterwards, she would fess up. Almost certainly.

"Do you mind if I have a look at your car?" she asks with a friendly smile. "We are looking at all red Toyotas in town and are checking for front-end damage. It'll just take a minute, and I'll shoot a couple of photographs, too."

"Of course, you can. It's parked around the other side of the house, by the woodshed."

Jo leads the way. They walk back through the garden gate, past the front of the house, where a white Volvo is parked underneath an old cherry tree.

"Paul, my husband, parks here, next to the garage," Jo explains. "The garage is crowded with wheeled things and tools, of course, so he likes to think that the tree provides weather shelter for his car." She turns to Luci and winks. "But you know how much crows and sparrows like cherries, right? So, for most of the summer, his car is covered in bird shit and pits." She laughs.

"My car's around the side." Jo laughs again. "It's silly, really. There's a small opening on this side of the woodshed, and I always park right in front of it so that no opportunistic bear can surprise me when I come for a bit of firewood from the other side." She points to her car, which is nosed right against the wall of an outbuilding, at the far side of the house.

Luci takes an involuntary breath. The red RAV's bumper touches the rough-hewn wall of the shed, and she can see even from here the scratches and small indentations all along the side of the right fender.

"Oh. It appears you use the well-known Braille method to park," she manages to joke, although she doesn't find this funny at all. These cars, unloved and used for utility alone, are a nightmare for forensic investigators. She sighs into Jo's snicker. She also notes that the car is parked so far away from the house that it could come and go without notice.

"Jo, I have to get access to the front of the vehicle. Could you pull it back a ways, please?"

"No problem."

Jo opens the driver's door without unlocking it and gets behind the wheel with youthful ease. She must be well in her seventies but talks and moves like a much younger woman. Luci is reminded of Lily Tomlin.

When the car moves backwards, its tires are almost soundless on the soft ground that is covered in wood chips and saw dust.

"Will that do?" Jo calls as she exits the car.

"Perfect, thank you," Luci replies and walks toward the RAV's front. It is as bad as she'd expected. The entire fascia of Jo's car is scratched up. It tells the story of years of driving along forest roads and too narrow pathways, of inattentive turns, tiny fender-benders, items falling out of arms or off garage shelves onto a once-gleaming hood. Luci sinks into a squat to inspect the area closer. Many of the scratches are rusty and can therefore be eliminated from the current investigation. But there are also some fresh marks in the red lacquer near the right fender, as well as chipped and scratched bits around the right headlight and signal lights. The bumper cover is lacerated extensively on the right side from years of "parking by Braille," using lampposts, concrete barriers, flowerpots, and tree stumps.

"It's a bit of a mess, isn't it," Jo says glumly.

"It sure is." Luci points to what appears to be the newest markings in the red paint. "Look here, Jo, these marks are pretty fresh. And here, just a centimeter to the left, that looks like it could be concrete. Have you hit anything in a parking lot this past week?"

Jo guffaws. "Sorry, I know this is no laughing matter. But the way I drive, well, I probably hit something or other every second day." She bends over from the waist and scrutinizes the area Luci is indicating. "You're right, that gray fleck does look like cement. Maybe from the new flowerpots they put up in the parking lot of our very first mall."

"You hit one of those?"

"Nico did. A day or two ago. He was practicing parallel parking in the lot with his grandfather. He told me about it, but I never even looked at it." Jo shrugs. "The front of a car is for collecting bugs and protecting the passengers."

Luci frowns. "And Nico is…?"

"My grandson. He's fifteen and keen to get his learner's license. He drives almost every day when he's up here."

It is illegal for a person of any age to drive a car in a public space without a license, but Luci doesn't admonish the older woman. Her job is to gather information.

"And is Nico here now?"

"Yeah, last week before school starts again."

"Can I meet him?"

Jo seems to consider this.

"He's off with his grandfather. They likely won't be back till late. If it's important that you speak with him, you could come back tomorrow. We're taking him home to Vancouver later this weekend. School starts Tuesday."

Luci makes some notes. "Yes, I'll come back tomorrow morning. What time will you all be up?"

Jo laughs. "Me at five-thirty, Paul at six, Nico seldom before nine. Take your pick."

Luci tucks the information away. Household with three drivers. "Okay, good to know. I'll grab my gear. Shine some light, take some pictures. Also, do you consent to me taking a few small lacquer samples?"

"Knock yourself out. I think bits of paint might fall off every time I drive, anyway."

"Alright. I'll be about fifteen minutes."

"Why don't you come inside when you're done?" Jo says and turns to go. "I'll put the kettle on. Tea or coffee?"

They settle on fresh mint tea and Jo goes inside while Luci takes a bunch of photographs of the car's passenger side and several frontal shots, as well. The newest-looking fender mangle doesn't sit quite right with her. Maybe because it is exactly where a fiber of Lena's rainbow pajamas could have been lodged, or maybe it's because the fresh scratches are at just the same height as a little girl, riding a small bicycle, would be. She takes some measurements, too, and documents the exact distances between the relevant markers and points. This Toyota is the first one to come close to what the team hopes to find, and Luci consciously tucks her good feelings about Josephine Nelson aside and gives the car her professional attention. When she has done all that she can, she walks up the front steps and knocks on the door.

"Come on in," Jo shouts from the kitchen when she hears the knock, "and leave your boots on."

Luci soon sits at her kitchen table in a bay window over-looking the garden. "You sure have it made here," she says, "what a beautiful spot."

"Some days, I could sit here from sunup to sundown," Jo replies, "and watch the world go by, or rather come to. Everything eventually comes through here, all sorts of critters and birds, occasionally even a black bear looking to share my berries."

"A window into a different kind of world," Luci murmurs and Jo smiles at her.

A kindred spirit, she thinks. *I'd hang out with you if you lived here.*

Luci sips at her honeyed and fragrant tea, then puts the cup down and pulls her notebook and pen from her shirt pocket.

She takes a deep breath.

"Look, Jo, I'll be honest with you. Some of the most recent damage on the front of your car is obviously from a cement block or some similar object, and I have no reason to doubt you on that. But it is also consistent with a successful attempt to cover up traces that could have occurred if the car had struck something else, before." She holds up a hand as Jo opens her mouth.

"Just hear me out, please. The girl's accident was just that, an accident. We are confident that she rolled through the intersection without obeying the traffic signal and that she was struck by a slow-moving vehicle. A Barcelona Red Toyota, which would have sustained minor front-end damage, likely to the passenger side fender. So, we are looking at all Toyotas here in town, and will move on to those on the highway cameras if we can't match a local car to the metal fragments we collected at the scene."

Jo leans back in her chair, keeping her eyes steady on Luci, her hands loose on either side of her full teacup. She didn't expect this level of frankness. Weren't police supposed to play their cards close to their chest? Why is this one so forthright?

"So, Jo, your car matches on all counts, I'm afraid," Luci continues. "Here is a household with more than one adult, meaning that either you or your husband could have been driving, with the other either unaware or protectively lying. Don't get mad at me now, I'm just laying out the way we think about these cases. Add to that the teen who just happens to be practicing for his learner's, and we have three potential drivers. The car, which matches the suspect vehicle, appears to have 'conveniently,'" Luci inserts the requisite air quotes with her fingers, "met a flowerpot the day of, or after, the accident." She sits back and curls her hands around her cup. "You see how this looks to someone like me, don't you?"

Jo shifts in her seat, keeping her eyes trained on Luci. *No, this woman is no longer the type I want for a friend. This new one, sitting across the table and drinking tea with honey from an earthenware mug I bought at a farmer's market only a year ago and give to guests because it's neither chipped nor tea-stained, seems more of a calculating harpy. Just look at the way she taps each point on her fingers, as though inventorying a roll call of my guilt. Where in the world do police get off making such assumptions? Give a girl a uniform and she thinks she can make wild accusations right here in my kitchen?* Jo holds her gaze steady, forces her hands to lie still. This is not the time or place for a temper tantrum, that much is clear. "I will never look at the world through cop eyes, but yes, I hear what you're saying. So, what comes next?"

"The paint samples from your and all the other red Toyotas we're looking at will be examined at an RCMP lab. Paint and lacquer comparison isn't quite like DNA, but the lab will be able to determine if a sample comes from the same batch of cars, painted in the same facility at roughly the same time. But first, let's talk about the timeline for a minute. The accident probably happened shortly after six, Wednesday morning. Were you up at that time?"

Jo adds some horizontal lines to her forehead as she pretends to mull this over. "Yes," she says eventually, "I had gotten out of bed at about five. Was here, in the kitchen, drinking my first cup of coffee. A little while later, after Paul had joined me, we heard the sirens."

"Are you certain that Paul was still in bed when you made your first cup of coffee?"

Jo smiles and makes a little harrumph at the back of her throat. "Paul sleeps like a baby. He takes a sleeping pill every night around ten or eleven and is snoring well before midnight. He rarely opens his eyes before his alarm goes off at six."

"So, he would not be a witness to your being at home, then?"

Jo's eyes widen, and she gives Luci a look of irritation. "Now see, that's uncalled for. This level of suspicion, this assumption that people are lying to you. You are sitting at my table, drinking my tea, we are having a grand old time chatting, and you throw this at me, this skepticism that I am anything but forthright? That's not cool, Corporal Miller."

"I know, believe me, Jo, and I am sorry. All I can say is that, as a police officer, it is my job to look for proof, the kind I can document." Luci shrugs and moves her chair back a little, creating more distance between them. "My first impression of you, Jo, is that I like you. But that's all it is, a first impression. I don't know you, don't know what makes you tick and who you are. Maybe you are a saint, maybe you rob banks, or maybe you lie easily to protect yourself or the ones you love. The thing is that I don't know."

Silence rises between them like an invisible wall, and they regard each other with set expressions.

Finally, Jo sighs. "I don't really care about your first impression of me or whether you like me. I'm not twelve anymore. I care that when I say to you that I was here in my kitchen Wednesday morning, drinking coffee, you have the gall to ask me for verification. I don't feel good when someone so openly and brazenly doubts my integrity." She hesitates for a moment and then goes on. "It's like when they ask you in a store to leave your bag or pack at the counter. I know that they lose a gazillion dollars to shoplifting and imagine they are doing all they can to limit such losses, but still. I am deeply insulted when they imply that I am a thief. Or could be one. It's an affront."

"Alright, let's start over," Luci says. "I can't take back my question, but let's leave that and talk about your grandson for a second. Did you see him in his bed that morning?"

Jo sits quietly, looking straight at Luci. But in her mind, she's sitting before a doctor. Any one of a hundred or more strangers who became Ollie's doctor because they were on call that night. Or they were the new resident. The new-to-Ollie doctors would hear her talk but never truly listen, never trust her knowledge and expertise of Oliver's symptoms and illness. They were I-have-seen-it-all ER docs, residents, or interns with little experience with CF kids; they hid their ignorance or lack of expertise behind professional arrogance and ordered diagnostics that were a waste of time while Ollie's color went from pale to ashen. These doctors leafed mechanically through Ollie's massive chart and missed the highlighted part about which anti-fungal medication had been spot-on three times previously and should be used first. They were the doctors who, with their conceit and arrogance, had honed Jo's sense of protection into a formidable advocacy skill. She veers toward it now, routinely and competently, as easily as breathing.

"No, I did not see Nico. He is fifteen, he sleeps with his door closed. He looked sleepy and disheveled when he came downstairs at about nine or so, asking for waffles. He ate five or six. Do you think he could have had such a good appetite if he had just killed a child?"

Her tone sharpens ever so slightly, her eyes radiating steel. "Look, Corporal, I think you should leave. You have your pictures and I told you what I know. If you have to come back to speak to Paul or Nico or both, then come here tomorrow at about ten in the morning. I'll let Nico know to get up early."

If Luci is surprised about Jo's shift in tone and demeanor, she doesn't let on. She rises gracefully from her seat, thanks Jo for the excellent tea, and walks out of the house. As she descends the front steps, she turns around and looks at Jo, who stands in the open front door. "I am sorry that my questions upset you, Jo. Hope the rest of your day will smooth your ruffled feathers."

CHAPTER SIXTEEN

THE HIKE

Jo slips behind the wheel and carefully backs out of the driveway. She shudders and bile rises in her throat when she thinks about the insinuation that this very car might have caused the worst that could happen to a family. The cop had said Lena Newman's death had been an accident, may not even have been an intentional hit-and-run, but still, it was hard to fathom that she, that *her* car, could be accused of such.

She remembers how fatal a common cold could have been to Oliver when he was young, and how much rancor she'd felt about careless hospital visitors who brought their disgusting germs in with them. *How dare they set foot outside their own four walls if they have as much as a runny nose?* she had thought often. How dare they threaten her son's life with their sore throat? This anger at everyone and everything had consumed and sustained her for years. She could live on anger, better than on worry and fear, anyway. It was righteous and had given her the strength and endurance to become a strong advocate for Ollie. Later, after the successful transplant, she had been infinitely glad to let the anger go. She had, with joy and reverence, rediscovered her happier, gentler, good-humored self.

She thinks about the Newmans and their anger toward the person who had caused their girl's death. They would be angry after they were done being stunned. In the center of their grief, there would be rage. Would it matter, in the end, if they had a name or a face to direct it at? Had it even occurred to her to ask the nurses which child's visitor had brought this new bout of cold to the pediatric ward? Or which doctor, nurse, lab tech, or child life specialist had not bothered to wash their hands before entering Oliver's room? And this rage that she'd felt, that she had always thought of as beneficial in her dealings with the myriad medical specialists and the bureaucracies of the health-care industry, had that anger not been useful exactly because she didn't have a singular face to direct it toward? Her fury had been a blanket, not a spear; or sometimes a soapbox to stand on, but never a weapon. Would it be so for the Newmans? Would never knowing who had been the driver of the red car spare them a lifetime of hate?

Jo noses slowly into Louise's laneway, opens the driver's door, and pats Samson, the Newfie, who had excitedly circled the car.

"Sorry it took me so long," she calls out to her friend who appears behind the garden gate. "Sam's extra excited. We'll go for a big hike, then. Ta-da!" Jo walks around the car to open the rear door and the ungainly dog jumps into the boot and makes himself comfortable.

Seven years ago, not long after Jo and Paul had moved to Oyster Hill, Louise Reynolds had been little more than a passing acquaintance. Then she'd broken her ankle and asked on Facebook if anyone would take her dog to the beach for an hour every day. Jo, who still hiked for lichen sightings and swam in the ocean regularly, stepped up enthusiastically. What better outdoor companion than a big, lumbering, goofy dog? Since then, she and Samson meet every other day, rain or shine, and either head to the beach or into the mountains. Today, Jo drives to the parking lot of the large provincial park that begins just north of town, where hiking trails stretch some twenty-five miles in all directions. Jo and Sam love it here; she allows him to roam freely, knows that Samson is old enough to no longer feel the desire to chase every scent, and he rewards her trust with his companionable silence, walking heel for long stretches. Jo talks to him, shares her triumphs and grievances with him, tries jokes, and practices lines and comebacks.

Today, she tells him of the policewoman's visit. "If you can call that kind of nosey, suggestive interrogation a visit, even." How she had felt a spark between herself and the cop. When Luci had first walked into her backyard—after Jo had moved past the initial fear that Paul had been hurt riding his scooter to the grocery store, which Jo has never felt is safe for a man approaching seventy-five—Jo had thought to herself that here was a woman she could like. Though the cop is "on loan," as she had called it, she probably lives in Vancouver. But Jo knows how precious the recognition of a kindred spirit is. "I moved around so much," she tells Samson around a mouthful of energy bar while he eyes her solemnly, waiting for his own treat. "A fresh start every few years, losing neighbors, friends, colleagues. All their lives carry on just as well without you; you hear that when you call for birthdays or Christmas, but you have to start from scratch. It's not easy making friends."

In truth, she never had the energy or the time. It had to happen by itself, along the way, as it had with Ilse, whom she still sees once or twice a year. Others were more episodic, confined to a specific place or time—CF parents, nurses, physical therapists, neighbors, fellow dispatchers. Close relationships, warm and intimate even, but the bonds never got a chance to strengthen into lasting friendships before one thing or another to do with Oliver's illness forced Jo to pull up stakes again.

"This Luci Miller—she had something. Humor, intelligence, forthrightness, and vitality. All stuff I admire. And then she has to accuse me of lying. What a crapshoot." And Jo had reacted as she always does when she perceives her family under threat: closed ranks. Pulled back her outstretched hand and went into defender mode.

"Ollie used to call me Gorilla Mom when I got this way. He had seen a classic Tarzan movie where there was a fight between an old alpha gorilla and young Tarzan with much chest banging, glaring, and roaring. Ollie was in stitches and kept laughing that I was exactly like that with doctors. Not very flattering, come to think of it, but I could dish it out back then, believe you me." She hadn't chest-banged with Luci, or roared, but she had uninvited her right out of her house and pulled back hard. Why had she reacted so strongly? Why had the corporal's questions raised such an ire, such a strong defensive response?

Jo knows why but doesn't dare to tell even Samson. Some words, once spoken aloud, go forth into the world and create a life on their own. Some thoughts, or even just wisps of inklings, must never be put into words.

"I think that I have breast cancer," she says to Samson instead, as they near the parking lot. Had she really waited almost two hours into the hike to finally give voice to this new…reality? Samson is tired and doesn't even raise his huge head to gift her a baleful look. He just lumbers on, in full awareness of the car's proximity and its cargo of treats and water. "I haven't even told Paul yet," she continues and slows her steps as the weight on her sternum tips the scale and a sob expands in her throat. She and Paul are as intimate with each other's bodies as two people can be—this bodily sharing had resulted in decades of satisfying and sometimes outrageous sex, had foretold pregnancy to Paul when Jo had still not known that she was even late, had allowed them to witness the other age and in so doing, removed all vanity and shame. But now she is secretive;

this cancer is hers. She doesn't want to share it and, least of all, be cajoled or pummeled into a treatment she is not ready for. Isn't even ready to contemplate. First, she needs to take time to become familiar with the lump. That is enough for now. "Paul would not understand," she tells Samson's backside. "He has swallowed the early-detection message hook, line, and sinker. That may be expedient for the medical industry, but it does nothing for me." She stops to gaze at some mushrooms, a beautiful *Pholiota* cluster nestled perfectly in the center of forked fir branches, close to the ground. She pulls her phone from her seat pocket and snaps pictures while Samson waits, his tongue hanging limply. Is he getting too old for a two-hour hike up a steep mountainside?

"Not to worry, my old friend," she murmurs and walks over to stroke his neck and shoulder. "We'll go to the beach next time. And maybe we'll head for the Kinnikinnick trails the week after—they're not as steep."

CHAPTER SEVENTEEN

LUNCH BREAK

Luci heads to the next address on her list. Good grief, that woman had turned from sugar and spice to cranky in mere seconds and had delivered the only pushback Luci had encountered so far today. Most people have been keen to help the police and allow their red Toyota to be ruled out; understood that the process of elimination would, eventually, lead to the person who had caused a child in their midst to die. Another elderly woman, Regine Herbertson, had offered photographs on her phone as proof that the right fender had been scratched up weeks ago during a family party involving a multitude of kids on pogo sticks and had not been the slightest bit offended. In fact, she'd been glad she could proffer the pics, irrefutably dated by her phone's software. So, what makes one person bristle when another has not the least bit of objection? By nature of her work, Luci tends to lean toward suspicion; the concept that a person is innocent until proven otherwise may apply to the way things are handled in court, but a police officer worth her salt uses a different sort of barometer to measure potential guilt, and so she tucks

Jo Nelson into a mental column titled *hiding something* and vows to return the next morning promptly at ten to question the husband and grandson.

By two, Luci arrives at the detachment. Danielle and Luci ready their collection of metal shard samples for the lab. Chain of custody rules forbid sending any evidence by courier or post, so they place their labeled and sealed bags into the station's safe until they can collect the remainder before delivering the lot to the Vancouver lab. But now, because of the relocation plans, everything will be passed on to Edmonton or Ottawa. *Whose bright idea was that?* Luci wonders. They compare their lists and create a schedule for the remaining eight local red Toyotas to be checked as well as their driver's whereabouts Wednesday morning at six.

The office administrator, Millie Scutari, has laid out a tray of homemade sandwiches, a box of Tim Hortons apple fritters, and an enormous thermos of coffee, and they eat while they wait for Jagwir. The two constables who had gone out with him to Gordon Machensky's place had returned and reported that Jags was off to the Horseshoe Bay ferry terminal to examine Machensky's Toyota.

"He'll tell you all about it," Miriam Humphreys says, eyeing the apple fritters with longing before giving in, pulling up a chair, and laying out a napkin on the table in lieu of a plate. "My mouth thanks you, Millie, and my heart and soul, too, but my hips aren't all that grateful," she calls loud enough for the office assistant to hear in the next room. Then she sinks her teeth into the sweet treat. "It went okay," she says a minute later. "The dog turned out to be a bullmastiff, six years old, very well trained. When Machensky is relaxed and in the room with him, Hero is a pussy cat. He's obviously been trained to guard the house with noise but was friendly enough with us."

"How about the owner? Was he friendly, too?" Luci asks.

"No, not exactly. Rather tight-lipped, rude even, but eventually compliant. I'm familiar with him. Often, when he goes to the pub, he rides his bike, and I've pulled him over a couple times for not wearing a helmet or having a working light, but I've never given him a ticket, so he has no beef with me. When he did answer Constable Malik's questions, he addressed me, every time." Constable Humphreys smirks and licks the specks of sugar gathered on her lips.

"He is an asshole, alright. Would only ever answer a question on the third or fourth go-around, and always waited till pushed, till he'd riled Constable Malik up by a few notches. Then he'd give him a morsel that was just enough to answer but lacking any real information, then he clammed up again. It was like chewing an apple through a letterbox." She laughs and gets up to pour some coffee into her tumbler. She raises her eyebrows, but both Luci and Danielle decline. They've had their fair share of caffeine today and switched to water after lunch.

"Your guy was good, though. Firm and patient, never rose to the bait. In the end, he was squatting to pet the dog and asking questions in a kind of soothing, singsong way, like he was talking to Hero, not to his owner. That seemed to work; Machensky relaxed a little and spat out a bit more. Gave up the location of the car and because it's parked in a public parking lot, we left it at that, and your colleague went off to have a look at it. Should be back any minute."

As if on cue, they hear Jag's laughter and Millie's exuberant giggle.

"Millie's the best, a true original," Constable Humphreys grins. "She's smarter than any of us and quicker, too, comes up with one-liners like nobody's business. We're all killing ourselves to one-up her but she's got our number every time. Keeps us sharp."

Luci thinks that if more RCMP detachments had a Millie, they'd all be better off. Intelligence and humor and warmth—you don't need to be Einstein to understand those qualities go a long way in difficult circumstances. Many times, when she was still working rural postings, colleagues and office staff had been sullen or loutish or both. Young people, out of their comfort zone geographically, heady with the power of their uniform, and not a parent or mentor in sight. They behaved badly simply because they could and egged each other on, to boot. Nasty times. She shudders at the recollection but it doesn't linger. It's good fortune to have found a workplace she enjoys and feels comfortable in. And the crew here in Oyster Hill are doing it right: every single officer has been good to work with and Millie, well, she's the icing on the cake.

Jags walks into the conference room, a wide smile plastered on his face.

"Can't say that it's in the bag, but Machensky's car is looking mighty fine right about now." He pours coffee into a paper cup, carefully adds milk and sugar, then pulls up a chair and selects a sandwich.

"So, he works as a contractor for a Norwegian fish farm company that operates several large, on-land tank farms here on the coast. I think he studied engineering but am not sure if he completed his degree or not. Anyway, this company manufactures their own recirculating systems and trains only a handful of people on the ground to fix and maintain them, to safeguard their proprietary technology, I suppose." Jags takes a bite from his roast beef sandwich and smiles contentedly while he chews, then washes everything down with coffee.

"When some bit of machinery malfunctions," he says more solemnly, "he flies out to have a look. More often than not, he uninstalls it, loads it onto a barge, and brings it to Horseshoe Bay. He drives the thing back to his property in his truck and works on it in the Quonset." He pauses to take another huge bite and chews quickly.

"But he doesn't always fly out to diagnose the issue. Sometimes he tells them on the phone to ship the thing down here. So, he mostly keeps the flat-back at the ferry. When a pump or a filter or what-have-you arrive on the barge, he drives himself to Horseshoe Bay in the Toyota, then takes the truck with the part back to his place. He fixes the thing, brings it back to the ferry dock, leaves the truck, and goes home in the Toyota. That's why it's parked there now."

"Does he lease a permanent parking spot from the ferry corporation?" asks Luci.

"Ah, see, I knew you'd ask me that. How public is public, is a leased parking spot private, and do I need a search warrant?" Jags laughs when Luci nods.

"I phoned Rudd on the way, and he checked with legal." Jags wipes his lips with a paper napkin. "Remind me to thank Millie for lunch. She didn't have to do that, bring all that food and coffee. How sweet is that? Rudd calls back not ten minutes later and gives me the go-ahead. Apparently, a rented or leased parking spot, when out in the open, is still considered public, whereas a rented or leased garage, even if only partially enclosed, is private. Go figure. So I get there, find the Toyota and…guess what?" He looks at Danielle, Miriam, and Luci in turn, eyebrows raised.

"It has front-end damage consistent with a kid-on-a-bicycle-sized impact?" Danielle says.

"Ten points Danielle, it does. But that's not all. What else?"

"One of the pink streamers is lodged behind the fender?"

"Close, so close." Jagwir looks serious all of a sudden and his tone becomes somber. "I found two embedded fiber threads. One yellow, one blue. Lena was wearing rainbow pajamas, so they could be a match. Could be. Hard to say. I looked at them through a forty lens and they appear to be a natural, smooth fiber, like cotton, but I didn't carry any sample threads from Lena's pj's with me, so couldn't compare."

"Are we doing it now?" Danielle asks with sudden urgency, her eyes glinting.

"No, not us," Luci replies immediately. "If we conclude the fibers are a match with Lena's clothes, we ought to arrest and charge Machensky, but the match will have to be verified by the lab before any of it can be used in court. If the lab is as backed up as Rudd indicated, then we might find ourselves in court with the doer but without the evidence to convict."

"Yeah, exactly." Jags nods and consults his notebook. "Rudd said the same thing. Because Machensky has stable employment and lives in his own mortgage-free home, he's considered a very low flight risk. Rudd thinks it's better to leave things be, carry on, and wait for conclusive results that can be used as evidence in court."

"Carry on...what does that mean? Does he want us to keep checking local red Toyotas? How about the highway cam list Ki-woo sent? Are we checking it or leaving it?" Danielle looks at Luci, then at Jagwir.

"Well...I guess it means we'll stick to our plan," Luci answers slowly. "Jags, if you leave now, you could maybe grab an evening flight to Edmonton. Check with Rudd on your way. If you press the sample into the lab tech's hands, they might process it a bit quicker. Tell them we need it for an active investigation, that the public is at risk from a DUI driver on the loose." She turns to Danielle. "We'll process the remaining eight cars here, do a couple of interviews in the morning, then head back, too. Have a weekend. Then start on the highway cam list Monday morning."

"Sounds as though your geologist is still in town? Saturday night fever?" Danielle laughs and gets up from her chair. "Okay, that's fine by me." She turns to Jags and bumps him lightly on the upper arm. "Good work, Constable Malik. Well done. And you'll be looking to get a dog now, right?"

"You have no idea how relieved I was to see that Hero is quite nice, in the daylight. He never barked at us when we arrived. Wagged his tail, even."

CHAPTER EIGHTEEN

LOBARIA PULMONARIA

Paul and Nico have spent the day helping the Weatheralls on their small farm and will feast there on fresh spuds, corn, and barbecue, and so Jo makes herself a large salad, using all fresh bounty from her garden, including a bit of leftover seed garlic. She boils a couple of soft eggs and butters a thick slice of rye. Ah, what decadence. Strong-flavored vegetables, a runny, still-warm yolk, and the earthy texture of whole grain…a meal fit for a queen. Jo savors her dinner at the kitchen table, where she watches the sky turn from orange to crimson to layers of dark gray, then gets up to put the kettle on.

When she steps into the hallway, she feels the chill. The last couple of evenings have been crisp. She heads back through the kitchen, pulls on her oversized muck boots, and carefully descends the stairs into the garden. They've laid in an enormous woodpile next to the chicken coop, and the sensor lights come on as she approaches, a keen ear tilted toward the orchard trees. Autumn bears are fattening up for hibernation and occasionally nose around their human neighbors' gardens for fallen apples, plums, pears, and left-on-the-vine grapes and berries. Jo can't even remember the last time she ran, or moved with some speed, anyway. Well, you can't outrun a predator, no matter how young and nimble you are.

Jo is keenly aware that her senses are as old as her joints, and that her former ability to smell a wild animal or hear a small twig crack under a heavy paw has diminished with the years, so she remains on high alert while piling a dozen pieces of seasoned, split hemlock into the canvas log carrier. Kindling is already piled in a cast-iron box behind the large wood stove in the living room. All through winter, the stove never cools down and she proofs her loaves of bread in that box. When they had moved into this house almost ten years ago, Paul had cut several through-holes atop the inside walls and placed small fans inside to pull the heat through the entire house, then they had uninstalled the old oil furnace. It's not a big house, barely fourteen hundred square feet, but it is plenty large enough for the two of them to rattle around, and it has a nice guest room upstairs, to boot. One day, when they are really old, they'll move their bedroom downstairs, into the room her studio now occupies.

Jo sighs at the thought, as she always does. What will she do if she cannot draw and paint? When arthritis and failing eyesight overcome her will? How will she be able to fill the idle hours and keep her brain elastic if she cannot obsess over hues, textures, and techniques anymore? Take today, for example. After that annoying visit with the policewoman and the restorative walk with Samson, Jo's evening had stretched in front of her enticingly, solitary hours to be spent appreciating food, foremost and always her favorite, and paint. There is a plate-finished Bristol sheet waiting for her, and for the last few hours, she's been thinking about the many green and gray-green tones of the lung lichen, imagined scumbling the different shades of mint, jade, and olive to effect indistinct layering and of sprinkling salt into the wet paint for texture.

The kindling soars into orange flames and Jo feeds several chunks of dried bark until she feels a strong radiance of heat on her face, then she adds two large pieces of wood and closes the stove door. She opens the vent almost all the way to encourage a vigorous burn and sets herself a mental note to add more wood before shutting herself inside her studio, where she'll forget about the fire, bears, rye bread, and everything else.

She climbs the stairs to close the barely open window in their bedroom, then sidles over to the guest room. The door is ajar, and a light blue shine emanates from the darkness. She grins. "Gran can show you a thing or two about your computer, laddie," she mumbles as she enters the room, closes the wide-open window, and sits at his desk. She has taken all manner of computer courses over the years, including software programming and web design, and just this past summer, a coding class offered for free through the library and taught by a summer-visiting whiz kid from Seattle. She knows that Nico didn't choose the correct power-saving option and is just about to remedy this for him when the laptop monitor jumps from the generic desktop display to Nico's last search screen. "Oh boy, and we're also having a talk about privacy and lock options," Jo laughs and then uses all her willpower to not cruise around Nico's search history. She had snooped in Oliver's things always, had thought that she had the right to unfettered access to all information pertaining to her son's life because she had been the one responsible for his survival. Overbearing, domineering, presumptuous, invasive, lacking respect...she had been all of those things and more. Of course she had. But she doesn't have to be that way with Nico, can let him be his own, private person. She leaves his computer settings be and closes the door behind her.

When she walks by the wood stove next, its heat draws her close. She kneels on the floor, adjusts the vent holes to their smallest setting, and sits back on an old horsehair pillow. The fire's warmth caresses her face, and she stares into the dancing flames, hugging her knees.

A soreness spreads through her chest, a heaviness that radi-ates into her whole body. *Oliver.* Could it be that he'd been the driver of the hit-and-run car? Is it even conceivable? Thoughts of his hurried leaving that morning have danced through her mind since the policewoman told her they were looking for a red car. Oliver's car is red, just like hers. He had left that morn-ing just before six; tired from an uncomfortable night spent on the pull-out, distracted and stressed about the upcoming meeting in Calgary. His preferred route along the old Gibsons road would have taken him right through the Eagles Nest sub-division—Jo remembers his endless complaints about delays and detours during more than two years of construction there. She sees him driving that dark morning when heavy clouds obscured the waning moonlight, yawning, rubbing his eyes. Sees a small girl on a small bicycle in front of the red hood, vanishing as suddenly as she had appeared.

No, it isn't possible! But what if it is? Would he tell her? Would he ask her for advice? They haven't talked since that morning; would she hear it in his voice? What if he hadn't no-ticed? How loud a noise does a small body make? Little girls are like a puff of wind. It'd be like brushing against shrubbery branches or driving through a pothole. He might not know. An accident in Oyster Hill doesn't make the Vancouver papers, so how would he even know about Lena Newman? Would she have to tell him about it?

The fire's orange flames dance and mesmerize. Jo gets up from the floor, slowly and gracelessly, grunting with the effort. Greens are calling to her.

But first, there is charcoal. For a few minutes, Jo sits in front of the large, white-bright Bristol paper and gathers her focus. Then she selects a dulled 2B pencil and begins to deftly draw the outlines of roughly textured old pine bark, lightly in-timating fissures and deep cracks. The first piece of the triptych is only charcoal; a dense, detailed, lifelike rendering of Lobaria pulmonaria growing over dimpled, mossy rock surfaces. The plant is old and dry, imbued with gray and hints of decay. For this second panel, in charcoal and watercolor, Jo wants the deep umber, syrup, and pecan shades of the bark to contrast with the lively and luscious greens of healthy, young lungwort lichen. Dappled sunlight will reach into its shady home, drops from a recent rainfall will glisten in the craters of its lobes. Jo sees the piece in every exquisite detail while working on the bark foundation deep into the night.

Lungworts are so named because their appearance is said to be like that of human lungs. As a new mom who had dispatched for the Port Alberni fire department until a week before her due date, Jo might have agreed with this comparison. But now, as a veteran student of pulmonology, after seeing hundreds of photos, illustrations, X-rays, and scans, and even after holding pieces of a real human lung in her hands during an anatomy class at the university morgue, she can no longer see any resemblance. Young, healthy Lobaria pulmonaria is dimpled and lobed on the surface, and the leaves are rather rigid in structure, unlike healthy lung tissue, which is smooth, stretchy, and pliant. Old, dying lungwort is paper thin, dry, and crumbly whereas unhealthy lungs, Oliver's lungs, were mucky, scarred, necrotic black, whole segments blocked off with sticky, moldering, toxic goo. Kids with cystic fibrosis, she had learned that first night in the hospital's library, can't keep their mucus thin and slippery, the way it's supposed to be. Because of an altered chemical process to do with salt, ducts and glands get clogged and the fluid that is supposed to go through backs up behind, instead. Lung tissue fills up with fluid, and pooled wetness in a warm, dark tank is like Nirvana to bugs. So, Oliver had lung infections, over and over again, sometimes with bugs that the doctors knew how to fight, sometimes with bacteria and even fungus that were hard to recognize. When that happened, and when they had to wait for days for lab cultures to identify the bacterial agent and the corresponding antibiotics, Oliver's lungs became so clogged that he could barely breathe and needed round-the-clock oxygen. His skin would become pale and paper thin, translucent even, and his eyes infinite pools of supplication. He would half sit in his hospital bed, a plastic intravenous cannula attached to his limp arm, oxygen tubing in his nostrils or a mask covering almost his whole face, sometimes a gastrointestinal feeding tube would snake underneath the blankets into his stomach. Jo sat by his bed then, reading *Peter Pan* and *Treasure Island*, later books by Roald Dahl, Kenneth Oppel, and Eoin Colfer, double-checking every medication that the nurses administered around the clock, waylaying the pediatrician or respiratory specialist with questions and suggestions. She coaxed Ollie through his physio sessions, which became painful and debilitating when he was this sick, and supplemented the meager hospital rations with loaded milkshakes, jars of peanut butter, and salty chips. Because the thick mucus their bodies produce also affects digestion and nutrient absorption, CF kids, universally recognizable by their small stature, need a ridiculously high-calorie diet to maintain basic weight. Keeping Ollie fed, *well* fed, was a full-time job by itself.

When Ollie wasn't almost dying at the hospital, Jo and Paul administered all his medications, four times a day plus enzymes with every meal, and inhalers with physio. They performed his hour-long physio sessions at least twice per day, pounding on his back and chest to dislodge the mucus. They emptied and cleaned ten thousand spit basins. They went to his schools at the beginning of every year, to give presentations about cystic fibrosis and explain that his lengthy and violent coughing fits were not something to be scared of, it was just his way to keep his airways clear. That he was not contagious and could play contact sports. When he was fifteen and entered high school, Jo mentioned during her talk that his kisses were salty, and when he came home later that day, he went ballistic and forbade her to ever set foot into his classroom again.

She laughs at the memory of an infuriated Oliver, red-faced and stammering with outrage and embarrassment while cleaning her brushes and palettes. She doesn't know or care what time it is, but the thick pine branch stretches across the 23x29 Bristol in absolute lifelike fashion, its bark reddish brown, thick, and scaly. Tomorrow, she'll lay the lichen across it, overpainting most of the detail she has worked for hours to achieve.

CHAPTER NINETEEN

PREPARATION

In the morning, Jo and Paul sit at their kitchen table, the window curtain closed to keep the absolute darkness at bay.

"Nico sure can work hard when he puts his mind to it,"
Paul says, absentmindedly stirring the spoon around his bowl of
oatmeal. "We finished tilling the potato field by midafternoon.
Everyone else was still busy with apples, quinces, and grapes,
so Nico suggested we start cutting down the cornfield." Paul
looks up at her, his bright blue eyes aglow with amusement.
"We got a couple machetes from the barn and went to town.
Oh my, Jo, you should have seen him. It takes quite a bit of
oomph to whack a dried corn stalk, and you have to bend over
far so you get right close to the ground, but Nico went along
the rows at full tilt." He laughs and licks his spoon. "What
a gift to be young and healthy. Before I'd done half a dozen,
Nico had the entire row lying flat on the ground, the stumps
no longer than three inches. He kind of whooped when he
got to the end, and then he just kept on going, kept circling
the field." Paul leans back in his chair. "He sure wasn't the kid
that Oliver complains about so much. The one who doesn't

help around the house, is sullen and uncooperative. That corn patch is as big as half a football field and Nico didn't stop until he was finished. I kept up, initially, but then I seemed to be in his way, so I began to bundle up the stalks, instead. I could see that his arm was killing him, and he grimaced every time he straightened up, but he finished the job. Was so tired, he could barely eat anything when we all sat down for supper, and then Fred loaded his bike into the truck and drove him home." He chuckles again. "When I came in just after ten, the light in his room was out and I didn't hear a peep. Bet he'll sleep till noon today."

"He can't," Jo says and tells Paul about Corporal Miller and her interest in the RAV and in meeting Nico.

"Hogwash," her husband mutters. "I get that they have to tick their boxes, but hell, going after a fifteen-year-old kid? That's grasping."

"I looked it up," Jo replies. "Legally, we can refuse to give permission, but only to buy time to get a lawyer or a counselor or the parents involved. We can't hold the police off indefinitely. So, we might as well go ahead with it."

"He doesn't know about this yet? Or did you see him last night when he got home?"

"No, I didn't hear him. Was busy with a trunk."

"For the triptych?"

While they finish eating, they talk about Jo's painting and Dr. Robichaud, who's definitely a long way past retirement age. Then, the conversation loops back to Nico.

"You should have seen him out there yesterday. He has a real eye for priorities; went to whoever looked to be needing help, didn't balk at being the gopher, was respectful and charming with everyone."

"So not the son Ollie and Gina are having such trouble with?"

"I don't know." Paul wipes a hand over his face, scratches at his ear. "I think they're having trouble with him because he's a teenager, he's being surly and testy and pushing boundaries with them. But there seem to be no issues at all when he's with us, so doesn't that show he knows just fine how to behave? When he's here, we leave him be, and he's just great." He shakes his head. "I wish they would cut him some slack."

"It's no wonder Oliver is a bit of a disciplinarian," Jo says, her eyes traveling through the kitchen window and far into the past. "Ollie learned from early on to abide by the rules."

"Because his life depended on it," Paul says.

"Yeah, but to a kid's development, the reasons for their parent's rigidity don't matter. Ollie had us as parenting models, and we had to be firm in so many ways. With ourselves, too."

She takes hold of Paul's hand, caresses it with her finger. "We lost a lot of our softness, our playfulness, too."

Paul smiles wistfully. "Sure did. From one day to the next, life became all work and no play." He sighs. "So, you say Oliver is hard on Nico because that's the only way to parent he knows. Do you think he might also be a bit jealous of his freewheeling, spirited, super-healthy teenage son?"

"Jealous," Jo scoffs. "What kind of parent would begrudge their kid's health and happiness?" A memory comes to her then, of herself, kneeling next to Ollie's crib in their small home in Port Alberni, just days after receiving the diagnosis of cystic fibrosis. "Help him," she had beseeched a god she didn't believe in, "or at least help me to protect him." She could barely talk, could hardly breathe, so girdled did she feel from dread and a pervasive sense of powerlessness. "Give him health, that's all I'm asking for, just some basic health for my baby."

Jo waves an imaginary stop sign at the humiliating memory, scoffs at her younger, feeble self.

"Nico ever tell you what he wants to study?" she asks to change the subject, reaching for her third cup of coffee.

"Funny," Paul laughs, "we talked about that yesterday, over spuds. You remember how entranced he used to be by all things war and military?"

Jo shudders: how could she forget? For two long summers, when he was eleven and twelve, Nico could be seen goose-stepping around the yard, shouting military command phrases and, when he tired of that, watching every war movie he could get his underaged hands on.

"Well, he still seems to idolize that kind of work," Paul continues. "He's thinking of joining the air force. No small wonder, *Top Gun* is still one of his all-time favorite movies. But yesterday, he also talked about politics. Seems as though his mother's success has intrigued him. He wants to work on her campaign—that seems to draw him back to the city more than the thought of school."

"Politics?" Jo is incredulous. "Nico hates politics. Every time I want to draw him into a conversation about the environment or Canada's nasty history regarding Indigenous Peoples, he can't leave the room fast enough." Her forehead wrinkles as she contemplates what she has just said. "Mmh, maybe that is because he doesn't agree with my opinion and doesn't know how to argue his own yet."

Paul looks at her questioningly.

"Sounds like you have some catching up to do with your grandson, Jo. Nico has grown up, he's matured a lot in the past year. He's growing into a young man right in front of you."

"He is," Jo replies with a slight defensive edge, "but to me, he's still baby Nico. I haven't really seen him as an older teen before. And now he's leaving tomorrow, so my chance to hang out with almost adult Nico is gone for the year."

"There are four hours in the car coming up, tomorrow," Paul smiles.

Except that Nico, like every teenager, will spend the entire drive sitting quietly in the back seat, absorbed in his phone.

Jo gets up and puts her dishes next to the sink before returning to the table. She bends toward Paul and kisses him lightly on the lips. "I'll get dressed. Would you mind boiling some eggs for sandwiches? Think I'll get him up soon so he can be awake and ready for the cop at ten."

She drags a very reluctant Nico out of bed and even sweet-talks him into the shower. When he comes into the kitchen just before nine, Jo has egg sandwiches ready and a thermos of hot chocolate. Paul is whistling outside in the chicken coop.

"Let's go for a quick walk, Nico," Jo says, handing her grandson his puffy, oversized jacket. "Something important has come up. Let's eat and talk."

She turns and leaves through the back door, heads through the orchard, and opens the gate at the far end before turning to see if her grandson is even there. Nico, looking sullen, is right behind her, chewing on the remnants of the first sandwich. They step through the gate onto a pathway that lopes around a knobby hill, a huge cedar stand, and some fields before circling back toward the village.

Jo takes a deep breath. "The police came by yesterday to examine the car. They believe that the little girl on the bicycle was hit by a red Toyota, exactly like mine. When they asked me about where I'd been that morning, they didn't believe my answer, and so they also won't believe that you and your grandfather had been home and in bed."

"There must be hundreds of red Toyotas in the area," Nico shrugs, "how can they suspect a nice old grandma?" He grasps her elbow and hugs it to his side affectionately, the seriousness of the topic already waking him up. "Maybe they saw the scratched fender and jumped to conclusions. Did you tell them you have a habit of bumping into things?" He shrugs and arches his eyebrows. "Oh, and me, too. Did you tell them I hit that concrete container in the parking lot that night?"

"Of course I did. They called it convenient," Jo replies. She was beginning to get a bit testy. "Nico, did you take the car for a joyride that morning? Tell me the truth."

"Oh my God, of course not!" he says. "Gran, really, I would never take your car without asking. And if I'd had an accident, if I'd *hurt* someone, you'd be the first person I'd come to. Like I always do." He stops, as if to hug her, but Jo walks on, pretending not to notice. She hates being a disciplinarian with Nico. When Ollie had been fifteen, he had wild mood swings and was surly and belligerent far more often than not. Instead of avoiding him and giving him space, Jo had to hound him hard to keep up with the routine and the meds, to keep sharing with her when even a small thing just didn't feel right. Ollie's puberty had pushed her to the very limits of her ability to remain loving and kind, and later she had truly believed she wouldn't ever have to lock horns with her grandson during his adolescence. She just wants to let him be. But how can she, now that the police are knocking on their door?

"I wanted to have this time with you so that you can rid yourself of that irritated tone and defensiveness," she says seriously. "The cops are coming this morning to talk to you. Be polite, be firm, stand by your truth, and don't waiver. I'll be there, too, but they will want to question you, not me. The important thing will be that you don't lose your temper. It's hard to stay on point if you get all emotional and angry."

"Gran," he grabs her elbow again but not affectionately, like before. "Wait a minute. You sound like you think I'm guilty. What's going on?"

Jo turns to fully face him. Her features are set, her eyes cold, her mouth a thin, straight line. She feels herself turning into Ollie's angry Gorilla Mom. She's taken this stance against so many doctors, but never before with her grandson. Is she being fair? Nico is only fifteen, for Christ's sake. "I'm not sure, Nico. All I know is that the cop's visit yesterday irritated me. And that if you say something wrong to her this morning, we'll be dragged in deeper. And I also don't want you to mention this to your father. Not one word."

Color runs up Nico's face. "So that's what this is about. Your precious Oliver!" he sputters, eyes narrowed, and he turns away from Jo, heading toward the house in long strides. "You seem all kind and caring until the truth comes out. As fucking always, you only care about Dad."

He is yards ahead and doesn't see his grandmother's eyes soften. "Of course I care about you, my boy," she calls after him. "Now, please wait for me. I've not finished." She waits until Nico stops walking and uses the moment it takes her to catch up to him to lay her next words out in her head.

"I want you to be awake and prepared before being questioned by the police. That is neither devious nor wrong. And yes, I want to protect your father from being pulled into this, if I can. He's got enough on his plate, and if we can see to it that no further stress is added, then we are looking out for him. That is a normal family standard, trust me." Jo reaches up, turns Nico's sullen face toward her, and smiles warmly. "I love you and care for you, that is always true."

It's just that my love for your father goes beyond the ordinary.
She admonishes herself for the thought a moment later. Because you're not supposed to rank love.

CHAPTER TWENTY

OLLIE ALMOST DIES IN MONTREAL

1995

"Mom!"

In twenty years, Jo has heard every cadence and intonation of that word, and this one sounds nervous with a hint of panic. As though he's just realized he has waited too long to call out. Her eyes fly open.

She's in a dorm room. She and Oliver came to Montreal yesterday and checked into one of Concordia's family residences for orientation week. The university offered Oliver a scholarship for its three-year bachelor's degree program in journalism, a fact he'd kept from his parents for a month before asking Jo if she would buy him a plane ticket. Of course she had insisted on coming along, and Ollie, kind and generous to a fault, had readily agreed.

He calls again, quieter now, more plaintive. Jo vaults out of bed and hurries into the bathroom without knocking. The room is steamy; the water is on full blast in the shower, the curtain open, Ollie sits on the lid of the toilet, elbows on his knees, head dangling. Bright red blood drips from his mouth onto a scrunched-up towel on the floor. Jo understands immediately: Ollie's "normal" mucus-clearing cough had changed into something more strenuous when he'd lain in bed, so he came to the bathroom to make steam to help his coughing become more productive, reach deeper. In so doing, something had ruptured inside his lungs, either a bit of frail tissue or, worse, he had blown a hole in a bronchial artery. She eyes the towel and tries to guess the amount of blood.

"How long?"

"It just started a minute or two ago. Feels bad. I'm afraid to cough. It feels like I'll hack up a huge amount of blood if I do."

Jo looks at him closely. Ollie is pale; paler than he was earlier in the evening when they had dinner at an amazing Moroccan hole-in-the-wall just down the street. Paler than he'd been when they went to bed. Tiny beads of sweat glisten at his hairline and below his eyes. His long, thin fingers tremble.

She imagines a broken artery inside his lung, pumping blood into the scarred tissues normally reserved for air. She imagines the blood level rising as though inside a clear, glass bottle.

"Cough," she demands. "Cough hard."

She grabs a spittoon, one of five they travel with. One for the bathroom, two by the bedside, one each for the kitchen and living room if they stay in a borrowed or rented home. They are wide-mouthed, hard plastic bowls with a handle on either side and can hold about eight ounces. When Ollie coughs next, she holds the spittoon below his chin, and the blood overflows the bowl and drips to the towel below.

Little bleeds are common; a few red spots on tissue paper, no big deal, it'll last for an hour, never longer. Moderate bleeds have happened three times; each time they traveled to the nearest hospital, and each time the bleeding stopped on its own and they were home within a couple of hours. A massive hemoptysis had only occurred once before when Ollie was fourteen, and Dr. Robichaud had been there to fix it. It had been scary, but so had everything else been, always, so the event had slipped into the recesses of Jo's memory, together with worst-case pneumonias, a worst-ever bout of diarrhea, and lowest-ever blood sugar. Now, vivid images of Ollie—as white as his bedsheets, intubated, comatose, tubes emerging from his neck, stomach, and groin—flood her mind.

Jo races to the next dorm and hammers on the door. When a sleepy-looking young man opens, she speaks calmly.

"Do you know the street address of this building?"

He nods and begins to speak, but she gestures for him to be quiet and holds her phone out to him.

"Call 9-1-1. Tell them a boy in the next room is bleeding. He's losing consciousness. He's pale and not breathing well. Call now! Then go downstairs, open the door, and wait for the ambulance there."

She waits until he murmurs assent, glances at her phone to make sure it's unlocked, thrusts it into his hand and turns.

"Hurry."

She returns to the bathroom. "Little coughs," she says to Ollie, "so blood doesn't pool in your lungs. Keep coughing it out." She takes the blood-filled spittoon from the floor in between his feet and replaces it with another.

She grabs their emergency bag from the closet. It holds Ollie's medical chart, forty-eight hours of all his current meds, pajamas for both of them, slippers for her, charging cables for their phones, her gum, and Nescafé. She finds her purse, then gets dressed hurriedly. All the while she keeps talking to Ollie, who remains seated in the bathroom, occasionally spitting blood into the yellow receptacle. It is almost full by the time paramedics hurry into their dorm. She answers their questions while retrieving her phone from the next-door student.

"Thank you," she says, "*merci beaucoup*. You've been a great help."

Montreal. Her French is rudimentary, enough for cab rides and dinner orders but completely inadequate to speak about Ollie's medical history. Or to understand medical jargon. One of the paramedics speaks fluent English, hopefully the triage nurse will, too.

She needn't have worried. Everyone speaks English with her, French to a semiconscious Ollie and among themselves. She feels somewhat on the fringes but is not bothered. The staff know their job and she aims to stay out of their way as they work to stabilize Ollie.

Soon he has plasma products and fluids running through two IVs, blood and blood gases are drawn, and a bedside X-ray is done. The ER doc, a young, Black woman with startling, light green eyes turns to her.

"You're lucky," she says, "the pulmonologist on call is Dr. Lafayette. He's one of the good ones."

Luck should not have anything to do with it, she thinks, *they should all be "good ones;" well-trained, sharp experts. Who hires the last in class?*

Lucien Lafayette arrives half an hour later. He is tall, broad-shouldered, exceedingly good-looking, and smells of aftershave. *Who shaves before rushing to save a dying boy?* He strides into the trauma room and stands at the foot of the stretcher, then looks directly at Jo without addressing her.

"How much fluid has he had?" he asks in French.

"Fifteen hundred cc of normal saline, five hundred dextrose, four units O negative, two plasma," the nurse standing beside him reels off. Jo only understands because she had time to read the labels on the bags of fluid hanging on the tall IV pole.

"Blood pressure?"

"Stable at one-o-five, tachy at one-forty. Systolic was ninety when he came in, heart rate was almost two hundred. He stabilized well."

"He is young," the doctor replies and looks at Ollie for the first time, then back at Jo. "Is this his first big bleed?"

"His second," she replies in English. "They embolized five vessels then. The notes are in Oliver's travel chart, which I gave to the triage nurse. October 10, 1989."

The doctor frowns, then turns to one of the nurses at Ollie's side.

"Prep him for a bronchoscopy in the OR. Do it quickly." He turns to leave, but Jo calls out sharply.

"Dr. Lafayette. A moment please."

He looks over his shoulder. "*Oui?*"

Jo takes a deep breath, her diaphragm pushing against a suddenly heavy weight in her middle. The way this doctor acts is familiar from encounters with countless medical professionals in hospitals and at conferences. His facial expression is haughty, his mannerisms exclaim that he can do no wrong, that patients are lucky to get him, the very excellent superman doc! He has hardly looked at Ollie and is underwhelming Jo with his first treatment choice. She must get him to listen to her, really listen, without antagonizing him. She motions for him to come back into the room and takes a few steps to stay out of the way of the nurses.

"*Je ne parle pas Français et je ne peux pas avoir une conversation médical avec vous. Est-ce que c'est possible nous parlons Anglais?*" (I don't speak French and I cannot have a medical conversation with you. Is it possible we speak English?)

"*Naturellement,*" he says a bit sourly. "Please, go ahead."

"Dr. Lafayette, my name is Josephine Nelson, and I am Oliver's medical decision-maker. Every treatment decision has to be run by me and I have to consent. I do not consent to a bronchoscopy at this time." She exhales slowly through pursed lips, waiting for this medical marvel in front of her to puff up. He does not disappoint.

"Madame Nelson, you are an ignorant woman. First, a bronchoscopy is not just a treatment but also a diagnostic procedure and second, it is your son's only chance. He is bleeding massively, and the involved blood vessels are large. The sooner I can get in there, visualize the damaged arteries, and repair them, the better his chances to survive."

"Bronchoscopies are risky because the scope may rupture tissue further. Please consider the use of CT angiography to localize the site," Jo responds, adopting Ilse's calm, measured science-speak. "It's noninvasive and shows you the entirety of his bronchial arterial anatomy, including the aortobronchial collaterals. Dr. Robichaud made a note of an unusual collateralization to the right subclavian artery in Ollie's chart and also found at least one ectopic. Please take a moment to read his notes."

"The longer I take to read, Madame Nelson, the longer your son will have to wait for me to stop the bleeding," the doctor replies, sounding less obstinate. *Maybe he's beginning to actually hear her.* She decides to press on.

"The reason why I prefer you take the least invasive route, doctor, is that Oliver has colonized *Burkholderia cepacia* but has had no infection from it for three years. It sits somewhere in his lungs, encapsulated and not bothering anything. By performing a bronchoscopy, whether you use a flexible or a rigid scope, you increase the risk of rupturing the fragile tissue and the bacteria being released into his system. Many studies show an increased risk of sepsis from tissue rupture during scoping when compared to CT exploration."

He looks at her, hard. This is maybe the first moment that he truly sees her. She can see the wheels turning behind his eyes. This uncouth woman in rumpled, ill-fitting clothing has done her research, knows what she's speaking about. She's not wringing her hands, moaning, and crying like other parents, doesn't pull on his sleeve to entreat him to save her little angel. She argues like a medical pro. There could be a medical malpractice suit in the offing if he ignores her and then something goes wrong. Of course, something can go wrong with CT angiography, too, or during embolization, but then she can't sue him for ignoring her advice, or for not reading the entirety of this boy's one-thousand-page chart. He sighs warily.

"Dr. Lafayette, please reconsider," she pushes still. "I've had time to research this hospital's angio capabilities. Montreal General has bought a two-million-dollar biplane system only four years ago, and I checked with cardio already—they have no booked procedures tonight. You could have Oliver up there in fifteen minutes."

"You read studies and think that makes you an expert. You know your son and his medical history and believe that only you have the right answers." Dr. Lafayette smirks and shakes his head. "A recent study by Stoller showed convincingly that bronchoscopy, performed promptly during a massive hemoptysis, is the superior method to find the sites of bleeding, especially in collateral vessels."

"I read that one, too," Jo counters immediately. "That study's subjects were ninety percent cancer patients with pleural neoplasms. Of course angiography cannot detect bleeding vessels in encapsulated carcinomas." *I have him*, she thinks, *he knows now that I'm up to date, now he must see that I'm right.* But the handsome doctor's gaze does not soften, and his entire countenance continues to express arrogance and superiority.

Jo draws herself up, stands as tall as possible, and plays her last card.

"I see that I cannot convince you. I will call Dr. Robichaud in Vancouver—he is Ollie's primary pulmonologist. Will you agree to talk to him? I'll consent to any decision you two arrive at together."

"And if I don't?"

"I'll have Ollie moved to McGill. The paramedic said it's a ten-minute drive."

And here it is, the standoff. How many times has she stood at this kind of juncture? Has given everything she has, has thrown all her weight around, and then has to wait and wait for the final decision to be made by another. Will he or won't he? Why is it up to some conceited schmuck to decide, anyway? Why can't she arrive with her bleeding-out and drowning-in-his-own-blood son at an emergency room and demand, and be given, the treatment she knows is best for Ollie right then? Her face reflects nothing; her features are set rigid lest she screams. She maintains eye contact and waits for Dr. Lucien Lafayette to make up his mind.

He doesn't even speak to her. He turns and walks to the central desk in the ER. Jo follows and hears him tell the clerk to reserve the angio theater and to call in the team. Then he stalks to a long desk off to the side, sits behind it, grabs Ollie's blue travel chart, and begins to read.

Jo returns to Ollie's side, and a compassionate nurse, who must have noticed her trembling legs, brings her a chair. She sits gratefully, feels worn to the nub. So much could have gone wrong. How could she have antagonized this important doctor who would soon guide a steel catheter into her son's lungs. And yet, she would have to square up with him again because she wants to be in the room for this procedure. Wants to look at the screen, wants to see the bleeding leaks inside her Ollie, wants to witness this doctor's skill at repairing them. And should he not be able to, she needs to be there, holding Ollie's hand, when he dies.

This is it, she thinks. *Another moment of truth. Ollie might die.* She pulls out her phone and touches Paul's number.

CHAPTER TWENTY-ONE
THE INTERVIEW

Luci Miller leans against her black SUV in front of the driveway, chatting with Paul when Jo and Nico return to the house. "Hellos" and "Good mornings" are exchanged before an awkward pause. Then Luci jokes that she has come early, not because she suspects Jo of ushering everyone out of the house before ten, but simply because that's how her day has fallen out.

She had been on speakerphone with Rudd around nine when he was at the Toyota dealership in Kerrisdale, where the paint specialist assured them of the scientific prowess of his software. Then, moments after he held the tiny fragment Rudd had handed him under the scanner, he confirmed the color to be genuine, factory-issued Barcelona Red Metallic.

"Are you saying that you can tell the difference between original Toyota paint and after-market products?" Luci asked excitedly.

"Well, *I* can't," the tech answered, "but the software can. Factory paint has a specific molecule added, which is totally proprietary and not even I know what it is, but the software is designed to search for it. So yes, your piece of metal here is from a genuine Toyota. And I can do you one better," he continued, with obvious satisfaction. "The car in question is a pre-2014 model. Another bit of info marked here. Paint molecule composition changes every now and again. The chemists never tell us scrubs what they're doing, but they're obliged to update the software accordingly."

He chuckled and Rudd switched the phone's speaker off. "There you have it, Miller," he said, sounding pleased and relieved, "this takes about half of your red locals out of the equation. Unless Gill or Jags and Dani come up with anything new, Machensky or your old lady driver are sitting pretty." He hummed a few melody bars before continuing. "Alright Miller, keep up the good work. And have a nice weekend. I'll be clocked out later when you guys get back. Something about a wine-tasting weekend that starts early." He sighed theatrically and cut the connection.

Danielle and Luci had disqualified every post-2014 Toyota off their lists and suddenly, the weekend was only a couple of visits away. That was why Luci arrived early at the Nelson house. That…and curiosity. Something about Jo had struck her in hindsight, but try as she might, she could not put her finger on it. Last night, after dinner with her colleagues in a pizza joint ten miles out of town, Luci went over her transcription notes several times and tried to recollect every turn of phrase and every facial expression Jo had shared. At the outset, there had been delight and curiosity, but they gave way to caution and prickly defensiveness. That she had seen, anyway. Underneath all that, there was something else, something steely and hard she could not qualify. Had it been protectionism? Furtiveness? Fear? An intrinsic guardedness that had nothing to do with her, the police, or the accident at all but was an attribute of Jo's personality? Luci keeps smiling at Jo and thinks that she might learn more today.

Jo and Paul hover as Luci questions Nico. The interview is entirely voluntary, as Luci mentions when she introduces herself formally to Nico, and which Jo pointedly repeats when she and Paul give their consent. The grandparents' heads move as though they are watching a tennis game, from Luci to Nico and back. Repeat. The exchange between cop and teen goes fairly predictably, all things considered.

"Did your grandma tell you I was here yesterday?"

"Yes."

"Had you heard about the accident on O'Reilley?"

"Yes."

"Can you tell me what you know about it?"

"Only what my grandparents discussed over dinner."

"What did they say?" Luci prompts.

"That a little girl had been killed in an accident and that she had been on her bicycle. And that they don't know the parents."

"Have you ever met the Newmans?"

"No, I don't know too many people here in Oyster Hill," he says.

"Don't you come up every summer?"

"Yes, but I hang out here, with Gran and Grumps. Sometimes, my grandpa and I go to the Interior together, camping and picking fruit."

"So, you had never met the little girl, Lena Newman, either?"

"No. Why would you ask me that?"

"Have you ever driven your grandparents' car without one of them in the passenger seat?"

Nico turns his head to look at Jo. She nods.

"Not usually, no. But sometimes they step out of the car, like in a parking lot or in the forest, and I drive on my own for a few minutes." He grins. "And here in the driveway. I must have driven that car a hundred times up and down the driveway by myself."

"Since when are you practicing driving?"

"Only since this summer. I'll turn sixteen next week."

"How many times have you driven your grandparents' car? Outside of this property?"

Nico shrugs. "Maybe fifteen, twenty times. Mostly on this street and over toward the park. One time in the schoolyard, but there was nobody there. I mean, no kids."

"And in the parking lot by the mall."

"Yeah, a couple of days ago."

Luci nods. "Tell me about that."

"Grumps let me drive from the house to the mall." Nico grins and looks at Paul. "I mean Grandpa. It's not far, maybe a mile. It was after dinner. When we got there, I practiced driving backward and parallel parking. At some point, Grumps got out of the car to sort of wave me closer to the curb, you know, like those workers at airports do. It was funny." Nico laughs.

Luci waits a second, then asks, "And then?"

"Well, we were both facing the sun, so maybe he didn't see what was going on, but he waved for me to roll forward, so I did, but then the car hit the planter."

"What did you do?"

"I stomped on the brake, what do you think?"

"Sometimes, inexperienced drivers push on the gas pedal, instead, in a sort of instinctive knee-jerk reaction. But you hit the brake."

"Yes."

"Was your grandfather angry?"

"No." Nico laughs. "He thought it was his fault. Which it was, when you think about it. He waved me forward."

"What did your grandmother say when you came home?"

"That it's no big deal. It's like the thousandth dent on that car."

Luci writes in her notebook. Draws the moment out. "If it had been you, for argument's sake, who hit that little girl, how would you have reacted? What would you have done?"

"Whoa, wait a sec, I didn't do it."

"Humor me. How would you behave after something like that?"

Paul clears his throat. "Corporal Miller, I don't think that's an okay question to ask a fifteen-year-old boy."

"My bad. Nico, when you have messed up with something before, at school or somewhere at home, how did you react?"

Nico's expression has gone surly. "My parents used to be like helicopter parents. I could never get away with anything."

Interesting, Luci thinks. "And now?"

"Well, I don't tell them everything, if that's what you mean. But if I had done something really terrible, like what you're suggesting, I would definitely call my mom."

"You're sure?"

"Yes, totally. My mom is great. She always knows what to do."

"Like your grandmother."

"Exactly. Those two are the same."

Jo's eyes follow her as Luci folds her notebook and slides it and her pen into her shirt pocket. "Thanks for answering all of my questions, Nico, that's it for now. If I have any others later on, I'll be in touch. I'll get your contact info from your grandparents in a minute."

"I can give you that right now," Nico says, and Luci pulls her notebook back out and hands it to him. "Jot down the street address, phone number, and email, too, please."

While Nico completes this task, Luci turns to Paul.

"And, of course, you corroborate everything Nico just said?" She notes his crossed arms, tightness of his expression, the flattened lips.

Paul Nelson exhales loudly, then draws a deep breath. When he speaks, his voice is quiet.

"Nico is like any other kid. He loves to learn new things. This summer, he's been up three or four times. We let him drive in Jo's car because it's an automatic. He creeps along at twenty or thirty. Mostly in the driveway. Occasionally in an empty parking lot. What's the harm?"

"And the planter? At the mall?"

Paul looks away as if embarrassed. "He was going back and forth along the curb, getting a feel for how much to turn the steering wheel to achieve the right angle. I was near the rear left fender and didn't notice we had crept along the sidewalk quite a bit. When I waved him to go forward and try the whole maneuver again, I hadn't noticed the car had almost reached the end of the lane. There's a low planter before the bike lane and Nico rolled right into it. In fact, it's so low, I hadn't seen it at all."

"You heard the crunch?"

"Yes," Paul says, "it was a definite impact."

Nico hands Luci her notebook and asks if he can leave now.

"Sure, we're all done here," she replies and smiles. "Thank you for your time. Hope you have a great school year coming up."

Nico and Paul turn together and don't see that Luci was about to extend her hand. They head into the garage, and Jo and Luci stand silently beside each other to watch them emerge moments later on their two-wheelers and disappear down the street.

"Phew," Jo says, smiling now, "talk about bundles of energy. I feel like I need to sit down."

"Just before you go in…" Luci says, managing to sound blasé. "If the chip from your car turns out to be a positive match, the fact that you allow your underage, unlicensed grandson to drive unsupervised will become front and center in the investigation. We might charge you under the Motor Vehicle Act. You're looking at a five-hundred-dollar fine and a week suspension, on average."

"If the chip from my car turns out to be a match," Jo answers, her lips drawn tight and her chin raised, "a minor infraction like that will be the least of my problems."

They look at each other like prize fighters before a match, all steely eyes and resolve, neither willing to back down. At last, Jo inclines her head.

"Tell me this: how long before you can clear our name, rule us out as murderers who'd leave a bleeding child in the curb to die?"

"Jo, I don't think of any of you in that way. I just think this car might have a story to tell." That, and the fact that they didn't exactly have a multitude of other suspect vehicles, but Luci doesn't say that. She looks at Jo with as open an expression as she can muster, hoping to leave the door open a crack.

"How long?" Jo repeats.

"It'll be at least a few months," Luci answers and Jo's face registers surprise.

"So, the neighborhood and the whole town will think of us as suspects until Christmas, at least," she murmurs, looking out toward the coast. "No wonder police reputation gets worse every year. This is a terrible way to treat people."

"We're pretty discreet, actually. And don't forget that, since the accident happened, we've interviewed almost a hundred people, have checked almost forty cars, and we aren't done yet. I'm not singling you out, and none of your neighbors have reason to believe that I am."

Jo stares at her coldly and asks if she's needed out here any longer.

"No, but please, take my card. I know that you're upset, but if you need to talk to me or come across anything that you want me to know about, get in touch. Please." Luci takes a card from her back pocket and holds it out.

"Oh, what the heck, why not," the older woman mumbles and takes it. "What's your real name, anyway? Nobody's parents call their daughter Luci."

"Lucinda. My parents are rabid country fans. Lucinda Williams is their queen. I'm forever grateful they didn't feel quite so strongly about Ms. Parton."

Jo turns to go but cannot suppress a wide grin. "Corporal Dolly…well, that does have a nice ring to it."

CHAPTER TWENTY-TWO

OLIVER

"That's all folks! Remember, everything is funny as long as it happens to someone else." Luci and Grant groan in unison, then whoop, whistle, and clap with the rest of the packed club before turning back to their drinks. The comedians have been funny as all get-out: one was witty and had them in stitches with punchy one-liners, another self-deprecating with so much dry humor that Luci's emotional barometer had swung between mirth and empathetic chagrin. The host was lame though, undeniably unfunny, but they cheered and clapped and laughed at all of it anyway. Luci takes Grant's hand, beams a wide smile, and kisses every one of his knuckles. A man who laughs generously at asinine jokes is her type of guy. Ditto for the one who takes a busted date with an easy smile and then shows up on time for the next one, Yuk Yuk's tickets in hand. She leans into his scent and warmth and slides her hand along his thigh. "How about we head out?"

"Your place or my hotel room? I've had four days to imagine all the marvelous sex we could have had, so this night is not for sleeping."

When they had met at that exhibition at the Anthropology Museum only about a month ago, their attraction had been instantaneous. Luci couldn't take her eyes off his scenic pictures while she was wholly mesmerized by his stories. In turn, he wanted to know every detail about her photos, which largely comprised animal shots, with one exception: a series of frames depicting an avalanche in claustrophobic detail. "If you weren't standing right in front of me, I would assume the photographer hadn't made it out of there alive," Grant had said, touching her lightly on the hand. "Would you tell me the story over a glass of wine?"

It had happened after one of those terrible house calls, after the deliverance of the worst news, hours after her shift had ended and she should have gone to bed—but who could sleep when you'd just officiated as the harbinger of death? She'd filled up one of the detachment's snowmobiles, packed a thermos of hot, black tea with a slug of rum, extra fuel, an emergency blanket, a flashlight, an avalanche beacon, her Nikon, and then set out into the land. The mountains exhaled frosty air, clusters of impossibly bright stars seemed to hold the cloud scads at bay, and yesterday's massive snowfall had supplied an undulating, inviting path into oblivion. *Better than getting drunk in my quarters*, she thought as a wolf plaint shivered over the snow. She followed the valley for almost two hours, then mounted a pass, soon another. The ride consumed her, her attention laser-focused on her surroundings, the sound and feel of the snow, the language of the wind, the changing scenery. Dark storm clouds rolled in over the peaks and then descended the mountain flanks, and she quickly sought shelter against a massive rock that nestled amongst century-old evergreens. The force of the wind pushed the snow-laden clouds to the valley's bottom, and the whole bowl erupted in a tempest of snow and ice, the wind howling in a screaming frenzy. *This*, she thought, *this!* Although she felt safe in the cradle of rock and wood shelter, she offered herself to the fury, opened herself to its might, wanted nothing more than to be scrubbed raw and her existence confirmed. She was *alive.*

The self-made storm petered out as soon as the cloud had dumped its load, then trailing winds pushed through and were followed by absolute stillness. Luci wrestled herself out from the half-foot of snow and vegetation debris that had blasted over her and stared at the magnificent scene: craggy, snow- and ice-helmed mountain peaks all around her, the glistening, smooth snow cover, the hundred-foot-tall spruce and pine along the slope, a wide sky, luminous with a bright, silver moon, the densely starred Milky Way, and a shimmering, fragile band of green luminescence. Just as she turned toward the snowmobile to dig out her camera, she heard it. A sonorous cracking sound, deep and rumbling, like when she pressed the release button on the pub's pool table and the hard balls poltered into the retrieval slot, only much, much louder. The lumbering roll turned into a booming roar as she fumbled in the pack and retrieved the Nikon, turned and began to snap the avalanche's descent. She didn't feel the cold on her bare hands, didn't fear for her life, which was now truly in danger should the massive amount of roiling snow and ice reach her natural shelter. Later, she reasoned that she knew all along that there was no place she could have run to at that moment, not that running in so much fresh snow would have been possible anyway, but in truth, all rational thought had been suspended when she'd offered herself to the elements and dared the universe to show her the meaning of life.

It took her an hour after the avalanche had worn itself out toward the middle of the valley before she had dug out the snowmobile, and she didn't make it back to Dawson until well into the afternoon. That night, exhausted and muscle-sore, she couldn't sleep but stared at the ceiling over her bunk. She needed a way out!

Only after she'd been accepted into Vancouver's CARS section, had completed the specialized training course, and had joined Rudd's team, had she developed several large prints of the avalanche pictures and submitted them to nature magazines and exhibitions. The showing where she and Grant met had been her third, and although she now has a portfolio of hundreds of very good to excellent nature shots, the capture of the plummeting mountainside in the moon-, star- and northern lights–lit valley is the one people talk about. Her breakthrough shot.

Luci drags herself into the office on Labor Day Monday morning with obvious reluctance. She'd showered at home but goes for another icy blast in the locker room. Then she puts on a pressed uniform, tidies her shoulder-length blond hair in its updo, and applies Nars' *Jungle Red* lipstick. Right outside the changeroom lives the CARS coffee vending machine, a sleek apparition of chromed steel, buttons, and dials the brass had bought them last year. Luci instructs it to deliver her third espresso today and heads to the fourth floor, where the large open office awaits. Ki-woo laughs at her from her neat desk next to the window.

"Killer lipstick, wet hair, coffee, elevator instead of stairs… I'd say you had a great weekend with your helicopter guy, eh?"

"If you're such a good detective, how come you rarely stray from your desk, eh?"

"That's exactly why. Fieldwork is for you grubs who have to touch something to believe it exists. Between my brain and my computer, we've got most everything covered." Ki-woo beams widely and watches Luci walk across to her desk. "Hi, colleague-friend, are you fully here now?"

"As present as ever and reporting for duty. Where is everybody?"

"Team one was called out at three in the morning. Porsche versus bridge pier. Guess who won? And Rudd, Danielle, and Jagwir were hardly in the building when Richmond called."

"Did they leave word for me?"

"Yeah, Rudd suggested we work on the highway cam list. I started on it Friday afternoon but haven't got far."

Office work seems like just the ticket for this morning, and Luci slips gratefully into her chair. She pulls Ki-woo's list up on her screen and sees that ten rows already have a green check mark in the first column. She reads the eleventh line:

> highway 101, exit # 82, southbound, 06:17, Wed. 09/7/19. Red Toyota Corolla, 2011, GHP 230, registered to: Brian Young, sole driver, DOB 08/16/1978. 912 Lakeview Drive, Kamloops, BC. DUI Apr. '98, speed x3 '98, '00, '04, non-fault ICBC claims x3 '01, '09, '15; partial fault claim x1.

Luci picks up the phone and dials Brian Young's number. He answers on the third ring.

"Yup?"

"Mr. Young, my name is Luci Miller, I'm a traffic investigator and have a couple of questions about your Corolla. Are you somewhere where you can speak freely?"

"Sure am. Late breakfast at home. Corn flakes if you must know."

"There was a fatal hit-and-run in Oyster Hill on Wednesday morning, and a red Toyota was involved. We have images of your car near Oyster Hill around the time of the accident. Would you mind telling me if you diverted off the highway that morning?"

"Wow, this is very Orwellian. You guys being able to keep tabs like that. Well, let me think for a sec…yes, Wednesday morning I was heading to Van from Lund. Left about five…. I like those early morning drives. You gotta keep your eyes peeled for wildlife, but other than that, there's very little traffic. Anyway, I didn't stop before Langdale, to catch the first ferry."

"You're sure? No Timmies?"

He laughs. "No Timmies. I pack a thermos and sandwich, have breakfast on the boat."

"Okay, thank you for cooperating. Not everyone does. We investigate many hit-and-runs by elimination…there are a limited number of red Toyotas around. Can I ask you for one more thing?"

"Sure. What's that?"

"Would you mind stopping by your local detachment this morning so one of the officers can take a picture of your fender? Won't take more than five."

"Wow, that's tricky. You sure this is important?"

"Yes, I am. Wouldn't ask you otherwise, Mr. Young. We have about a hundred vehicles to look at all over the province, and we want to examine them for front-end damage ASAP before body shops get involved. If you get yours photographed this morning, I'm down to ninety-nine. That would be great."

The man sighs deeply and manages to sound put out. Luci thinks about Lena Newman's parents. She'd called on them before leaving Oyster Hill Saturday afternoon. Stephan Gill had come along and made introductions at the door. Lorna Newman was a petite woman with long, dark blond hair, enormous eyes, and shoulders that fell forward as though pulled by a string from her belt buckle. Stephan had told her that on Wednesday, at the scene of the accident, she'd screamed so loud that ravens in the surrounding trees had fled from their perches in alarm; now she was muted in grief. Her husband Mike stood erect, shook Stephan and Luci's hands, and held on with an iron grip. When he'd held Lena to his chest, wailing and shouting, he had seemed a big man, a high-school-football kind of guy with an athletic build. Now he was diminished, faltering, his voice barely a whisper. "What have you learned?" he wanted to know. "Do you know who did this?"

"Mr. Young, can I count on you doing the right thing here?" Luci asks into the silence.

"Yeah sure, I'll do it. I can be there before noon."

Luci thanks the man, then phones the Kamloops detachment and speaks to the duty sergeant. After she ends the call, she adds a green check mark to row eleven and calls the next number.

Just before noon, with her thoughts heading toward the various lunch options, she reads row twenty-seven.

> highway 101, exit # 77, southbound, 06:20, Wed. 09/7/19. Red Toyota Matrix, 2013, BXR 375, registered to: Oliver Nelson, DOB 03/02/1975. 2759 W 6th Ave, Vancouver. non-fault ICBC claims x2 '94, 02.
>
> Secondary driver: Ginevra Nelson, née Moretti, DOB 10/15/1979. same address. At-fault 3 vehicle collision 2008, DWDC, 6 points, 3-month suspension.

Luci blinks several times and reads the lines again. Dammit! She inputs the address into her phone and gets quickly out of her chair.

"Ki-woo, I've got something. This guy in row twenty-seven, Oliver Nelson.... I'm already looking at his mother and his son as potential doers. His mom's car is a BRM RAV with recent front-end damage. Apparently, the grandson, Oliver's son, struck a cement planter in a parking lot on Wednesday evening. I interviewed both him and his grandmother and she is evasive as hell, and the kid's story isn't adding up either. I thought they were suspicious, but now here's Oliver, their son and father, also in a BRM Toyota, also in the vicinity at the time of the hit-and-run. Maybe they were protecting him. I gotta go see this guy and check him out. And his car."

"Do you want company?" Ki-woo asks politely while getting up and sliding her jacket on. "And can we pick up something to eat on the way?"

▰▰▰▰▰

Luci sits in the passenger seat of the black Subaru and knots her brow in angry concentration. Why had Josephine Nelson lied to her? She had never mentioned that her son had left, in a red car no less, at that crucial time in the morning. Not a word! And had then been aggravated about Luci's lack of trust, her request for proof. Had lectured her on forthrightness and integrity. The nerve of the woman. What a hag!

The house at 2759 West 6th Avenue is a gentrified, three-story town house with a Montreal-type staircase leading up to the front door. The garden must have been amazing in the summer; there are dozens of shrubs and bushes with spent flower buds, and several large ceramic pots line the brick walkway. A climbing rose on a large trellis still blinks with a few yellow-orange blossoms, and the abundance of lush plantings continues down the side of the house, likely into a large back garden. *Must be nice to have so much time for gardening*, Luci thinks as they make their way up the wide, steep stone stairs. She knocks loudly but only silence responds.

"Maybe someone's in the back. Gardeners spend a lot of time in the fall readying for the spring growing season," Ki-woo offers, and Luci looks at her in astonishment. Her colleague shares a tiny two-bedroom with a roommate, and her parents live in a very modern condo in Burnaby, the steel and glass capital of the region. Ki-woo laughs. "I read gardening magazines in the bathtub. It's relaxing."

They walk along a row of raised beds with tomato cages, a few forlorn yellow-hued fruit still clinging to the vine. The gate into the back has a complicated mechanism, and it takes Luci a moment to figure out how to open it when suddenly a man appears on the other side of it.

"Can I help you?" he asks, guarded but not unfriendly.

"Oh, hi there. Are you Oliver Nelson?" Luci asks, aiming to keep the surprise from her voice and facial expression. The man in front of her, even through the gate slats, looks nothing like his mother or son, who are both tall with brownish hair and fair complexion. This man is around fifty, rotund and ruddy, an unkempt beard covering his face and throat. He wears rubber boots and an Australian-type waxed work jacket. Maybe the gardener.

"Nah, I'm not. Who might you be?"

"My name is Luci Miller. I'm a corporal with the RCMP's collision analysis team."

"And I am Constable Ki-woo Park. Could you tell us please where we can find Mr. Nelson at this hour?"

He eyes them speculatively and makes no move to open the gate. "He's at work."

"It's a holiday," Luci replies.

"Not for you and him, it's not." The man smiles broadly.

"Do you have the address, please?" Ki-woo remains polite, an affable smile anchored in place.

"It's down by Powell-Clarke. I've been there but don't know the street address by name."

"How about the company name then," Luci cuts in, her tone steelier than Ki-woo's; she has reached the dregs of today's allotment of patience.

"Look for Enviga," the man answers and turns away. Apparently, he has a rare aptitude for non-curiosity and more important things to do than to help the police with their inquiries.

"Thank you," Ki-woo calls politely toward the retreating back, and they return to their car.

"Enviga is a brand of meal-replacement drinks," Luci reads out loud from her handheld as they make their way to the industrial area just east of downtown. "Founded in 2002 as a kitchen-shop type venture by Saaz Chauhan and Oliver Nelson. Ah, here is the bio: Oliver Nelson had a double lung transplant in 2000 and his friend, Saaz, a nutritionist, created a super nutritious smoothie blend that not only kept him alive but helped Oliver to an almost miraculous recovery. Apparently, half the people who get a lung transplant because they have cystic fibrosis die anyway, but Oliver did well. Real well. There are pictures of him here, running and biking and skiing. He looks like a million bucks."

Without their nav app, they would have never found the place. There are no signs for Enviga, save a letter-sized sticker on a small door in the rear of a nondescript industrial building. A diminutive woman who looks to be Vietnamese opens the door and, addressing only Ki-woo and never even looking at Luci at all, gestures for them to wait by the adjacent loading dock before closing the door again. After a couple of minutes, a rumble announces the opening of the roll-up, and a man wearing a pair of dark dress shoes, light brown canvas pants, a leather belt with a fancy buckle, and finally, a red polo shirt open at the neck, emerges. Oliver Nelson is of medium height, well proportioned, muscular but not hefty, with thin, soft brown hair above a wide, expressionless face.

"Yes, what is it now?" he asks curtly.

Luci and Ki-woo exchange an astonished glance before Luci speaks.

"Good afternoon, Mr. Nelson. We are with the RCMP's collision analysis team. We'd like to talk to you about your car, your Matrix. Do you have it here?"

"We told you guys yesterday that Gina will take a cab to the airport. Why do you need to check my car now?"

He sounds put out, angry. The space between his eyes dissects into vertical lines and his shoulders slide back. Luci had seen that exact sequence of movements only a few days ago, in Oyster Hill.

"Mr. Nelson, I don't follow. Our query has nothing to do with your wife or her transportation needs. We are here as part of an investigation into a fatal hit-and-run that happened last Wednesday morning in Oyster Hill." She pauses, wants to give this man time to sort through what he heard.

His eyes, the same color and shape as his mother's, widen. Annoyance turns to worry. "Excuse me? Are my parents okay?"

"Yes, your family is fine. A little girl on a bicycle was hit by a red car and we have determined the color to be proprietary to Toyota. We are checking every red Toyota that showed up on the highway cams that morning. Your Matrix was one of them."

"So, you're not with my wife's protection detail." His countenance shifts back to irritation.

Ki-woo exhales. "Sorry, what?"

"Your colleagues have been to the house twice in the past week. Talking to Gina and me about safety procedures. During the election. I assumed you were following up." Oliver looks at their perplexed expressions, his brows rise into a perfect arch. "My wife, Gina, is running in the federal election. As an MP."

"Oh, now I understand." Ki-woo laughs. "It's a case of a police pile-up." She giggles at her joke. Oliver does not. His features remain stern and unyielding. His mother's son. Focused. Uncompromising. Defensive? Or intentionally distracting?

Luci extends her arm, wills him to shake her hand. He does, with practiced routine. She learns nothing from the medium grip, the single up-down movement, the dry skin, the quick withdrawal. A businessman's shake. Or that of a politician's husband.

"My name is Luci Miller. This is Ki-woo Park. Yes, we are RCMP, but we don't know anything about the other members' visits to your house and we're from a totally different unit. Our concern is with the motor vehicle accident that occurred at approximately six in the morning last Wednesday, August 28, in the Eagles Nest subdivision in Oyster Hill. A little girl died in the collision and the driver did not remain at the scene. We have examined highway cameras at the north and south ramps of Oyster Hill and found several dozen red Toyotas in the area." She breathes and forces herself to slow down. Oliver is listening intently.

"It's our job to look at every one of those cars and to check for any signs of a recent accident. If we can rule your Matrix out at a glance, we'll do so. If we can't, we'll take a tiny lacquer sample and send it to the lab for comparison."

Luci pauses, waits for Oliver to respond. He remains silent but has begun to rock ever so slightly on his feet. He folds his arms across his chest and smooths his face into an expressionless mask. He reminds Luci of her Grade Eight math teacher, Mr. Jorgess. The kids had called him Mr. Joyless. He still doesn't answer them, but appears to be assessing them, as they are him.

"Is your car here, Mr. Nelson? The sooner we look at it, the sooner we'll be out of your hair." Ki-woo doesn't sound giggly anymore. Luci knows this tone of voice. Her colleague is becoming miffed.

Finally, Oliver speaks. "My car is not here. I rent a refrigerated truck twice per week. To make deliveries to the various grocery stores around town." He turns and points to a midsized van with the logo of a local brewery all over the sides. "I parked my car at the warehouse when I picked this one up an hour ago." Oliver looks directly at Luci, then at Ki-woo. "Them renting me their truck until I can afford my own is a favor. A big one. So, I don't think I want to send the cavalry into their parking lot."

He coughs into his hand. Looks down. Luci wonders if that is just an old habit or if he is still concerned about what he might cough up, even twenty years after the transplant. Did that cure him or just buy him a couple more decades? She has no idea.

"Look guys, I have to go back to work. If I am not in there hustling, I'm not earning any money. No earnings, no taxes, no raises for the local constabulary."

He smirks and looks at the pavement between Luci and Ki-woo. "If you want to look at my car, you can come back here tomorrow between ten and noon. That's the best I can do." He turns to leave.

"Mr. Nelson!" Luci's voice slices through the air like a Japanese throwing star. She waits until the man halts and half-turns toward her. "We are investigating a serious crime. Your cooperation in this matter is an expected act of citizenship and, if withheld, might be compelled by a judge." Oliver Nelson turns his back and continues to walk toward the roll-up. "It won't take us long to get a search warrant and show up at your business friend's warehouse with a cohort of marked cars and officers," Luci continues. "That would, ultimately, be more em-barrassing and damaging, no?"

He's now back inside his building. As the door slides from top to bottom, they see his legs and feet vanishing into the rear.

"That went well." Ki-woo hands their car keys to Luci. "Here. I like it when you drive angry. It's like a ride at the fair."

Luci takes a deep breath. Then another. She fake-smiles at Ki-woo. "Okay, I'll bite. But you get on the horn with Rudd and get us a search warrant. I'll buy you lunch at Gain Wah if you talk him into it."

"No, no search warrant," Sergeant Rudd's voice fills the car as they weave their way through East Van. "He invited you to examine his vehicle tomorrow morning. So, what's he going to do before then?

Take it to a body shop to have front-end damage fixed overnight? Or is he going to ram someone in a fender bender to murky the waters? So what? If the lacquer sample is a match, it's a match. Nothing he can do about it in twenty-four hours."

The Subaru comes to a jarring stop behind a MINI that sports a gleaming Union Jack paint job but has no brake lights. Luci swears loudly and Rudd chuckles over the speakers.

"Easy, Corporal. Ask yourself why you're so riled about this guy. And you two should have lunch somewhere and relax. Then come see me when you get back here. You'll probably want to carry on with the cam cars in the afternoon, but check in with me, anyway. We'll have a laugh."

Egg fried rice and spicy green beans go a long way toward improving Luci's mood, but she can't shake a sense of aggravation. About Oliver Nelson's blasé bearing, his arrogance and dismissive attitude. Not one word from him that expressed concern or empathy about the death of a little girl. "But mostly, I'm mad about his mother withholding information," she says to Ki-woo around a mouthful. "I must have spent an hour at least with that woman. You'd think she would have mentioned her son being on the road with a Barcelona Red car that morning."

"No parent in their right mind would volunteer that information," Ki-woo answers. "My parents would have their hands chopped off before telling the police anything bad about me. To them, giving up their kid to the authorities would be the ultimate betrayal of family honor. Maybe your old lady has Asian sensibilities?"

"Nah, she's pretty WASP. But controlling, too. Needing to be in charge. Obviously, that extends to information. Anyway," Luci shrugs and pours fragrant jasmine tea into their small cups, "what did you make of Oliver Nelson?"

"Well, he was angry right away, but if the VIP-PD have been at his house twice and he thought we were them…it's no wonder he got irritated. Those protection detail dudes can be incredibly annoying. I would be, too, if I ever got stuck there." Ki-woo grimaces and lifts her bowl higher to shove a glutenous heap of saucy noodles into her mouth.

"True. Once he came out of the starting holes pissed, he couldn't very well turn on the charm a minute later. I get that. But still...." Luci sips her tea and looks past Ki-woo at the little restaurant's packed tables.

"His reluctance to have us examine his car in another person's place of business is understandable, too, you know," Ki-woo continues. "Imagine just starting out with your own company and having an established businessperson lend you a helping hand...you wouldn't want to jeopardize their support with even a hint of wrongdoing. A criminal investigation, even if they haven't done anything, can ruin a person's reputation. Or at least damage it."

"So, you don't think Oliver Nelson behaved suspiciously?"

"No, I don't think he did. I think his attitude was normal, given the circumstances. And he did invite us to come back tomorrow. I felt that was reasonable. Many of the people whose cars we look at are unhappy about the police nosing about. That guy was just very open about it, that's all."

CHAPTER TWENTY-THREE

THE MATRIX

Oh, Oliver Nelson had not been hiding his aggravation, that's for sure. Luci mulls over the man's facial expressions as she sips her morning's first espresso. She can see English Bay from her window but barely registers the flat, gray expanse of the Pacific Ocean that, today, provides temporary anchorage to four behemoth cargo ships awaiting access to the Vancouver port. The bay is lined with walkways and bicycle paths, roads, parks, and beaches but Luci doesn't pay any heed to the morning's bustling activity seven stories below. Instead, she goes over every "Nelson" moment in her head and tries to pinpoint when exactly her acute spidey sense had begun to tingle. This is entirely Rudd's doing. He believes wholeheartedly in his investigator's instincts, and encourages the team to trust them, as well. Has given expansive lectures on mindfulness, on paying close attention to not only their interviewee's unconscious behavior, but to their own responses, as well.

"What happened when you took a half step backward? Did you consider me a threat and then consciously move to get out of my range?" he'd asked Jagwir during an interrogation "demonstration." Jagwir knew better than to interrupt Rudd. You can't stop a boulder from rolling down a mountain. "Exactly!" Rudd continued with exuberance, as though Jagwir had agreed. "Our bodies react instinctively. Half the time, we spend all our energy overriding our instincts. Societal pressures and all that. But as investigators, I want you to…no, you need to be attentive to your body. To every half step backwards, to goosebumps, rising neck hair, and all that other stuff. A dry mouth, a brain scratch, a sting pricking the skin and stitching inward. Something a suspect did or said, at that moment, half an hour ago, yesterday. Something alerted your ever-attentive brain, and now it's trying to get you to pay attention. That's called a niggle and you simply cannot be a detective without honoring those niggles!"

Luci had had a niggle about the Nelsons since her first encounter with Josephine. Something about that woman. And her grandson. And now her son. All three of them made her feel like she's missing a good deal during their conversations. The fact that she didn't get that sense with Paul is also curious and seems to support Rudd's contention. So, what did she miss during yesterday's encounter with Oliver?

He'd been justifiably put out about being repeatedly, and unexpectedly, pestered by police. Ki-woo was right. But many people would have felt a bit sheepish after realizing their error, might have apologized for lumping them together or for speaking rudely. Not Oliver Nelson. He just kept on being rude. Even walked away and shut the door in her face while she was still talking. First impression: moody jerk who has something to hide. Of course she'd wanted a search warrant.

After returning to the office and reviewing the incident with Rudd, who had opined that Oliver probably saw them as a distraction rather than a threat, Luci researched cystic fibrosis. How does one grow up, from birth, always being the center of attention? Not the admiring kind, mind you, but being dissected, assessed. A never-ending parade of white-clad medical people, studying. And no matter how nice they were at the time, the minute they left his hospital room, they would have forgotten him and turned to their next patient. What might that do to a person? To a teen? How does one live with the threat of imminent death over one's head for a quarter century? How does one develop social competence in an isolation room? Luci has come across enough people (and pets, for that matter—her first dog Lady being a perfect contender) with neurodiverse behaviors and understands that one person's rudeness is another's anxiety. Maybe Oliver Nelson, with his chronic illness and forever breathlessness, had his childhood so interrupted that his people skills remained rudimentary. And yet, he is a husband, father, business-partner.

Luci dives into these musings on their drive over to East Van. Ki-woo, behind the wheel, appends some of her early morning research findings. Mainly, that Oliver is in debt. That he and his wife rent the main floor of the house on West 6th Avenue. That he, therefore, has no collateral to get a business loan with. That Enviga runs on a shoestring budget and is jointly owned by Oliver and his friend Saaz. That he lives on a small disability pension. That his wife Gina left her hundred-K-plus job at the university to take part time work with the Climate Action Network and that she has since raised almost seventy thousand dollars for her election campaign, most of which has been contributed by various environmental groups and not, as Ki-woo notes pointedly, by her wealthy mother-in-law.

"The mother might be contributing with monthly checks, I don't really see how they can survive otherwise, raising a teenager no less. Oh, by the way," Ki-woo taps on the wheel in rhythm with her words, "the son started high school at West Point Grey, a private school, but left after just one year. He is now enrolled in the public school on Trafalgar."

They arrive at the single story, nondescript building that houses Oliver Nelson's business empire. The minuscule parking lot is empty. Luci cranes her neck to scan the street on both sides for the red Matrix but comes up empty. Where does he park? Is he not here yet? She looks at her watch, although she had just checked it a minute ago. They're right on time. "Must be nice to cruise into work halfway through the morning while your minions have been here since daybreak," she mumbles when she joins Ki-woo on the low landing. But unexpectedly, it's Oliver who opens the small door.

"Oh, hi," he says and steps outside, closing the door behind him. "Sorry, we try to keep all portals as closed as possible. During production hours."

To accommodate personal space, Luci descends the two steps and now looks up at Oliver. He's wearing white coveralls today, but no booties, gloves, or hairnet. Presumably, he'd taken those off before opening the door. Production morning then. But where is his car?

"Where's your car, Mr. Nelson?" Ki-woo asks in her friendliest tone.

"Yeah, sorry about that. It's not here." Oliver looks guilelessly at her.

"What do you mean it's not here? We had an agreement." Even to her own ears, Luci sounds petulant.

"I didn't get to swim yesterday," Oliver says. "I usually swim every evening for half an hour. It's good for my lungs." He takes a breath between each short sentence. Luci wants to contract her growing irritation in the face of his short-windedness, but impatience and indignation win out. She opens her mouth to tear a strip off him when Oliver continues.

"To make up for it, I ran this morning. I parked up by the PNE. I can draw you a map."

He makes to turn, reaches a hand for the door handle.

"You ran from the PNE? That's like seven miles." Ki-woo cannot hide her amazement. She regards jogging as a form of corporal punishment.

"It's about five and a half, yes. I like running. But I can't stand being on a treadmill."

142

He speaks in two-word sentences like Grandma Phil, who's nearing ninety, Luci thinks, her ire rising steadily, *but he runs five miles before work. What's going on here?* She knows better than to butt in. Teflon Ki-woo is sorting it.

"Do you need the keys?" He frowns, looking almost concerned. Maybe he has conveniently "lost" them? Wouldn't be the first time a hit-and-runner pulled this one. Luci takes another breath.

"No, we don't need the keys. If you could just give us the address." Ki-woo's voice exudes positive accommodation.

"Thirty-four hundred block Oxford Street. On the north side."

"Mr. Nelson." Luci can't help herself. Everything about this guy is irritating. "The highway cam shows your car at exit 77 twenty minutes after six. But your parents' house is closest to ramp 83. Do you mind me asking where you'd been?"

His eyes narrow slightly. She had jostled him with the abrupt change of direction. Interview technique 101.

"I take the same route every time. Stay on the old beach road for a while. Only get on the highway as a last resort. I prefer back roads."

Ki-woo and Luci exchange a glance. "We don't have a map of the area with us, but I would sure like to see which roads you were on before getting on the highway. Can we find you later this afternoon at your home address?"

He frowns, then scowls. Surprisingly, he turns to open the door. "Come inside then," he motions with his arm. "I'll draw you a map."

His office, just next to the loading bay and crowded with all the usual workplace accoutrement, is so tiny that Ki-woo and Luci

BARCELONA RED METALLIC

wait outside its door. The sound of voices and machines can be heard from the other side of a double-wide steel door. Here in the loading area, a forklift, half a dozen palettes, a few un-labeled drums, and some cardboard boxes jostle for space along the margins. The place is spotlessly clean. Rumbles, whirrs, and hisses billow softly through the closed double doors that lead, presumably, into the production rooms and every once in a while, they can hear people talking, a woman's laugh. After a couple of minutes, Oliver joins them and places a single sheet on top of one of the drums.

"Here's Robins Row. Where my parents live." He points with the tip of a ball pen.

"Then I turn right. Right again here. That leads to this long, curvy paved road. Here it crosses under the highway. Heads south, right along the beach. Then forks. I keep heading south, follow the road. Until here," he makes a mark on the printout with the pen, "when I get on this forestry road. For a couple of miles until it meets this road here. Then it's smooth sailing until the highway ramp here. From there, it's nothing but sheer rock. There are no secondary roads at all."

"Did you see your mother that morning before you left?" Luci asks, knowing the answer in her bones.

"Yeah, we had coffee together. She'd never not get up. That's not in her."

"How about her car? Did you see it in its parking spot?"

Oliver knots his brow in concentration. He looks maybe a bit older than his forty-four years, is a mere decade away from balding completely, and has stress lines furrowing around his eyes and chin. No wonder, Luci thinks, after what he's been through. But he looks robust and thriving, fit, with a summer tan and bright eyes the color of sky.

"I think I left through the back door. I usually do. From there, it's a straight line to where I park my car. Mom's car usually sits around the other side of the house. By the woodshed. I don't think I can say for sure. I guess it was there…because where else could it have been? She didn't report it stolen, did she?"

For the first time, he seems a bit rattled, unsure. He looks at them, in turn.

"No, she hasn't." Luci can't help herself to ask the obvious next question. "If her car would have been missing, wouldn't she have called you?"

"Probably not. She's used to keeping bad news from me. They brought my son home yesterday. Probably in my dad's car. I didn't see them. Was still here. But Nico didn't say anything. About a stolen car." He looks doubtful, seems to wonder if such news would have, indeed, trickled down to him.

He straightens and rubs his temple, his facial features now a study in concern. "So, there was an accident. You think my mom's car was involved? Or mine?"

"So far, we only know that it was a red Toyota, pre-2014, with factory paint. And there are a lot of them on the road."

"No kidding," Oliver answers with a laugh, his face brightening with relief. "When I bought the Matrix. I chose the same color as my mom's old beater. It's just so great. Like candy apple meets perfect lipstick."

He jots the parking spot address of his car on the back of the map he'd printed, presses two bottles of "the best midday pick-me-upper" into their hands, and watches them turn around in the lot before closing the door. Ki-woo and Luci sit quietly as they head over to East Hastings Street, which is crammed, of course. Rush hour in Vancouver lasts all day.

"We'll have to double check with a decent map at the office," Luci says, watching an un-helmeted bicyclist weave skillfully through lanes of cars and trucks. "But I got the sense that his route takes him right through Eagles Nest. Or at least very close to it."

Ki-woo opens her midsized glass bottle and takes a careful sip. "Oh, this is yummy. Creamy and chocolaty. What's yours?"

"Creamy and coffee-y. Delicious."

"Didn't he say there's no dairy or sugar in these?"

Luci reads the ingredients out loud, and they sip their drinks until they find Oliver's car on Oxford Street. Ki-woo halts just behind it and turns the light bar on. Luci gets the kit bag from the trunk and begins to examine the Matrix. It's covered in dirt specks, and there are several scratches and dents along the bumpers and fenders. Unsurprising, considering the owner habitually drives along unpaved forestry roads. She sighs as she takes several photographs, then motions for Ki-woo to join her.

"We won't be able to rule it out without a proper setup," she says, meaning that they'll have to set up lights and at least two cameras with macro lenses on tripods. It'll take an hour. "Look, it's scratched up and dirty and we're six days post-incident...."

Ki-woo pulls out her phone and dials the number on the business card Oliver had stapled to the map.

"Mr. Nelson, Constable Park here. I'm standing next to your car and there are some dents and scratches in the area where the victim would have made contact. We'll have to take some paint samples, which involves scraping a few small shards off...is that okay with you?" She listens for a moment, then replies, "Of course. We're definitely in an elimination process. We have no reason to suspect you of wrongdoing. It is only the presence of your vehicle in the vicinity of the incident that's giving us cause to examine it.... Okay, that's great. Thank you. We'll call you when we're done."

"He is odd...but also nice," she says to Luci.

Yes, Oliver Nelson is an odd fellow, Luci thinks. Who drives a scratched up BRM Toyota. And what about the curious case that Jo Nelson never even mentioned her son, his red Toyota, and the fact that he left that Wednesday morning before six at all? Not one word. Lying by omission. Now, why would an old woman do that?

The police. They're nosing about. Of course he doesn't worry, because the prisons are full of idiots and any normal person can outsmart the clunky law enforcement apparatus. Right, *law enforcement*. The cops are good at brute force and throwing their weight about, but do they have any real brains at all? Not that he'd ever heard. And besides, he's smarter than your average bear and surely has nothing to worry about. But here's the thing: it's exciting that they're sniffing around. Now it's a challenge. He hadn't foreseen this, but he likes how it makes him feel. The significance. The power.

CHAPTER TWENTY-FOUR

THE CITY BECKONS

After they've taken Nico back to Vancouver, Jo muses on their return trip that she misses the city.

"It's the crowds of all kinds of people, you know," she says to Paul when they are on the ferry, watching the rain form splotches on the windshield before running off in rivulets. "I feel energized when I'm on a sidewalk with a couple hundred others, everyone having a life and errands to run and places to come and go to. There's so much vitality in the city that it rubs off on me, and I feel more...well, more dynamic and vigorous, I guess. In small doses, it's like a really good coffee that gets you almost to the tingling point."

He nods to signal that he understands, but she knows he doesn't share the feeling. Paul had found his lotus land the moment they'd driven into Oyster Hill eight years ago now. He was sixty-five then, just retired from his last job as a power engineer with Halliwell. He had always worked in physical jobs, with large machines and groups of mostly men in overalls, oil jackets, and hard hats. A man's man, capable, proud, and generous, taciturn when quiet was called for, easy to laugh, make friends, fit in. He'd been a union rep all his working life; had learned to negotiate, push when gains could be made. When it had become clear just how sick Oliver was to become and how much turmoil would await, Paul had leaned into work and providing stability. He had done so doggedly, and he'd always been the space where Jo could be restful. Her pillar. Nine years after Ollie's successful transplant, six years after they acquired Gina as a daughter-in-law, four years after Nico was born healthy and robust, Paul had led Jo by the hand to the balcony of their town house in White Rock, had put his arm around her shoulders, and taken in a very deep breath.

"It's time, Jo," he'd said into the blue summer sky, and a shiny white seagull far above had squawked its consent. "We've lived for Oliver's care and treatment for more than thirty years and here he is now, married, a father, and in good enough health to keep going another thirty. You've moved the mountains they said couldn't be moved and the territory looks different now, Jo. We can step back now. Look after ourselves."

She had felt this, too, for a while now but had wanted it to be Paul to say it out loud. In case it would turn out to be a betrayal, it could not come from her.

For several months, they drove up and down the coast and looked at houses. Paul wanted a small-town feel, a home that stood among trees, a fishing boat at the dock, and Jo hoped for a studio room with natural light, Wi-Fi, and a large garden. When the realtor told them about the property on Robin's Row, Jo fell for the hue of the name and Paul remembered knowing the little hamlet on the Sunshine Coast, suspended between stony beaches and rocky mountainsides.

"Three hours by car, including the Langdale ferry," Jo mused, looking at pictures of a two-story, gabled, cedar-shingled house that stood proud in the center of a wide garden dotted with beds and a sizable orchard. In front of the house, an old cherry tree, as wide as it was tall, would lend much-needed shade in the summer, and then there was nothing but forest behind the couple of acres. "If Oliver needs us badly, we can probably even get out by plane; there's regular service up here during summer and skiing season, too." She marveled at her own words—at thinking in stretches of hours, not minutes. For the very first time in thirty-four years, she would live more than half an hour away from her Ollie-Golly, Goofy-Doofy. And from St. Paul's Hospital, where the CF clinic was and Dr. Robichaud. Who had moved from Victoria to Vancouver when Ollie had been sixteen because he couldn't refuse the offer to head the Pacific Lung Health Centre. The Nelsons had followed him, as had several other Island families with CF kids. A new school for Oliver's last two years, a new job for Paul, a different call center for Jo. New neighbors. A duplex close to the hospital for the three of them, then a series of townhomes in Greater Vancouver to cut down on commuting time, lastly, a small-town house in neighboring White Rock, after Ollie had moved in with Gina. Other parents experienced empty-nest syndrome; Jo and Paul never found any words to describe this new feeling.

"Untethered," Jo suggested.

"Cuckoo parents," replied Paul.

"Castaways."

"Geriatric ragamuffins."

"*Since You've Been Gone*," Jo laughed and put Kelly Clarkson's song on speaker, and they goofed and chorused until they embraced laughing, then hugged tighter, eyes brimming, allowing twin feelings of joy and sorrow, relief and fear, worry and triumph to overcome them. Jo cried hard and Paul held her tight in his arms, gave her the rock-solid she needed, and when he began to tremble and could no longer contain his tears, Jo led him to the couch and cradled him there, rocking and soothing him.

Now they're solidly ensconced in Oyster Hill, master and mistress of their life's rhythm. Paul has made friends with just about everybody, and his days are filled with coffee meets, softball coaching, and maintenance projects. He's got weekly poker at Mel's house and snooker night at the pub. Fishing weekends away. He helps build mountain bike trails in the region and is a volunteer firefighter.

Jo keeps to herself with her garden, cooking, and painting. She walks with Samson. Delivers casseroles to the local food bank and cookies to the church sale. Now that she is not driven by necessity and circumstance, she folds in on herself, wraps herself in a sort of prideful independence. Measures her days by steps taken between stove and studio.

But the city always invigorates. And she needs to know. Needs to spend time around Ollie to see what he knows or thinks he knows. Needs to follow up on that nasty, nervous sense she got the other day. Needs to figure things out.

And then there is the lump, of course. She's sure it's larger now than it was when she first felt it in late summer. When she had lain in the tub yesterday, she had looked at her floating breast for a long time and had either seen or imagined a slight bulge in the curved flesh just above where the pea had anchored itself. In the warm, soapy water, her fingers had glided smoothly over the bump and surrounding area. *The upper left quadrant*, as the medical speak would call it. She had shuddered in the warm water when she thought of the medical people who would soon touch her, instruct her, speak over and about her, assess her and recommend courses of treatment, cut and slice her, take her bodily sense and integrity from her and leave her scarred. Why would she want that? Why would she want to enter into that cold, technical, industrial world of modern medicine when the outcome was always going to be death anyway, either soonish from this cancer or in a few years from a different ailment. Would she allow them to cut and slice her if she got a crappy heart at eighty? Would she be that old woman on a hospital gurney in a hallway in some emergency department? The one whose vacant look belies the competence and brilliant life force she once possessed? She had shuddered again, had stood up in the tub too quickly, had to grab the wall and shower pole to steady herself. In all those years of advocating and fighting for Oliver, she had never once entertained the idea of being a patient herself. And she knew, then, dripping almond-scented water and feeling slightly dizzy, knew with absolute clarity and conviction, that she never could be. That she had fought that fight and would not, could not do it again.

"I think I'll come into the city more often in the next few months," she says casually while they watch the ferry attendant lower the ramp to the dock and Paul gets ready to start the car. "The live shows are calling to me, and I haven't done any gallery strolls forever. Maybe I'll rent an Airbnb for a few long weekends, what do you think?"

"I think I am already having enough of the big city feel, and we were barely in and out." Paul shakes his head. "You mind making plans without me?"

"No, not at all. This girl knows how to have fun on her own." Jo reclines and smiles.

She gets in touch with her agent and asks if a pre-Christmas show could be arranged somewhere in Vancouver. She has almost twenty new paintings, including the triptych and Estelle, the agent, can probably secure another twenty as loans, from previous buyers.

"If you want a successful Christmas sale," Estelle's honeyed sales-agent voice drips through the line, "we'll both have to work very fast and very hard, starting right now. I will have to charge you an extra three percent for all the overtime I'll be putting in for you."

Jo agrees and then sends an email to the print shop she has been using for the past five years. It'll take a dozen mails back and forth to settle on the right ink, paper, and finish for each painting, haggle over quantities and prices and COAs. It's a thrill, this compulsive urgency, and she smiles at the recognition. This is where she shines.

She makes neither a doctor's appointment nor books a mammogram. When Paul folds her into his arms, naked, at night, she makes sure to angle her upper arm to redirect his roaming hands away from the lump. She has too much on her mind just now to have this conversation with her man. It'll have to wait.

Within a week, thanks to a fortuitous cancelation, Estelle has organized a solo show in a prestigious downtown gallery to run from the first Friday in December until after New Year, and Jo has ordered dozens of prints in various sizes on paper made of layers of wood fiber, cotton, and agave, as well as some on canvas. She gets her RAV serviced and makes an appointment for late October to put winter tires on. She books two- and three-night stays at the Sylvia, her very favorite Vancouver hotel and at a couple of Airbnbs. Then she sends an email to Ilse. *Am heading to Seattle next Sunday to meet with a guy I met last summer at the local library. He teaches computers, and I need some lessons. He'll work with me in the mornings, Monday through Thursday, from eight till noon. If you are free-ish, I'll stay with you but will book a hotel if your calendar is full. —J*

The answer is in her inbox not ten minutes later. *Come. I am nine-to-five these days. Boss perks. Love, Ilse*

CHAPTER TWENTY-FIVE

THE WOLF

Luci transforms her banked overtime hours into a week off. Three days at Peril Creek on a solo photo shoot, then another three with Grant at a lodge in Bella Coola. Heaven.

She flies to Prince Rupert and charters a Grady-White, a center-consoled, thirty-two-foot cruiser with double Yamaha F300 outboards, a large bunk, a vac-flush head, and ten large, primed oxygen tanks in the hold. When she steers the powerful boat into the choppy waters of Porpoise Channel, she trills with delight. Out here in the wild is where her heart soars and all her senses come alive. She does city life and city work because one must, but the purpose of the grind is so that she can afford to do this: run a boat up the Skeena River for a couple of hours, then tug into successively smaller channels until the hidden shoals and sand banks bring her journey to an end. She ties up, has lunch, and then dons her diving gear to join thousands of salmon on their great spawning migration. In years past, she has come away with stunning pictures of not only leaping fish but also their predators, namely wolf, eagle, and bear. She swims upriver in her neoprene suit to a deep-water bowl about fifty yards across, perfectly round and smooth along its concave sides, and a depth of twenty yards. The bottom is muddy; there is no current down here to sweep debris into the river proper, and hundreds of years of accumulated deadfall have resulted in thick, fertile mud that supports teeming algae, undulating seagrass, and a myriad of other life-forms. Storms must angle into the dene above, because the towering cedar trees, whose roots practically grow into the river like mangroves, suddenly recede to pebble beaches all around the bowl. At the north end are cascades: an almost hundred-yards-long, flat-rocked stair-case that leads into a long, shallow, graveled riverbed—perfect spawning grounds for thousands upon thousands of returning salmon, steelhead, and trout.

Luci spends the next two full days here, swimming and diving for up to four hours at a time, snapping hundreds of pictures and then resting, eating, and sleeping on the boat neatly tied up to a mammoth fallen tree. At night, she sits in the boat's open cockpit and revels in the soundscape of a true forest. Branches of large trees rub against each other in the slightest breezes, producing a deep croaking sound, the burling calls of rutting sika bucks echo through the forest, nocturnal hunters such as raccoons and foxes yowl and screech, and when ravens fly along the creek's path through the forest, she can hear their wings flap. The migrating fish jump and splash right next to her boat in total darkness, and the occasional wolf or bear who comes to the creek for a midnight snack creates a mighty ruckus.

She jumps in her seat when a loud screech rips through the night and drops the bottle of Enviga she had been sipping. What sounds like a human scream is most likely the mating call of a cougar, but in the relative quiet of night, the shriek is as disruptive as a gunshot. She *tsks* at her nervy leap and has to use her flashlight to retrieve the now empty bottle of Oliver Nelson's meal replacement. She had brought three six-packs and they, together with a bag of trail mix and instant coffee, are sustaining her through the trip, despite her body's increased need for calories due to the long swimming and immersion hours in cold water. Amazing. The guy really has something here. With a bit of marketing and promoting, it should become as big as the ubiquitous Happy Planet smoothies, or kombucha sodas. Why hadn't she heard of Enviga before?

Luci is spending a lot of her vacation thinking about Oliver Nelson and his mother, and she is none too pleased about this. She prefers to leave work in the office and generally succeeds in doing just that. But not this case. There is just something about Josephine Nelson that rubs her against the grain, and her internal warning bells kept on jingling when she'd interviewed both Nico and Oliver. Something subtle, not tangible, was going on below the surface, and her instincts had picked it up. The same instinct she trusts her life to when out here in the wilderness, when snapping pictures not fifty meters away from a grizzly bear or sleeping soundly in a half-open boat in cougar territory. As an outdoor enthusiast who loves solitude, Luci has honed her ability to sense her surroundings, and she trusts her intuition completely. And so, she keeps thinking about mother and son Nelson; had, in fact, been contemplating the surreal coincidence of them both driving pre-2014 Barcelona Red Metallic Toyotas, when the love-hungry cougar had broken into her thoughts.

If Oliver had been the driver who'd hit the little girl and had subsequently told his mother, she, in turn, would do anything to protect him, of that Luci is sure. But what would protection mean, exactly? Josephine had struck her as forthright and honorable, so she would likely not counsel her son to lie. But that doesn't mean she would advise him to come forward, either. Maybe she would play to muddy the waters? To delay investigative results? To gain time? To draw suspicion on to herself? On to Nico? Serve up the grandson in favor of her beloved Ollie? Luci shakes her head. She is way off base, way out in la-la land, but that's okay. Allowing her thoughts to shoot off in all directions and looking with open curiosity at their landing places is a bona fide investigative skill, and she excels at this mental exercise. But it works only if she can keep free of any investment in potential outcomes and somehow, she feels that she is not entirely objective. Why not?

Because she likes Jo Nelson. A lot. Because she had felt an instant attraction when they'd met in the backyard at Robins Row. Because the woman's quick wit and sense of humor had drawn her in and then, when Josephine had turned suspicious and acerbic, she, Luci, had felt spurned. Had she? Well, rejection engenders hurt, that is normal for most any human encounter, and psychologists have a name for it. Social pain. Had she, Luci, felt rejected by Josephine Nelson, and that is why she is aiming to pin suspicion on her or on her son? Probably not, but the thought bears paying attention to. Rudd always cautions them to keep tabs on their emotional involvement throughout any investigation.

"You don't leave your personhood, your heart and soul, in the locker," he reminds them from time to time. "When you investigate people, you are the same person who absolutely hates to lose a card game, whose beloved grandfather just recently passed, the same person who failed their sergeant's exam for the first time, and the one whose life partner just walked out. You are full of intense and raw emotions every day you clock in for work, and where we asked you decades ago to leave your personal issues at home and come to work untainted, we know better now and ask, instead, that you are aware of who you are and where you're at. Your emotions, whether you keep them under guard or not, affect the way you interact with people, and how you perceive them."

Does Luci have an investigative bias against Josephine? Because she had felt spurned or because the older woman was indeed hiding something? For the hundredth time, Luci recalls their first meeting in the backyard of the Nelson home. Josephine had been hanging laundry, using a large spider and old-fashioned, wooden clothes pins that were dark with age. Her voice had been warm with friendliness when she'd called an invitation to come closer, her eyes had been wide and bright with curiosity. They had bantered a bit and then talked about the accident. Jo had expressed sadness for the parents of the little girl. Had spoken of her son, his illness, and the many parents she'd known who had lost children to that disease. Even after Luci had said that a recently scratched-up car in a household of several potential drivers raised police suspicion, Jo had parried with ease and had expressed displeasure at being lumped into a category, but true antagonism had only appeared when Luci had first asked about Nico. That was when the older woman became prickly and even hostile.

So, based on instinct alone, Luci would say that Josephine had not been defensive about herself. But she became adversarial when Luci indicated that Nico would be part of the investigation and then had failed completely to mention Oliver. Affront to protect the grandson, evasion to protect Oliver. The grandson could have driven either vehicle, the son would have been in the Matrix. Josephine, mother and grandmother, might have simply flexed her well-honed protective muscle. Maybe that was all there was to it. Maybe.

And then there were Luci's two interviews with Nico and Oliver. Neither had struck her as evasive or guilty. Nico had been open where other boys his age might be sullen or try to appear über-cool. And his father hadn't exactly been the poster boy for accommodation but had been sincere in his irritation. Would a man who'd been at death's door repeatedly be in full control of his emotions? Hell, yes. Could a man who'd cheated death several times be lying his heart out to escape persecution? Well, yes, of course. He'd be well trained to overcome, at all costs, the seemingly inevitable.

She shakes her head at her Nelson fixation. In all probability, it'll turn out that the driver that fateful morning was Machensky, the cantankerous town drunk who is, by any reckoning, on the very top of their suspect list. He had been uncooperative and evasive from the get-go and fits any cop's definition of a bad guy. Maybe the Edmonton lab will prove his guilt within a couple of weeks, and she can put him and the whole Nelson brood out of her mind. Luci sighs, stretches her neck, rolls her shoulders. The trees on either side of the creek are tall and allow her to see only a thin band of the clear night sky far above. She can make out the zigzaggy shape of the lizard constellation and, in an effort to clear her mind of the Nelsons, tries to recall the names of its four brightest stars. U Lacaerta, Alpha Lacaerta, M something, and D something. That's it. Her head is finished…it's time to call it a night.

The next day, she gets the shot she's dreamed of. She's in the bowl, her head and camera just half a meter below the water's surface. Close to the cascade's infall is a large, partially submerged boulder and in its lee rests a particularly gorgeous steelhead with a dark blue back, silvery belly and a wide, crimson band spanning the entire length of its body, which is as long as her arm and thrice as thick. The fish is resting, likely in anticipation of the mighty upsurge required to ascend the rocky staircase. If she times her own muscle responses just right, she'll capture its leap from the water with her lens just below the surface, or she may even breach to catch both worlds in one shot. In anticipation, she begins to shoot: her finger presses the shutter release button rhythmically, every sixth heartbeat. Her feet, leg, and back muscles move to bring her into position inches behind the steelhead, while her chest, shoulders, arms, and hands work to keep the camera perfectly stable.

A hint of a shadow above and a wolf's snout angles into the water. The steelhead explodes away. Luci can barely suppress the instinct to follow but stays utterly still instead, only her shutter finger speeding up. The wolf's face becomes larger; soon the entire wedge-shaped head is submerged. She recognizes the blended beige and yellow colors on both sides of the muzzle as belonging to a male teen, an inquisitive and playful fellow she had first photographed as a three-month-old pup two years ago. His distinctive ocher, almond-shaped eyes are wide open, and he seems to stare right into the camera, from half an arm's length away. The water's resistance pushes his lips back and reveals his canines so he appears to be grinning. She keeps shooting and resists the instinct to paddle backwards. The wolf is curious; he must have looked at her strobe lights for a while and finally decided to investigate. He pulls his head out of the water and then thrusts it back—his large, black, well-textured nose almost touching the lens. As a means of examination, he would bite the camera, but Luci knows wolves cannot hold their breath and therefore don't dive, and so she holds her position. She keeps shooting while changing the camera's angle in minuscule ways, careful not to make sudden or excessive movements. She is wholly mesmerized by the wolf's oh-so-close face and focuses on capturing light, water movement, oxygen floaters, and the tenacious fish on the perimeter but marvels, in the recesses of her awareness, at the fortune of this moment. Her finger keeps tapping the shutter, her heartbeat too fast to provide rhythm, her feet sway to maroon her in place, and the wolf's thirty-second air supply seems to last forever.

CHAPTER TWENTY-SIX

AT ILSE'S

"You and Oliver have always had such a strong bond—you were *so* in tune with one another, it was almost uncanny. So why can't you just ask him?" Ilse carefully places her long-stemmed wine glass on its coaster and leans back into the couch, all the while keeping her eyes trained on Jo. She has aged incredibly well; is elegant where Jo is solid and earthy, has a chic, all-silver bob, pearl earrings, and the permanently bemused bearing of the true academic, whereas Jo feels like a battle-worn soldier deep inside a muddy trench. Jo, still damp from the shower after a long day in Dave's computer lab, sighs deeply before taking a sip from her wine.

"It was easy being super-mom back when Ollie was a kid. I was in charge then, and we all knew it. In charge of him. Of his meds, his food and exercise, therapy sessions, his bowel movements for goodness's sake. He couldn't fart or blow his nose without me knowing about it. And that was when things were going well and he felt healthy." Jo smirks and moves a wayward strand of hair behind her ear. "I mean, that time when he ejaculated for the first time, at home in his bed, he called me into his room so we could examine the blob on his sheet. He asked me if it would be salty."

She guffaws and Ilse breaks into her trademark horse laugh; soon both women are laughing so hard they have to wipe tears off their cheeks and pause to catch their breath.

"He didn't."

"Oh yes, he did. Completely unperturbed, too. He was just that used to me examining his bodily fluids."

They both snort and roar with laughter again. They're sitting on Ilse's deep, extremely comfortable couch in her immaculate condo in Seattle's Beacon Hill neighborhood. Jo has been here all week, and they have dined out or brought in take-out each night. Tonight, Ilse has flash-fried a pound of prawns and served Caesar salad and cheese bread. They're on their second bottle of Chilean red and Jo has a ticket for tomorrow's noon flight back to Vancouver.

"It was like that again during the transplant year. Not the ejaculate," Jo grins before continuing, her gaze toward the window where the first raindrops of a predicted storm hit the glass panes, "but the absence of any boundaries. And again, in a way, when they were trying to get pregnant, and I did all that research, went along to some of his appointments and paid a good chunk of the IVF and embryonic testing, to boot." Jo shakes her head and sighs again. "No boundaries, really. Seems kinda unhealthy in hindsight."

"It's like that for all CF families. You figure it out as you go along. I hope you're not having any regrets about seeing your boy through it all?"

"No," Jo grimaces. "No regrets. He is alive, and that's all that counts. But Gina must have put her foot down around the time Nico was born. There are boundaries now, lots of them. I mean, don't get me wrong, we're close, and everybody loves each other, but Oliver is very much his own man now and holds his own counsel. He doesn't share himself with me any-more—he tells me the stuff he thinks I should know." Jo leans back into the soft cushion and looks at her friend of more than thirty years. "He is like any other adult son out there. A bit secretive and none too keen to share upsetting news."

"A fatal hit-and-run is a bit more than upsetting news, wouldn't you say?"

"The policewoman said the driver might not have noticed, even. And I am only thinking that it could have been Oliver because I know he likes to take that route through the new subdivision to the old Gibsons highway. I tell you, when she said Barcelona Red Metallic, my stomach lurched every which way." Jo frowns and lowers her head slightly. When she speaks again, her voice is so soft, Ilse has to lean in to hear her words.

"Back then, whenever Ollie wasn't in the house and I heard a siren blare, my immediate thought was always, *Oh no, it's Ollie.* A bleed, a mucus plug in his airway, a hockey stick in the chest, a car ran him over, a fire. Every conceivable mode of accidental death flashed through my mind, adrenaline would be pumping, and I'd be vibrating inside with anxiety until he came home from wherever he'd been, school or sports or a friend's house. I was in permanent, constant fear something might happen to him."

Ilse remains quiet, allowing the silence to be and her friend to gather the threads of her thoughts.

"I went to therapy about it. About my constant worry. She called them intrusive thoughts and basically taught me to stop them from happening. Taught me to visualize a traffic stop sign the moment a thought began to rear up and to banish it with that sign. Funny thing is it worked." Jo laughs and reaches for her glass. She drains it and places it back on its coaster. "Now a little kid is dead because she didn't know what a stop sign means, and every time I think that it might have been Oliver who ran her over, the visualized stop sign puts me at the scene of the accident, and I see his Matrix hit Lena Newman on her bike and drive off. Ugh!"

Ilse reaches for Jo's hand, which had curled into a fist. She takes it between her own hands, uncurls the fingers one by one, and strokes it softly. She waits until Jo's breathing is easy and slow.

"First off, you need to replace your traffic sign with something else. Something beautiful. A Mandala perhaps, or a swarm of bees or the Eiffel Tower. Anything will do, I imagine. Then you have to ask yourself a few questions. Is Oliver a decent driver? Is he an honest man? Is he someone who owns up to mistakes or is he a habitual liar? Could Oliver be the kind of person who kills a child and then lies about it? Who'd not allow that child's parents to find a bit of closure?"

Jo shakes her head at each question. "No, he is not that kind of man. He is a good person—kind and compassionate, caring and decent. But isn't that what the moms of pretty much every mass murderer in history say? Jim Jones's mother said her son was an angel."

"Jim Jones's mother didn't know her son the way you know Oliver. You really, really know Oliver. Jo, you have to trust your instincts on this, trust your heart. Let the police deal with the science of verification and all you need to do is listen to what your heart tells you."

But her heart is the crux of the problem. It had contracted hard when she first learned that a Barcelona Red Toyota was the car that had fled. Her heart had convulsed and then beat to the anxious rhythm of the silent incantation that was borne of muscle memory: *Oh no, it's Ollie.* He left at the right time, likes to take that road, drives the right car, was distracted that morning. It could have been Oliver. Who is kind and compassionate, but can also be rash, spiteful, egocentric, and shortsighted. Who she hasn't actually seen since the morning Lena Newman died alone by the curb of the road.

At five-thirty that dreadful morning, she'd made two cups of Nescafé, and they sat at the kitchen table, Ollie and her, in companionable silence. Oliver, who had brought Nico up on short notice to stay for a few days, and who would drive back to Vancouver, then take a plane to Calgary in early afternoon where he had an important sales meeting with the buyer for a large, nationwide supermarket chain. He was excited about the deal, which would quadruple his sales and pave the way into solidity, would show the banks that he was more than a one-trick pony and lead, at long last, to financing his much hoped-for expansion. He sat at the table and gathered himself for the task ahead. When he left, he kissed her on the cheek somewhat absentmindedly and left the back door open in his wake. She closed it slowly, worrying about the stress he was under. Stress is not good for anybody, but least so for someone with a set of donor lungs, someone who takes a handful of antirejection medication every day, whose immunity is frail at the best of times and who is at twice the risk of developing lymphoma or skin cancer than anyone else. Stress would boost his cardiac risks, could lead to asthma and Alzheimer's.

Jo doesn't share these thoughts with Ilse—it's enough to speak about her worries—naming them transforms fleeting thoughts into something more material, three-dimensional she can examine from all sides. Processing, they call it.

Should I tell Ilse about the lump? Jo considers this for a moment, then relegates the thought to the very back of her mind. She knows that her friend would, unequivocally, counsel her to visit her doctor immediately, or, more efficiently, arrange for Jo to see an oncologist first thing in the morning right here at Seattle's Cancer Clinic. *To hell with that.*

During the wait for her plane the next morning, Jo stands near a window onto the tarmac and watches the interminable rain fall impassively from a gray, heavy sky.

2000

The year of the transplant had been horrendous. First, there had been several months' worth of evaluation in Vancouver:

ventilation-perfusion scans, CT scans, pulmonary function tests, tissue typing, EKGs, blood tests, mental health workups, evaluations of emotional support determinants. Then Ollie is accepted to the transplant program, but not listed to actually receive a donor lung. To be listed, the transplant team has to accept you. The team in Toronto knows Ollie only on paper. The inclusion criteria aren't exactly clear, have never been spelled out, and this not-knowing increases their sense of power-lesness. They have to live in limbo, waiting for Ollie's quality of life to become unbearable. Lung transplants for CF kids are done as an end-stage procedure, a Hail Mary, so a person has to be quite sick but not so sick that they can't recover from the surgery.

They live for months in an elusive zone of no clear description. His breathing becomes so bad, he can't hike or swim anymore, he gets sick with lung infections more often, hospitalizations become more frequent and last longer; he has to give up his dorm room at university and move back home. Soon, he needs to use supplemental oxygen all the time, not just for physio and to recoup from a lengthy bout of breathlessness, but the cannula is stuck up his nose all day and night. His nose bleeds, of course, and becomes raw. His moods spiral out of control, and he starts on anti-anxiety meds. He had become used to being on campus, around peers, had a large crowd of friends and more than a few girlfriends. Now he is out in the burbs in his parents' house. Some of his more dedicated friends and his latest flame, Juliana, come round regularly, then less so. Ollie is an emotional mess, cranky, sore, dying, hopeless, angry. And always, always short of breath. No word from the transplant team. Then the second round of pretransplant assessment. All the same tests and a few others. Back and forth between Langley and the Lung Health Centre in downtown Vancouver two or three times per week. Rushing to make appointments on time, then sitting around, waiting endlessly. Hurry up and wait. Come back tomorrow. Come back next week.

And then the phone call. Yes, you're on the list. Your score is high enough (meaning your life is shitty enough). Come to Toronto, we need to do our own assessments here, start you on our pretransplant physio. You can expect a wait time of six to twelve months. During that time, you need to come to the center every week for evaluation. No, we cannot assist with getting you here. Not all insurers pay for pretransplant medevacs, you'll have to figure it out.

They get lucky. Some months ago, the Ottawa Art Gallery had approached Jo for a show, and so she phones and tells them she'd be delighted but would need help to find a year's lease in Toronto and a private plane with a medical team to bring her son. He is too sick to tolerate a six-day drive and has been turned away more than once from a commercial airport gate just for looking too pale. The gallery's wealthy patrons fall all over themselves to lend a hand (and a fully staffed converted Airbus), and so Jo and Ollie move into a fabulously furnished suite one block away from Toronto General in the spring of the new millennium.

Fasting, blood work. Six-minute walk tests. CT. ECG. Sputum cultures. LFTs. Echo. RNA MUGA, abdominal ultrasound. Meetings with Ollie's surgeons and anesthetists, a cardiologist, a nutritionist, a psychologist, and a physiotherapist. Also a doctor of bones. A doctor of kidneys. Nearly every body part is represented. Sessions with the pretransplant coordinator and social worker. Ollie has to defend his decision to be on the list, has to prove his support systems, has to reflect on his life's choices, decisions, and hopes in dozens of interviews. Jo and he feel like they are on trial. The team has to agree that he and his mother will behave, can handle the pressures both pre- and post-op, will be compliant with all that's asked of them. The team has to determine whether Ollie will put forth his best effort to survive. Whether he is worth the precious organ. Whether he understands, deep in his heart and soul, that someone, a person, is out there in the world right now, breathing through a pair of healthy, pink lungs that will later end up inside his body.

Jo has to submit her own health history and undergo a psychiatric evaluation.

Ollie makes friends with some members of the transplant support group that meets weekly. They do their twice-daily physio sessions together. With the exercise, his lung function improves. With new friends, he brightens. Is buoyant, hopeful, expectant. Jo is able to spend a bit of time in Ottawa; her show is due to open in November, and she is expected to do her part of marketing, to show up at art magazines' interviews, some hobnobbing luncheons. On a Monday, she flies to Boston to attend a CF conference but is called back the next day by a phone call from the hospital. Ollie has a major bleed in his lung, is in the ICU, has received a dozen blood transfusions. Prognosis uncertain.

This is Ollie's third major bleed. His lung tissue is so damaged and frail from repeat infections, colonized bugs and fungi, hardened globs of years-old mucus debris that a hearty cough can rupture it. If an organ comes in now, while he is bleeding, the surgery can go ahead, but if he develops a post-hemorrhage pneumonia, as he had done the previous time, they'll have to wait for it to clear up before he'll become eligible again. That might take months. Who knows. Who's to tell.

Up, down. Up, down. Repeat. Each loop, twist, and hill on the roller coaster repeated over and over, each time with a different mindset. Sometimes you are full of can-do attitude, you believe in yourself and your inner strength to survive, other times it catches you unawares and pummels you through all kinds of hell. Jo picks Paul up from the airport and leans into him for the half-hour taxi ride to the hospital, quietly weeping the whole way.

The doctors are able to stop the bleed and Ollie does not get pneumonia. He recovers well and quickly and is discharged by the end of the week. Paul, Jo, and Ollie celebrate by going on a harbor-front cruise in the evening, marvel at the impressive skyline, and eat soft caramel candies. Ollie's phone rings and Mallory Cobb, the transplant team coordinator, tells him that they have a pair of lungs for him. "Come back as soon as you can," she says, "we're assembling the team. Today is the day."

CHAPTER TWENTY-SEVEN

THE TRANSPLANT

2000

Jo had once figured out that Ollie has spent about twenty-five
thousand hours of his life inside hospitals, give or take. And she
about half that; at his bedside, in cafeterias, hallways, family rooms,
nurse's stations, doctor's offices. An average doctor, respiratory
therapist, or nurse would clock double that during a life-spanning
career. A big institute, like the massive Toronto General with its
hundreds of patients and thousands of workers, would absorb
millions upon millions of life's hours into its walls. One hour in
a person's life could hold so much vital force...when she thought
about this long enough, or vividly enough, she quickly became
overwhelmed by visions of energy-drenched walls, seeping with
pain, loss, and love, and yet holding up this grandiose temple to
the human insistence that brain and brawn can ultimately win the
fight against microbes, enzymes, and molecules.

They have to persuade the tour boat operator to take them back to the dock, then hail a taxi to the Ajmera Transplant Centre on University Boulevard. They walk through the double doors three abreast, Ollie between his parents, holding their hands in an iron grip. A week ago, he had almost bled out, had almost died, and this had prompted his father to drop everything and fly in. Now Paul's fortuitous presence binds and anchors them. He radiates hope and confidence, makes Jo smile despite her worries, and causes Ollie to draw his shoulders back and walk tall. This is their moment, and they would seize it, together, come hell or high water.

Of course, the night unfolds in banality and waiting. Hurry up and wait. They sit in a large waiting area, then are moved into a patient room. Ollie changes into the hospital pj's that lie folded at the foot of the bed, then an excited student nurse comes in and gives him a gown to put on, instead. Every member of the transplant team enters the room to check in, says a few encouraging or hopeful words about how it wouldn't be much longer now, then leaves as quickly as they had burst in. Jo feels her nerves jingle; the energy in the room has reached a simmering point. She looks at Oliver, who sits back in bed, eyes half closed, chest moving rapidly underneath the thin, light blue gown. Out of habit, she counts against the large clock on the wall. Twenty-two breaths in a fifteen-second segment. Eighty-eight breaths per minute. Sixteen for her. Eighty-eight for her son. His skin pale, his eyelids so thin she can see the blue veins in them, a slight blue tinge to his lips. Same for his nail beds on his long, too-slender fingers. Her boy looks ethereal and fragile. Is closer to death today than even earlier this week when he was bleeding out. That had been close, but they had been at that particular junction a few times before, and he had always pulled through. After all these years, they know the signs of pulling through: the slight pink on the top of his nose, the faint smirk at the corners of his lips, the twitch in his fingers. *I am still here and coming back. No worries.* But today is different. Today he could really die. Ollie is gathering himself for the task ahead, she knows. She has practiced the meditations with him hundreds of times in the past. Go to your favorite rock at the beach: the one that fits the curve of your spine to a tee. Slide your hands through the ground, feel the pebbles, the bits of seaweed, a chunk of beach wood under your fingers. Breathe the salty, humid air. Feel the sun's warmth on your face or a drift of cool fog. Now, visualize your surgical team. Dr. Lee. Dr. Rubaskova. Dr. Maggie. The nurses. The anesthetist. The folks who prepare the instruments, the ones who cleaned the OR for you. They are all there, crowding the space. Lending you their expertise and knowledge. They'll do their best work for you today. They are calm and professional. Here to do this work. You are safe in their hands.

But the whole thing is ludicrous. How can he be safe with his chest cracked wide open, his lungs removed, a heart and kidney machine attached to keep his organs alive during the twenty- or thirty-hour-long procedure while he lies, essentially dead, on that table? They'll fit new lungs into the space, connect all the tubes if the frail, damaged tissues of his body can be matched up to the vibrant, muscular, strong stuff of the healthy organ. And then they'll turn him back on, flip a switch, and wait for his engine to sputter back to life. All eyes on the monitors above his shrouded head. *Come on*, they'll murmur, *come on buddy, you can do it. Come on. Come on!* Jo shudders at the image. She waves an imaginary stop sign at it and the operating room disappears.

It is two in the morning before a nurse they've never met knocks and steps into the room. "Hi everyone, my name is Cynthia Robertson. I'm part of the team who recovered your lungs for you, and we brought them in about twenty minutes ago. I just wanted to tell you that they are healthy and pliable and beautiful and will serve you for many, many years. Congratulations." She is young and very pretty, with long, light hair, hazel eyes, freckles everywhere, and a wide, wide smile.

"The porter is outside, ready to take you to the OR. I just wanted a minute to tell you that your new lungs are absolutely gorgeous!" Cynthia laughs, steps closer, and lays a hand over Ollie's. She leans forward and says quietly, "Just think, when you wake up, you can breathe. Just think about that."

The porter comes in and readies the bed for transport, then he and Cynthia and three others wheel Ollie out of the room. Jo catches a glimpse of a sparkle in his eyes and a wan smile. He lifts his right hand and gives a thumbs-up, and then it is just her and Paul in the now very empty room. The door swings slowly closed.

What do you do while your son is temporarily dead?

They walk out of the center in a daze, not holding hands; both feeling so over-sensitized they're afraid their touch would burn the other. The air feels thick, their feet millstone-heavy, their minds crowded with hundreds of fragments of thoughts and images swirling wildly. Ollie and his A-okay thumbs-up. Ollie as a toddler in the sandbox underneath the stately Arbutus tree, in the yard of their first house in Port Alberni, a lifetime ago. Ollie as a teen: calmly discussing his own funeral plans but quivering with nervousness around Islay, his first girlfriend-to-be after Chloe. Ollie, breathless and beseeching, and Ollie the seal, swimming with assured strokes out into the bay. Ollie on the operating table, his body covered in drapes except for his torso, which is splayed wide open. Ollie graduating next year with a BA in journalism, a wide, proud smile splitting his face.

Silently, Jo and Paul walk among the very early risers along Toronto's city streets and find an open coffee shop. Jo slides into the booth and buries her face in her hands. How can one cope with this day? The interminable wait? Paul places a coffee in a white ceramic mug in front of her, followed by a piece of apple pie. Two forks. He sits across from her and digs in, his own coffee forgotten on the counter. The waitress brings it over, looks at them with hooded eyes.

"You folks have someone in the hospital?" she asks quietly, having recognized the utter helplessness and resignation in them. She fusses over them, refills their coffee, encourages Jo to order a stack of pancakes, makes sure their water glasses are refreshed every so often. Clucks and hums into their silence. Jo gives her a grateful hug when they leave to make room for the morning coffee crowd. She could have spent the whole day at that table, enveloped by kindness. By unspoken agreement, they walk toward the CN tower and then keep going until they reach the waterfront. They sit on a bench, huddled deep into their coats, and lean into each other's presence.

Somehow, the day passes. They go to the suite and have hot showers, try for an uneasy nap. By five in the evening, they have dinner out, then return to watch TV. Then it is eight o'clock, then nine, ten. They go walking. Find themselves at that same beach bench by midnight but it is too cold to sit there. An icy breeze comes off the lake, and the surf is building. A storm on the way. No word yet from the hospital. Jo checks her phone's battery status every twenty minutes. They walk back to the suite, their legs heavy with fatigue. They strip down to their underwear and crawl under the down comforter. Their hands and feet are like ice blocks, and they pull each other close and tight and eventually, their body heat spreads delicious warmth along their limbs. They remove their briefs and T-shirts and hold each other snug, wanting to touch and be touched everywhere at once. They cry and laugh and fumble their way to release. Then they sleep.

The call comes just before noon. Jo's phone rings loudly and she picks it up on the second ring. It's Dr. Lee, the lead surgeon. His voice booms energetically from the minuscule speaker, fills all the space around them with relief. "Fine, Mom and Dad, it all went fine! Hahaha, we're tired as dogs, but your boy did great. Sailed through it all." He talks on but Jo would never remember what else he says. Ollie lives. He has a new set of lungs inside him, and he lives.

It's during the early post-transplant months that Jo sees a new side to Oliver. He is ramped up on steroids, impatient to head home to BC, disappointed he isn't well enough to join his campus buddies for spring break, and cranky all the time. Short, rude, obnoxious. Yes, he can breathe better. Yes, all the tubes are off. Yes, he can walk for an hour on the treadmill without supplemental oxygen. Yes, his swallow is back and he can eat whatever he wants. Yes, the frightful amount of pills he has to take every day allows for a beer every now and again. Yes, Tracey Gould, a young woman he'd met last summer here in Toronto shows more than a passing interest and visits him almost every day. Yes, everything is going swimmingly, but Oliver is a bear, an outright douchebag, and Jo can't stand being around him. A psychologist on the transplant team suggests that she is part of the equation.

"You are not used to having an adult healthy son. You both just leaped out of the known-to-you environment of your previous relationship into something entirely new and different. He is no longer the kid with the lung problem. He is someone new. You both have to make huge adjustments in your expectations of one another."

Now, that is helpful.

Four months after the transplant, Jo and Ollie move back home. Again, food, exercise, and physio become the time-consuming mainstays of their lives, and they fall back into their previous routine. Jo cooks and bakes, takes Ollie hiking, sits on a log on the beach while he swims. As he comes off the steroids, his moods balance out and they find joy in each other again. His friend Saaz comes over almost every day and prepares smoothies in their old Osterizer, throwing handfuls of greens, butter, whey protein, maple syrup, and mango together. Ollie fills out every which way and grows two inches. At age twenty-five! The common cold is no longer a death threat. Thoughts, dreams, and plans for a future become staples of their conversations, and he returns to university. And then Gina happens. Ginevra Moretti, a marine biology student at UBC, who takes him on exciting double-hull zodiac trips into the Salish Sea to skim across the breaking swells and see, hear, and smell whales up close. Who studies his scarred torso and declares him "her" miracle man.

Does that mean he is no longer mine? Jo wonders. *If he is her miracle man, then that must mean he can no longer be my worry boy.*

And then he isn't.

CHAPTER TWENTY-EIGHT

A NIGHTMARISH MEMORY

He hasn't been to the pub in three months. He shops for his groceries in Gibsons now and buys his liquor there, too. A few times, he sleeps in the truck at the ferry dock, waiting for a broken machine part to be delivered on the barge. He doesn't like driving the red Toyota anymore, thinks about just taking the plates off and leaving it, but then worries that abandoning the car in the ferry lot might sour the already bad attitudes of the landing dock's crew. He needs them to be cordial, to give him space when he comes to load or unload, to not double-park behind his vehicles and then plead ignorance as to who has the keys to move the truck that blocks his. So many ways guys can be mean, underhanded jerks to each other. He just wants to be left alone to do his work. He's good at it, very good. He knows about machines and what they need. It's easy because machines need to run at ease. If something shifts somewhere, and now metal grinds on metal, well that's not an easy run anymore, is it? A speck of dirt, a bit of rust, sometimes a dead animal or plant growth. Water damage, a corroded bit of wiring, an ignoramus forcing a lever. These are all detriments, and he never fails to find the thing that went wrong in the first place and then caused a sequence of malfunctions. In turn, machines never fail to reward him for his care, his listening ear, his laser-sharp attention. They hum for him, shine for him, vibrate silently and endlessly.

He watches kids' movies about cartoon machines at his sister's house on Christmas, sitting wedged between nieces and nephews who turn their noses up at the presents he buys at the mega mall but delight in introducing their latest animation heroes to him. *WALL-E*, *Transformers*, *Big Hero 6*, *Cars*. They know what he loves and that he prefers to sit with them, in the corner of the couch with a beer, rather than at the table with the adults, turkey, and wine. He tells them that he sees the personality of each of the machines he works on, that he doesn't need cutesy eyes or cartoon teeth to know what they want.

"Machines are simple, you see, like you kids. Your parents give you food and sweets, warm clothes, toys to entertain you and make you think, they read to you at bedtime and teach you right from wrong. If they do all that, you grow up fine. It's the same with my machines. I give them oil and gas, fix their wheels and gears so they run smooth, keep their wires warm and snug with proper insulation. Machines and kids and dogs are easy to figure out." He turns his head slightly and nods in the direction of the dining room table. "It's the adults," he whispers conspiratorially and the kids grin and chuckle, but Gordon Machensky doesn't find this funny at all. "It's the adults who I can't figure out for the life of me."

He wants to visit the Newmans. Wants to give his condolences. He knows that all the village folk have been by their house, have left cards or food dishes at their door. Many of them probably don't even ring the bell. 'Cause what is there to say? What could he say to them? "Hi, my name is Gordon, and the police suspect me of having killed your kid"? Or, "Hi, my name is Gordon and my sister died when she was ten, and my family broke apart in splinters and cut and sliced at each other until we bled? I know what you're going through, and it is hell on earth and will never, ever get better." Or, "Hi, my name is Gordon, and I bought you some cabbage rolls at the M&M in Gibsons, and I hope none of you is allergic"? What would you say if you were dumb enough to ring the bell? He has visions of shaking the man's hand and conveying, with his eyes alone, that he feels sympathy for him and his loss. But what if the woman opens the door? He doesn't do well with looking women in the eye, is always afraid they'll see right into him, know his darkness, know his worst thoughts. He's got nothing for her.

He knows he'll never make that visit and so he'll try the graveyard, instead. He didn't go to the funeral, of course, because he only learned of the little girl's death a couple days before the service was held, and he was a mess for a week or more after the police had come to his house, twice, and accused him of having caused her death. He stayed in his workshop with his machines, for days after, slept on the cot, left only to fetch food and booze from the house. He couldn't focus enough to work, but he oiled and polished all his tools, gears, and parts. He kept Hero fed, of course, and lived on the cans of soup and Chef Boyardee he had in the pantry. He drank the bottle of vodka in the freezer, then the rum that he keeps in the shop for emergencies. After seven or eight days, he ran out of cans and bottles and had to drive to Gibsons. He filled the shopping cart to the brim and grabbed a couple of papers from beside the till. When he got back home, he stashed the groceries, the vodka, and beer, and returned a full bottle of rum to the lubrication cupboard in the Quonset. Then he made a ham and cheese sandwich, sat at the kitchen table, and read the local rag. There was a big story, with pictures, about the accident, the parents, the little brother, the birthday bicycle, the funeral. He cried. Hero came over and put his massive head on his leg in sympathy. Such an easy gesture for a dog to make, but he, Gordon, wouldn't be able to do that in a million years.

All of last week, he's had flashbacks. To what had happened in '78. He was just little then, barely in school, the local one-room in Crofton. He was the runt of the litter, and his siblings didn't let a day pass without reminding him. They pointed to his supposedly open shoelaces and then knocked his chin back with their fists when he was dumb enough to look down. They challenged him to an underwater hold-your-breath-as-long-as-you-can contest and then piled on top of him for so long, he almost drowned. Actually thought he had died, truly. Or they snatched his piece of sweet he had saved to savor later, in bed. Or, almost daily, they painted him the culprit to their father, who punished even mild mishaps, never mind what he did when you really fucked up. What he had done when John fucked up.

1978

John, Peter, Gabrielle, and Cathy all go to the big kids' school in Duncan. There's a yellow school bus that comes by their house every morning, actually comes right into their yard like they are important people who warrant door-to-door service. The bus driver is Mr. Hampton, who opens and closes the swishy doors with a big lever.

"Good morning, Gordon," he says when he sees him standing nearby.

"Good morning, Mr. Hampton," Gordon replies.

"When will you be old enough to come on the bus with your brothers and sisters?"

"One more year, Mr. Hampton."

"Well, I am looking forward to welcoming you aboard. Have a nice day, Gordon."

"You too, Mr. Hampton."

Then, one day, the bus doesn't show. Their father says the kids can stay home and help him with the chores. The school phones later that day to say that Mr. Hampton is sick and would Mr. Machensky be able to drive the bus for a few days, considering that he is a logging truck driver and certified. Their father declines politely, hangs the phone up, and then yells at them for going to a school where a stuck-up secretary thinks she can boss him around. He gives them a list of chores to do and drives away in his pickup. When he returns later, there are four bicycles in the truck bed. They're used and a bit rusty, need their chains oiled and a few tires patched, but they're nice bikes and serviceable. The kids are to ride to school from now on, a six-mile, hilly ride.

Peter's to ride in front, the girls in the middle, and John to bring up the rear. Single file all the way. The road is paved, with a fresh yellow center line, but no shoulder. They have to get up earlier than before, eat a bit more breakfast, can't get away with shoving a muffin or sandwich in their bag to eat on the bus. But their father is king, and their mother picks her battles scrupulously, and this isn't one of them. After a week, the whole thing has become routine. Gordon misses Mr. Hampton's friendly eyes and hearing the swish of the school bus door opening and closing. When he gets out of bed in the mornings, the big kids have already left. He wonders if his father will buy him a bicycle next year, too, or if he might allow the bus to come back.

Of course, you can tell children to ride single file for almost two hours every day but that doesn't mean that they will. Or that they'll ride in formation. On the day that it happened, John and Peter are riding way up front, side by side, talking and laughing. Cathy's not far behind, trying to keep up, and wanting to stay close to Peter, as always. They're twins and don't like to be apart. Gabrielle is last, has fallen behind, and no one has noticed that her rear light isn't working anymore. The morning is heavy with clouds and dew and layers of gray. The driver of a passing Volvo towing a big trailer sees Gabby too late and steers away from her in a reflex, which causes the trailer to jackknife. Just enough so that its tail corner brushes the bike. The driver keeps going, thinking he's avoided a collision. He casts a glance into the rearview mirror to check that the girl is still riding along, but the trailer load is too high, and when his eyes travel instinctively to the side-view mirror, he remembers that it had broken off months ago. Soon he overtakes a group of kids, their rear lights shining bright red in the morning's receding darkness.

It's a while before Cathy rings her bell furiously and shouts at her brothers that Gabby is no longer behind them. They turn around and ride back, expecting to see her sitting at the side of the road with a flat tire or a busted knee after a fall. But there is no sign of her. They ride almost all the way home, then turn again and begin to search in earnest. A soggy, gray-cloud-filtered light emerges, and they strain to look into the shadows, lee side of trees, blackberry picker's paths in the dense brambles. At last, their eyes fall on it: the wheel of a bicycle sticking out of the ditch water, surrounded by long grasses and cattail. They let their bikes fall every which way and run to the site. Gabby is under the bike, face down in the water. They scream, they lose their breath, they stare, spring into action. John and Peter lift the bike and throw it into the middle of the road, turn Gabby over. She turns easy, is floating in half a meter of water. Cathy stops oncoming cars and screams for help, an ambulance.

Gordon didn't know any of it. His mom had made him breakfast and then he walked to school. It's Thursday, math day for his Grade 4 class. He likes math, likes it best when the teacher, Miss Henschel, walks up and down between the desks, quietly and slowly reciting numbers. *Ten—add four—minus seven—plus thirteen—divided by two—times four—minus nine—divided by three....* You aren't allowed to use pen and paper, have to lean in to hear every word, have to juggle the numbers in your head and keep up. Gordon always, always keeps up until the last digit and his result is always, always right. He likes Thursdays and math class best.

When he comes home for lunch, his father's truck is in the yard and the bikes are piled in the rear. He can hear shouting from behind the house. He runs around the corner and peers into the backyard, which is really more of a field than a yard, even though his mother has claimed a corner to grow spuds and corn, and his father built a big fence around her crop to keep deer and bear from it. In the summer, a volleyball net stretches across, and John or Peter carve symmetrical lines with the red mower all over the grass.

John stands in the middle of the yard, his face pale with two dark red blotches on his cheeks. His clothes look dirty and messy and the front of his trousers is wet. He's sobbing, and rivers of tears and snot run down his face. His father is standing right in front of him, his back to Gordon. He is shouting and shouting, but Gordon can't make out the words. His father has a gun in his hands, the big, heavy shotgun. He sometimes allows Gordon to polish the barrel and Gordon enjoys running a smooth cloth up and down the shaft, seeing his own distorted image in its shine.

His father clutches the heavy gun in shaky hands, his finger curled around the trigger, and the muzzle is shoved into

John's neck so hard it looks as though it is right in his throat. Suddenly, Gordon can hear his words clearly.

"I will blow your fucking head off, you useless piece of shit! You dirty, lazy bastard! I gave you one job to do, one job, you useless piece of garbage, one single job and you couldn't even do that. You half-wit, you piece of shit, you miserable excuse for an older brother! I will shoot your head right off your useless body!"

John wails in helpless terror and his father keeps on shouting, his spittle landing in John's already sopping wet face. The boy crumples as his muscles give out, and his father looms over him, shotgun pressing into his neck, his finger ready to snuff out his firstborn's life. Gordon wants to scream, run to his brother to rescue and comfort him, run to his father to stop him, and run to his mother most of all, but he can't move from the spot next to the house. He stares in mute disbelief at the scene in front of him, his nine-year-old mind recording every impression to serve it up, its terror and helplessness, at every conceivable moment in his future life.

It does so now, as he stands in front of Lena Newman's grave in Oyster Hill. He is forty-one years and hundreds of miles removed from that sunny Thursday afternoon, but his father's voice, John's abject fear, and his own feeble passivity rear as ugly in his mind as ever.

"I'm sorry Gabby, I'm sorry John," he stutters between sobs, reaching, for the thousandth time, for something, anything, he could have done differently that day and comes up empty again. "I was too little to help you, I'm so sorry." And now he sobs in great, heaving howls, tears streaming down his cheeks, his whole body shaking so hard he has to unlock his knees and reach out for an old gravestone to steady himself. In time, he's able to reach into his trouser pants for a handkerchief, and he wipes his face with it, then blows his nose. The inside of his head seems to reverberate with indistinct noise, a cacophony of shrieks and shouts and rhythmic whirring, like turbine blades grinding on bent metal housing. He presses both hands to his ears, but that does nothing to quiet the clamor.

"I am sorry, little girl," he shouts at the heap of flowers and stuffies, then turns and walks quickly to his truck, which is parked just outside the graveyard gate. He yanks the door open so hard it ricochets against his shoulder, then clambers inside the cabin and falls on his seat. It is a long while later before he's able to turn the ignition key and leave.

CHAPTER TWENTY-NINE

THE CHASE

He looks at the picture every few hours. It's impossible to resist the urge to pull out his phone and gaze at her still features. From the moment he took the shot, he'd felt elation, a deep proprietary sense of satisfaction about the little girl who had been a stranger but is now his. The affinity he has for her is stronger than any feeling of love or belonging he encounters in his normal life and adds a delicious sense of accomplishment to every day.

Initially, it had baffled him that he wasn't curious about her life or her family. But then he had come to understand that she mattered only in death, in the death that he had wrought. And with that comes another knowing. That he will have to kill again. That the image of the little girl will wither in its power to fulfill him and that his innermost desire will compel him to do it again.

Already, when he pulls out his phone, the anticipatory joy to click to the most-often chosen JPEG feels slightly diminished.

A dog walker calls the local detachment to inform them that a man is behaving very oddly at the graveside of the little Newman girl. Everyone knows, of course, that the police are still looking for the hit-and-run driver, and Millie fields several calls a day about sightings of vehicles with front-end damage, never mind the folks who call to point a finger at a neighbor they have a beef with. She sighs and relates the information to Constable Miriam Humphreys, who is just returning from the highway.

Oyster Hill's cemetery is at the northwest corner of town, fronted by an old church and a small garden, both of which are maintained through prayer and volunteer labor alone, as there's no cleric of any kind in town. A thin, paved band circles the graveyard, and cars were bumper to bumper the day Lena Newman was laid to rest here in a very small, white coffin topped with pink carnations, baby's breath, and white lilies. Miriam Humphreys and Sergeant Gill had been there that day, scanning the crowd, the cars, and the encroaching woods surrounding the cemetery on three sides for any signs of guilt. Miriam wasn't sure what to look for but stood beside Sergeant Gill in attentive parade stance and listened to the priest from Gibsons, who had of course never met the Newmans, give an earnest and kind eulogy for a girl who had worried about being a good enough big sister. "She'll be Benjamin's sister and his angel now," the old man had pronounced before signaling the pallbearers to lower the casket into the ground. Then all of Lena's kindergarten class had stepped forward and lined the space around the coffin with helium balloons suspended on weights. In minutes, a bed of shiny, colorful polypropylene and metallized plastic balloons, bobbing and bumping in the slight breeze, had filled in the entire space where a solemn, dark, earthy hole had been.

Miriam turns into the graveyard's parking lot just as a white pickup is leaving on the far side. Without a doubt, it's Gordon Machensky; she has seen this truck parked in his driveway when she was there with handsome Jagwir from the CARS team, and she also easily recognizes Machensky's rather wild mop of graying hair behind the windshield. Hair like "Doc" Brown from *Back to the Future*, but without the goggle eyes and manic laugh, of course. Or the intellect. Machensky hasn't struck her as particularly bright. A drunken dullard, ill-mannered and rude. Who also owns and drives a red Toyota. Miriam hasn't heard anything about the lacquer sample Jagwir sent to the lab; she wonders for a moment if there is any news yet. The truck weaves down the road and sails right through the stop sign.

"Idiot!" she hisses angrily. "Drunk in the middle of the day, on the road in a metal killing machine, making a fool of yourself at the girl's grave. If that doesn't spell guilty, I don't know what does."

She turns on her light bar and follows the truck. When she gets close enough, she flicks the siren for a moment, then brings the police car's bumper closer. In most cases, that's plenty to convince a driver to pull over; sometimes they just hit the brakes in a panic, right there, in the middle of the road. Not Machensky, though, who steps on the gas, instead. He lays some high-pitched rubber on the road and swings around the next bend. He's now headed straight into town, and Miriam sees him roaring through yet another yield sign when she turns the corner. She gets on the com.

"In pursuit of a white four-by-four, Ford-150 flatbed, plate JSV 917, driven by Gordon Machensky. He fled my request to pull over. Suspect is believed to be impaired. History of not cooperating with police. He might have a weapon on him. Request assist."

Miriam pauses for a second. Calling out a potential weapon would bring her colleagues down hard on Machensky, maybe even put them at risk if they'd try to cut the truck off with their own vehicles. She hadn't seen any evidence of a weapon. Where had that notion come from? Well, too late now; she's said it. Damn.

"He's headed down Simpson Street from the graveyard, I am no longer following at speed. It's just about time for school to let out. Will head through town, then to his residence. Address is 1050 Peatt Road. Suspect lives alone, has aggressive guard dog on property."

Her eyes are flitting all over, trying to predict pedestrian movement. She isn't in high pursuit any longer but still drives way past fifty and the school day has ended for sure—there are kids all over the place. She keeps the light bar on and hopes the flashing red and blues will pierce the awareness of daydreamers. She feels her adrenaline pumping and asks herself why she's so excited. They know where the guy lives and have already determined he is a low flight risk. Metal samples from his car are already at the lab. So, what's the hurry? And why did she call Hero an aggressive guard dog? When they'd left Machensky's house that time with Jagwir, the dog had licked her wrist in farewell.

She stays on Simpson, slows as she crosses Second Street. Scans every which way. No sign of the flatbed. She turns right on First and heads north; the road narrows as soon as it passes the business district and is much too twisted to see more than a hundred yards ahead. No sign of Machensky.

Millie's voice fills the car. A storekeeper on First had called in to say a white truck was driving way too fast, heading north, and Constables Bromsky and Villeneuve are on their way, ETA less than five minutes.

"Get the Sergeant out, too," Miriam shouts. "I'm feeling kind of weird about this. He's got this house and the Quonset out on Peatt; it's like a compound in the bush. If he does have guns, we could be looking at an armed standoff."

She knows that Sergeant Gill listens to the scanner twenty-four-seven and is likely on his way already. That

Millie will now call the off-duty members plus the larger Gibsons detachment, who'll send a couple of cars, and may start looking for the nearest negotiator. Just in case. She has used all the right words to start the large machinery of serious law enforcement rolling. Why had she done that? Part of her brain had wanted to hold back, had whispered *Wait a minute. Machensky has no registered firearms, and no one has ever seen a gun on him.* It's pure conjecture. And his dog is sweet as can be, just really loud. But her worry and adrenaline and pissed-off-ness that he hadn't pulled over right away had overruled that small voice. In the academy, they'd learned to trust their instincts, to follow procedure to a tee and to never, ever seek out risk if a few more steps could ensure the safety of everyone involved. Control over the perp and safety for everyone else. That was the mantra.

Miriam stops at the Peatt Street turnoff. Should she wait here for reinforcement? The thought of confronting loony Machensky and his dog by herself, of requesting him to submit to a breathalyzer, brings slight nausea, but she is too ramped up to sit here in her car and wait. She decides to drive very slowly so that the others can catch up.

Despite her best efforts to stay off the gas, her cruiser rolls up to Machensky's driveway in just a few minutes. The white flatbed is there, a bit of steam rising into the cold November air. From where she sits in the car, no movement is visible anywhere. She imagines Hero, the massive mastiff, crouched behind one of the truck's wheels, ready to attack her the second she puts a foot on the ground. She imagines Machensky, wild hair sticking every which way, face angry and withdrawn, standing just to the side of the window, peering through the narrow gap between the blinds, and clutching a loaded American Ruger rifle. She opens her car door.

"Mr. Machensky!" she yells into the still air. "It's Constable Humphreys, RCMP. I saw you at the cemetery—you didn't look so good. Is everything okay?"

Only silence. The absence of barking weighs heavy. Her shouts have disturbed some crows who relocate noisily between pine and cedar branches. Someone's using a chainsaw in the distance.

"Mr. Machensky!" she shouts so loud her throat scratches. "I know you're home. I just saw the truck in town. Could you just come out so we can talk?"

No movement at either of the two windows facing front. Miriam wonders if the hairs on the back of her neck are really rising, the way she has seen it on TV, or if she's just imagining this happening as she steps around the hood of the cruiser. Her right hand aches to reach for her holster, but she forces both her arms to hang straight down, hands turned slightly out. *I come in peace.*

She calls out again and advances toward the front steps of the house. Just as she lifts a foot, she hears the bawl of a police siren. *Idiots!* Here she is making friendly, and they're coming in like the cavalry, bayonets at the ready. She turns and walks back to the road, signaling with her arms for her colleagues to turn off the blaring noise. Inside a minute, Bromsky, Villeneuve, and Sergeant Gill are exiting their vehicles.

Sergeant Gill takes command and Miriam feels instant relief. She still thinks that Machensky might have a gun and that his dog could attack, but it's less menacing now that there are four of them. *Band of brothers*, she thinks as she gives her report to Gill, *one for all and all for one.*

They split into two groups. Bromsky and Villeneuve take the house, Miriam and the Sergeant head over to the Quonset. They walk side by side along the wide driveway and she's grateful to be wearing her Kevlar vest. Gill had cautioned them that a man who hides is not at all the same as a man who forces a standoff.

"Tread lightly," he had said, "talk—don't whisper. Walk—don't sneak up. Don't draw your weapon unless you see one on him."

They arrive at the large shed. It's a dull, metal structure with no sign of life, surrounded on three sides by encroaching blackberry rambles. The long side faces a dirt yard, muddy after recent rains. Sergeant Gill studies the ground in front of the small entrance door.

"He's sure in and out a lot, and see, here are some paw prints. Maybe the dog is in there with him."

He pounds his fist against the door several times. *Bam! Bam! Bam!*

"Mr. Machensky!" Miriam shouts as loud as she can. "Are you in there? Come out, please. I'm worried about you."

A single bark emits from deep inside. They strain to listen. They can hear Peter and Doris at the house, banging on windows and doors, shouting. Miriam concentrates hard on the structure in front of her, lays her ear right on the metal. She can hear something, faint, but is unable to make out what the sounds are. Machine or human? Or dog? Is Hero locked in here to guard? But then he'd be making a racket right about now, wouldn't he?

"Sergeant," she whispers, then remembers his instruction to speak in normal tones and repeats, a bit louder, "Sergeant, I think I hear someone crying in there."

Stephan Gill raps on the door again, less loudly this time. "Mr. Machensky, Sergeant Gill here from the local RCMP detachment. Please talk to us." As an afterthought, he lays his hand on the lever and presses it down. The door opens.

Now they hear the dog advancing—his nails are clicking on the cement floor. When he whimpers, Miriam lowers herself into a squat. "Hey Hero, what's up big boy?" she croons and holds her hand out. The mastiff's head appears in the open-door space and then the large dog scampers over the raised threshold and right into Miriam, almost knocking her off her stance. He whines and yelps excitedly, licks her outstretched hands, then turns and lopes back into the Quonset. Sergeant Gill and Miriam exchange a worried glance and follow the dog inside.

The interior is brightly lit. Several wire-encased fluorescent light bars hang from the ceiling and illuminate workbenches in the center of the large open space and dozens of shelf units all along the perimeter. Boxes made of wood or cardboard are everywhere, presumably holding machine parts and tools, and parts and gadgets of every size and description line the shelves, hang off rows of hooks, are scattered on gleaming surfaces. Everything is neat and impressively organized; the scents of machine oil, acetylene, and diesel hang heavy in the air. And then they hear the unmistakable sound of crying. Hero, who had stood inside the door as if to welcome them inside, now runs off toward the far back of the large hall, and the two humans follow him slowly, their eyes scanning the walls and rows of shelves for hiding places. But Gordon Machensky is not hiding, nor is he a threat. They find him sitting on an old car seat that is nestled inside what could be a large turbine housing. The dog lowers his head and licks the man's face, then turns around, looks balefully at Miriam, and whines. She crouches and lays a hand on Gordon Machensky's knee.

"Hey Gordon, it's alright. We're here now. We can help."

CHAPTER THIRTY

DOUBT

Just like the news of the accident that claimed little Lena's life had spread like wildfire, the word of an arrest in the case races through town. Jo has already heard two wildly differing versions by the time her neighbor, Garrett Minniefield, enters her kitchen through the back door. As always, he doesn't bother to knock but takes his boots off laboriously before coming inside and, as always, Jo has a cup of coffee and a freshly baked muffin ready for him.

"Have you heard?" the old man asks after he's found his way through half the muffin and drained his cup. "They arrested a fellow for the Newman hit-and-run. Just yesterday. He's in cells downtown."

Jo harrumphs inwardly at the use of the word "downtown" to designate the huddle of buildings at the village's core but remains silent. Garrett had been Millie Scutari's father-in-law once and may have this story right from the horse's mouth, as the saying goes, and she wants to know the truth. Has the person responsible for Lena Newman's death really been identified?

"It's a nutter from out by the salt marsh. A guy who works with machine parts from the fish farms. He drives back and forth to the ferry terminal all the time, at all hours of the day. They saw him carrying on at the graveyard and chased him all through town. I think there was a standoff at his place and then they brought him in, yesterday afternoon, and locked him up. He's still there."

He thanks her for the refill of steaming coffee and eyes the basket holding the muffins meaningfully. Jo sets one on his plate and leans back. You can't hurry old Garrett. His coffee *klatsch* with her, three times per week and sometimes including Paul, is the extent of his social life if you don't count the visiting nurse or the kid who mows his big lawn. Garrett's wife Barbara died two years ago, and now he waffles between looking for a new housemate or moving to Calgary, where his only son lives with a wife and two children. In the summer, Jo had set up eHarmony and Silver Singles apps for Garrett on his phone and since then, there's been a definite improvement in his mood, a bounce in his step. Perhaps you don't need to actually pick a person at all; maybe just the act of looking and long-distance flirting is enough to lift a person's spirit. Just as long as he doesn't send his money to a shyster in Eastern Europe. She had made him promise to check in with her or Paul as soon as someone solicits him for cash.

"Millie told me that he had a breakdown of some sort about the death of the little girl, was crying endlessly. The paramedics checked him out and declared him fit, so they're keeping him in cells until tomorrow when a detective will come up to inter-rogate him. Apparently, he's already confessed to the local cops. Has taken a shine to the girl officer, the one with the short hair, and she has his dog now, a big, dangerous-looking brute." Garrett smacks his lips and washes down the last muffin bite with coffee. "It's silly, really. What if he goes to jail? She'll be stuck with a dog she never asked for."

For the rest of the day, Jo's nerves are taut. She burns the roasting yams for dinner. She gripes at an innocuous remark Paul makes about a favorable article regarding Vancouver's new MP Gina Nelson in a nationwide magazine. She breaks two soft pencil leads and ruins an almost-finished drawing of a pale green *Pseudocyphellaria rainierensis*, or old-growth speckle belly. *Who gives such ridiculous names to an innocent lichen?* she thinks angrily, crumples the entire sheet in her hands, and throws it at the studio door.

Since the day that policewoman came into her backyard, Jo has worried that Oliver might have been the driver. The car, the color, the time of day, the street where it happened—it all fit. Her Oliver! Portentous fear had slipped over her like a glove. At first, she couldn't even give words to her feeling of unease; it took days before she was able to name her fears. And since then, she has been unable to ask Ollie straight out. She knows that she would know, with absolute certainty, from his answer. If he'd lied or not. If he'd had a guilty conscience. If he'd hide behind a mask of words and smiles.

What if his answer is yes? *Yes, Mom, it was me. Yes, I killed a little girl, but it was an accident—she came from nowhere and I hardly saw her, then panicked and drove off. Yes, I killed a little girl by accident and have been too cowardly to tell anyone. Yes, I killed a little girl, but my new business is just launching, and I can't take my focus off it for a minute. Yes, I killed a little girl but negative publicity about a fatal hit-and-run would shut Enviga down before I ever really got started.*

And where would that leave her? She, who'd spent her entire life protecting him? She, whose every task for endless years had been to keep him alive. She, who had decided early on to dispense with normal child-rearing methods and to just shower her son with love, love, love. When you believe that your child will die young, you don't give a hoot about preparing them for adulthood. Never once had there been a time-out for Ollie. Or a dessert withheld. No fervent wish left unfulfilled. No harsh words. No punishments.

Everyone knew that Oliver lived because of her. So, she was equally responsible for the *how* of his life, not just the life itself. Had she raised an egocentric, careless killer? Who had she fought so hard for all these years? If Oliver had been the driver who didn't stop or accept responsibility, then she was to blame. If she had been so blinded by the relentlessness of fighting for his life that she'd sacrificed parenting him for character development, then she was to blame.

And what if it had been him, but he truly didn't know? What if he'd been looking down at the tape deck at that moment? Out the driver's side window at a bit of pink in the sky? If it had been him, but he didn't know about it, then this was not about his character. What was it about, then? Would Lena Newman's parents really suffer any less if they knew the name of the driver?

And what if it wasn't Oliver, anyway? Some other person in a red car at that time in that area? The one waiting in cells right now? If she asked Ollie outright, he'd see her doubt, realize she thought it possible. And like everything else she'd ever thought possible, he'd take it on, would quickly come round to believing it himself. That he could kill a child and hide it. Because he trusts her more than anyone, her doubt would sentence him.

She can't find a way forward. It's been more than three months since the accident, and her mind has not yielded. When she went to Seattle, she learned how to "hack" computers. About malware and foxholes and, with the instructor's help, she was able to attach a bit of exploitative software to an email she sent Oliver. It gave her unfettered entry to his data. Since then, she has examined every last file in his system, looking for a diary of sorts.

He used to keep one, had needed an outlet for his rant-ings. Hospitals don't tolerate anger and rage; even moodiness is frowned upon. Throw an empty plastic cup at the wall, and the counselor will be in your room that afternoon; throw it at the door after an unpleasant exchange with a nurse, and your chart will be decorated with a purple sticker, universally under-stood in the healthcare industry to denote violence. Oliver had learned as a ten-year-old to always make nice in the hospital, and that attitude had secured countless favors, solicitude, and double ice cream portions. His wrath, worry, frustration, fear, despair, and disgust went into his diary; first as monster pic-tures, then words. *I HATE this fucking asshole doctor. She knows nothing about anything, I want someone fat to sit on her chest and fart for an hour!!* When Oliver was a teen, he filled pages and pages with angry and forlorn observations about the shittiness of life as a CFer:

Abandon all hope ye who enter here.

Lighten up. It's just life. It'll be over before you know it.

My soul feels endangered by my body.

Riding through the turbulence of my disease like the horseman of the apocalypse.

I hate the impending sense of doom.

People are always looking at my cannulas, my IVs, my scars, my G-tube…not at ME!

I think about that very last breath. Sucking for air. Pulling and pulling and getting nothing. I think about my chest muscles ripping and burning, absolutely useless. No air. Just black.

I'm thirteen now. I've reached my halfway mark.

If you're talking about someone's psychological health, I'm guessing that pretty much the worst thing you can do is confine them to a hospital bed in a room by themselves and then wake them up every three hours to find out how they're doing. It's not waterboarding, but it's close.

How does it feel to have your very existence always in doubt? Pretty fucking awful, that's how.

Sometimes I wake up coughing so hard that I'm scared I'll choke to death. I keep myself awake, petrified that if I fall asleep, I won't be alive in the morning.

Did you ever stop to think about how the words coughing and coffin sound the same?

Jo doesn't find a diary anywhere in his electronic orbit. Oliver uses social media, like everyone younger than her these days. He exchanges his thoughts with others, is hopeful and buoyant one day, bewildered and perturbed the next. She notices that he is most considerate and encouraging with kids and teenagers who contact him to ask about life after transplant. He is patient, sensitive, friendly. He is her Ollie.

A few weeks after Seattle, Jo had a secret meeting with Saaz Chauhan, Oliver's friend and business partner. Saaz had been Ollie's first roommate at university and had quickly become his best friend. He'd studied nutrition as a premed and discovered that diet was more integral to health than peddling pharmaceuticals or snipping away at body parts. Ollie became his guinea pig and, ultimately, his proudest achievement. Had it not been for Saaz and his relentless search for nutritious superfoods that were easy on the digestive system and pancreas in particular, and also helped Ollie's ravaged body to rebuild cells, fibers, and muscle tissue, the posttransplant period might easily have had a different outcome. Only about a third of double lung transplant recipients survive ten years—Ollie is closing in on twenty.

"Have you noticed anything unusual in his demeanor lately?" she'd asked Saaz when they met at a coffee shop in Vancouver. Considering the many times they'd fretted together at Ollie's bedside, Saaz didn't even raise an eyebrow; he just shook his head and said that the business was about to expand and that Oliver, as chief negotiator and resource allocator, was taxed highly during this phase but seemed to be coping.

"We all have his back, all the time, and one of us would've noticed if anything was amiss. There are no secrets in this crew, believe me, Jo. He's solid."

This resounding endorsement did nothing to quell her doubts. That afternoon she nosed behind the PNE grounds until she found Ollie's car. She'd even brought a magnifying glass, crouched down, and examined the front right fender inch by inch. There were scratches aplenty, tiny and bigger dents, mud, and bits of rust. Oliver has never had any care for his cars and spends the bare minimum on car maintenance. It shows. She is none the wiser after this effort.

But now someone else has been arrested. Has confessed. This changes everything, of course. She can let go of the nagging doubts and fears she's entertained for months. Can get back to sleeping solidly, to a head full of green, preparing for the upcoming show.

And she can concentrate on the lump. Which has grown noticeably bigger, even just in the past three months. Now there is a dull ache when her fingers push too insistently. She imagines a hard node, about the size of a hazelnut, behaving like Oliver once did, when he was little more than a cluster of cells. He'd grown those cells ever faster, had soon finagled to get his own blood supply, had expanded his limbs, had pushed her anatomy out of the way, had created a space for himself to somersault. This cancer is wont to do the same, isn't it? It will grow, festoon itself with red arteries and blue veins, it will push and shove at her. And it is so close to her heart. When she'd been pregnant, her organs around the growing baby had been walloped and squashed. Depending on where his feet and hands were pummeling her intestines, she'd suffered from constipation or diarrhea or gas; if he pressed on her stomach, she became nauseated and was, sometimes for days at a time, unable to eat more than a morsel. When he kicked her pancreas, her system flooded with insulin, and her moods and energy fluctuated all over the place. Her bladder shrank to the size of a walnut. This cancer lump, so close to her heart, will cause worse, that is for sure.

She feels ready for it. She is seventy-five, practically closing in on eighty. What is in her future but waiting to die? Or worse, a nursing home. Soon, shaky hands and failing eyesight will steal her artistry, and sore hips or unsteady legs will curtail mobility. Oliver is holding his own, has a new, younger support system now in Gina and Nico and true friends, and they will be at his side when he needs them. They won't be as unfailing and meticulous as she has been, but they'll do the best they can, and she just has to trust that that will be good enough. And Paul will be fine, of that she is certain. Paul has always been at ease in the world.

On the edge of her PC, where various yellow sticky notes jostle for space, Jo has taped a condensed Elizabeth Barrett Browning poem:

Enough!
So tired, so tired, my heart and I!
Yet who complains? My heart and I?
In this abundant earth no doubt
Is little room for things worn out:
Disdain them, break them, throw them by
And if before the days grew rough
We once were loved, used—well enough,
I think, we've fared, my heart and I.

Her eyes travel to the small, white paper square often and each time she reads these lines, she feels the certainty within her solidify.

CHAPTER THIRTY-ONE

ANOTHER INTERVIEW

The Oyster Hill fatal hit-and-run has become Luci's case. It happens with all their investigations: one team member takes the lead. Either due to rank—the sloggiest are fobbed off to the lowest on the totem pole, or because Jags, who loves the limelight, gets the ones with highest press interest. Or they fall to the member first on the scene, or last, for that matter. Sometimes, one of them will get drawn in deeper than the others, will be affected by something at the scene or by someone inside all that mangled metal. Rudd not only allows this to happen but encourages the "investigative vigor" that results from a certain level of personal involvement because, he says, it also gives their work a level of motivation that, as first responders, they're taught to eschew: the personal bias.

"You remember Mrs. Kaur, don't you, the lady in the old Pinto? She was rear-ended at speed on the Viaduct, her car exploded, and we chalked it up to Ford's most infamous design flaw. End of story. But I happen to have a grandmother whose birthday is the same day as Mrs. Kaur's, I gnawed at the case and couldn't let it go as rote. And you guys all caught the bug and looked a tad closer. Not because of any investigative instinct or a promotion carrot, but because you wanted to do right by me. To stand by me. That was the motivation. And only then did we really look at the other vehicle, the rear-ender, and found the shotty brake job. Found that the Rooney garage had not only installed parts bought on the black market but had used unlicensed and untrained labor to do it. We saved a lot of lives the day we shut those crooks down and had we blocked out our personal bias, we would've missed it."

Rudd beamed at each of them with parental pride and leaned forward. He was welcoming their newest member, Danielle, that day and had launched into one of his famous lectures with his usual enthusiasm.

"All I'm saying is that personal bias is not your enemy—don't avoid it at all costs. If it spurs you to do deeper work, you can even let it guide you to some extent. The important thing is that you share it with us, with the whole team. Because we can keep it real for you. The team has the distance, the objectivity, to discern the difference between you wanting to do your very best work in reverence to a person or a family or your own history, and you getting sucked into some kind of Faustian nightmare."

They stopped him there to explain *Faustian nightmare*, but the message had been clear enough. Trust your instincts. Don't become an automaton. Think with your heart. Put in for a reason, put in for the team.

They name their cases by the vehicle involved. The Pinto case. The Egg Truck case. The BMW case. The Camper Van case. And, periodically, the name changes. Ki-woo's Volvo. Jag's School Bus. Luci's BRM, short for Barcelona Red Metallic.

And so, it comes as no surprise that Sergeant Rudd asks Luci to come along to Oyster Hill to interview Gordon Machensky. They take a float plane to Gibsons Landing and borrow an unmarked car from the local detachment. The Tragically Hip's "Bobcaygeon" blasts from the speakers when Luci turns the ignition on, and they listen to an album's worth of Gord Downie's poetic lyrics at full volume until they reach Oyster Hill. Millie Scutari greets them like family when they enter the building, and Stephan Gill steps out of his office to shake their hands.

"To tell you the truth, I'm not sure this is our guy," he says. "As I told you on the phone, he behaved suspiciously at the Newman girl's graveside, and we brought him in for questioning. But even though he cries a lot and goes on about being sorry.... I think he might be referring to a different accident altogether. It's hard to piece anything intelligible together... he's really not making much sense."

"Was he high or coming down off something?" Luci asks.

"When we got him into a cruiser yesterday, out at his place, he blew zero-point-three on the breathalyzer, and the medics took blood samples in the rig. The clinic lab tested for EtOH, THC, meth, opiates, cocaine, psilocybin. With the exception of alcohol, all came back negative."

"What does it look like to you if not a guilt-induced psychotic episode?" Rudd asks.

"Oh, it's guilt, alright. That much is clear. I just don't think it's about Lena Newman. But he's calmer today. Millie brought homemade breakfast for him, and he ate it all. Downed two cups of coffee and washed up a bit. Constable Humphreys brought the dog in for a visit. Nobody talked to him about accidents or cars this morning—we basically treated him like a cousin after a bender. He's as good as he gets for you."

Stephan Gill opens a door into a narrow hallway. Four steel doors, two on either side. Everything is beige. Three of the doors have small windows and hinged pass-throughs, the last door to the left is plain and Luci assumes it's a shower room. Sometimes, prisoners spend up to a week in these small holding cells and begin to fester. If there's enough sympathetic staff, they get to wash up properly under streams of hot water. If they behave like assholes, well, there's a tiny sink and a mini soap bar in the cell. Suit yourself.

The window in the cell door has no glass but deeply embedded wire instead. Luci's friend and colleague, Darren, once took a fist in the eye through one before the wire screen was installed service-wide. The punch broke several orbital bones and sent a career-ending shard into Darren's frontal lobe. Now Luci keeps her distance when she peers through the window.

The man sitting on the cement bench bears no resemblance to the angry, quarrelsome curmudgeon who had threatened to sic his dog on her, Jags, and Danielle that night. This guy is trying to sink into himself, to disappear into a black hole of his own making. His previously wild mane is combed neatly back, and the still-wet ends have painted a dark collar onto his T-shirt. He sits on the edge of the bench, elbows on his knees, hands dangling between his legs, and stares at the beige wall. Although he's still, his breath is rapid and his neck vein pulses. His face is a study in grief: eyes and cheeks awash in tears, nose running freely, half-open mouth emanating soft sobs. Gordon Machensky must have heard them walk down the echoing hallway but gives no sign that he's aware of their presence.

Rudd turns to Stephan Gill. "Do you want to bring him to the interview room?" he asks quietly. "Miller and I can wait there." Luci agrees. Three additional bodies in the small cell might make matters worse for a man at the end of his tether, and the Sergeant nods in agreement. "That'd be best."

The interview room is no more ambient but is about triple the size of the holding cell. Rudd and Luci sit on two folding chairs against the wall, leaving the most possible distance from the chair on the other side of a small table that's bolted to the floor in the center of the room. These places are designed to intimidate, put pressure on a suspect, create a foreboding atmosphere that increases insecurity and fear, and both Luci and Rudd have made good use of this in the past. But today they wish they had couches, friendly wallpaper, and an open window to allow in sunshine and birdsong. Machensky's despair is so tangible; it's obvious that solace and comfort will be more effective than any intimidation techniques.

Millie steps into the room and places a large plastic cup on the table, then lays a small hand towel next to it.

"I got him a beer from the pub," she says and smirks when she sees their surprised expressions. "Come on, you know he needs one just to get by on a good day. Stephan thought it was a good idea, but I'll take it away if you don't agree."

"No, leave it," Rudd says quickly. "Thanks, Millie, that's great."

Luci gazes at the camera in the corner. Any self-respecting defense lawyer will have a heyday with the deliberate use of alcohol to elicit a confession from a distraught suspect, but she doesn't object. Working with Rudd means not only thinking outside of the box but living there. Besides, if Machensky is the driver they're looking for, then the metal shard sample from his Toyota will match and a botched interview won't sink the case. She hopes.

Now, the two men they're waiting for appear in the doorway. Sergeant Gill has a hand on Machensky's elbow and seems to prod him slightly to set one foot in front of the other. Machensky is wearing clean sneakers, gray sweatpants, a Harley T-shirt, and an open black hoodie. The clothes are worn and fit him well, so the officers must have picked up a clean set from his house. Very decent of them. They really are treating him like a cousin. The Sergeant nods at Rudd then leaves the room and closes the door quietly behind him.

Rudd gets to his feet and steps forward, hand extended.

"Good morning, Mr. Machensky." He waits until the man looks at the proffered hand, considers it, and then slowly extends his own for a limp, reluctant shake.

"I'm Sergeant Rudinsky and this here is Corporal Miller. We've come up from Vancouver to ask you a couple of questions. Please, have a seat."

Machensky doesn't look at them; he lowers himself onto the indicated chair, rounds his shoulders, lets his hands dangle between his legs, and drops his head.

Rudd returns to his own chair. "Mr. Machensky, as you know, there was a terrible accident in the subdivision in late August that caused the death of a little girl. We've determined that the car was most likely a red Toyota, and we secured lacquer samples from all such local cars to compare them to shards found at the scene. Your car was among those. Then we learned that yesterday, you appeared at the little girl's graveside. You were seen to be very distraught and emotional. Would it be possible for you to tell us what happened?" He speaks quietly and calmly, enunciates all his words clearly. When he's finished, he leans back and waits for the sad man to process what he has heard.

After a long silence, Rudd leans forward a bit. "Gordon?"

"I got to thinking about Gabby." The words are so quiet and spoken to the floor that they would not have caught them at all if they hadn't already been straining to hear.

"Who is Gabby, Gordon?" Rudd's voice is very gentle.

Machensky draws a shuddering breath. "Gabby was run over by a car. She was just a little girl, too."

"Is Gabby your daughter, Gordon?" Luci loves that Rudd uses the present tense and shoots him an appreciative glance. Then she fixes her concentration back on Gordon Machensky.

"My sister. She was hit from behind on her bicycle. She was riding to school." Another convulsive breath and then his shoulders begin to shake. "She fell into a ditch and drowned."

Rudd sighs audibly. "What a horrible tragedy. I am so sorry, Gordon." He waits a moment, then adds, "Where did this happen?"

"In Crofton, on the Island. A long time ago."

"And you've been thinking about it since Lena Newman's accident?"

"Yes." A moment passes. "Thinking about it makes my head hurt. There are flashes and noise in my head. I can't think." He leans forward and takes a gulp of beer, then uses the towel to wipe his face and blow his nose. He puts the towel on his lap.

"Gordon," Rudd's voice is soft. "Why did you visit Lena Newman's grave? You hadn't gone to the funeral."

"I would have. I should have. It would have been the right thing to do. But I got drunk after...." He shoots a look at Luci and grimaces. "After you lot came to my house and accused me. I was very upset. I didn't know that a little girl on a bicycle had died. That made me upset. I drank a lot."

He takes another, longer gulp from the beer in front of him, then keeps the plastic cup in his hands. "Because I hadn't been to the funeral, I wanted to go to the house. To give condolences. But I was afraid. Maybe the parents thought it was my fault." He pauses, sips, swallows. "Maybe you lot had told them that it was me." He scowls, lifts his head, looks straight at Luci. His eyes are red-rimmed, bloodshot, and cloudy, the lids heavy.

"But it wasn't me. I was at home, sleeping like I told you." He drinks deeply.

"So, you went to Lena Newman's graveside instead of going to the house. Did you leave flowers or a teddy or a card?" Rudd asks.

"No card, no flowers."

"And then you got overwhelmed by your feelings of grief for Gabby?"

"It went bad for my family after that. Really bad."

Sip.

"My father blamed my oldest brother, almost killed him. My mother blamed my father and kicked him out of the house. Divorced him. Then she had to work all the time to make ends meet, and we hardly ever saw either of them."

Sip.

Luci texts Millie, asks for another beer.

"My father started drinking, got laid off, then he went to the mainland. Got hired as a log driver on the Fraser. Was too old, of course, and too drunk, and not nimble enough. One day he fell between a bunch of logs and never came up."

Gulp.

"My mother turned hard. Drank too much, too."

He makes to sip, sighs when he sees the bottom of the cup, places it on the table slowly. Then he hunches his shoulders and lowers his head. It looks like the dime in the animated puppet clown has run its course.

Luci clears her throat. "Mr. Machensky, about that night at your place. I'm sorry that we gave you the impression we were accusing you. We must have not expressed ourselves correctly. All we knew was it was likely a red Toyota that was involved in the accident. We took samples from almost forty red cars in Oyster Hill. We didn't mean to single you out. I apologize."

The sad man does not respond, but Luci is glad she got that off her chest, regardless. They had been aggressive that night because they felt intimidated by the dog, the darkness, and the seclusion of the place. Yes, Machensky had been uncooperative and behaved like a prick, but haven't we all been taught that offence is the best defense? Now that she's glimpsing the depth of his pain, Luci feels only compassion.

"Gordon, just to get this clear: when you were crying at the graveside, you cried for your sister and for your family?" Rudd leans forward and tries unsuccessfully to make eye contact. "The people who saw you there thought they heard you say you were sorry." The tall man doesn't move, gives no indication he's heard Rudd. "That you were sorry to have caused her death."

"No." He shakes his head. "Not that. I'm sorry I couldn't help, after." Gordon Machensky raises his head and stares at Rudd, his eyes suddenly clear and wide open.

"You mull something over and over, for years, then decades. You go over every little inch of what happened, what you saw and did and didn't do. And as you grow and see clearer, and you begin to understand, you also think of all the things you could have done if you'd only been smarter. Because, at sixteen or thirty or forty, you know the answers, and you bash your head in that you hadn't seen something so obvious when you needed to see it."

There is a quiet knock on the door and Millie peers inside. Luci nods and the empty plastic cup is exchanged for a full one. Rudd smiles. Gordon takes a drink, puts the cup back on the table.

"I was a stupid kid, didn't know how to be extra nice to my brothers and sister after the accident. All little kids are selfish, I know that, but I also know that it wouldn't have taken much to show a bit of kindness at the time. But I didn't. As my family fell to pieces around me, I just carried on with math class and wanting the right kind of jelly on my peanut butter sandwich."

Sip.

"How old were you?" Rudd asks.

"Six."

Sip.

"And Gabby?"

"Nine."

Rudd sighs.

Sip.

"Gordon, what would you have done if you had been the driver who caused that accident in August?"

Gulp. "I would have killed myself."

He lifts his head and looks at them, and Luci and Rudd see that he means those words.

Sip.

Sip.

CHAPTER THIRTY-TWO

SITTING IN GRIEF

Miriam Humphreys is only too glad to reunite Hero with his person. The dog almost topples Gordon Machensky when he jumps at him outside the police station. A comical, high-pitched whine rises from his muzzle; a canine equivalent to shouting with joy.

"Looks like he's pretty keen to be heading home with you," Miriam says and then offers man and dog a ride. Machensky declines.

"I've had enough of your lot. We'll walk."

An unscheduled float plane with plenty of empty seats will leave Oyster Hill at two for the city, and Sergeant Gill offers to take the borrowed car back to Gibsons for them. He and Rudd will write up the interview report and subsequent release of their only suspect thus far, and Luci volunteers to visit the Newmans. "I want to let them know where we're at and what to expect, or rather not expect, over the Christmas season," she explains. "Meet you at the dock, boss."

Luci knocks on the door of 51 Crescent View. In response, a dog begins to bark, a toddler wails, and a woman shouts something unintelligible. She waits. Soon footsteps approach, and then the door opens wide. Luci stares at the woman in astonishment, the rehearsed greeting for Lorna Newman stuck in her throat.

"Oh, hello Corporal," Jo Nelson says quietly, her blue-gray eyes sparkling with amusement. "Would you mind waiting a minute while I check with Lorna if it's okay to invite you in just now?"

The older woman doesn't wait for an answer but turns around, leaving the door ajar. Luci stares after her, mind buzzing. During their last encounter, their spark of friendship had been snuffed out as the police officer followed both instinct and evidence, and a mama bear stood up on hind legs to shield her cubs. And now this. A totally unexpected chance meet and a welcoming smile full of warmth. Go figure. And what is Jo Nelson doing here?

Jo returns and waves Luci in before reaching the door to pull it wide open. "Come in, Corporal Luci Miller, you're just in time for cinnamon buns. Little Benjamin is in a sharing mood."

Right. That's the delicious smell that had wafted around her as she stood waiting by the door. Cinnamon buns. Her mom's favorite dessert. Luci smiles instinctively as she enters the hallway and closes the door behind her. Her mom made the best ones; had taught her to pour a little bit of warm cream in the pan just before baking to create the most incredibly luscious rolls.

"He didn't sound to be in a sharing mood just now when I knocked on the door," she replies to Jo's back.

"He got frustrated because he can't hold on to his truck and fill his face at the same time," Jo laughs and steps into a large, bright kitchen where warm, yeasty baking smells mingle with the aroma of fresh coffee. And wet dog. Lorna Newman, hair cut short since Luci last saw her, glances over her shoulder in greeting while securing the tray on her son's high chair.

"Hi, Corporal Miller. Did your nose lead you here?"

"Sure did. Brought my mother's cinnamon buns to mind so vividly my mouth is watering."

"Ours too. We'll have to give his highness his due, and then we can all dig in. Come on, Benny, don't be ridiculous."

Luci looks at the baby. He's a wide-eyed toddler now, one hand clutching a little red and white plastic truck and the other a doughy chunk of pastry which is obviously a remnant of a larger piece that has left sticky traces all over his face. His mother is trying to clean him up, but he's having none of it and evades the napkin with flailing arms and full body contortions, alternately gurgling and wailing. When he catches sight of Luci, he stops moving in surprise, and Lorna is able to wipe his cheeks.

"Hi Benny," Luci smiles widely and waves her hand. "You've got it made, I see."

Lorna approaches, her hand outstretched in greeting. Her previously dark blond hair is now chestnut, with sparkling red highlights cut in a very short, elfin style which compliments her delicate features and blue-green eyes. She smiles broadly at Luci, her cheeks flushed, her yellow T-shirt accentuating a light, residual summer tan. She takes Luci's hand and pulls her farther into the room.

"Come in and sit right here, on the bar stool. I'll get you a cup of something and a fresh bun. Would you like water, too?"

Luci sits where Lorna indicates, nods yes to coffee and again to water, accepts a small plate with a sticky bun, and watches the two women move about the kitchen, chatting with each other, her, and Benny, getting glasses, cups, plates, and cutlery for everyone. Jo is at home in this kitchen, knows where all the gadgets are, wipes Benjamin's face when she walks by him, unconsciously closes a drawer with her hip while turning to a different task. Hadn't she said, back in August, that she had never met the Newmans? A spike of unease needles the recesses of Luci's mind, and she silently vows to come back to it later, when she's alone, or perhaps with Rudd, who pays close attention to instincts.

When there's a lull and Benny is absorbed by his efforts to stuff sticky dough into the window of his truck, Luci compliments Lorna on her new hairdo.

"It's the elfin cut I wanted Lena to have. I always thought it was the best do for her red hair and freckles, but she loved her curls and I couldn't sway her."

So you look into the mirror and see her, Luci thinks. *How is that helpful with moving forward?*

"Now, when I see myself, I can imagine how she might have looked as an older teen. Sometimes I say, 'Good morning, Lena,' and am happy when she smiles back at me." Lorna grimaces, cheerfully. "I know it makes me sound like a lunatic, but it's comforting to have an ongoing relationship with Lena, one that'll last through the ages. Through her ages."

There is sorrow in her eyes, but a genuine smile plays around her lips when she turns to hand a sippy cup with water to Benjamin. He grabs at it with both hands and drinks deeply; toy truck and sweet treat forgotten for the moment.

"Lena is everywhere in this house," Lorna continues, folding her hands around her coffee cup. "In every room, every one of Benny's hand-me-down toys, every wall because she helped us choose the colors, every memory of everything. She is with me more clearly and somehow more alive even, if that is possible. It's as though her passing somehow distilled her into something clearer, purer than she could have ever been as a real child."

As if on cue, the real child in the room decides that it is time to leave the confines of the high chair. His belly is full, his thirst quenched, and his nervous system reacts to the sugar hit: it is time to move. When his mother doesn't pull him out of the enclosure immediately, Benny breaks out in a mighty wail and throws his upper body backwards violently. Lorna gets up and looks at Jo, then at Luci.

"Shall we head into the living room? He can play on the floor for half an hour, then he'll go down for his nap. Bring your coffee and plates."

Jo produces a tray from behind the fridge and piles cups, plates, and napkins on it. She turns to follow Lorna when she catches sight of Luci watching her.

"I come once a week. There are others, too. We help with the baby, cooking, baking, laundry, cleaning. Take the car for an oil change. Walk the dog. The pram. Mike went back to work in mid-October and Lorna's parents were only here for a week or so. She doesn't like to be alone a lot."

Lorna sits on the floor in front of the couch and is building a tower of colorful wooden blocks. Benny watches her, bides his time, knows that the longer he waits the more satisfying the gratification of toppling the growing structure will be. His face displays the effort of constraint. Jo puts the tray on the low coffee table at the other end of the sofa and sits next to Lorna, Luci sinks into an upholstered armchair facing them.

"You'd never know it, but this town is full of people who've lost children," Lorna says quietly. "During the funeral and the weeks after, more and more folks came up to me, laid their hand on my arm, and said they knew what I was going through because it had happened to them, too. Miscarriages, allergic reactions, drugs, cancer, traffic accidents, drownings, falls from trees, a teen suicide. I learned that being a parent is hell waiting to happen."

Benny begins to gurgle, then his face opens up, and he laughs in a series of hiccuping burbles and chuckles. He barrels on hands and knees toward the block structure his mother builds and shrieks with excitement and laughter as it topples over. When she grabs him into a hug, he wiggles out of her arms and crawls back to his starting point. With no little effort, he turns and flops onto his padded bum, then raises his gaze to his mother's eyes. *Again*, his look and demeanor say clearly. *Again!*

Lorna keeps talking about the town reaching out and supporting her family after Lena's death while the game of tower building and destruction continues. Benny's antics throughout are funny and entertaining, but also a balm, an island of unadulterated joy in an ocean of grief.

"I like being with Jo best." Lorna sets a little plush elephant on the top of the tower and removes it immediately when Benny roars in disgust. "She knows how a child's death derails everything, but it hasn't happened to her. It makes her feel safer than the others. Like she can keep me safe, too. Weird, I know, but there it is. As a newly grieving mother, I get to live out my weirdest thoughts. It's like I have a carte blanche for kookiness."

Benny has tired of the game and crawls across the room, in search of mischief. He finds James, the retriever, who, Lorna says, never seems to let him out of his sight since Lena's disappearance, and grabs at his fur before plunking into a seat beside the big dog. Lorna walks over and holds the elephant out. Benny takes it and leans into the dog, plush toy in both hands and eyes fixed on his mama who now joins Jo on the couch.

"Corporal Miller, we've carried on as though you're a neighbor come over for coffee. Sorry about that. Why are you really here?"

"I came to tell you that the man who'd been arrested yesterday has been let go. He's not been ruled out as the driver—we're still waiting to hear back from the lab about the fifty or so lacquer samples that were sent in. He'd been arrested for being uncooperative and somewhat impaired, but that all cleared up this morning during an interview."

"I heard that he'd confessed," Jo blurts.

Luci spreads her hands. "Rumor mill," she says. "He never confessed to anything, but he did have a breakdown relating to a historic event in his family."

"So, the police are no closer to finding the driver than you were three months ago?" Lorna asks.

"That is correct. I am sorry."

Lorna's features express resignation and perhaps mild anger, but Jo looks indifferent, although her eyes never leave Luci.

"We were told in August that wait times would be extensive while the new lab is under construction," Luci goes on, "but none of us realized how much the results would be delayed. I talked to the Chief Forensic Director in Edmonton yesterday, and he didn't have any good news about how long it will take them to clear their backlog. I'm sorry," Luci repeats. "He said about three months still." The polite voice at the other end of the phone had also said the lab triages its cases by an algorithm he wasn't about to get into details about, but that it generally didn't favor traffic accidents.

Lorna shrugs in a deliberate, exaggerated movement and sighs. "What does it matter, really?" She looks to Benjamin who sits contentedly and drowsy against the dog, eyes half closed, hands around the elephant, a tiny spit bubble balancing on his lower lip. "I have dreams sometimes where I see the car, but the driver is always shrouded, shadowy, hidden, and that's not the part of the dream that makes me wake in a sweat, believe me. And what will happen when you finally arrest someone, anyway? They'll get fined, most likely, and may lose their license for a bit. Big fucking deal, if you pardon my language."

She turns and holds Luci in a tight gaze. "We don't really care, to tell you the truth. It's too soon for us to think about others, other potential victims of this driver, even. Mike goes through the motions at work, and then he comes home, and we look at Benny. Always look at Benny. Every little bit that we have inside of us that's not sad or angry or hopeless we give to Benny. There's nothing else." Her voice lowers to a whisper. "When Benny is sleeping, we just stare at the wall. That's it. That's all we do. Stare at the wall."

Luci nods slowly. What is there to say? She sinks into the silence of the room until she becomes aware of the smallest sounds. The dog's breathing, the baby's sleepy snuffles, the sound of swallowing from Jo drinking the last of her coffee. An old-fashioned clock on the mantelpiece ticking.

At the front door, Luci turns to Jo. "I didn't see your car here when I arrived."

Jo points to the beige Vespa. "I take Paul's bike when I come here. I couldn't imagine parking my red Toyota outside their door."

"Of course."

Luci takes a step, then turns and looks at the older woman. "Jo, when we spoke back in August, why was it you never mentioned that your son had been here that morning in his red Matrix?"

Jo smiles tightly. "Because I like to see my tax dollars at work and knew you'd figure it out?" She waves at Luci's indignation. "Corporal Dolly, lighten up, will you? After spending a few hours with Lorna, I feel the need to crack a joke. I meant no offence."

"How long do you stay?" Luci asks.

"Till Mike comes home. Sometimes I join them for dinner. A couple of times, Paul has come, too. He and Mike get on well. They have a lot in common and Paul's the right kind of calm for this. He'll teach Mike how to play boules in the spring and then maybe ask him to join the league." Her voice lowers.

"Once you bury your child somewhere, you can never leave. Mike and Lorna will never move. Not for their careers, not for Benjamin's schooling, not to chase a dream in Hollywood or Costa Rica. They have become Oyster Hill lifers now. This is it. End of the line. Anchored here forever by a small grave."

Luci nods. Of course.

"Please, Jo, tell me why you didn't mention Oliver to us back then."

The other woman sighs. Frowning, she takes a deep breath, then lets it out slowly. Luci waits.

"I've thought and spoken for Oliver for forty years. His lung transplant and subsequent health allowed us to live separate lives and to both of us, it felt like we were conjoined twins being cut apart. We had been that integral to one another. He needed me for his survival, for every medical encounter, for every crisis, and I needed him just as much, for meaning and purpose and spirit. Now we practice, like you would practice any new skill, to live apart, to not immediately reach out to the other when something unexpected happens. Oliver needed to learn to take his troubles to Gina or Saaz. I needed to learn not to call every day to check in. My hand went to the phone a thousand times in those first few months. The day I canceled my subscriptions to a dozen medical journals, I drank a whole bottle of wine and cried myself to sleep."

They stop in front of Luci's borrowed police car. Jo turns and leans against the fender, her arms wrapped tightly around herself. Her large eyes are ringed with deep crow's feet at the temples, but her expression remains somber.

"It was easier for Ollie. He had a new life, so many firsts, so many long-held dreams and goals now within arm's reach. He was drunk on living and shed his old life like a snake leaves its skin behind. But I struggled to find new purpose. The move up here helped—the house and garden take a lot of my time. But that, and even my painting, it's only skin deep—I can take it or leave it." Jo's voice deepens, her eyes losing focus. "I'm used to being suffused with urgency, concern, care. That Ollie would be okay was like the DNA of my every cell and to not have that any more was emptying me, was turning me inside out. I even went to addiction counseling for a while, thought they could teach me some tools that might make it easier to rid myself of constantly thinking about Ollie, even subconsciously." She shakes her head and smiles. "It didn't help, really. I lied to both Paul and Ollie, told them it was becoming easier, that my thoughts were less and less saturated with Ollie's care. I pulled the pretending off so well, they've fully accepted I'm living my best life here in Oyster Hill, retired and happy, fulfilled by my garden."

It's a gray December day; cool but not brisk, low clouds in a dozen shades of pale hang low and dampen the air; the dense vegetation all around them exhales its abundant moisture. They can hear crows and seagulls gathering on beaches to feast on high-tide detritus, and just now, a passing ship sounds a warning blast as it rounds the tip of a nearby island. A raven soars overhead, calling its sonorous gurgling croak, and Luci can hear faint car and truck sounds from the nearby highway. She keeps her eyes fastened on the woman in front of her as she seems to struggle to maintain composure.

"But that's not true," Jo continues. She sounds bitter now, angry even. "Saving Ollie, preventing that disease from taking him, that was my best life. It made me strong and smart and resourceful. There was purpose and meaning in everything I did. And now, without that, everything else is bland, beige, boring, banal." Jo barks a laugh. "The proverbial B-side of life. The lesser. Everything seems to be less now.

"Anyway." She straightens, loosens her arms from their tight grasp around her midriff and shakes them out. "That's why I didn't mention Oliver and his red car to you. I'm practicing nescience. Not talking about him if I can help it."

Except that you told me all about your precious son, just not that he was driving near the accident site in his Barcelona Red Metallic Matrix right about the right time, Luci thinks but doesn't say. Instead, she holds out her hand. "And we figured it out ourselves, anyway. No worries, Jo, no hard feelings. I was just curious."

And as if all is easy between them, Jo smiles. "Come to my show if you have time," she says and takes the proffered hand in hers. "Ian Tan Art Gallery on Granville. Opening night is Friday. Black tie and all that. Dress up and bring a date. It'll be nice to see you in something other than your uniform."

CHAPTER THIRTY-THREE

OPENING NIGHT

"Do you remember when we talked about a Faustian pact?" Luci asks Rudd when they're airborne on their twenty-minute flight to Vancouver. "Josephine Nelson reminds me of that. She spent her whole adult life working to keep her son alive. And now that he's healthy and thriving almost twenty years posttransplant, she can't live with the result. Not that she's unhappy that he's well, I don't mean that, but she told me she feels empty inside, robbed of purpose. I believed it, too, when she spoke, but then," Luci pulls her brows together in concentration, "she turns on a dime, appears fully settled and in harmony with her surroundings one moment, superior the next, then bitchy and stubborn, and later, expansive and generous. She's got tons of layers and seems able to draw them around herself. Maybe that's artistic manipulation? I don't get her at all. She irks me, but I also like her."

Rudd doesn't appear to have heard; he stares intently out the window. They're flying close to the snow-covered ridges of the Tantalus Range, the last untamed mountain span before the descent into Vancouver. He waits until the plane banks, then turns to his colleague.

"The way you describe your conversation, I get the sense she was stonewalling your question. After forty years of arguing with medical professionals, many of them high up on the hierarchy ladder, Josephine Nelson is a skilled negotiator who knows how to handle awkward situations. She evaded answering your very direct question by giving you a cock-and-bull story about the hardship of retirement."

"That's how you read it?"

"Yes, and you do, too. Otherwise, it wouldn't gall you so. And you just called her a manipulator yourself." Rudd stretches his legs as far as they'll go and rolls his shoulders. The RCMP corporate credit card buys them seats on Canadian carriers at a reduced rate, and most ticket agents will assign them to business class. Not that it matters on such a short flight, but stretching one's limbs is always appreciated. He groans like a contented Cheshire.

"Stay on her. Something is going on there, your instincts are clearly telling you. Go to that gallery opening and keep drawing her out. It may be that what she's hiding has nothing to do with the hit-and-run, but chasing after your sixth sense hones your investigative skills, at the very least." He smiles widely and his eyes sparkle. "Getting to play cat and mouse with a suspect is the funnest part of the job, isn't it? See what you can figure out."

As luck would have it, Grant is in town for the weekend. He wants to go to the Christmas Market and the epic toy store on Granville Island. Something about ferrying Santa in a helicopter to the outlying communities up north and needing more toys. He's delighted to have a chance to dress up, rents a royal blue three-piece on Friday afternoon, and then they take their time showering and getting ready.

"Did you google her?" Grant asks in the elevator, holding Luci's hand and looking at her appreciatively. She knows she looks amazing in her pink cashmere and long, dark brown velvet skirt. She released her blond mop from its customary ponytail, and curls cascade all over; there's mascara, smoky eye shadow, glossy lipstick, a bit of rouge, and dangling earrings, all finished off with gloriously high heels. She's turned out as good as it gets and feels girlish and special. Maybe she could just have fun instead of working Josephine Nelson?

"Yes, I did. She's a big wheel in the arts community. She started out as a lichen cataloger, then illustrator, then painter. She sells internationally—her paintings fetch ten thousand and more." Luci hooks her arm through Grant's and leans into him. They have decided to walk; the gallery is only about six blocks from her building, and it's dry and crisp in the wintry air. The sidewalks are swamped with Christmas shoppers and weekend revelers; crowds of people in hockey jerseys are heading toward Rogers Arena.

"I have to admit that I spent more time looking at her work than her bio. Her paintings are beautiful. Can't wait to see the originals under gallery light."

They arrive fashionably late. The brightly lit gallery seems to be full of people; most are holding glasses, and a few black-suited servers are roaming with bottles and trays of finger food.

"Oh yes," Grant says, "a true hoity-toity! Let's mingle away."

Luci follows the light and color within a sweep of other guests. The drawings and paintings don't seem to have been mounted in any particular order: charcoal hangs next to watercolor, a large tree in a lichen suit next to a microscopic examination of substrate. Luci is enchanted. She has closely looked at lichen before but is now aware of how much she has not seen. The sheer range of color, shape, and structure of Josephine Nelson's favorite *objet d'art* is immense: shapes range from speckles of dust over leafy, hairy, crusty lobes to convoluted, bushy phallic shapes, and the colors cover the entire palette. There are dark brown barks overlaid by a blanket of shimmering green and ocher lichen that look like succulents with inch-high red protrusions; there's a filigree of verdant tendrils over shiny-wet black rocks with moss-like growth and cement-gray pebbles. Some are underwater, some in rain, and others are sun-kissed. Luci circles the first room, then the second. She receives a glass of red from a passing server and an artist's bio replete with price sheet from a young staffer. Wow! That triptych was commissioned for seventy-five thousand. The one she likes best, the *old man's beard* nestled across the distinct red skin of arbutus goes for a measly twelve thousand. Yikes. This is definitely not the occasion to indulge in a Christmas present for herself.

She sees Jo standing with a group of people near the back of the largest room. The woman looks regal, matriarchal. She wears a green silk dress and jacket, a lavender shawl, yellow pumps. Her gray, longish hair is swept into an elegant bun, and she has donned a silver necklace, shimmering earrings, and even some rouge. She looks spectacular. Oliver and Gina are standing next to her and Luci spots Nico sitting on a low couch just behind them, immersed in his phone, of course. As Luci raises her glass to take a sip of wine, Jo's eyes catch hers and the older woman smiles, then waves. Luci lowers her glass and walks toward her.

"Corporal Miller, what a pleasure to see you. Thank you for coming to my show." Jo pulls her into a welcoming embrace and even kisses her cheek lightly. Then she turns sideways, keeping one hand on Luci's arm, and gestures toward Oliver with the other.

"I'd like you to meet my son."

When Oliver turns his eyes on her, a friendly, guileless smile on his open face, Luci extends her hand in greeting. He doesn't take it, even steps back when shocked recognition floods his features. Just like she had in September, Luci marvels at the likeness of mother and son's frowns and expressions of scorn. Oliver's eyes narrow, two vertical lines appear between his brows and others furrow his forehead, the smile upends, and his lips press tightly together.

"Officer," he says, and Luci clearly hears the repressed rage in his voice, "what the hell?"

Luci withdraws her hand after a moment's hesitation and looks cooly at one of her main suspects. "Your mother invited me, Mr. Nelson."

His eyes dart to Jo and Luci half-turns quickly to catch the expression on Jo's face. When she sees only mild amusement, she wonders at the older woman's ability to veil her thoughts.

"Oliver!" Jo admonishes her son and allows a bit of steel to surge into her voice. "Corporal Miller is here as a friend. Please be gracious."

Oliver breathes noisily, holds his mother's gaze for a moment, then looks back at Luci. "She threatened me, you know," he hisses. "Like a schoolyard bully."

"That's her job," his mother answers cooly, as though Luci wasn't standing right there. "I imagine that cranking the heat up is a useful tool for an investigator."

Jo laughs as though she had made a joke and takes Luci by the arm, turning both of them away from Oliver. "Have you seen the triptych yet, Corporal Dolly?" she asks, indicating the adjoining room with her chin and leading Luci toward it. "I wouldn't mind hearing your thoughts on it."

When they stop to accept new glasses from a passing server, a loutish group of people move into the space around Jo, and the room swells with ambient noise. Luci disengages as soon as it seems polite and steps into a quieter area. It's not exactly claustrophobic in here, but the energy in the gallery seems to vibrate. Her senses are wide open because she's on a quasi-work assignment—it's easy to feel overwhelmed by all that noise, laughter, pushing, and everyone's apparent desire to be seen. She wishes Rudd were here in her stead, his gregariousness would fit right in. He would draw Jo into an animated conversation about her artistry, charm Oliver by congratulating him on his business success and ask him a thousand questions about the highs and lows of entrepreneurship, and he'd engage and charm Gina Nelson, the earnest politician. Rudd would small talk forever and then emerge with stunning observations about everyone. He likes people and delights in looking for what makes a person tick.

Luci watches Jo and her family. The matriarch is clearly in her element. She beams at the adoring crowd and reaches out to embrace and kiss anyone who ventures into her range. Her laughter soars, her eyes sparkle with amusement, her cheeks are flushed. Oliver orbits her like the moon circles the Earth: he refills her water glass, finds Kleenex when she spills some on herself while talking animatedly, smiles and shakes hands with everyone she wants to introduce him to. Gina is much quieter and less focused on her immediate family; she seems to know most people by name and allows herself to be drawn into one-on-one conversations. Luci hasn't seen Paul yet but imagines he's here somewhere, perhaps giving someone a guided, interpretive tour of his wife's luminous art. Then her eyes fall on Nico. He still sits on the couch with a large Android in his hands; the plate of sandwiches on the small table beside him is now empty, next to two open bottles of beer. Are the parents letting their fifteen-year-old drink? Luci exchanges her wine glass yet again and walks over to him.

"Hey, Nico," she says lightly as she lowers herself onto the seat next to him. "I can see you're fascinated by your gran's artwork."

The corners of his lips rise slightly and Nico scoots over an inch, by way of welcome. Luci settles next to him and sighs contentedly.

"This is better than that," she indicates the room full of people with a nod. "I really like her work, but all those pesky folks are getting in the way."

"Vanbourgerites," the boy mutters and Luci laughs.

"Clever," she acknowledges. "Also, Philistines?"

"No, that word is used wrong, anyway. Philistines were a warrior tribe. Back some three thousand years. Goliath was a Philistine."

"Oh, I thought he was Egyptian."

"No, the Philistines fought the Egyptians. And won a lot, even though they were a small tribe. They fought the Israelites, too," he adds.

"You know your way around history. Major in antiquity much?"

"I'm interested in everything. History, politics, science, art, photography. I like to learn."

Luci raises her eyebrows. She hadn't taken the boy for a studious type when she'd first met him. He has the build of an athlete, with wide shoulders and long limbs, and his confident, even cocky, attitude during their interview led her to slot him into an undeserved category. Her least favorite one.

"Photography?" she asks. "What are you into?"

"Architectural photography mostly—urban, street, cityscapes, that kind of stuff."

"So, you probably use an older, large format view camera with tilt and shift lenses to capture things like large buildings?"

"Yes." Nico shoots her a sideways glance. "My dad studied journalism and sidelined in photography. I got his Deardorff clone, five by seven, with a Wollensak lens. And a Fuji GFX100. And I use this Huawei Pro for everyday." He indicates his Android.

Luci nods. "The best. Do you have any shots on there you'd let me look at?"

"Sure. But I'll be selective."

"Of course," Luci laughs. "I'm curious about your art, not nosey about your life."

They scoot a bit closer and bend over Nico's phone. He shows her shots of the library, the Museum of Anthropology, the Parq, Westbank's Vancouver House, the Evergreen. He's used light and shadow to explore details as much as the whole. Luci is impressed and says so. When Nico angles the screen away to scroll through some pics he'd rather not share, she takes out her own phone and opens her picture library. She shows him the wolf-under-water shots that had turned out even better than she'd hoped. It's Nico's turn to raise his eyebrows.

"Wow," he exclaims loudly. "Do you have an underwater drone?"

She tells him about diving and shows him other under-water images. Salmon, seals, sea lions, a giant squid. Nico asks about continuous lights versus strobes underwater, then shows her some very good pics he took inside the aquarium. They angle their heads over their phones, scroll and tap, show their favorites, exclaim in praise and appreciation. Their legs touch and Luci is aware of her comfort in sharing space with an open-minded, curious teen. Her visits with her nieces and nephews are like this: comfortable and easy.

"You're not picking on my grandson again, Corporal?"

Jo Nelson slides around the short end of the couch and lowers herself into the corner. As Luci turns toward her, she feels the cushion under her shift slightly and knows without looking that Nico took the opportunity to scram. She sighs.

"No, Jo. In fact, your paintings inspired us to discover we share a common interest."

"You mean photography?"

"Yes. Nico's got quite an eye for lines and angles. Impressive."

Jo raises her eyebrows. "Nico let you see his pictures?" The laughter in her eyes vanishes, and her lips form a thin line. She looks put out. "He only ever lets me see the ones he prints. And that only since I put up the money so he could convert their attic space into a darkroom. He's usually very secretive with his photographs." She lowers her shoulders and squints at Luci. "How did you get him to show them to you?"

Luci laughs uneasily. Did Jo have too much to drink? Is she one of those sad drunks, the type who mopes and feels sorry for themselves?

"It's common not to show your works in progress. I imagine you do the same. But I'm a semiprofessional photographer myself, so we just shared a few of the ones we're proud of. Don't worry, Gran—I'm not muscling in on your turf. Scout's honor." Luci laughs again, hoping to turn the mood. Jeez, this woman seems to take offence at everything. *That's what I get for relaxing in the kid's company and forgetting I'm here to work*, she thinks, and realigns herself accordingly. *Alright then, Missus Josephine Nelson, control freak extraordinaire, let's draw you out.*

Jo's features have smoothed, and she reclines into the backrest, her hands falling to her thighs. "I'm knackered. It's a lot of work being nice."

"How often do you do this kind of thing?" Luci asks.

"You mean art shows, or opening nights? Both rarely—it's been ten years or more since I worked a crowd this size." Jo sighs and shifts her bottom and legs into a more comfortable position. "It's gratifying and invigorating, yes, and I'll sell a bunch tonight, for sure, but I much prefer my studio at home, or the hikes it takes to find specimens and let my agent do the selling." She points to a tall, angular, slightly over-made-up woman of intermediate age who wears three thousand dollars' worth of silk and leather.

"That's her over there, Estelle Jambor. I'd introduce you, but she's talking to someone who's got actual money. Best not to disturb them."

"I've seen your whole family but not Paul. Did he stay in Oyster Hill?"

"No, he was here earlier. You must have arrived after he left. He said he felt a cold coming on and didn't want to pass his germs around with the canapés, so he went back to the hotel. I bet he's in the bar, watching a game, and having a grand time."

"The Canucks are playing a home game against the Red Wings," Luci says. "If you time your exit here just right, you may get into a bar just as the fans pour out of the arena. Fun people-watching."

"Only if they win. I remember the Stanley Cup riots and once was enough for me. I don't think I'll go courting a bunch of rioting hooligans tonight."

Luci feels similar. "I honestly think you could peace-keep the lot of them with a look. You have heaps of natural authority about you."

Jo laughs. "There's nothing natural about it, believe me, Corporal Dolly." She pauses, looks around the room where well-dressed and well-heeled Vanbourgerites admire her work and pay tribute to her artistry. "I know I can be forceful and make others do my bidding, but I wasn't always like that. I started out being really easygoing. Wide-eyed, naive, compliant even. A yielder."

She turns back to Luci, her gaze unfocused. "My mother was a war bride from England—she came to Quebec on the *Aquitania* in 1944. I was an infant, obviously don't remember a thing, but our lives were fairly unsettled for a long time. My mom and dad had this massive war romance in London but then didn't get along as husband and wife in Canada, and moved and separated several times. I remember being anxious as a kid, worried and nervous, waiting for the next bad thing to happen. We were living in Saskatoon when I graduated high school and I married Trevor, my prom date, and settled in to be a good housewife." Jo's eyes begin to sparkle and a smile raises the corners of her mouth. "But then the sixties happened, and women's lib, Janis Joplin and Gloria Steinem. Wearing an apron on 24 Street North became untenable when San

Francisco kept calling, so I left Trevor and went west. Made it as far as Portland where I fell for a peacenik who became a draft dodger and who took me back across the border to British Columbia. We lived in Vancouver, in Penticton and Nelson, then on Lasqueti Island. The hippie life. Hand to mouth, day to day, not a care in the world except world peace."

Luci nods imperceptibly, keeps her attention focused on Jo, and shuts out the ambient voices all around them as best as possible. Hopefully, no one would come interrupt them now that Jo was reflecting so freely.

"We became involved in timber conservation. In the early seventies, with a new NDP government, the movement to change forestry practices gathered steam. We went to Moresby Island and the Nitinat to be pesky, blocked logging roads, talked to reporters whenever we could find any. Even engaged in a bit of what they now call ecoterrorism: poured sugar into the logging truck tanks, punctured tires, and that sort of thing. Pretty harmless by today's standards, but we felt daring and very antiestablishment. Then we went to Victoria to speak to actual politicians.

"My peacenik and I drifted apart. He became sloppy and drunk, and I realized that there could be more to life than making him happy. More and more often, he'd stay home to feed the chicken, and I hitchhiked and bussed to gathering points. I became good at organizing people and haranguing politicians. I learned to study and to prepare for meets by reading and learning as much as I could. Then, this one time, I was researching sulphate effluents from paper mills into ocean waters and went to MacMillan Bloedel in Port Alberni to see for myself. And I met Paul."

"He was a protester, too?" Luci knows the answer because Paul had told her that warmish, sun-speckled morning she'd waited with him outside their house in Oyster Hill for Nico and Jo to return from their walk. Paul had been friendly and genial and had told stories of his vocation as a working stiff.

"Oh God, no!" Jo laughs dryly. "Paul was the enemy. A mill worker and proud of it. He happened to see me get off the bus in the mill's parking lot and knew right away I didn't belong there. He beetled out to shield me from the foreman and manager who were a bully and a creep, respectively, as he put it. Paul understood what I wanted, and he showed me around, pretending I was his girlfriend. He pretended so well it took me all but two days to trade him in for the peacenik."

"She couldn't resist my roughneck, woodsy charm," Paul says quietly from behind them before leaning over the couch's backrest to kiss Jo lightly on her cheek. "Or my good looks, for that matter," he grins and winks at Luci.

"Oh Paul, you came back. How lovely of you." Jo reaches out and caresses his cheek, then shimmies over and pats the seat next to her. "Come join us for the telling of tales."

As envisioned by his wife, Paul had been at the hotel bar, nursing a hot buttered rum and watching the hockey game. When it was clear the Vancouver Canucks would lose, he decided to return to the gallery and accompany his wife safely back to their hotel. "It wouldn't do for a dame half sotted on Prosecco to wander the sidewalks when the rabid hockey crowd comes swarming from the gates," he muses with a wry smile.

As if on cue, Luci sees Grant approaching. "I'll be leaving, too. Thank you for inviting me, Jo, it's been a real treat. I'll never hike another forest without paying attention to the lichen. Your artistry brings them to light in all their hidden beauty."

She wanted to say "infinitesimal" but didn't trust her tongue with the difficult word. The two women embrace awkwardly while seated, then Luci rises and shakes hands with Paul before joining Grant, who slides his arm around her waist and pulls her close.

"A nightcap at the Outcry while we talk about the shiny, pretty people we met here tonight?" he suggests, and Luci grins.

"Sounds perfect. I just have to use the bathroom."

She slips through the knots of Vanbourgerites mingling in the foyer and quickly walks through the gallery to the back room.

As she enters the discreet passage to the washrooms, she hears male voices ahead. Angry voices. Fragmented sentences. *Jerk… behavior…ever…don't you dare…disappointment….* Then the door to the men's bathroom is flung open and crashes against the wall. Oliver Nelson is caught on the shoulder by the ricocheting wood but doesn't appear to notice. His face is contorted in fury, and he brushes past her in the narrow passage seemingly without registering her presence, and hurriedly disappears around the corner. Luci had pressed her back to the wall to avoid a collision and stares after him. What had gotten mild-mannered sonny boy so riled up? Was there even someone in the men's? Or does this guy deal with pressure by blasting his head off in front of the mirror? Wow.

Luci has had a couple of very good glasses of red wine and snickers to herself. The best intelligence comes from the pisser, old cops had always told her. And they weren't half wrong about it, were they? She already knew Oliver Nelson could be an arrogant jerk, now she'd witnessed an outburst of rage that had, at least temporarily, fully consumed him. Interesting.

She pulls open the door to the ladies' when she hears sounds from the other room. Somebody stepping on the lever pedal of the garbage can and the metal lid banging against the wall behind. Somebody had been in there with Oliver. She tries to recapture the words she'd heard…*behavior…disappointment.* Those aren't normal fighting words, but a person might hiss them at their own image. Or…at their kid. They're parental words. Oliver had been yelling at Nico. Had reamed his kid out in the gallery bathroom between rounds of making nice with the adults and paying guests. Not just an arrogant jerk with anger management issues, but a devious schemer, to boot. Glib. Luci stands hesitantly by the door, unsure if she should check on Nico. Teenage egos are fragile at the best of times, let alone after a parent loses his cool.

She knocks on the men's door. "Nico, is that you? It's Luci. The photographer."

Nothing breaks the silence.

"Nico, are you okay?"

She thinks she hears a sniffle. Hard to say with all that ambient background noise of the gallery rooms emptying out. Luci imagines the tall teenager standing behind the door, gulping back a sob lest he be discovered in a moment of humiliation. Remembers what it had felt like to have an adult step through the thin mantle of privacy you so desperately draw around yourself.

Luci leaves quietly, her own bladder forgotten. There are still small huddles of people clustered here and there, but the gallery rooms have emptied out enough so she can stride right through. Enough with working Jo and her family. The rest of the night is hers and hers alone.

CHAPTER THIRTY-FOUR

ON GUARD

Of the seventeen paintings that had been for sale, nine sold the night of the opening and another four during the two weeks since. Not to mention almost sixty prints. Jo feels rich and successful and glides along on cloud nine for days. She may disdain working the crowd but feels replenished after four days in the city. Paul's cold never came to fruition, so the two of them visited the large, open-air Christmas Market in Jack Poole Plaza, walked Stanley Park, then took the "Bright Nights Christmas Train" and *ooh*ed and *aah*ed with a hundred starry-eyed kids over each and every magical light presentation. They ate at their favorite restaurants and had breakfast in bed, off a trolley.

Now Christmas is less than a week away and Jo sits at her desk, her laptop open in front of her. She's supposed to be writing Christmas cards and notes of appreciation to buyers and patrons—Estelle had given her a lengthy list—but Jo can't get in the mood. Instead, she checks if Nico has opened her email yet. She sent it to him yesterday: a quick "hello" and two articles about the benefits of formal driver's ed, as well as a link to the highest-rated driving school in his neighborhood. She had carefully embedded a bit of malicious code in the attachment, following the step-by-step instructions she'd learned in Seattle, and which she'd already used to infiltrate Oliver's devices. She had rifled countless hours looking for anything relating to the accident in Oyster Hill. A file with a collection of newspaper articles, a search history about the laws pertaining to hit-and-runs, or an emotional diary entry. Her search had yielded nothing.

The diary Oliver had kept as a kid had literally been an open book into his innermost thoughts. At seven, he kept a tally of who had guest appearances on *Sesame Street* and *Pee-Wee's Playhouse*, jotted down Inspector Gadget's missions and locales, kept tabs on GI Joe's weaponry. At twelve, he wrote about his favorite MTV videos and then morphed seamlessly into sexual fantasies. Jo read all of it and Ollie never found out. She never used her surreptitious knowledge overtly and never shared anything with his father, either. She read Ollie's journals for the same reason she bullied his doctors into showing her his X-rays instead of just telling her what they'd seen in the films: she had a pathological need to know. How could she keep him alive, against all scientific prophecy, if she missed anything important? Who was to know which information would prove vital? Although the steps of her son's disease progression could be outlined in broad strokes, the medical community professed repeatedly that they could not predict every eventuality, every setback, every outcome. As much as Jo appreciated Dr. Robichaud and Ilse and all the other expertly and urgently working scientists who labored to uncover the genetic fingerprint of cystic fibrosis and, therewith, future treatment options, she knew in her heart and soul and bones that Ollie's survival lay in her hands. Every innocuous decision about Ollie's care, such as which private physiotherapist to hire, whether to go on vacation far from a nearby hospital, which drug trial to pursue, even which caloric booster to pack into his daily lunch, could throw a long shadow over just how short his life might be cut.

Everyone, from Paul and Oliver himself, to Ilse and all of his doctors and caregivers, thought he would die as a kid, a teen, or a young adult. *Twenty-six and a half* had loomed large and became an absolute in their eyes. But not in hers. She worked to keep him alive. She wasn't overinvested in his medical care because she wanted to ensure that she had done enough, had been a good enough parent to a terminal kid, as one of her therapists had suggested. No, not that. She was holding on tight to the reins of his medical care because she wanted her son to be un-terminal, to have decades of life, to live to old age.

And yet.

1990

She stands in the fourth-floor hallway of BC Children's Hospital in Vancouver. It's almost midnight; the corridor looms eerie and empty. The long walls are painted in pastel yellows and greens and adorned with fantastical Dr. Seuss characters. Horton and Yertle smile encouragingly, Vlad Vladikoff is more aloof, and Thing One and Thing Two frame the door to the family room. The fourth floor is home to the oncology department, and the family room is where doctors impart the worst news to pale, exhausted parents. There are two long couches to crumple upon in a heap, thick carpets to muffle the sound of screaming, large, soft pillows to punch or hold in a death grip against one's breaking heart, and a highfalutin stereo that plays a never-ending loop of soothing music and meditative nature sounds. When Jo hears the unmistakable beat of Technotronic seep through the not-so-soundproof door, she winces. Turn it down, she wants to hiss, shush, be quiet, someone might come down the hallway at any time.

But Ollie and Chloe have chosen wisely. The hallway's heavy, double swinging door with rubber insulation is closed to the patient rooms and nurses' stations on the other side. Only doctors' and therapists' offices are on this end of the corridor and, barring any nighttime emergencies, there's no reason anyone should come by the family room and hear the uncharacteristic electronic hip-hop reverberating behind the closed doors. But here she is, just in case, guarding her son's first sexual encounter.

Jo grins as the words "coitus interruptus" float into her mind, the standard birth control method before the pill, and remembers her own teenage fumblings with Stuart Whitmaker in his parents' bedroom, of all places. She'd had only the vaguest idea of what to expect when the massive boy had put his hand over her breast and asked if she wanted to lie with him, but she'd agreed immediately because she wanted to know what all the fuss was about. How fortunate that Stuart had been a kind boy, caring and sensitive, and experienced already, at sixteen.

She had been fifteen and derived immense pleasure from sex, then and in all the years since. To lose oneself in sheer sensation, to give and receive in the most open, intimate ways, to watch the miracle of orgasm unfold in another's eyes; Jo had embraced the joy of sex long before the famous namesake's book arrived on the shelves of daring libraries. As she guards the family room's door against any potential disturbance during her son's first foray into lovemaking, Jo hopes that Ollie will have the time of his life.

She had found out about this tryst from his diary while he slept. He writes in it more when he's in the hospital, during unfathomably long days with nothing to do but receive intravenous medication and chest physio. A pneumonia bad enough to warrant hospitalization usually sees him sleeping exhaustively for a day or two, then, after the first round of three or four different antibiotics, he rallies, turns from pale to pink, from silent to chatty, from listless to ravenous, but has to stay bedbound for days. Sometimes as many as seven. Doctor's orders.

Ollie and Chloe have been friends for almost five years. They became pen pals after Horst, the German physiotherapist who worked exclusively with CF kids, had moved from Smithers, where Chloe lived, to Vancouver, and suggested Ollie write to her. Horst's instincts had been spot-on: Ollie and Chloe hit it off immediately. They wrote to each other daily and still found much to talk about on the phone after six p.m. or on weekends when long-distance charges were less. When they were fourteen, Paul and Jo had driven Ollie the four hundred miles up to Smithers for a supervised in-person visit. Supervised, because cross-contamination between CF kids is as high-risk as it gets, on par with unprotected sex between barflies and lounge lizards. And so, they were told not to touch, not to be too close, and to turn away from one another when coughing, but children being children, they couldn't be trusted to obey the cruel rules. There'd always been at least one adult in the room, trailed along to the ice cream parlor, or sat, out of earshot, on a riverside bench nearby. As far as a budding teenage romance was concerned, circumstances could not have been more awkward.

Now they're both at BC Children's. Chloe arrived five days ago by air ambulance. Her mucus-plugged pancreas was stalling and Dr. Gregorio Fernandez, the anointed Holy Grail of endocrine wizardry at the pediatric super center, is sorting out her insulin regimen. It'll take at least two weeks. After her first night here, which was touch-and-go according to her parents, Chloe has bounced back and is now her usual energetic, slightly aloof self. As much as a fifteen-year-old girl at death's door can be aloof, that is, while her boyfriend is lying in his bed three doors down the hall with a crappy pneumonia that had plummeted his lung function to less than thirty percent. Ollie must have caught a bug on their flight back home from Montreal, where he had been enrolled in a clinical trial for almost a year. The minute he began to improve, Ollie and Chloe started making plans. They phoned each other's rooms incessantly, bribed other kids to pass notes, and rolled their eyes at doctors and nurses who cautioned them over and over not to enter the other's room.

"Both your lungs are colonized with the usual bugs," Dr. Paul said earnestly to Ollie, who was looking out the window. "But Chloe has also been infected with Burkholderia cepacia, which is an aerobic gram-negative bacillus that is very, very hard to treat, impossible to eradicate, and which might preclude a person from receiving a donor transplant one day. This is a very bad bug to get, Ollie, and I must warn you, in the strongest terms, to be *very* cautious when interacting with your friend. I'm sorry."

Ollie didn't care. He'd heard about B. Cepacia all his life and knew every hospitalization increased his chances of catching it, regardless of who he came in contact with. And besides, Chloe had sent him an inducement only a complete idiot would spurn.

Jo saw the invitation. A small drawing Ollie had glued into his diary. The once-folded square of thin paper has been straightened meticulously and the creases smoothed with care. He left the opposite page bare, so as not to risk graphite or ink smudges.

It's a punctilious drawing of a vulva. Perhaps a generic version, perhaps a likeness of Chloe's own, drawn with expert skill: rosy flesh curves and curls and bows in correct, if plush, anatomical detail. And over this, Chloe has painted a transparent red rose, its center pistil shadowing the clitoris. It is beautiful, artful, provocative and, for any teenage boy, achingly arousing. Jo admires the artistry of this very candid drawing as much as its unmistakable power. Unsurprisingly, the following diary pages are filled with longing and their planned rendezvous.

After reading the latest entry, Jo had slipped the leatherbound journal back into its hiding place below the stack of graphic novels in the bottom drawer of the nightstand. For all his early maturity, Ollie has a guileless, almost naive quality about him; it would never occur to him to hide his diary because he'd never suspect her of betrayal. She'd settled back into the comfortable couch and looked at her son. In sleep, and at the tail end of a bad bout of pneumonia, he looked very young and fragile. The nurses kept the head of the bed on a steep incline and secured pillows under both his arms to maximize lung expansion. They wedged a larger pillow under his knees to keep Ollie from sliding, turning his hospital bed into a makeshift recliner. His head lolled to one side, and a thin trace of drool ran from the corner of his mouth. He was very still, except for his rapidly moving chest. His parted lips were dry, his skin pale and so luminous she could see the blue riverbeds of his veins near his temples.

He looked like a boy who might die any minute. In the quiet of the hospital room, in the stillness of night, and in the solitude of a parent watching a sleeping child, Jo could allow the truth to settle in close. Ollie could die today, next month, long before he ever got to twenty-six and a half. Statistically, this was probable and, looking at him in the dim light, even realistic. Next time, his lung function might slip even lower, or a catastrophic hemorrhage might burst his fragile bronchial arteries and drown him in his own blood. Or an infection with B. Cepacia might become the last straw in their fifteen-year-long fight against the inevitable. The doctors and nurses were right: they must do everything they can to limit Ollie's exposure. Of course they were right.

Then the beauty and innocence of that drawing had floated back into her mind. Who else but Chloe to open Ollie's world? Should Ollie's only, and last, foray into sensuality really be a picture? What if he dies next month? Next year? Wouldn't it be more life-affirming for these two budding youths to explore their sexuality within the trusted intimacy of their years-long friendship? Could there be a more perfect pairing than best friends who care deeply about each other?

Jo kissed her still-sleeping son on the cheek, waved to the nurses on her way out, then phoned Paul to wish him good night. She had dinner at a Vietnamese restaurant on Heather Street, then walked about in Queen Elizabeth Park until it was time. The diary had been specific: Ollie and Chloe would wait until after the ten o'clock meds, after the nurses would retreat behind their desks and immerse themselves in paperwork. They would wait until the ward settled into quiet and semidarkness. Then they'd sneak out of their rooms and find their way to the family room on the fourth floor. Ollie would bring some decent tunes.

She paces the hallway, expecting nurses and hospital security staff to emerge from the elevators on the other side of the double doors. Imagines herself blocking them with outstretched arms, whispering that they are too late, that breathable bugs have already been inhaled, that there is no point in tearing the young lovers apart now. Think of Romeo and Juliet, she would hiss, think of the one thing that was taken from you a long time ago and that you still pine over. Leave them be!

But nobody comes. It's after midnight now and the whole hospital seems to be in slumber. *That's it*, she thinks, *they've gotten away with it. Young love prevails, and if Ollie dies in three months from a B. Cepacia infection, I alone will be to blame.* But this is a fleeting, sarcastic thought. As she leaves the hospital to return home, she laughs in her joy that these two kids might find a hidden source of delight in their treacherous bodies.

CHAPTER THIRTY-FIVE

YOU CAN NEVER UNSEE

Nico had not only opened the attachment she'd sent him on his Android, but had saved it in the cloud, linking all his devices. *She has unfettered access.* What's more, his computers and phone are completely unprotected. Passwords are deviations of names and numbers that are embarrassingly easy to guess, he uses neither firewalls nor encryption, and his hardware's default credentials are still the original factory setting. *Silly boy.* She looks for his photographs, irked to no end that her grandson shared his passion with a stranger over her. She, who had given boundless amounts of time, energy, and money over the years to support his various interests and wishes, was being pushed out into the cold. *You've got another thing coming if you think this old girl is a wallflower,* she thinks in indignation as she begins to open his picture files.

The master hacker in Seattle had cautioned her about changing any settings when roaming around other people's computers. "It's much safer to move files to your own hard drive, especially when you're trying to find something in huge amounts of data. If you bring them home, you can view them in order of date or topic or last-opened, then you can sort them in a way that makes the most sense for you. You can't do any of that when you stay in their house, so to speak." He'd installed the "send anywhere" app on her laptop and had practiced with her how to enter six-digit key codes on the host's and her own device and then quickly send hundreds of files across the ether without leaving a single trace. Then he'd taught her how to work around a host's passwords once the files enter a different domain. Brilliant.

Jo mutters about her grandson's lack of security and over-abundance of naive trust as she sends thousands of picture files from his laptop, PC, and Android to her own hard drive in a matter of minutes, then sorts them into folders by date. Her computer has software to adapt images to improve the picture resolution, so Nico's photographs will look better for her than even he can get them. Jo smirks, then starts at the beginning.

Family pictures. Nico received his first phone for his tenth birthday and begins to shoot. The cake. His buddies. Coco, the black and white Cocker Spaniel. People and places on his way to school. More buddies. Teachers. Selfies. Jo changes the settings so all pictures show as thumbnails. In this manner, she scrolls through the years of artless snapping until she sees shots of scenery. First nature photography, when Nico is about thirteen, then the images morph into cityscapes. Buildings, roads, public art viewed from unusual angles. Also defaced and altered public art. Jo zooms in on some of those but it's impossible to tell whether Nico just captured the mischief after it happened or if he had a hand in the vandalism. Some of it's funny, actually. The iconic laughing men in English Bay are sporting dildos, the bronze sparrows in the Olympic Village are banded, the flank of the enormous metal deer at the North Van rec center is covered in red paint, like a successful hunt.

The blood theme continues for hundreds of photographs. Red paint pours over sculptures and portraits, drips from sunflower heads, pools on a dinner plate, covers a LEGO police station in its entirety, with only the word "police" showing clearly. Then there are real wounds. Bright red blood runs down a tanned, young leg, presumably Nico's, and into a white sport sock. A buddy's bloody nose. Varieties of sports injuries, including someone's nasty compound leg fracture. Then she opens an entire folder of screen grabs, all depicting mayhem, mutilation, desecration, terror. There is obviously a place in cyber world where real-time pictures of accidents, captured by thrill-seeking rubbernecks, are not filtered out. Neither are the videos of beheadings and other atrocities ISIS used to send into the world. Nico, in all his apparent digital fumbling, must have found his way there and captured image after image. Why? Is this normal teenage boy behavior for Gen Z? Is he testing his sensitivity? Jo bites her lips in disgust and anger, then closes and deletes the entire file.

August 2018. Nico is becoming more adept with different lenses, drawing out shadows, accentuating angles and perspective. His cityscapes, especially, take on the veneer of artistry. Jo scrolls through hundreds of images of familiar façades and buildings. The young photographer shows, clearly, what casual glances so easily miss. He not only has an eye for beauty but also for originality and simplicity; sometimes manages to capture all of it in a single shot. Impressive.

October 2018. Coco paces and leaps around the yard. The beach. That girl loved retrieving sticks from the waves and would swim out no matter how far. What a trooper. Here she is all tail wagging and proud and here…Jo squints, clicks on the pic to enlarge it, and leans into the monitor. What the hell? It's Coco, underwater, her flank pressed against the pebbly ground with a hand, her head turned toward the camera, eyes huge, pleading and confused. The picture quality is lousy, but its content is unmistakable. Nico had held his dog underwater with one hand, then snapped a picture of her struggle with the other. You bastard! The little dog's terror leaps from the screen, the photograph is powerfully visceral. Jo minimizes it and lets her gaze run over dozens of thumbnails before she sees Coco again. She clicks to enlarge.

The little black Cocker Spaniel with a white fur patch on her chest and three white ankle socks is dead. Unmistakably. There's quite a lot of blood and even some visible tendon and bone. Oliver had told her that their dog had been run over by a car just outside the house, but in this picture.... Jo takes a deep, shuddering breath and leans back in her chair. Coco looks as though someone had taken a sledgehammer to her—she seems mutilated. Could such severe injuries to every part of her body really have been caused by a car? Or was this something else entirely? She scrolls back to the photograph that shows Coco being confined underwater, the look of terror in her eyes a vivid plea. It's dated October fourth. And back to her bloodied corpse on the grass. October tenth.

Jo closes the pirated folder and takes a minute to move all of Nico's pictures on her device into a secure cache, then follows the sequence of steps to gain access to his laptop again. She searches for all documents, downloads, and search histories that had been active between October fourth and tenth of last year and copies those files, then repeats for his Android and desktop computer. Holy cow, there's a lot of data.

A heaviness slides into her middle, a familiar sense of dread and Jo stops to breathe. You can never unsee, never unlearn. The pictures of the dead dog have unsettled her, and she has a nasty, sour suspicion that Nico had cruelly abused his dog. That's what it looks like. She can leave it at that, can't she? It will color how she interacts with him over the next while, but in time, these feelings will fade and she'll be able to embrace her grandson with genuine love again. Don't most kids act out as teens, push boundaries, test limits? It's not so long ago that animal cruelty, in the form of pinned insects and licensed dog fights, was commonplace, no? Maybe this was a one-time offence. Maybe her interpretation is absurd. Maybe Nico took those pics to document the extent of injuries a careless driver had caused. Maybe Coco had been entangled by some seaweed and Nico's hand on her flank had been lifting her, not pushing her down. She can still let this go.

Can't she?

She wants to. God, does she want to.

But no. Of course, she must know. That's how she's lived her entire life, even if her gut is telling her she'll hate what she'll find. Jo leaves her studio, takes a one-person supper from the freezer, and places it on the counter together with a note telling Paul that she's engrossed in a complicated painting and won't join him. She fixes a big pot of tea and returns to her workstation.

She organizes all the hacked data into folders and begins to read. She deletes every innocuous page and shuffles compromising, suspicious, or outright disgusting material under separate headings. There is no shortage of disgusting material. Nico had googled animal cruelty, had discoursed with self-professed "zoosadists," and had tried to gain access to a website on the dark web that shared torture videos. The material she finds is so disturbing that Jo is simultaneously sickened and frantic to see more. How far does this go? How unimaginably bad? She returns to Nico's devices and searches all his data to present day.

At some point, Paul knocks gently on the studio door and wishes her a good night. Her pot of tea sits cold and un-touched. Her skin is clammy and tight. Jo is unaware of the soreness spreading through her tired back and shoulders, of the need to go to the bathroom. She sits motionless, staring at the screen, and clicks through a series of Nico's blog posts. *Click, click, click.*

> February 14, 2018: Gave myself a Valentine's today.
> A good one. Last night, I set the alarm and got up at
> four. Poured three buckets of water over the steps,
> nice and slowly. Waited twenty minutes and poured
> one more. Just to be on the safe side. Then this

morning, rode over to Lambrick Park and climbed on the playground structure. You can see the house from there, especially now, without the leaves. Mom came out just like always: her arms full and in a hurry. She wiped out on the top step, her briefcase and stuff flying as she tried to hold onto something, but she's too high to reach the railing. Down she goes and smacks on the sidewalk. It was a pretty good riff, even if I say so myself. People came and helped her up, chased her papers for her. Then somebody got Dad out and he was his usual useless tit. Eventually, Mom decided this was not going to be a workday and limped back up in the house. She and Dad were gone when I came home from school. Saaz came over, and we watched movies and made sandwiches with weird pickles and sprouts on them. They tasted good, though. Later, Mom and Dad came home and cried a lot and said I was no longer getting a little sister or brother. Bull's-eye!

The thing is, they are baby killers, too. They had three babies in tubes, frozen, waiting at the lab. Then they decided to use one and to "destroy" the other two if this one takes. That's the actual word they used: destroy. Like they are some kind of Einsatzgruppe.

May 28, 2019: I AM GUCCI! PHAT! BADASS! Man that was intense. We were in that abandoned factory on Wilmot. Roger had some serious Stardust and Tweak and a couple of girls showed up, trading blow jobs. The chinky passed right out and we all got to dip our dicks. Wow! My first real time and it was intense. The guys were hooting and hollering when I shot my load and I felt like home, like I belong. It was awesome.

But then the other chick started to freak out and scream because chinky didn't wake up. Like, not at all. Eyes open and blue all over. Roger belted the loud one around for a bit, then gave her some smack and sent her packing. The guys were all duh, I don't know what to do, so I had my moment of glory. Told them to steal a car, drive it and the dead girl to Abbotsford where all the gang killings are, and set both on fire in a field. The cops will take it as a typical gang hit. It was very intense, this driving around for an hour, with a corpse in the trunk, let me tell you. But it all worked out beautifully and now the guys know me. And I have a new notch.

August 26, 2019: Dad is such an asshole! I can't believe him. I had all these plans with the guys, nothing special, just hanging around. But important, because I want this connection to stay solid, even if I have to start at Trafalgar now. Another asinine worst-ever-dad move. He's such a loser! Anyway, he says I have to go to Oyster Hill for the rest of the week. Apparently, Momsy is too busy to be a mom and Dad is flying east for b-u-s-i-n-e-s-s. What a shitload of bull.

Did he ever give me what I wanted? Don't think so. Like when he said he'd take me to a barber, where they give you hot towels and a close shave with a real blade. I've really been wanting to do that, but of course, Dad says one thing and then does another. Goes to physio or the clinic, or meetings or whatever, and he didn't even teach me how to shave myself. YouTube is a better Dad than mine.

August 28, 2019: UN-FUCKING-BELIEVABLE!!!

December 11, 2019: It's been over three months and I can still vividly see the kid disappear below the red fender. Glorious! I think about it all the time and when I look at the after-pics, I feel like Jake Sully who morphs wholly into his avatar through the magic of Pandora. But where Sully becomes almost ten-foot tall, with blue skin and yellow eyes and the coolest tats ever, I transformed in more subtle ways, but no less powerful. And everyone sees it. Guys in Trafalgar are treating me okay, want to hang out. Even my parents are beginning to see me, to show some respect. Not that they matter so much anymore. This is weird, right? For all my life, they were my everything, but without much reciprocation, and now that I don't need them anymore, they come around, they see me, congratulate me on my accomplishments, want to spend time with me. Lepers!

December 15, 2019: That fucking Sarah Gilbertson! She's the slut who blowed everyone for smack, she and her friend Akira, who lit up the field in Abbottsford. Sarah cleaned herself up, I guess she missed a half year and is now back at Alexander's High. But the other day, I saw her here, at Trafalgar. Hanging with some girls by the back entrance. What the fuck is that all about?

Things have changed for me, with guys here in school and with Roger's gang, too. They totally treat me with 'spect. And my parents are coming around, like I said. But girls are different. They still don't seem to want anything to do with me. I don't get it. I'm good-looking. My features are symmetrical, I'm tall, have decent muscles, have all my teeth, a good haircut...but girls take one look at me and that's it.

What the hell? What makes me different from Sean, who has pimples and greasy hair but has been going steady with girls since Grade Eight? Or Rob? The dude likes to pick cherries. I'm not even friends with them, so can't ask them outright how they do it, but I hear them talking to their mates. Shit, everyone here has mates and best friends and buddies and a whole other set in the fucking lacrosse and ball teams and steady girlfriends or a roster of wannabe lays...but I have nobody. Except Roger and his druggy band of nerds and I'm supposed to lick their boots for letting me hang with them? Maybe I should tell them about slutty Sarah. Maybe we should shut her up for good.

When, at last, Jo stirs, every movement hurts. Her entire body feels stiff and getting up from the chair is a clumsy, painful affair. Jo tries to pull a deep breath into herself but finds her middle unyielding, tight.

I closed off my heart to you, and with it my ability to breathe.

Before she leaves her studio to stand outside in sub-zero temperatures, staring unseeing at the garden and orchard, her heart as frozen as her fingertips are about to become, she organizes all of the horrific content of her night-long search under five headings, then moves each file, together with the corresponding photographs, onto separate memory sticks with tiny printed labels: Nico's blog, animal cruelty, white power (names, discussions, forums), incel (forums, Sara Gilbertson and Akira Ishida), Lena Newman.

CHAPTER THIRTY-SIX

WALKING WITH SAMSON

Jo lies on the couch next to the roaring fireplace. She was able to build a fire when she returned from the back porch, her hands shaking, her movements clumsy, but the task so routine her limbs completed it on their own. Now she's wrapped in two wool blankets, shivering with cold and fatigue, yawning uncontrollably. She's dimly aware it's almost time to make breakfast, but her mind is too wrought with fragmented thoughts and images to function in any coordinated way. So, she curls into herself, unable to close her eyes, because there, in the darkness, she finds the pictures she wishes she'd never seen.

Time passes in this way. She doesn't know how much. Eventually, she summons all her willpower to slump off the couch and into the bathroom. She sits heavy on the bowl, her shoulders sag forward and her elbows dig into her thighs. What she has uncovered about Nico, about who and what he is, is the worst imaginable. Revulsion, rage, and fear grip her, obliterating all space in which to form coherent thoughts. Then one notion surfaces through the fog: she mustn't tell Paul. He'll find her here, upset beyond what he has ever witnessed, and he'll pry until she shares all she has learned. She mustn't allow that to happen. Paul is a straight shooter; he'll call the police before she'll even finish speaking. And she doesn't want the police to know. Not yet. They'll take her story, then leave her with the burden of knowing before they destroy her family. No, the control must stay with her. Now that she knows, she needs time and space to think. This, she can do. Never panic, never allow the heat of emotions to dictate actions. Instead, think. About next steps and their consequences. About what is needed to shape a fallout that is survivable.

She strips naked and steps into the shower. As she learned from her mother a lifetime ago, she alternates between hot and cold, hot and cold, hot and cold. Her senses are so muted and foggy she hardly notices the difference, but she keeps moving the lever from right to left, left to right. After a long while, Jo begins to feel the needle pricks of the cold water, then the almost unbearable scald, and soon the shocking twin discomforts begin to penetrate her awareness.

Like an old car on a cold, wet morning, her engine begins to sputter.

When Paul comes down, he finds Jo sitting at the kitchen table, hands curled around a cup of instant, and his porridge fixings on the stove.

"Morning love," he says amiably and leans over, kissing the top of her head. "You didn't come to bed last night?"

"I started a shrubby fruticose and had such trouble with it. A dozen false starts before I got even the outline right." Jo yawns, drains her cup, and hands it to Paul. "Would you mind fixing me another? I'm bone tired."

"Sure. Let's see, here. Two teaspoons of instant for a full cup?"

"Please."

Jo sits quietly and watches her husband prepare his oatmeal. She feels slightly nauseated at the thought of food but nods when Paul offers to make her some breakfast. The scent of toast fills the kitchen. Paul butters two golden slices for her, smooths on some raspberry jam, and then cuts the bread into little soldiers, as his mother had done for him when he wasn't feeling well. By the time he sits across from her at the table, Jo's appetite has returned, and she begins to eat.

"I'll grab Samson this morning. A vigorous hike up the mountain is just what I need. Will you bring in the tree today?"

"Yes, I was thinking just that. We can decorate it this afternoon. Some Christmas tunes, a bit of mulled wine. It'll be nice."

"It's a big walk today, my friend. We have a lot to sort out." The amiable Newfie lopes from the RAV's boot and waits patiently until Jo outfits herself with shawl, toque, gloves, and a thermos with hot and sweetened ginger tea, loops the leash across her shoulders, locks the car, and stashes the key deep inside the front pocket of her pants. They set off on the three-mile trail that meanders along the not-too-steep slopes of Trill Hill. Usually, they begin their walk at a brisk pace, but Samson's companion trudges today and he falls back to walk beside her.

She tells him everything. About the morning she and Paul heard the ambulance wail, Luci Miller's visits that seem so portent in hindsight, Nico's apparent fender-bender in the mall's parking lot that had been a lie like everything else that's come out of her grandson's mouth in the past five years. Her budding friendship with Lorna Newman.

"But none of that is the worst of it, Sam. The worst is that this will destroy Oliver."

She stops to catch her breath. She's been talking and walking uphill for the better part of an hour and now has to pause every few minutes. It's cold, probably just above freezing, but the hike has warmed her through. If the thin strands of cloud bunch up over the course of the day, perhaps it'll snow. A white Christmas would be nice.

She snorts. "Here I am hankering for Christmas, Sam. What the hell is wrong with me? How do I tell my son that he's raised a failed human? That *his son* is a monster? And what do you think will happen then? The police, of course. Charges. Hit-and-run or intentional vehicular manslaughter and God knows what else. The press will eat it up. Son of an MP. It'll be the end of both their careers. It'll be the end of their lives. Nothing but stress and worries from here on in. Weekend visits to the prison. Big press coverage every time parole comes up. Christ, Nico is a teen…he'll be out at twenty-one? I have no idea how long we jail kids for the worst crimes, but it won't be long enough for this kid. And then what?"

There must be books on the subject. How do parents and families of headline-makers cope? Surely, some must have written about life after knowing? Or do they all just drown in the morass of regret, guilt, and shame? Every monster in human disguise on this planet has parents, siblings, grandparents, aunties, uncles, and cousins. Sometimes a wife. Sometimes children. "I don't mean normal assholes," she says to Samson, who is sensitive about cussing and looks at her balefully. "Not the reactionary type who lashes out or are just plain dumb.

Whose only coping skill is to yell and smash something. No, I mean truly bad people. People like Nico, who go around purposefully causing pain. Who revel in their so-called superiority by really hurting people." She walks silently for a while, huffing in earnest through the last stretch of the climb.

When they reach the summit, Samson veers off toward the lookout. He knows he has time to leisurely sniff about for scent trails of wildlife and other visiting dogs. Up here, Jo imagines the forest floor tells stories of passing deer and bear, of an owl's meal, a squirrel's desperate search for its hidden walnut stash. The large dog meanders here and there, interested in all the stories shrubs, tree trunks, needle piles, and burrows have to tell, the acrid scents of animal droppings or the last hint of elk musk buried beneath a pile of rotting leaves.

Jo takes in the sight. An opaque midday sun kisses the water three hundred yards below, causing silver sparks to ride tiny crests and giving the calm surface a glistening shine. The strong currents in this formidable strait shepherd seaweed and flotsam into undulating lines. Ripples and eddies variegate the water into all manner of slate-gray, silver, blue, green, and black. Despite the cold of winter and the threat of snow, small fishing and pleasure boats, tugs, three freighters, and even some kayakers explore the coastline. Who knows what swims below them? These waters are home to whales, sea lions, and porpoises but also to the world's largest octopus, biggest barnacles, and huge anemones, never mind the humungous Humboldt squid and scores of other sea creatures. All her life, Jo has been interested in what lies beneath the ocean's surface and yet she has never dived once. Would she be brave enough to try it now, in her dotage? She has seen aspiring divers in the deep end of the pool in Gibsons; decked out in black and blue neoprene suits, learning how to breathe through a mouthpiece. It had seemed safe enough; safer, anyway, than jumping off the dock into the ocean's depth.

Errant thoughts drift in and out of Jo's mind as she overlooks the scenery below. So much beauty. Yet, the question of what to do about Nico overrides all other thoughts. What should she do? What must be done? And when does it need to be done by? How much time can she carve out before she has to share what she now knows? Who needs to be protected from this the most? How?

When she and Samson return to the parking lot and Jo digs out the car keys from her pocket, she has arrived only at one answer. Her foremost duty, as it has always been, is to protect her Ollie.

Later, she sits in the studio.

> *Dear Sarah,*
> *You don't know me, but I am the grandmother of one of the boys who hurt you and your friend Akira. I found out on my own, and he doesn't know that I know yet. I'm sorry for what happened to you.*
> *I have looked through all the newspapers from that time and have found only one police report about having identified the body in the burned-out car as Akira Ishida. The way the article read, it sounds as though the police took her death as yet another casualty of local gang warfare. I'm guessing you haven't told anyone what really happened that day. As a mother, I think Akira's parents would want to learn why their daughter's life was taken.*
> *It may be shame that stops you, or guilt or fear. I understand all those feelings...have worn*

guilt and shame like a too-heavy blanket and know it can smother you.

And then there is the anger and rage at the men who did this. I cannot call them boys because their crime was adult, and they deserve to be punished for it.

I will see to my grandson. I promise you that.

I wanted you to know this. That I know what happened, that you're not alone, and that it was wrong. And for my grandson, for who and what he is, I am sorry.

Find someone to talk to.

And forgive yourself, for your sake, and for Akira's.

J.

CHAPTER THIRTY-SEVEN

BORN A PERFECT CHILD

After she returns from her walk with Samson, Jo and Paul decorate the tree with the same baubles they've used for over thirty years. They carefully unwrap glass icicles and fragile colored orbs and hook them over the branch tips of the ten-foot noble fir, string popcorn garlands and tinsel, and top the whole affair with a golden Gabriel, the heavenly trumpet player. An assortment of beeswax candles on a side table in place of a nativity scene. At the end of it, Paul plugs in the lights, and they sit on the couch, admiring their handiwork. Jo leans into Paul's shoulder and sighs deeply.

"Pretty as always," she murmurs. "And festive and maybe even a bit emotional. I think I'm getting a trifle sappy in my old age."

"You and me both, baby." Paul slips his arm around her shoulder and pulls her close. "Every year it gets more nostalgic, with more fond memories. Am feeling a bit sentimental myself."

They sit in quiet contemplation. Jo feels tired and worn but no longer panicky. The rawness from the morning has transformed into a leaden weight, uncomfortable below her sternum. She imagines it to be a globe of dark energy that spins slowly and gathers all stray thoughts, deliberations, and unfermented plans into itself. She still has not even a hint of an idea how to proceed with Nico but this bodily heaviness tells her that she needs time to allow the answers to come to her. *Business as usual*, she thinks warily, *I'll just have to fake it for a while.*

Over the next few days, they bake. Paul loves Christmas baking and every year produces an astounding array of cakes and cookies to give away as presents and to share with neighbors. Jo creates a colorful gingerbread house for the annual village competition at the library. They share the kitchen space amiably, wash each other's dishes, wait their turn at the mixer, move away from the countertop when the other needs it to knead. They listen to the radio's cheesy seasonal tunes and then blast those into the stratosphere with an AC/DC album played at full volume. They drink more rum than they mix into the batter. They laugh, dance, and sing, lick each other's spoons and nibble on still-warm cookies.

The weight in her middle grows heavier each day.

If she tells Paul, he'll call the police. No doubt. There is no universe in which he wouldn't reach for the phone and the "proper" authorities.

If she tells Oliver, he won't know what to do at all, but will simply break under the weight. He, who has survived the unimaginable, will not be able to reach for his strength because he believes that Nico is the good and healthy thing that came from him.

After the successful transplant and Ollie's near-miraculous transition to almost perfect health, he and Gina had started to talk about babies. Why shouldn't they have? CFers were walking around with new lungs all over the planet, some already for ten years, and the research into optimal treatments for continued health after organ transplantation was in full swing and promised new milestones. Who knew anything those days? Maybe he'd live to be seventy!

Oliver was infertile, of course, but not because his body couldn't produce healthy sperm. It could, and it did, and Jo spent a fairly uncomfortable afternoon listening to Ollie's detailed description of his well-functioning anatomy. He was so excited about the mere idea of being a father that he veered instinctively back into the comfort zone that had existed between them when he was younger. Oversharing. "Everything works like it should, and Gina is totally healthy, and so all we really have to do is extract the sperm and then put it where it would normally go, anyway. No big deal," he'd told her.

He came to Jo for moral support, medical know-how, and also money, because he wanted not only his sperm to be genetically tested and altered for cystic fibrosis, but also the eventual fetus. That kind of testing was available in the States and cost a small fortune. "It can rule out not only CF, but all sorts of other inherited diseases. Imagine not having to worry about your kid being born with hemophilia or getting muscular dystrophy or heart disease. We can totally ensure our child would be one hundred percent healthy. Just imagine!"

But you wouldn't exist! she wanted to shout. *If such testing had been around in the seventies, should I have aborted you? You wouldn't be here!* She couldn't think past the monstrosity of it and stared at her son who, oblivious to her shocked bewilderment, talked on. "Did you know that Italians have the most diverse DNA on the planet? I don't really understand why that is, but higher molecular diversity means a higher chance of good health. So, if they take my CF gene out and then with Gina's massively diverse DNA, we'd have a perfect baby!"

When she'd looked into the future, she hadn't seen an auburn-locked miracle child on the swing. Instead, she'd seen her Ollie wilting under the strains of parenthood. *Family is hard*, she'd thought. *Can't you see the toll it's taken on your father and me? Don't you understand the unfathomable weight of fear and stress and sorrow we had to shoulder because we decided that having a child was what we wanted? Sure, you might get lucky and conceive a ten-toed wunder-baby, but she can still get leukemia at four. Or drown at ten. Or fall under the spell of drugs by fourteen. And that'll be your burden to carry, forever and a day. There is no escape, my boy, from parenthood, once you sign up.* She wanted to say this all aloud to her son, but didn't.

Instead, she told him, "It's not really fair to the child, is it, when you won't live long enough to see him graduate."

"But I might," Oliver replied with an edge of steel in his voice. "I just might."

She didn't mind the money. She had it, in no small part thanks to Ollie's treacherous body. Lichen and her artistry would have never entered her life if it hadn't been for her boy and his sticky lungs. So, Jo paid for the extensive genetic profiling. And then Nico was born a perfectly healthy child. Eight pounds and six ounces. Apgar score of ten. He hit all his developmental milestones on target and showered his besotted family with sweet, never salty, kisses. He was smart and funny and felt like a miracle. Sometimes, Jo looked at him in wonder and marveled that this boy had made all of it worthwhile.

Jo thinks about those moments of enchantment now, when she is sitting on the couch with Paul, mugs of mulled wine in hand, Nat King Cole's *Christmas Song* floating softly through the cookie-scented rooms. How wrong she had been. Oliver's miracle baby has taken his optimal health and his middle-class privilege to mean that the world owes him. And now the piper wants to be paid. Jo knows that the price will be too high.

"Remember when Ollie had that big bleed in Montreal?" For the past three days, she has blurted out random thoughts whenever she skates too close to the edge of telling Paul everything. Keeping secrets is hard.

"How could I forget?" Paul answers, his voice soft. "I believe I'd argued strenuously against going to uni in a place where the medical system is so different and he doesn't even speak the language. It was horrible that he had to learn the hard way."

"I was just thinking about the doctor, Lucien Lafayette," Jo continues. "He was amazingly good. I watched the whole procedure, although he resented me being in the room, but he was just so skilled. He had the perfect sense of timing when to inject a little more, when to pull back the catheter, when to advance through a difficult, knotty branch. It was artistry in motion. I should have probably sent him a Christmas card."

"There's still time," Paul chuckles.

CHAPTER THIRTY-EIGHT

CHRISTMAS VACATION IN BRANDON

Sergeant Rudinsky has very firm ideas about just what makes a good workplace, and he never fails to negotiate with the brass. So, rotating between holidays, each team gets vacation time together, just in case members want to vacation together or invite each other to their weddings in far-flung, sunny destinations. No one is getting married this time around, but it's their turn to have Christmas and New Year's off, and Rudd's team has been making plans for months. Rudd and his husband are off to Rio de Janeiro, Danielle and her boyfriend of two years are heading to an ice hotel in Quebec. Jagwir's entire multi-generational family is going skiing in Fernie, and Ki-woo and her roommate Lorraine are headed for bottomless jugs of margaritas along Mexican beaches.

Luci goes home. She arrives in Brandon with bags of Christmas gifts for her nieces and nephews, her sisters and brothers, her in-law sibs, her parents, and Grandma Phyllis. Phil for short. It's Phil who pulls everyone home for Christmas; whose infectious joy about Gumdrop cake and family visits acts like elastic in the ties that unite them. Phil, who had been born

Ruslana Onyshchenko in Pavlograd, Ukraine in the middle of the Second World War and who had transformed into Phyllis Powell, the good-natured matriarch of a sprawling Prairie family. Every Christmas, the Powell, Steadman, Miller, and Oulette clans gather from all reaches of the continent and descend on Brandon. They camp in bunk beds and pull-outs in the original homestead still hobby-farmed by one grandkid, they rent Airbnbs and hotel rooms, are never too shy to ask old neighbors for shelter, and fight over who gets to stay in the family rooms in Phil's retirement residence. Phil's kids are home for the holidays.

Luci had considered, for about thirty seconds, to invite Grant. His parents live in Charlottetown on Prince Edward Island but spend their winters in Florida. Grant says he'd rather dive naked into a tank of Piranhas than spend even one week in a seaside retirement community where golf carts have license plates. And so he would have been, technically, available but.... Luci looks around the crammed living room where beer-fueled conversations meander from politics to church and state, card games and puzzles coexist in tight spaces, and two teens, wearing elaborate headgear, are immersed in virtual reality gamery. In the kitchenette, aproned aunties wield spoons, beat batter into submission, sing and drink, and drink and sing. Grant would love this, would be welcomed raucously, and would fold himself with ease into the large group. But is she ready for this? Luci doesn't want to bring a different guy every Christmas and isn't sure yet whether Grant will stick around. Or if she'll want him to. If they're good for each other long-term. So far, they're having a blast, are smitten and compatible in temperaments and interests. Luci feels the heat of a blush spread across her neck as she remembers their last date. Grant had been studying her body like he examines maps; learning her topography by sight and feel, he wants to know how her skin reacts to every touch, every breath and flicker of tongue. They had showered together just before he drove her to the airport and Grant had lathered her whole body in sudsy, slippery foam, and then....

"Aunt Luce, can you French braid my hair?" Giselle, her twelve-year-old niece plops onto the couch beside her and holds out elastics. "I tried to do it myself but my arms get tired."

Luci laughs and banishes her X-rated thoughts before leaning into the task. When she looks up, she sees that Grandma Phil, on her perch in the easy chair next to the fireplace, anchored a wistful smile onto her face, before falling into slumber.

CHAPTER THIRTY-NINE

CHRISTMAS

Oyster Hill is splendidly snowed in on Christmas day, but the highway department does its job and keeps the roads passable. Everyone in town who has a pickup truck also seems to have a snowplow attachment, and most residents walk around with handheld sand and salt distributors. An un-treed hill behind the fire hall is perfect for sledding and Ms. Johnson, in time-honored tradition, receives four cords of split firewood in exchange for her duck pond becoming the communal rink. Dads install sideboards and string lights, neighbors bring benches and propane firepits. In this little town, Christmas is as picture-perfect as a Hallmark card.

Gina has no difficulty driving up the hill in her 2018 Land Rover, and the Nelson family share a magnificent meal and thoughtful and quite expensive gifts. Nico is beside himself when he finds the photograph of a blue Ford Fiesta in his card, a gift from his parents, and a gift certificate for twelve driver's ed classes, specifically including night lessons and driving in snow and ice, which is a present from his grandparents.

"You guys, this is awesome," he repeats over and over. "Just awesome!"

The car, which apparently had been named one of the safest for young drivers, will be ready for pickup on January fifth, and Nico jokes that he'll barely be able to eat until then, before putting away a large bowl of trifle with vanilla ice cream.

Jo had been a nervous wreck before Ollie, Gina, and Nico arrived, fearing she might burst the second they all climbed out of the car. But miraculously, she is as cool as a cucumber; she hugs Ollie hard, Gina less so, and ruffles Nico's hair in the way he hates, smiling widely. If food is a form of love, then it would speak for her, and she had been cooking up a storm for Ollie, pouring her guilt for suspecting him into bubbling pots and pans. She is, of course, aware that her throat tightens every time she looks at her grandson, that she cannot hold him or sit close to him, but no one else notices and the mood in the house is merry, amiable, and kind.

After everyone goes to bed—Paul wearing his new blue flannel Christmas pajamas, Ollie and Gina in the double bed in Nico's room, and Nico himself on the couch in the living room—Jo sits in her studio and stares hard at green. Her chest is so tight that she has to force air to move in and out, has to push, like through a too-small straw, for her belly to expand. Every exhale has to drive through the knot of despair and hate inside her chest. Yes, she hates Nico. What he has become. The person in his pictures and blogs. In the discussions he archived with other hateable people on male dominance, white supremacy, able-mindedness, able-bodiedness. She's had time to consider, and she is very certain that Nico's hate-filled tirades are more than juvenile boundary-pushing. Way more. Infinitely more. He has become the monster. The kind who rapes an unconscious, dying girl. Who drives a big, heavy truck into a crowd. The type that shoots into groups of kids or women or families. Her grandson is a true monster and she must stop him. Not only that, but she must, at all cost, prevent

Ollie from following her down this rabbit hole. Her Ollie-Golly, Goofy-Doofy. Who could have been killed a thousand times over by a bug so small you need a microscope to see it. Or a raspy cough that tears a shred of tissue. Or if his heart had failed in the transplant surgery. Ollie, who has survived so much, has weathered so many storms. But he has no mettle for this. How could he? How could anyone? It will destroy him. He'll trace every parental decision, every rebuke, every time-out, every "go-to-your-room" back to himself, will search every instance where he could have acted differently. Heck, he will even question the medically-assisted retrieval of his sperm and will always, undoubtedly, arrive at the conclusion that every parent comes to: *It is my fault. I did this.* Ollie will believe, of that she is certain, that he survived cystic fibrosis only to fail at fatherhood. And in time, he will trace it back to her, too. *You made me survive,* his eyes will accuse, *and see what happened.*

It gets easier to pretend after Ollie and Gina leave. Gina, who had become Canada's newest MP exactly five and a half weeks ago, has to return to Ottawa on Boxing Day, so Oliver takes her to the Sechelt airport at six in the morning and carries on from there to the city. Nico will stay for a few days and enjoy the peace and quiet of a small-town Christmas. Paul has promised to take him snowshoeing, and the Weatheralls, their hobby-farm friends, want Nico to come out for a couple of hayrides. Jo will deliver him to Vancouver on the twenty-seventh.

Until then, she vows to live moment-by-moment, putting her years-long meditation practice to good use inside the sealed vacuum of her own knowing. The house looks and smells festive and is stuffed with joy and laughter. They play board games, bake even more cookies, cook even more food. They visit with friends and neighbors, tell long-winded, ridiculous stories about frozen water nymphs, octopuses in boxing rings, and Ogopogo, the green-scaled lake monster of the Okanagan. They dance to old records and watch all their favorite Christmas movies while eating popcorn and drinking mulled plum wine. It's a glorious holiday.

In the morning, Paul starts the RAV for her and lets it warm up. He scrapes all the hoar frost off the windows and puts an extra car blanket into the boot. Jo takes a thermos of chai with her, and Nico places his large travel bag into the trunk.

"Bye, Grumps," he says and gives his grandfather a warm hug. "Thanks for everything and have a very happy New Year."

"You too, Nico. Drive carefully."

Nico grins happily and slides into the passenger seat, Jo hugs Paul tight.

"I love you forever," she says and Paul replies, "I love you too, Jo," meaning it, as always.

Jo and Nico drive silently for a while, and when Jo enters on to the highway, Nico clears his throat.

"Everything okay, Gran? You're quiet."

His grandmother doesn't respond. She stares straight ahead, her jawline set. White knuckles on the steering wheel.

"Gran, are you ill? Maybe we should turn around and go back. Grumps can drive me."

"Nico." Her voice seems scratchy. Maybe that's why the sound of his name rings like an accusation. "I know what you did. All of it."

His grandmother's features remain stony. Hard. Her voice cuts into him like a blade.

"The dog, Nico. You drowned poor Coco and then you beat her to death."

How could she know that? Nico swallows, looks away from Gran.

"And the girls. Sarah and Akira."

A whirling sensation twists in his stomach. Like a gyroscope swinging and turning. He feels sick.

"And Lena Newman."

"Gran, what are you saying?" His voice is squeaky. He wants to swallow and clear his throat, but the skin inside his mouth is parched. He wants to turn his head to look at her, but his muscles won't obey. He sits muted and unmoving. *How is this possible?*

"I'm saying I know who you are, and that your father is not to be blamed."

His grandmother's voice is like a hammer. *Bam. Bam. Bam.* He wants to put his hands against his ears, but his arms hang limply by his side.

"And I have cancer. Near my heart. I don't think I can survive it."

Cancer? What? The tightness that had gripped his body is loosening. He takes a shuddering breath. So, this is a deathbed confessional? She wants to take their secrets to the grave? Her last wish is his promise to reform?

"Gran, I can explain. Roger and his gang bullied me. I wanted to go to the police and tell, but they threatened me."

He had this one down pat, had laid it out in his brain if the police ever came calling. Everyone knew Roger was the leader of his little group. And so, he would take the fall.

"Actually, I'm kind of glad you found out. I can finally talk about it." He thinks for a moment. "Maybe, if you wouldn't mind, you could come to the police with me? Help me?" He turns to look at her, opens his eyes wide to appear vulnerable and hopeful, sets his mouth straight like he understands the seriousness of the situation. Inside his head though, panic roils. "Gran, how do you even know?"

She slides her hand into her coat pocket and when she brings it back out, her fingers are closed around something. She reaches over and drops the contents into his lap. Nico stares at several flash drives. He picks one up and reads the printed label. *Lena Newman.* He drops it as though it burns his fingers. He grabs another: *Nico's blog.* Nico turns sideways, looks at his grandmother open-mouthed, all theatrics forgotten.

"I found out because I hacked your computer," Gran says, her face a mask of bitter resolve. "That's how I learned what you really are." She keeps her hands on the steering wheel, her eyes on the road. Her lips barely move when she continues. "Everything I found, everything damaging to you, is on those five memory sticks. All the evidence a prosecutor could dream of."

"Are you taking me home, Gran?" Nico's voice is hoarse. "Or to the police?"

She doesn't answer. Her jaw is set so hard, he can see the little bone knob on the top of her cheek. They drive on in silence.

When they arrive at the ferry terminal in Langdale, Nico waits until the car stops at the ticket booth, opens the door, and bolts toward the washroom. The single stall is open, and the metal door clangs when he slams it shut and locks himself in. Now, here in the confined space that reeks of sweat and urine, he stands uncomfortably close to the none-too-clean toilet bowl and tries to force himself to breathe deeply.

Holy fuck, old grannie has him by the balls. His grandmother is fierce and smart, he kind of admires her, she stands head and shoulders above his parents when she commits, but now... this...is she going to unload all her steel on him? Drag him to the Vancouver police station and rat him out? But then why give him the sticks? He opens his clenched fist and stares at the small plastic pieces. His blog! Gran had read his blog. Made *copies* of it. Nico can't breathe, and a caustic burn scratches the back of his eyeballs. He had never held back on his blog, had poured his disgust and hate into it, but he had also exaggerated. Wanted to sound bigger and badder than he was. Painted himself terminator steel gray when he was, at best, only a hanger-on. And the kid on the bike was a true accident, no intention involved. An accident.

He drops two of the flash drives into the grimy bowl and flushes, waits until the tank is full again, and then sluices with the other three. Then he takes the first truly deep breath in ages, no longer noticing the reek. Surely, Gran had given him the sticks as a warning. She'll want to talk about it, make him confess and regret and promise so that she can go to her grave in peace. He can give her that. They can talk all the way home and of course she'll never tell his parents. That goes without saying. She'll do anything to prevent her precious Oliver from stressing out. This whole thing will be their secret and she'll lord it over him...but then, she said she has cancer, so it won't be for long.

Nico exits the stall and stares numbly at the guy in a suit washing his hands. He hadn't even heard anyone come into the washroom, let alone use the urinal.

"Hey kid, you alright? You're mighty pale around the gills."

"Fuck off." Nico wants to shout but his voice comes out like a whisper. He gives the guy the finger, but even that gesture comes off mostly lame. He turns to walk out of the john and pulls on the heavy door. He has misjudged the placement of his feet and the door catches him on the shoulder with a painful whack and grazes his temple. Shit, he's losing it. *Hold it together*, he admonishes himself, *this is Gran. She gets pissed sometimes but never for long and she sounds like a bear and can take your head off over spilled milk, but she is Gran. An old woman who's going to die soon.*

He feels relief at that, not sorrow. On the way to the red RAV, now parked in line for the ferry, he sees his grandmother's shape in the driver's seat and does what she taught him eons ago. Can even hear her voice inside his head: *When you're feeling upset, do an emotional inventory. Name your feelings. Are they anger or sadness, shame or humiliation? What brought the reaction on? What lies behind it? Is it helpful to you, or to the situation, to act on this feeling now? Or can you moderate your instinctual response?*

So, he is fucking angry. Because she stuck her nose into his private business. Not that a blog is one hundred percent private, but he posts under an alias in a dark web forum. What was she even doing there? He has every right to be angry and he'll tell her.

And he's scared, admittedly. If she talks to the police, he'll be in hip-deep shit, although, a good lawyer will make it go away. He hadn't killed the kid on purpose—just couldn't hit the brakes fast enough. And he ran because he doesn't have a learner's yet and isn't supposed to be in a car by himself. A misdemeanor, or whatever. And the thing with the girls—well, he was definitely being coerced into participating. Everyone at Point Grey knows he's a loner, excluded by his peers, that he fell in with Roger's clique by default.

So, what's the worst that can happen? No more holidays at Gran and Grumps. About time. His parents will hate him, but he hated them first, so no loss. The kids in Trafalgar will ignore him, but he's used to that, already. So, overall, no big deal. He can handle it.

As he walks the narrow space between all the parked cars waiting to board the ferry, he slows. Maybe sitting in dead silence and Gran's furious mood-fog is not what he needs right now. He saunters right by her car, wants to kick at the tire but holds it in. Instead, he glares at her with all his fury, but she's angled away, looking out over the water, and doesn't even see him. Nico carries on slowly, angrier, sidles between two massive commercial trucks, and emerges next to the foot passenger waiting room. He slouches inside, hurls himself into a seat, and glowers at a wall strewn with pamphlets.

It's no wonder artists of all stripes move to this place, Jo thinks as she watches the late morning sun striate the hazy clouds. Coastal humidity lends colors and pastels at this latitude not seen elsewhere. Faint blue, rose, and lilac filters over the misty rainforest, over massive rocky shores, and onto the calm, glassy surface of the ocean. Everywhere her gaze falls, she sees precious beauty and her heart aches with the pain of loss.

She wonders if Nico will return to the car. He might catch a ride with any one of the many drivers in the lot; a well-mannered, clean-cut kid like Nico who can spin a story would have no problem getting a lift into town. No matter. It's a gorgeous day and now that she's sure of what she must do, she will find an opportunity, whether that day is today or not. Certainty has given her composure, has allowed her heart to settle into a calm, steady rhythm, has freed her lungs into easy expansion. Her resolve will not weaken.

Nico boards the ferry on foot, watches out of the corner of his eyes that his grandmother drives on, as well. That car. The red RAV. The sight of it had jolted him with pleasure all through the holidays, but now he feels only reluctance as he approaches the open driver's side window.

"Do you want to talk about it?"

She doesn't answer, stares straight ahead.

"Gran, I can take a bus on the other side. Just pop the trunk for me, okay?"

She turns her head then. Looks at him so long, he lowers his eyes. Her face is a mask—he doesn't remember ever seeing her this flat. He wants to turn and walk away but can't. He feels trapped by her cold eyes.

"No," she says quietly in a voice he doesn't recognize, "no bus. I'll drive you home."

He walks around the car, slides into the passenger seat. Breathes as slow as he can. Moves words around in his brain, prepares answers. For her, his parents, the police. People will come with accusations and questions. He'd better get ready.

They drive off the boat and before the many lanes of traffic converge for the highway, Jo pulls over to allow all the impatient ferry passengers to shoot by. She rummages in her purse and brings out a small glass jar. Before leaving home, she had filled it with her most favorite Christmas treat. She takes one and puts it in her mouth, closes her eyes as the sweet chocolate begins to melt and is chased by the sharp tang of ginger. John Lennon's Christmas song plays in her head. She turns to look at Nico. He's slouched over his phone, avoiding her gaze and any conversation. There's nothing to talk about, anyway. She hands him a small napkin parcel from her purse, which he takes without raising his head. Shortbread from his grandfather.

Jo pulls up the steep, long hill, and when they emerge into the open, the ocean's glossy surface shimmers several hundred yards below. The curvy four-lane highway is built into the side of massive rock walls and granite boulders that reach skyward from the ocean waters. Early settlers might have looked for mountain passes to traverse, but the Stó:lō peoples of old had carved out trading routes along these cliffs hundreds of years ago, and the newcomers had eventually built the aptly named Sea to Sky highway. Driving along here, Jo always feels close to heaven, feels as though she soars like an eagle. She watches Oliver's son, still crouched forward, chewing, eyes on the small screen. At sixteen, he is taller than his father ever was, with long legs and arms that suggest another growth spurt is yet to come. His hair is walnut brown and curls a bit at the tips when he allows it to grow past his ears. He is winter-pale and seems to sink into himself in the passenger seat. She looks ahead, onto the road. A sharp curve is coming up, after which, as she knows, there is a long, flat expanse for a quarter mile marking the summit before the highway plunges into the city. Jo takes a long breath, negotiates the curve, then turns her head again.

"Nico." Her voice is sharp. "I'm not sorry. I have thought and thought about what to do. This is the only way."

Her foot pushes on the accelerator as she watches Nico raise his head, confused and alarmed. Then she wrenches the wheel over.

At twenty minutes after twelve, on December twenty-seventh, the 9-1-1 call center of the Squamish-Lillooet Regional District receives a flurry of calls about a red car that has gone off the cliff on the Upper Levels Highway. It must have wiped out on black ice, although, when witnesses are questioned later, no one remembers seeing the car spin or slide. Several vehicles pull over and people converge on the unbarricaded ledge to peer down. The rocky, ice- and snow-covered slope is incredibly steep, and the tumbling car has created a trail of destruction, leaving scraped granite and broken trees in its wake. The onlookers cannot see where the vehicle has landed or if there might be any survivors. Forty minutes later, soon after search and rescue personnel begin to rappel down the rocky façade and shortly after the helicopter arrives to hover above the scene, the operation's status is changed to a recovery mission.

CHAPTER FORTY

LUCI IN THE CAVE OF DIAMONDS

Luci stares open-mouthed at the kaleidoscope of blue. Patterned facets of ice swirl and flow in undulating waves, the crystal reflecting the wintry sunlight above her in brilliant shades of blue. It's overwhelming. Her heart thumps forcefully, her throat burns with the cold, and tears of wonder press at the backs of her eyes. Her legs shake uncontrollably after the arduous hike, and she leans heavily on her trekking poles. If only her body would still so her brain can take in the indescribable beauty surrounding her.

They had left the kayaks near the tidewater entrance of the glacier, had put on their hard hats, packed their crampons, and set out across the glacial moraine, an area where centuries of rock and dirt convene into a field of uneven debris. Once they reached the ice field, they spiked their shoes and angled northeast, following Grant's handheld GPS. He'd marked out this route last summer but warned that the glacier's constant movement might have shifted the entrance of the cavern or even collapsed the entire cave.

"There are no guarantees with glaciers," he'd explained. "Everything is in constant motion, from the accumulating rain and snowfall on top to the fluctuating melting points from seasonal shifts and climate change. Glaciers are fluid and unstable, and ice caves are unpredictable."

She'd wanted to go anyway, of course. What's life without risk? Grant had taken pictures from inside the icy grotto in the summer; they're so otherworldly, so surreal that she'd jumped at the chance to come herself. The forecast for the southwestern corner of the Yukon predicted clear skies for a week or more, so Luci changed her ticket and flew from Brandon to Whitehorse for the last few days of her vacation.

Grant had prepped his Bell helicopter and outfitted it with clothing, food, and kayaks, and they went out in morning darkness, due north-northwest. After two hours, they landed north of Destruction Bay and slipped their kayaks into the frigid waters of the Donjek River before sunrise, just after eleven o'clock. Now they'll have four and a half hours of daylight. Half an hour hard paddle to the moraine, an hour hike, at least, to where the cave's entrance had been, half an hour wiggle room to find its new location, and another inside, if they're lucky enough to find it, and then the hurry back. But don't hurry too fast...a misstep into a glacier's crevasse would spell disaster, so they'll have to move with the greatest of care, always.

They set out into the river in the leaden light of dawn, cross the fissured ice field with their dim shadows shortening noticeably. Before they reach the GPS-indicated spot, Grant whoops with joy and points excitedly at an indistinct gray mass just in front of him.

"Here it is, it shifted about a hundred meters downstream."

An ice cave is a labyrinth or dome of ice forming inside a glacier over a stream of melting water in the summer. The warm water vapor rises and melts the skin of ice above, causing it to drip into the flowing river. All summer long, this slow and steady process hollows out the inside of the dome and the patterned ceiling recedes in undulating waves. The higher the ceiling, the thinner the remaining ice, and the more sunlight can penetrate and suffuse, if there isn't a meter of fresh snow. If the snow doesn't break the weakened ceiling.

They are lucky. The cave is cathedral-like and the sun, now approaching its zenith, low to the horizon as it is, shines brilliantly through smooth, faceted layers of blue ice. Everything inside is blue, blue, blue. Eternal and ephemeral, ice from millennia ago in a cave that might be gone in weeks. Ancient and newborn. After a few moments, Luci's breath regulates. Her eyes cast about this surreal world where every shade of blue reflects from crystal formations and sculptures. She is aware of an alien kind of silence that blends with echoing sounds from deep within the ice. She stands still and stares in wonder.

After what seems to her like just minutes, Grant touches her arm.

"We've got to go, Luci. Our time is up."

Her senses are still so overwhelmed she barely hears him. But her training as a police officer has primed her to follow orders, and this allows her to shift focus. Like drawers, she shuts her unfiltered intake of sights, scents, and sounds, wipes her mittened hands across her face to interrupt the languid settling of vapors on her skin. Grant had cautioned her that hiking across the moraine in darkness is foolhardy at best. The ever-shifting ground opens fissures and crevasses underneath a deceptively thin layer of ice, and a fractured tibia would only be the beginning of all manner of misfortune resulting from a misstep on the glacier after dark.

"We may feel like outdoorsy type of people," he'd said, holding solemn eye contact during his prep speech this morning after they'd strapped into their seats. "But we're city folks, by and large. We're not used to being out on the land after dark and have no skillset, no tools, and no smarts about being out there in total darkness. We're okay in the bird without daylight, but not on the glacier."

"You're the pilot," she had said genially, meaning it, and this is what she remembers now, as she stands rooted in the blue effervescence of light.

"Did anything ever develop in that hit-and-run involving the painter? The one whose art show we went to?" Grant nuzzles her neck, holding her tightly from behind as Luci is washing up the last of their dishes. They're in Whitehorse, the day following their excursion to the ice cave, and they haven't left Grant's apartment all day. She'll be flying home tonight to start work tomorrow morning. Grant is helping her shift her focus from vacation to work. *Thanks a lot.* She sighs.

"Nothing yet. I can't shake the feeling that someone from the Nelson family was the driver, but which one?"

She turns to face him and begins to count on her still-wet fingers.

"It could be Jo herself, of course. She talks a good talk about being sensitive to family pain, but she also lies. She's definitely hiding stuff. Maybe those things have nothing to do with the hit-and-run, but every time I meet her, she's running circles around me in an effort to muddy the waters. I can't see her reason to be out in her car at six in the morning, but maybe that's part of what she's keeping close to her chest? If her car is a match and she continues to be less than forthcoming, then she moves into the prime suspect slot."

Luci taps her middle finger.

"It could be Paul. The silent background guy. He's not quite doddery enough to not have noticed the bump, so we'd have to assume he was aware and fled. But, and I asked a pharmacist about this, he is taking a sleeping pill every night. Do that for too long and you might suffer blackouts during which you could very well be driving a car. Jo would lie to protect him, of course. But why would he be out in his wife's car to begin with? I asked at the local service station, and he's never seen driving the RAV."

Ring finger.

"Then there's Nico. He's in that teenage phase where they look guilty no matter what. A bit awkward, unsure, reluctant. Not super keen to bare his soul. He has motive to drive his gran's car in secret because he just likes to drive. Maybe he takes the RAV for a spin late at night or early in the morning all the time. That's unlikely, but it could still be true. He comes over the hill and is too inexperienced to react with speed. Hits her, then panics, of course, and hightails it home to hide under the covers of his still-warm bed."

Pinkie.

"Oliver. He drives a Barcelona Red Metallic Matrix. He was on the road that morning and would have come right through the subdivision. He was under-slept, stressed, and in a hurry. His mother lied about him being there by omission and he didn't come forward to the police about it, either. He says because he never learned about the accident and Lena Newman, but whatever. Words are cheap." She thinks about Oliver's enraged face after he emerged from the washroom at the gallery. About the sound that could have been a teenager trying to swallow his tears.

Luci finishes packing her bag when she returns to the earlier conversation. "If it's Oliver and the lab comes back with a positive match to the Matrix, the case is in the bag because Oliver is the sole driver. If it's the RAV, we're still none the wiser unless someone begins to talk truth. If everyone keeps lying, we'll charge Jo as the car's owner."

"What if it was Nico?"

"If he confesses, he'll be charged and go to juvie court. Jail time is unlikely, rather community hours, a fine, and a lengthy driving prohibition. If he and Jo continue to lie and Jo gets charged and convicted on circumstantial evidence, she'll go to prison. A couple of years, perhaps."

"Wow." Grant looks at her, frowning. "That would be a pretty messed-up message for a teenager if his grandmother goes to prison to protect him." He puts air quotes around the word "protect." "That would be truly warped. From how you describe her, I didn't get that she's out to lunch. You think she might let it come to that?"

Luci remembers Jo holding out her wrists, laughing, mischief flashing in her eyes, asking to be handcuffed and taken to a nice jail where she would meet new friends and have a wretched affair with a guard. And she remembers the tight line of Jo's mouth when the older woman felt threatened by Luci's questions, the cold look, the way her expression had set into granite, how her words had become bullets: fast, hard, and delivered to maim.

"I honestly don't know. I think she might walk across corpses when it suits her. She told me that protecting Oliver had been her life's purpose—maybe that extends to Nico. Maybe she knows that Nico drove that morning and is revving up her defensive shields out of habit?"

Luci thinks about Jo and her family on the two-hour flight to Vancouver. Charming Paul, talented Nico, abstruse Oliver, and scheming Jo. If only one of them is pulling the wool over her eyes, then it must be Jo. If it's another, then they're conspiring with her and eventually, their stories will crack. She begins to lay out interview questions for all four Nelsons in her mind.

CHAPTER FORTY-ONE

TERRIBLE NEWS

The next morning, she learns that she won't be interviewing anyone. When she opens her inbox just minutes before eight, a message from the Edmonton lab catches her eye right away. The results must be in! This is weeks earlier than she'd anticipated and she smiles as she opens the mail. It's like a Christmas present.

But it isn't. A Veronica Sterling, Corporal at the Edmonton Forensic Science Centre, informs her in neutral tones that six of her specimens sent from the Vancouver lab had become contaminated with other samples in the same shipment and please resubmit the relevant paint samples in a timely manner, with the bags sealed and packaged according to service-wide standards. Kind regards. The terse message is followed by an itemized and numerical list. Among the six:

4. MVASEP72019O.H.BC-DA20. Paint shards removed with sterilized tweezers near right headlight of red RAV4. HJT 556. Registered owner: Josephine Nelson. DL 8396271. 09/08/2019. LM

Luci slams her hand on the desk and swears loudly. No fucking way! These six samples had been in the last bag from Oyster Hill, and she knows she had processed them exactly the same as thousands of other samples before. Although she could do it blindfolded and with one hand tied to her back, she still pays attention to the process, places items into receptacles with care, seals the bags immediately, and then labels them. Six clear, plastic bags containing a few minuscule shards, plus the tweezers or pick used to remove them, bundled into a larger bag which she had also sealed and labeled. She's still glowering at her screen when Jag's hand falls on her shoulder.

"What's up, buttercup? What gets you all riled first thing in the morning?"

Luci points at the monitor. "Look. I haven't had an issue like this for two years. What the hell happened?"

Jagwir leans in and frowns, clearing his throat.

"Could be anything, Luce. One of the picks slid out of its sheath during transport and punctured the bag. A piece of broken glass or a knife dropped through the whole thing. A fire in the transport van. They must be double-busy there, with Vancouver sending all their cases. Probably didn't get a bump in staff. So, people cut corners, mistakes are made, and un-intended stuff happens. Sorry it happened to you."

"If you have to go to Oyster Hill to retake samples, I can come with, to help and for company. Everything I've got going here can wait until tomorrow," Ki-woo offers.

Luci shakes her head, mollified by her colleagues' solicitous support.

"Nah, thanks guys, I'll deal with it. My bad, perhaps, or theirs, but I'll eat it." She laughs joylessly. "I know for sure that there's no point in calling Edmonton and pleading my case.... The labs log when they reject a sample and can't undo that. No prosecutor would touch it with a ten-foot pole." She sighs.

"Do you want me to phone the helicopter to see if there's a ride available?" Ki-woo asks.

"Oh great, thanks Ki-woo. I'll call the folks in Oyster Hill to find out where they and their cars are today. Hopefully, it'll be just a quick in and out."

Ki-woo and Luci take to the phones, and Jagwir returns to his desk. Twelve members are working quietly this morning; team Rudd has yet to be called out to a new case since they returned from their winter break and are assisting teams Kaur and Taylor with the legwork on their holiday cases. Every year, the accident toll of the festive season is high: CARS logged almost seventeen hundred crashes in the province between Christmas Eve and January 3; of those, nine hundred fall into the RCMP's jurisdiction and the other half are investigated by municipal police. Of the nine hundred, twelve had fatalities and more than a hundred accidents had considerable injuries. The Vancouver section is working fifty-eight of these and every head in the office leans into their screens, murmuring into their headsets.

Luci puts the receiver down and stares into space. Doesn't hear the chatter and snippets of conversations all around her. Hears, instead, Paul Nelson's affectless voice.

"Haven't you heard?" he'd said, with no hint of surprise in his tone. "Jo died a few days ago. Last Friday. While she was driving Nico back to Vancouver. Her first car accident ever." Paul had sobbed then, a short, explosive yowl that stopped as abruptly as it started. In the shocked silence, she heard only his ragged breathing, his fight to control his throat muscles. Then she had managed to pull some words out of her toolbox; after all, she was accustomed to interacting with bereaved families.

The platitudes meant nothing, and that had bothered her because she'd liked Jo and felt her loss. Was stunned, actually, that this vibrant, cranky, skilled, humorous, quick-witted woman was no more. So dumbfounded that she didn't even ask Paul about Nico. Had he died, too? Or is he in the hospital? What a sardonic turn of events if his father now has to spend weeks or months or years of his life watching over his injured son. Luci sits still for a long time, replaying the instances with Josephine in her mind, seeing the older woman through the filter of loss which erases all annoyance she'd felt and leaves only admiration, sorrow, and a hint of gladness that they'd met. Then she turns toward her computer.

Sergeant Rudd looks up when a hand touches his shoulder. Luci stands next to him and the light brown eyes in her unusually pale face are huge.

"Team meet in the conference room, stat," she says tonelessly, hardly moving her lips. Then she turns and repeats her message to Ki-woo, Jags, and Danielle. Less than ten minutes later, they're all assembled in the large conference room around an oblong mahogany table. The morning's dull gray light through the huge windows sets the tone. Luci leans on her elbows, stands only after Danielle closes the door.

"I called the Nelsons in Oyster Hill about half an hour ago to set up a time for me to retake some paint samples," she begins after her team has settled into their chairs and looks at her expectantly. "You'll remember that Josephine's RAV had three potential drivers and significant front-end damage. That car was 'number one' on the probable list."

She pauses. No one interrupts as she gathers her thoughts.

"Josephine's husband answered the call. He said that his wife had had an accident in the RAV, five days ago. Went off the road on the Sea to Sky, just south of Tunnel Point where there's a short section without guard rails. She died in the crash, as did her grandson Nico."

Luci pauses, allowing the quiet of the morning-gray room to settle around them. Rudd clucks sympathetically.

"I couldn't ask him about the car, just gave condolences and hung up soon after. Then I talked to Sergeant Taylor—his team worked the site. He said by the time they were called in, the midday sun had dried up any spots of black ice that might have been there and that there was no oil residue on the pavement. That's in the file. But he also added that the road was as dry as it could be, that there wasn't even any dampness in the treed section just a hundred yards north." She looks at her notebook in front of her. "I talked to Miles Cobb, the Fire Chief in North Van. They coordinated the recovery mission. Chief Cobb designated the vehicle as 'unrecoverable' and ordered no efforts shall be undertaken to winch the RAV up or to approach seaside. This is to be reassessed by next spring, after the last of the snow melts and after the spring rain season. He said that particular section of cliffside is prone to rockslides."

Luci looks at her attentive teammates and continues, "Chief Cobb told me that driver and passenger had been seat-belted, that Josephine Nelson had been behind the wheel. So, I just can't figure this out. What on earth would cause a seasoned driver to go down that cliff if the road is straight and dry as can be? And, to make matters worse, her car is high on the list for the Newman case and now I can't access it for a second sample." Luci breathes out forcefully, feels irritation and sadness swirl in equal measures. "I don't know how to proceed," she finishes, eyes on her notebook.

They sit for a long while and brainstorm. Could they ask the Northshore Search and Rescue Team to rappel down to the car and take a sample? Could they request an autopsy on Ms. Nelson to determine if she'd suffered an adverse medical event? Would a judge compel Ms. Nelson's will in case this had been a planned suicide? But surely, Luci and Jagwir object simultaneously, if she had been planning such a thing, she would have gone over the edge on her way back from Vancouver, after she dropped off Oliver's son. And if it had been her and her car who caused Lena Newman's death, Luci added, the Josephine Nelson she'd encountered over the course of their investigation would have admitted to it. Of that she feels suddenly certain. As certain as a person can be.

In the end, Rudd suggests that the five red Toyotas in Oyster Hill which are accessible for sampling should be processed as soon as possible. And after that, Luci would be needed to dig into work here, because CARS' ratio between files and available manpower was beginning to skew dangerously into overload.

And that is that.

Luci continues to chew on all of this on her way home and long into the night. One thing alone crystallizes with clarity: that she had been more suspicious of Josephine being the driver in the hit-and-run before her death, not after, unlike almost the entire team. Rudd and Danielle, but also Ki-woo to some degree, had all leaned into the possibility that Josephine Nelson had been their "doer," that perhaps she had a medical condition, that perhaps her grandson had argued or accused her and caused a moment of distraction. But Luci cannot accept this. The woman knew how to focus her attention over hours—her paintings spoke to that. She could handle herself in emergencies and knew how to prioritize. If an argument had erupted in the car, Jo would have pulled over. And she certainly had not been the suicidal type. No way.

Luci mulls and grates and knows she may never find the answers. And is aware that, by allowing herself to grieve for a woman she had only ever met a handful of times, she loses objectivity. And that she feels more like a friend left behind than an investigator.

CHAPTER FORTY-TWO

A LAST VISIT

Two weeks later, Luci receives a call from Sergeant Gill from Oyster Hill.

"Corporal Miller, how are you?" he asks with his broad baritone. "Hope I didn't catch you at a bad time."

"Not at all, Sergeant. Just having coffee with the gang. What can I do you for?"

"Well, the Newmans have rung again, asking if there was any news. What do you suggest I tell them this time?"

Luci motions an apology to her colleagues and gets up to walk to a quieter part of the office.

"Sergeant, maybe I should come up and we'll visit them together. Sit in their living room and talk truth. How does that sound?"

"That sounds about right, Corporal. When can you come up?"

"I'll be there the day after tomorrow, by one in the afternoon at the latest. Meet you at the detachment?"

She bums a ride on the RCMP helicopter to Sechelt, borrows a marked car from there, and walks into Stephan Gill's office at a quarter past noon. He raises his eyebrows mockingly.

"The early bird gets a slice of my dessert. Look closely, it's part of the world's oldest Christmas stollen."

Luci laughs. "Town folks regifting to the local peacekeepers?"

"Got that right, Corporal. How was your holiday?"

They chat amicably for a while and then turn to the matter at hand.

"Miriam told me that you'd been up, a couple of weeks ago, to take more samples. Anything come of that?"

"Nothing," Luci responds, blushing slightly as she remembers the affronted and accusing faces of the various car owners when she explained that the original samples had somehow been contaminated. "The Edmonton lab processed those immediately upon receipt," which in Luci's mind was as good as an admission of guilt but she left that unsaid. Sergeant Gill has been around long enough to pick up on that himself. "But they all came back negative."

"I don't have a problem being honest with the Newmans," she continues. "And I don't think it's fair to leave them hanging in the wind any longer, anyway. Are they expecting us?" Luci learns that they are.

Luci and Sergeant Gill drive to Crescent View Road and are cooly but politely welcomed by Lorna and Mark Newman. Luci notes an absence of Christmas ornaments or lights outside, which reminds her, viscerally, that this was the family's first Christmas after Lena's death. It had probably been a somber occasion. She follows their hosts on stockinged feet. There are no baking or coffee smells from the kitchen today, and Mark ushers them into the undecorated living room. The baby, Benny, is nowhere to be seen or heard. Luci and Stephan Gill sink onto the edges of chairs while Lena's parents sit on the couch, hips touching, and gaze expectantly at her.

"Mr. and Ms. Newman, thank you for making time for us. I am afraid that I have no real news for you, but I would like to discuss what's been happening."

She takes a deep breath and, when no one else says anything, continues. "We did not find the car that struck Lena. As you know, we found some paint chips on the road and also minuscule ones on the bicycle itself, so we knew that they hadn't come from a different collision. The chips were confirmed to be from a red Toyota, so we checked all locally registered cars in that category without finding a match. And I mean that we checked them. We went to all the addresses and sometimes to people's workplaces until we could strike every last one off our list. I'm pointing this out not to boast about our work, but because I don't want you to wonder, in the future, every time you see a red Toyota driving down the street or parked outside the post office in town. It has been checked and it was not the car we're looking for. In some cases where we couldn't determine visually, we took paint and metal samples, but none matched what we took off the street that morning."

Mark interrupts. "Don't all cars from a certain year get painted with the same paint? Even allowing for different production lines and equipment, how is one 2000 Camry different from the other?"

"It's the base coat that would differ in relation to factory site and year, as well as microscopic airborne contaminants in between the layers of base, color, and lacquer," Luci replies. "The paint may be the same, but the dust that day in the room or even a worker sneezing inside the sealed paint box prior to application…those are the markers the lab is looking for when they analyze for comparison."

Luci pauses, sitting in the silence.

"The traffic unit also checked the highway cameras," the sergeant continues, "and we checked all the red Toyotas from out-of-towners who had come into or through Oyster Hill that day or during a couple of days before or after Lena's death. And by checking, I mean that a cop went to the house and inspected the car for damage. If there were any signs of anything, they took pictures and sent them to Corporal Miller."

"But nothing came of those, either," Luci picks up the thread. "The lab results had been delayed, due to unforeseen circumstances, but since a couple of days ago, we've received the last results of everything we had sent in." She spreads her hands. "I'm sorry, Mr. and Ms. Newman. We have not been able to find the car."

"Will you keep looking?" Lorna asks quietly. Her eyes are impossibly large and dulled. Dark semicircles spread below them, giving her pale face a masked appearance. She looks so tired and worn, Luci is regretting her impetus to visit here today. The first Christmas after Lena's death in their postcard-perfect village must have knocked the stuffing out of her and Mark. Luci trains her eyes on a picture of Lena and Benny that holds pride of place on the mantel behind Lorna's head.

"Not in the way we have, as in checking evidence against potential matches. We are out of both at this time. But if new information comes to light, such as a witness statement, then, of course, we'd open the investigation again."

There is not much else to say, and Luci and Stephan leave the sad house soon after. They walk quietly to their car.

"Why didn't you mention the Nelson car?" Sergeant Gill asks.

"What would have been the point?" Luci says with a hint of anger. "The samples I had sent in are unusable. Jo and Nico's accident happened before we could get out to collect another one. And now the RAV hangs in some trees on an unapproachable cliffside. Who knows what it'll look like by the spring. After months of snow and rain and lightning strikes. No judge in their right mind would accept the samples. Besides, a storm or two could dislodge the car and hurl it into the ocean."

"And you hadn't let us know about her because…" the sergeant asks quietly.

"Because I had nothing other than my gut," Luci shoots back, defiant and angry. *And because I'd liked her*, she thinks. "It was just one among many, at that time. There was nothing more evidentiary or conclusive about Jo Nelson's RAV than there had been about a dozen other Toyotas with recent front-end damage. We were in the process of elimination, nothing to share with you yet."

They get into the car. Sergeant Gill sits in the driver's seat, his hand on the key, but he hasn't turned it over. Luci puts her seat belt on and turns to face him.

"I don't know, Sergeant. It was a judgment call. I thought if I tell them about Jo's car.… I know that Paul is friendly with them and he and they might grow close now, after Jo's accident, in mutual support. What good would it do to share our thoughts without evidence and proof? And maybe I didn't want to look like a loser whose outfit can't even keep crime scene samples safe and separate." She waits a moment and then asks, "What would you have done?"

EPILOGUE

Katherine Ramirez holds her hands underneath the powerful, skin-pummeling blast of hot air and sighs deeply. The heat is welcome and she lingers, despite the obnoxious noise of the machine. A day before Valentine's, it's barely above freezing today, and the icy outfall from the Arctic nips through the old walls of Trafalgar School and invades classrooms, offices, and even the cafeteria. The custodian, Jesse, is doing all he can to keep the brick and granite building from frosting over, but this year, his efforts prove futile. It's ridiculously cold and drafty everywhere, except here, in the student bathroom on the second floor.

Teachers are prohibited from using student bathrooms, but Kath gets away with it, namely because the rule clearly states "teachers," not "staff." And so, she nips in here when nature calls, the four-stall loo just around the corner from her office. She usually manages to time her pee breaks during regular class hours and rarely encounters any students in here. The last time, in late September, was when she'd come out into the hallway to find Nicholas Nelson standing right outside. He had given

CHRISTINE COSACK

her an eyeful of such radiant loathing that she'd come to a startled stop. They had stood there for a moment, the student unflinching, his eyes unblinking and steadfast on hers—cold, dissecting, hateful. Kath hadn't had her professional counselor mantle on, was only just herself, bustling to the loo last minute, but the boy's ardent hostility aimed directly at her had unnerved her, and she moved quickly away, back to the safety of her office, and felt the relief wash over her when her door became a barrier.

What on earth was going on in that boy? She hadn't met Nicholas yet; he had just transferred into Grade 10 from Point Grey at the beginning of the school year. Transfers from private schools weren't that unusual. Sometimes parents ran out of money, other times students were expelled for not meeting expectations. For that reason alone, Kath felt that private schools should be banned completely, never mind that her tax dollars were hard at work supporting a weeding and filtering system that only served the already privileged. If rich people wanted to invest into a first-tier education for their kids, so be it, but those schools should not suck up government dollars that were so desperately needed elsewhere. And here was Nicholas Nelson, a hoity-toity kid from West Point Grey, standing outside the Trafalgar High School bathroom, filled with hate.

Kath had searched for his file. There wasn't much there. Nico lived in the catchment area of Kitsilano, both his parent's names were on the registration form. His grades were average to better, especially in languages and art. No reason was given for his leaving Point Grey. She had placed a call to Point Grey's counseling office and Jennifer Lundquist had called her back just a few hours later.

"Of course, I can't divulge much," Jennifer had said. Kath knew her by sight from some shared in-services and conferences, but they weren't really acquainted. Even so, she was pretty sure the tone in Jennifer's voice suggested urgency.

"There are a lot of rumors about Nico Nelson. He hung with a group of older boys who are pretty heavy into truancy and drugs, but their parents are rich enough to smooth everything over. Nico's parents are not that well off, so he's taking the fall. A couple of girls came forward and complained about sexual interference and assault, all relating to that group of boys around Roger Hutchinson. Allegations only, you hear, nothing ever went to court." The Point Grey counselor had gone silent for a long moment.

"A few girls talked to me about it. They thought that they were given Rohypnol or something similar. They were certain that they'd been assaulted, felt sore in their vulva, had bruises, woke up nude. But they refused to take their allegations out of the counseling office. Nothing ever came of it."

Jennifer had told her as much as she could within the limits of their professional conduct obligations. Then Kath had updated Nicholas Nelson's file accordingly. If he were to transfer again, his next school would know right off the bat that he was a bad egg. Kath had no compulsion to protect sexual predators. She stopped using the bathroom around the corner from her office and began to ask a few, carefully worded questions of all kids who came to see her. Girls and boys.

And then Nico died. In a horrible traffic crash. They were told on the first day of class after Christmas, and Kath had added extra office hours and invited kids to come talk to her. *Sometimes, when disaster befalls a peer, someone just like us, someone from our midst, we get worried that it could happen to us, too*, she had written in a memorandum the office sent to all students' email accounts. *Come see me if you want to talk about your experiences in the face of this tragedy.*

Over the past five weeks, some new faces had appeared in her office. Kids who hadn't sought her out before now came to talk about their interactions with Nicholas Nelson. DoubleN, as he liked to be addressed. Some kids had only met him once but had that experience etched into their memories, similar to Kath's own encounter outside the bathroom. Nico had certainly been intense. Intensely angry, is what she hears these days.

"He actually snarled at me to shut up or he'd bash my head against the wall," one girl had said tonelessly, staring at the one wall in Kath's office that was left entirely blank exactly for this purpose. "I mean, you could feel that he meant it."

Others said, "He totally creeped me out. Just by the way he looked at us. At our bodies."

"Nobody liked him."

"I like coming to school again, now that DoubleN is gone."

"I always thought I'm a good person. Now I'm not sure. 'Cause I'm glad he died."

One girl, Sarah Gilbertson, also a recent transfer from Point Grey, had sat in Kath's office for an hour, crying. That had been in early January. Since then, Sarah had come by twice more, but hadn't said anything at all. Just sat in the armchair by the window and stared. Kath had provided tissues, tea, and cookies and had clucked sympathetically. Maybe the girl will talk next time.

There is a police officer standing outside her office door when Kath rounds the corner. The woman is tall with blond hair in a ponytail and broad shoulders above a long, lean frame. The fingers of her right hand are tapping a rhythm on her thighs, and she looks expectantly at the approaching Kath.

"Are you Katherine Ramirez, the counselor?" she asks, not smiling.

Kath nods and takes the door key from her trouser pocket. It's not the first time the police have come calling and she knows better than to begin a conversation in the hallway. School hallways might as well be megaphones.

"Yes, I am," she says after they enter her office and Kath has closed the door. She points to the hard-back chair in front of her desk, not to the two comfy recliners nestled by the window. "Please have a seat. What brings you here today?"

"Thanks for making the time," the officer responds. "My name is Luci Miller. One of your students died in a traffic accident six weeks ago and although we're not actively investigating the accident per se, it puzzles me greatly." The officer's brown eyes fasten keenly on Kath while she speaks. "Nicholas Nelson and his grandmother Josephine drove off a perfectly straight piece of highway on a clear, sunny day. The road was dry. There were no break marks."

The officer looks away for a moment, sighs, then continues, "To tell you the truth, the car was subject to a hit-and-run investigation at the time. During that investigation, I interviewed both Jo Nelson and Nico, as well as other members of their family." She sighs again, leans forward, but keeps her eyes fastened on Kath. "This accident on the Sea to Sky doesn't sit right with me. It haunts me day and night. My boss has given me permission to look deeper into the victim's histories. That's why I am coming to you. Maybe you can help me understand what happened."

ACKNOWLEDGMENTS

T.S. Eliot said, "Immature poets imitate; mature poets steal…" and this writer stole a lot. Expressions, metaphors, euphemisms, and whole phrases from other writers and many, many experiences shared by people living with illness. You were patients then, and I your nurse, and so there'll be no name-calling here. But you have my gratitude all the same: for your trust and your words and your willingness to teach, no matter your exhaustion.

The late Anne Bushnell shared her extraordinary artistry.

Paul Underhill went public with his story of survival and with Rumble, Canada's best Supershake.

The early readers who weighed in with questions, suggestions, and support: Arnold Porter, Laura Anderson, Madeline Walker, Melanie Carlsen, Michelle Sims, Kerry Jacox, Carolyn Parsons, Heidi Tiedemann Darroch. Thank you.

Thank you to Erin Ruff.

The team at Second Story Press did all the heavy lifting. They helped to make the story better, they polished and designed, and they are the ones to bring you this book. They are Margie Wolfe, Jordan Ryder, Beatrice Glickman, Phuong Truong, Emma Rodgers, Laura Atherton, April Masongsong, Michaela Stephen, Kate Earnshaw. And to Shannon Whibbs, the editor—thank you.

My heart to Morty and Dan.

March 2024
Christine Cosack

ABOUT THE AUTHOR

Christine Cosack is a debut author in her sixties who once wore the moniker "Seahag" with pride. She lives and works on the traditional, unceded territories of the ləkʷəŋən People on Southern Vancouver Island. She had long careers in social work and nursing, always working with families in situations of extrema, and is thankful for the privilege to bear witness to the vast, ardent depths of the human heart.